Praise for

MARK ANDREW OLSEN and *The Watchers*

"Olsen delivers an entertaining thriller likely to be enjoyed especially by fans of the spiritual warfare genre."

—*Publishers Weekly*

"Mark Andrew Olsen blasts open the door into the world of the supernatural with this gripping and suspenseful novel. Readers won't be able to put this book down as Olsen weaves an exciting story filled with rich history, wonderful imagery, and intense characters."

—*Romantic Times*

"From California to the jungles of Nigeria to the holy city of Jerusalem, *The Watchers* is a wild ride of action-packed suspense. Not since Frank Peretti's *This Present Darkness* and Ted Dekker's Martyr's Song series have I read a book that so compellingly weaves the spiritual world—visions of heaven and the battle between angels and demons—into the physical."

—Sheryl Root, *ArmchairInterviews.com*

"Olsen manages to include glimpses into the spirit world without sounding like he's imitating past works, and occasionally providing truly moving moments of insight. Recommended."

—Tim Frankovich, *ChristianFictionReview.com*

THE
WARRIORS

Books by Mark Andrew Olsen

[1]with Tommy Tenney   [2]with John Bevere

MARK ANDREW OLSEN

THE WARRIORS

BETHANYHOUSE
MINNEAPOLIS, MINNESOTA

Published by Bethany House Publishers
11400 Hampshire Avenue South
Bloomington, Minnesota 55438

Bethany House Publishers is a division of
Baker Publishing Group, Grand Rapids, Michigan.

Printed in the United States of America

ISBN 978-0-7642-0657-3

Library of Congress has cataloged the hardcover edition as follows:

Olsen, Mark Andrew.
  The warriors / Mark Andrew Olsen.
    p. cm.
  ISBN 978-0-7642-0274-2 (alk. paper)
  1. Spiritual warfare—Fiction. 2. Special forces (Military science)—Fiction. 3. Secret societies—Fiction. 4. Prayer—Fiction. I. Title.

PS3615.L73W36 2008
813'.6—dc22

2007043450

To our beloved

Emma-Le Olsen,

born in your mother's heart,

more beautiful and precious to us

than all the Pearls of China

MARK ANDREW OLSEN, acclaimed author of the supernatural thriller *The Watchers*, also collaborated on bestsellers *Hadassah*, *The Hadassah Covenant*, *The Road Home*, and *Rescued*. Mark grew up in France, the son of missionaries, and is a Professional Writing graduate of Baylor University. He and his wife, Connie, live in Colorado Springs with their three children.

THE WARRIORS

Our hope in God is greater than our desire to please men; beware how you draw down upon yourselves this anger by persecuting us; for remember that, if God so wills it, all the forces you have assembled against us will nothing avail.

—Entreaty of Waldensian leaders John Campo and John Besiderio to a papal legate leading an army of religious cleansing, 1488, La Torre, Italy

A bitter thing, a lamentable thing, a thing horrible to think of and terrible to hear, a detestable crime, an execrable evil, an abominable act, a repulsive disgrace, a thing almost inhuman, indeed alien to all humanity, has, thanks to the reports of several trustworthy persons, reached our ears, smiting us grievously and causing us to tremble with the utmost horrors.

—The Mandate of Maubuisson, pronounced against the Knights Templar, 1307, Notre Dame Cathedral, Paris

CHAPTER

_01

TOWER OF CONSTANCE, AIGUES—MORTES, PROVENCE,
FRANCE—A.D. 1353

The condemned lay hunched over the dungeon floor to carve his last words, using a beak pried from the carcass of a seagull. He breathed deeply and bent even lower, blowing dust off the letters, when something caused him to freeze.

He cocked his head to one side. Slowly closed his eyes. Then exhaled the breath, slow and trembling.

It was not a new noise that had alarmed him, but rather a new quiet. The ringing of hammer blows outside had ceased. He nodded faintly, absorbing the terrible truth.

The *carpentiers* had finished his execution stake.

He glanced over at his three brethren huddled in the cell's far corner and staring darkly at the stone floor. None had uttered a word since hearing their friends' death howls the day before. This morning their gazes were hollow with fear, for fresh sounds of doom seemed everywhere. From outside their window slits floated the growing clamor of a mob surrounding the gallows. From the guards' room below he could hear the clanging of swords and the curses of returning soldiers.

The hour of their death was upon them.

He sighed and fought back a misting in his eyes. The men's wasted appearance would never betray it, but they were the last known members of the once proudest and most feared military order in the world: The Poor Fellow Soldiers of Christ, Knights of the Temple of Solomon.

Knights Templar.

How far the mighty had fallen! Only a century ago, his forebears had sailed as heroes in the king's own ships from the quays of this very town, Aigues-Mortes, as crusaders sworn to the recapture of Jerusalem. The king himself, along with his cardinals, had stood by, tossing them tearful waves and bids of "Godspeed." The same offices that today condemned their order as devil worshipers and deviants, slaughtered its members and hunted down all who refused to flee until only these four doomed men remained.

He shook his head and willed himself not to sully his final moments with bitter thoughts.

Reading again what he had written, he caressed the words with his fingertips, then bowed his head for a long moment. Thankfully, the limestone had proven softer to pierce than he had thought possible, allowing him to inscribe the words of this most important message over the course of the last three days. He carefully turned the stone over, concealing his work, then returned it to its place in the floor with a dull thud. The soldiers would notice nothing amiss.

As to who would ever read his words and when, he would leave that task up to Almighty God. He who had inspired them would surely bring a reader in due time.

Forty minutes later, the carver of the message did indeed burn alongside his three fellow Templars, staring calm and upright through the flames even as his brethren writhed and lofted stomach-churning howls.

Some of those watching testified that, during his horrific final moments, the man looked heavenward with the beatific smile of a saint. A few of those near the front fell to their knees and began crossing themselves in repentance of their earlier taunts.

Finally it was over. Within the hour, farmers had carted off the charred remains and fed them to their swine. Peasants looted the pyre for kindling. By evening, coastal winds had chased off the remaining ashes and swept them into the nearby marshes of the Camargue. Three days later, the dead man's odd demeanor had been exhausted as conversation fodder. A week later it was forgotten.

Years passed, too numerous to describe. Prisoners came and went, as did many more such executions. Through it all, the dead man's hidden message went undiscovered. Yet somehow, against all logic and human reason, an awareness of its existence seemed to linger through the ages.

Only the Tower itself survived the passage of time intact. Eventually, the structure's dark renown would spread across Provence and all of France, whispered of as the bleakest of earthly hells, its only abundant feature the misery of those inhabiting that dreaded second floor.

The Middle Ages dragged on, and the Tower's oppressive presence worsened still. Centuries flowed around the dismal sight of the pale, weather-stained edifice thrust up into fog and clear blue sky alike as a soaring rebuke to the very notion of mercy. Indeed, every era of the second millennium would dawn upon the Tower, confining some wretched soul or other, usually of marginal guilt—petty thieves, indigents, prisoners of conscience, the royally disfavored, the politically unfortunate. Most would leave as withered cadavers laid out on slat boards, swathed under heaps of the town's famous sea salts.

Years after their imprisonment, Tower survivors would find it difficult to describe the place's horrors. They would struggle to capture the density of the resignation that seemed to drip from its chamber's ceiling. Or the depth of gloom that clung to its barren limestone walls. Or a despair even more pungent than the brine-scented winds that flowed through its narrow windows from the swamps and salt beds around Aigues-Mortes.

A name that, in the old Provençal, fittingly meant *Dead Waters*.

With a very few of its inmates, however, the Tower and its notorious bleakness had wrought a far different, even opposite effect. The grim atmosphere seemed to focus hearts and minds on eternal things. It appeared to wear away the barriers separating this world from the next. And, in one or two cases, it seemed to provoke astonishing manifestations of the spiritual.

It happened in the case of the Templar and his mysterious inscription in the floor stone. It also happened nearly three hundred years after his death, when the Tower was converted to a women's prison.

During this period, the Tower housed the inmates for whom it would become most famous: a group of Huguenot women, including the heroines Marie Durand and Anne Salieges. The latter would be remembered for surviving a seventy-one-year imprisonment, begun when she was an infant in her mother's arms. The former was celebrated for carving RESIST in the Tower's stone with her adolescent fingernail and for nurturing the prisoners' defiance.

Every morning, the Chief of the Watch would grumble up his obligatory offer of clemency in exchange for the women renouncing their Protestant faith. Every morning, Marie would shout down their refusal.

They would be released decades later, broken and stumbling old stalwarts, yet Marie Durand's engraving would remain to become one of the most celebrated ever left by a woman's hand.

But the other, far longer and more provocative message, carved and hidden in that same chamber by a Knight Templar three centuries before, would lie undetected and yet supernaturally whispered about for eons.

Translated, its opening lines would read as follows:

A Call to War

The stillness and solitude of this place have sharpened my sight and allowed me a wondrous revelation. I have been shown things of which most mortals know but a glimpse. I have beheld the battlefronts of a vast and ancient war.

I may be called a soldier, yet in the face of this war I know nothing. I am less than a spectator. This is a war beyond all things, beyond all conflicts, beyond time itself.

Do not be deceived, for although my words may bear the ring of legend, they describe truth of a supreme order. Truth so monumental that by comparison the reality of our present travails, the urgency of our earthly Crusades, are as trifling as the grains of salt upon these nearby shores. Truth of such magnitude that it could alter the course of a conflict which has engulfed heaven and earth since before the dawn of history.

CHAPTER
_2

TORA BORA, AFGHANISTAN, MALAWA CAVE COMPLEX—
DECEMBER 2001

Seven hundred years later, a new world power found itself waging another war rooted in religious and spiritual conflicts.

The three-month anniversary of 9/11 had almost arrived, and America had just lost what history would call the Battle of Tora Bora. Five hours earlier, amidst one of the most devastating conventional bombing campaigns and the most intensive manhunts in the annals of modern warfare, Osama bin Laden had disappeared—melted into the White Mountains of eastern Afghanistan.

The loser had no explanation for what had happened, no likely or even reasonable scenario.

It did, however, have one final deathblow to unleash.

Lumbering through a cloudless sky seven thousand feet above the White Mountains of Afghanistan, a U.S. Air Force MC-130 Combat Talon lowered its rear door. Instantly, its cargo bay filled with a roar of wind. Within seconds the aircraft's massive jaw stood fully open, its interior lights twinkling in vain against a sea of darkness.

Inside the aircraft, hugely muscled American airmen groaned. A massive, gleaming metal cylinder glided away from their shoulders and slid along a wooden pallet.

One of them heaved a bunch of cloth into the night. The wind caught it and snapped the fabric into a canopy, mimicking the shape of a small parachute. Ropes tied to its corners quivered tautly back into the aircraft, working to drag their payload down the ramp and out over the void.

The bomb swung ponderously into a nose-first attitude. Its pallet tumbled away, as useless as the static release wire now waving wildly in the wind. The fifteen-thousand-pound behemoth, resembling a miniature lunar command module, swayed into its descent.

Frosty wisps trailed along the giant's flanks, along with a plume of freezing vapor from its nose. For several long seconds the bomb plummeted through the aeries of night, anchoring its trajectory with tiny corrections of its copper arrowlike snout.

The final hundred feet whooshed by in an instant.

Thirty-two al-Qaeda warriors sitting watch on the mountainside heard a sudden rushing sound and looked up. The moonless night revealed only a fleeting reflection of stars along the bomb's polished sides.

The BLU-82 Commando Vault, as America's most lethal non-nuclear bomb was called, landed dead center of their location.

In a millisecond its fuse extender grazed the Afghan dust and transmitted the impact back into the warhead. Inside, a spark no larger than a match head flared to life beneath a pool of explosive slurry. The spark ignited a cascading tide of fuel that thumped into fire. Night flashed into day. Death exploded outward with the power of the sun.

All the air within a half mile shrieked inwards, its pressure collapsed from the normal fourteen pounds per square inch to a pulverizing one thousand. The bomb's shock wave roared through the terrorists and ignited their bodies into dancing columns of flame. Just as quickly the human torches imploded into glowing scarecrows and floated apart in scarlet ribbons of clotted ash.

Thousands of feet above the scene, pilots in the retreating plane, silently appalled, peered down on concentric rings of fire bathing their target in an orange and gold preview of hell.

One thousand yards from the spot of impact, a twenty-year-old al-Qaeda lookout named Rahmad paused from fleeing an underground horror to raise his head above the ground.

Rahmad found another terror awaiting him on the surface.

A sound he could never have imagined in his darkest night-mares caused the dust-covered youth to cover his ears. He shook his head. Was this the sound of apocalypse? He thrilled for a second, for surely the end of the world had come. Bin Laden had just escaped, and now Allah must have arrived to blow the hated Americans off the face of the earth. The best part was, Rahmad would never have to return to that cave. He would never again have to face the bestial presence that had whisked bin Laden who knows where, the fear of which had driven him up here to the surface.

Rahmad turned in the direction of the awesome roar and blinked against a sudden radiance. His mouth opened of its own accord, and he lowered his hands as the sounds of death swirled in his brain. He heard brief screams pepper the slope as the wretches were overtaken. He heard their bodies burn with a sound like kindling. He heard the sheet of fire crackle on toward him.

He felt it approach like a living thing. A beast. A being with a murderous will to find and kill him.

His face fell. No, this was not the end of the world—just the end of *his* world, racing toward him at four hundred feet per second.

He glanced back toward the hole at his feet which, even at night, gaped blacker than a bottomless well. Then he glanced back up, wrestling with an awful choice. Should he duck back inside for cover, or escape the horror pursuing him?

He looked down at his feet and stifled a scream. The presence from below had not given up its chase. It was rising through the cave opening.

The young man made his choice. He jumped away from the portal and embraced the fate he found least dreadful. Then he turned back—he couldn't help the impulse—and watched the sheet of flame close the gap, reach out, and almost lunge for him.

He felt the soles of his feet start to combust. Unbearable heat rolled over his back. Flames sucked at the whole length of his body. He felt his flesh turn to liquid. He screamed, but there was no air, no breath to make the sound. Agony made his hands constrict and claw the dirt mere inches from the pit.

But he did not scream because of the pain.

He screamed because that something, that *someone*, had now completely exited the cave entrance. He did not see it. But he felt its approach.

Its foulness made the flames seem like a solace.

He felt his organs begin to melt and the holocaust around him grow dim in his eyes. His eyelids fluttered shut. A part of him detached itself—something he had never felt connected to him before, something faint and fluttering and unbearably vital to who he was.

Rahmad looked down on a burning corpse and calmly recognized it as his own. He realized he was no longer inside his body, but with this departing spirit. *His soul*, he realized. He wanted to float, to rise up into the oblivion of night . . .

But the presence from underground wanted him. He felt it wrap around his being like a curling tongue. The closer it came, the more revulsion engulfed him. The more its loathsome desire made him want to flee back into his carbonized shell of a body.

Then, with a sudden intake like a drawing of breath, he was inside it.

Part of it.

One.

———

A hateful, unearthly presence, older than the mountains.

A cesspool of ancient vengeance. A bottomless well of resentment and rage.

It moved over the scorched earth and sucked in more souls from the smoldering cadavers, one after another, gleaning, inhaling them into a gullet, which, had it been carnal and visible to the eye, would have caused any human observer to retch in disgust and fear. Hardly pausing at the rapture of its feeding, it floated farther along the mountainside, seeking to satisfy a ravenous, unquenchable hunger for human spirits.

The presence growled in rage, uttering a rumble so low that only the most sensitive seismograph would have detected it in the physical world. But no instrument could have captured the hatred its sound embodied. The rage. This night marked the end of the being's refuge. For centuries Afghanistan had played an exquisite host. It had been perfect. The eternal hatreds. The willing pawns to inhabit. The endless wars for carrion. The veil of spiritual darkness for cover.

But now the Americans were blowing its playground to bits. Killing its home.

The so-called Western world has provoked me one time too many. Yet it is weak. More vulnerable than ever before. The time for a final onslaught has come at last.

Time to unleash hell on earth.

CHAPTER
_3

Operation Mystic Sender began silently, at sunset, with four tiny shooting stars igniting the azimuth of a darkening sky. Only an observer armed with the most powerful optics could have made out bodies plummeting there, nearly twelve thousand feet high amidst the dying sun's glow. The onlooker would have even less chance of spotting the aircraft that had released them, for twilight rendered the U.S. Air Force tanker essentially invisible, a lofty silhouette camouflaged by nightfall.

As they approached earth, the falling shapes lost their glow, turning into black dots that vanished against the outline of mountains. Their parachutes popped open at barely three thousand feet—a HALO or *high altitude, low opening* jump. A high altitude release followed by free-fall until almost the last moment. And that meant only one thing.

Special Forces.

For Jon Ferrugia, designated Mystic Three and accordingly third in line of the parachuting commandos, the jump was more than a list of statistics. To him, it was a plunge into exhilaration—the abandon of free-fall, the wind buffeting his limbs, the sea of gray peaks swaying beneath him with no sign of man from horizon to horizon. Beyond all else, he reveled in the thrill of being back in the proverbial saddle, once more jumping fully armed from a U.S. military aircraft with a righteous mission before him.

The helmet did not reveal it, but Jon was grinning from ear to ear. It had been a while.

Within seconds, however, the man immediately flushed the ecstasy from his conscious mind and willed himself back to discipline. His thoughts instinctively filled with ground rules and contingencies for the operation ahead.

He replayed his commander's words, mentally returning to that first briefing back in the Bagram bunker two weeks ago, still hung over by a twenty-hour plane trip that had begun as nothing more than a phone call, a muttered code word, and his own stammered, almost reflexive acceptance. A forlorn meeting in a folding chair in his civilian clothes, still jet-lagged, surrounded by three other strangers just as bleary and uninformed as he.

"Welcome to Operation Mystic Sender," the colonel had said in a hushed tone, as if even he could not speak of it too loudly. "In case you guys haven't figured it out yet, you're all freelancers. You're all here courtesy of the Activity."

The Intelligence Activity. The very sound of that name had caused Jon to rouse himself. It had taken him years to learn that the Activity was the working title of an elite group supplying independent intelligence to the Joint Special Operations Command. The group was as legendary as it was covert. Even in Jon's considerable black-ops experience, it had rarely been more than a shadow, a fleeting name quickly spoken and just as swiftly ignored.

The colonel continued. "We picked freelancers for a very specific reason. The operation for which you've been hired is a hero project of the highest order, and unconventional to say the least. In fact, it's riddled with so many risk factors and red flags that although we need top people on the job—the reason we hired you—the mission demands maximum deniability. You will absolutely forget all about this op as soon as you've completed it and gone home. That is to say, even more quickly than usual."

The officer turned to a large easel and pulled back its protective black covering with a papery clatter. The newly exposed sheet revealed a large map titled *Tora Bora*, flanked by a collage of topographical map and satellite imagery riddled with superimposed red lines and labels.

"Our target is the caves of Tora Bora. You may know that three major military ops have tried to pacify this area, starting with the Battle of the Caves back in '01 and ending with Operation Jawbreaker. None have fully succeeded. To this day, every general alive wants to go down as the man who pacified Tora Bora and finally figured out how in the world Osama slipped through our fingers. That question is one of the great mysteries of the modern age. Right up there with the Bermuda Triangle and whoever it was that sanctioned JFK. Which, by the way, I will never tell."

The men around snickered in response, but the colonel never smiled. In fact, he seemed to glower at his own levity.

"But I'm not kidding, men. NRO has a spy bird tasked 24/7 on Tora Bora alone. I don't know of another single spot that rates its own full-time recon satellite. Gotta be the most scrutinized place on the planet. And that brings us to our problem at hand."

The colonel scooted a leg up over the tabletop and affected a casual pose. Jon found the body language unconvincing—a calculated attempt whose awkwardness betrayed exactly what the colonel had sought to conceal.

Anxiety. Uncertainty.

"The locals have avoided this area for decades, long before any outsiders showed up. They've got stories that would make your hair curl—that is, if you believe half of them. According to them, those caves were places of death. Only the most hardcore Taliban and al-Qaeda would even come close to them, let alone climb inside. We always believed the terrorists dug the tunnels fairly recently, but now it turns out they only widened them. Those passages have been there for centuries. In fact, there's no historical record of who built them in the first place. We've got stories from local shepherds and passersby about horses and livestock herds going mad and stampeding away from the area. Human disappearances, of which we've documented twelve in the last year alone. Child sacrifice. When we started watching the entrances themselves, our sensors picked up things that, well, aren't supposed to happen."

The commander's expression acquired a morose, even resentful cast, as though being forced to say such things were a punishment beyond endurance.

"Heat signatures more intense than what you'd see coming off a city block in January. Electromagnetic firestorms that don't compute into anything coherent, but crank out more interference than the sun. Unexplainable noises at all times of day and night. Sounds that aren't human, according to NSA computers, but not created by any device known to man. Two months ago we sent in a robot loaded with full spectrum analyzers and sensors of every kind. Here's what happened."

He turned to a large plasma screen behind him and punched a remote. The eerie glow revealed the grainy image of a ragged cave tunnel bouncing slowly as the robot-mounted camera lurched forward.

Without warning, a firestorm of vague and jagged light erupted on-screen. The scene veered sideways and a screeching *beep* assaulted their ears. Cave walls started to spin past them in a dizzying whirl.

Then came a sound that made Jon's blood run cold. It was a roar resembling that of a lion yet much deeper, more powerful, infinitely more savage. A sound beyond anything he had ever heard before. A sound that tried to yank him to another place, another time, another part of his life he needed desperately to forget just now.

He fought a shudder and strained to recover his concentration.

The monitor went black.

The colonel switched it off and turned to face them with a countenance even more somber than before.

"Here's the clincher. We sent men in already, a three-man squad. They never came back. After that point, it was considered too dangerous, and the priority level dropped after it was ruled bin Laden was no longer inside. For some reason, the tide's changed, and now the brass wants a full exploration.

"Operation Mystic Sender is officially a recon, gentlemen. But it's probably one of the most unconventional recons ever sanctioned by our country, even on such a secret basis. You're not necessarily going in to engage al-Qaeda, although that could certainly happen. You're going in on a blind reconnoiter. You may not encounter any physical resistance whatsoever. Or you may encounter something this army has never seen before. Nobody knows. But we're gonna send you men in equipped with every possible sensor and weapon you can carry."

He nodded to his audience, his face grimmer by the second.

"You've been handpicked for your experience and expertise. This squad includes a cave specialist, a sensor geek, a weapons and tactical man, and one of the best comm men I've ever worked with. We're gonna back you up with every asset at our disposal. Everything from a thermobaric cave-buster bomb to real-time video monitoring to Corner Shot rifles to helo extract on standby. Even a Spectre gunship in case anyone threatens the perimeter. But make no mistake, we are sending you in alone. You're going in, and you're not turning back until you've found the answers. And no one has the foggiest notion of who your enemy will be, let alone what you'll actually find."

Jon's parachute inflated and yanked him away from the memory of his commander's warning. The backlash returned him instantly to the immediate challenges of landing safely on the side of a mountain officially classified as *unsecured*. Grimacing at the tug of the cords at his chest and midsection, he aimed wide glances all about him. On every side, taut squares of camouflaged nylon and careening rock faces reminded him to be on his highest alert.

He told himself that these few seconds, before the mission's official beginning, were also some of its most dangerous. A bad landing on treacherous terrain, not to mention detection by hostiles, could knock him out of the action, or given the small size of his team, even ruin the op from its first moments.

He peered down and glided into a wide turn to keep his third place in line—fifteen seconds, no more no less, between himself and number two. Their leader had already disappeared onto the chosen site: a small notch straddling the junction of two boulder-strewn slopes. The number two man had just pulled in his chute and ducked out of his path. It was time to come in.

Pulling down on his toggle lines, he felt his chute slow its descent and level into its pre-landing flare. He tried in vain to keep the rocky terrain fully in sight, but with little light and few reference points with which to orient his approach, the ground seemed to rush at him twice as fast as usual. And the sharp angles of the slopes certainly didn't help his reckoning.

He rushed into the target area, correcting furiously with sharp tugs on the lines. A gust blew into his canopy just as he prepared to touch earth, tossing him skyward a few dozen yards. Just as quickly he fell again.

This time there was no reprieve. Narrowly missing a boulder to his right, he struck the ground hard. Pain shot through his leg joints. He landed solidly on both feet and winced as his knees fell forward and struck a sharp stone. With a pull of his valve cords, the canopy deflated and came to rest at his feet.

A close call.

He sighed in relief and swiftly began gathering up the fabric. Quickly landing and stowing his chute was another vital imperative; the towering profile of a floating canopy would broadcast his arrival to the enemy. Not to mention threaten to drag him across the landscape with the least gust of errant wind.

Looking up, he saw the last airborne chute floating past on his left, on course for a safe landing behind him. His first two comrades had already taken up positions to his right, scoping out their ingress point just a few hundred yards upslope. He pulled on his helmet and his infrared goggles, shrugged over his Corner Shot machine gun—hinged in the middle to shoot around corners—and joined them.

He took cover behind an outcropping and lensed the way ahead. Nothing. The mountains were so bare and desolate that he might as well have been staring at the moon. The stillness was odd, considering that right before departure the commander had described their destination as lighting up U.S. military sensors like a Christmas tree.

With a raised fist and one first, silent step, the squad moved forward.

CHAPTER

_4

Pentagon records would later show that Operation Mystic Sender's four-man squad entered a hole labeled *Tunnel 9* at ten minutes after sunset, a time selected to give their approach the benefit of waning daylight, followed swiftly by darkness. And once they entered the tunnel, they would be invisible to the outside world. What their commander had not told the squad members, however, was that a primary reason for their concealment was not only hiding the mission from Afghan eyes but from the eyes of their own countrymen.

The truth was, Operation Mystic Sender had been deemed far too vague and risky for the tastes of the U.S. military. As a result, knowledge of this freelance op had been even more tightly contained than any of its soldiers were told. Not only was the mission to enter the caves kept hidden from the locals, but also from every American unit not actively involved in its support. Most of the usual eyes and ears trained on this place had been temporarily redirected under the pretext of a top-secret weapons test.

Initially at least, these precautions proved unnecessary. To the relief of both squad members and their commanders, Operation Mystic Sender encountered zero resistance and zero outside detection on its way to the cave mouth.

At 7:24 p.m. Afghanistan time, squad leader Mike Griffith, Mystic One, once again pumped his right fist in the air and three dark figures crawled behind him into the ten-foot-wide aperture in the side of Orkutz Mountain.

Jon Ferrugia predictably found their first thirty feet the slowest going. To avoid creating an outline against the lighter night sky behind them, the men had been obliged to keep crawling those first thirty feet into the cave itself.

Ferrugia could not recall ever feeling more concealed. His face and neck were painted pitch-black. Also black were his clothing, boots, weapons, and other equipment—all of him made to be anti-reflective, invisible.

He took a deep breath and his first whiff of fetid dust sent an alarm up and down his spine. A vague sort of warning, unease. Many years back, when Jon Ferrugia had been in his prime and his instincts razor-sharp, he would have immediately trusted the response as a reliable warning that something was wrong.

Today he wasn't so sure. Certainly not confident enough to risk throwing a wrench into an op like this one. And yet, he reminded himself, he was the squad's tactics man, recruited for his fighting skills and knowledge of how to prevail in the heat of battle. Did he really have the right to withhold his strongest instincts from the others, when those very instincts were the reason for his presence?

Pulling himself over a bed of sharp rocks, Ferrugia felt his knees being poked mercilessly. He gritted his teeth in frustration. It didn't help that the mission itself was so stinking fuzzy. And creepy. Fact was, he had been tempted to stand up and resign on the spot when the colonel had finished his initial briefing. The mission's objectives had sounded like a lose-lose proposition to him. He'd never heard of a unit of the U.S. government, covert or conventional, being asked to carry out such an ill-defined assignment. In his experience, successful missions always began with clear and achievable goals. But none of the other men had budged, and a surge of professional and masculine pride had anchored him in place.

Now, smack-dab in the thick of things, adrenaline suddenly turbocharged his limbs in a visceral confirmation that he'd made the right choice after all. Resigned to the mission, he clenched his jaw and focused his gaze into the cave, the black gullet of stone yawning before him . . .

He frowned. Why did it feel as if he were moving straight into the jaws of a predator? As though what loomed ahead were not so much an opening in a mountain but a large and hungry throat?

Finally, as he proceeded deeper into the cave, he felt the shadow pass over him like a weighted veil. He was now beyond the outdoor glow of night, well away from the cave's entrance. His head began to swim—vertigo from the high jump, he told himself. Then he realized his heart was racing. He breathed in deeply, trying to calm down, but the draught of air only filled his mouth with the mustiness of undisturbed dust, dry and sulfuric. He felt nausea rise up in his stomach as he fought back the horrible taste.

He was losing it!

He ordered himself to remain focused, remembering that what lay just ahead could be decisive. Odds were, any improvised explosives or booby traps would detonate somewhere in the next few yards or minutes.

He looked up at the tunnel snaking on ahead, a black hole. Never before had he experienced such a sense of darkness being this thick and palpable. He felt as if he'd immersed himself into a pool of thick, oily tar.

Just then, one of life's most familiar sensations lit up his brain.

I'm being watched.

But he shrugged off the feeling. After all, the squad's point man was equipped with a thermal sight more sensitive than his own state-of-the-art sensor. If they were moving forward at all, then the only possible foreign presence in the cave would have to be the squad itself.

It now occurred to him that the cave mouth had been much smaller than he'd originally imagined. The insight troubled him, for it meant his imagination was distorting vitally important calculations. He needed his senses to be accurate, at their highest pitch. He had to face it—*he'd grown soft*. Frustration wrenched his insides into a bitter knot. He hadn't been away *that* long. But apparently long enough to steal his edge.

Finally he saw Mystic One's black-clad figure stand up, his hand cupped in the signal for the others to follow. Jon strained to remain silent as he rose to his feet. He grimaced and stretched his arms, his muscles resenting both the posture and the jagged surface. Mystic One formed a V with his index and middle finger and motioned ahead. That meant a double-file column formation.

It was easy to see why: the passage was too narrow for the wedge grouping they had hoped to adopt.

Jon Ferrugia forced himself to take a long, deep breath. He had fought in many dark and claustrophobic spaces, from Middle Eastern back alleys to tight slot canyons on moonless nights. But no caves. Nothing like this, ever. Nothing this exposed, this vulnerable, this bereft of tactical advantages. He felt short of breath, hemmed in. He looked around and realized he had no escape route other than making a U-turn and going back the way he'd come. The very thought made him want to run away.

He checked his weapon, tightening his grip on the machine gun, inwardly vowing never to step foot in such a place again.

CHAPTER

_5

Six thousand miles away, beside an open window whose curtain obscured a bright ocean view, a blond twenty-five-year-old woman sitting cross-legged on her bed winced suddenly. She appeared to be in pain. She raised her hand to her heart, then closed her eyes and kept them shut.

She grimaced as though some waking dream were tormenting her, yet continued to keep her eyes closed, watching it. As distressing as it was to keep witnessing the pictures playing within her mind, she dared not turn away.

Quick and assured, her hands reached out, grasped her Bible, and lifted the book to her chest. Still grimacing, she held it to herself even more tightly, like a shield against the images afflicting her soul.

TUNNEL 9, TORA BORA, AFGHANISTAN

"Man, I hate this place."

Jon Ferrugia jumped at the words' clarity and sheer loudness. The voice belonged to Mystic Two, and the words were as bright and immediate as if whisked through the cavern's stifling blackness and spoken directly into Jon's brain. Small wonder, for they had reached him courtesy of the squad's short-range comm network, channeled through a tiny earpiece and a two-inch plastic wand nestled behind his ear. He'd nearly forgotten its presence.

Jon bristled, for the comm network had remained totally silent until now. It had been deployed for emergencies only, intended as a backup in the event they became separated from each other. The only advantage of using it now would be the ability to communicate in the lowest of whispers. Anything other than an outright crisis was supposed to be conveyed through hand or face motions. Those were the rules, emphatically conveyed by their superiors.

More surprising still, Jon thought, was that Mystic Two would have broken those rules in order to utter such a banal statement. The sentiment was irrelevant and, worse yet, unprofessional. Jon shot him a glance. The soldier's head turned, but the fuzzy infrared of Jon's goggles made a closer look at his features too difficult.

"Gettin' creeped out back here," said Mystic Four. "I'd rather be on point."

"Quiet, men," growled Mystic One. "Let's go."

Jon exhaled a breath, grateful the leader had stepped in to restore protocol. This didn't feel like a mission that should tolerate lax discipline. He now remembered why he had strongly preferred solo missions in the latter part of his career. He spent enough energy just dealing with the mission itself and staying alive without having to contend with the careless mistakes of others.

He fell in as they formed the column and began to walk, still using only their goggles for vision.

Jon quickly lost track of time. It seemed he'd been trudging into the belly of the mountain forever. One heavy step onto cold stone and rubble, followed by another, in an unending procession. While his eyes slowly adjusted to the eerie infrared glow, he felt a strange disorientation, as though losing his memory of ever having been outdoors. Soon he lost his sense of backward and forward, east, west, south, and north. He felt he'd forgotten the vividness of daylight. He breathed in and out, trying to clear his mind.

He fought to maintain his concentration, but his thoughts veered off into the realm of evil. He thought he could smell it and taste it on his tongue like a bitter secretion. Without intending to, he replayed some of the darkest stories he had ever heard, those of horror films, novels, bloody campfire sagas. He pictured the gore he could splatter on these cave walls with but a twitch of his index finger against the tiny metal trigger of his machine gun. In a split second, the men around him would be . . .

Stop that! he warned himself. *What's the matter with you?*

A few dozen steps later he glimpsed something—a motion, the fleeting afterimage of sudden movement upon his retina. He felt not so much alarmed as terrified.

What he'd seen whisked back memories Jon had sworn to forget. Memories attached to matters he had insisted on leaving at home, as far away from this mission as possible.

Memories of a young woman, beautiful, who was thousands of miles away.

When he saw the awful thing again a moment later, he impulsively yanked off his goggles and let them drop with what his imagination magnified into an echoing *thud*. In the same motion he swiftly raised his weapon.

This time he'd seen it for real. No mistake.

A face, if you could call it that. Eyes, and a mouth of sorts. The hideous verdict of his optic nerves threw his heart into a gallop, tightening his every muscle in a vicious clench.

He had not seen anything like this in months. Not since Africa.

"Mystic Three, what is it?"

He looked over at Mystic One, source of the question. In a perfect reflex, the leader had already shouldered his own SAW machine gun and was lighting up the cave wall ahead of Jon with the red dot of his laser sights.

Jon swallowed hard and furrowed his brow. A knot of hesitation abruptly gripped his will. He wasn't prepared yet.

"Can't tell you right now."

"What do you mean? You're tactics. I want to know."

"Sorry. I haven't fully processed the data yet. Give me a minute."

The leader glared at him for several long seconds. More than long enough for his displeasure to sink in. "You do that."

The leader then spun on his heels and resumed formation. Studiously avoiding eye contact with Jon, the other commandos turned and silently continued their journey deeper into the tunnel, their world nothing more than dimly reflecting darkness. They rounded a corner and the walls widened a little, leading into a small chamber that included two chairs, an empty ammo box, scattered refuse.

While they paused and the other men lit up the objects with the dancing trails of their gun sights, Jon closed his eyes and

struggled to regain control of his thoughts. He wasn't equipped
to accept what he was feeling, let alone what he'd seen. He had
worked hard to erect a wall that separated the two provinces of
his understanding. The two were not supposed to meet.

At least not here. Not now.

And yet he couldn't escape the fact that the mission at hand
was a highly unorthodox exploration of unexplainable phenomena.
How would he do his job if he refused to acknowledge what his
whole being now screamed at him?

A sound. That roar again, dim in the distance. He ignored
the cascade of shudders down his spine and jerked his head
sideways.

"Hear that?" he asked with a glance at Mystic One.

Mystic One shook his head. "Hear what, Three?"

Time to come clean.

"A roaring sound."

"Like an animal?"

"No."

"Human?"

A pause. "No."

Mystic One was glaring at him again. "You okay?" he asked,
stepping closer to Jon. "Your head in the game?"

"Affirmative," Jon replied in his best military grunt. "That's
the problem."

"So what is it? Do you know?"

Jon considered his response.

"I order you to answer me," said One.

Jon frowned. Mystic One's lips appeared to be moving fast.
Jon heard a low grumble but could make out nothing. He pulled
off his radio headset.

". . . answer me," One repeated with a whisper.

Jon finally realized the problem. "Comm's out," he said out loud.

"What?" said One. He yanked off his own headset. "Our comm's dead. Mystic Four, you're our last link with the outside."

Mystic One threw the apparatus to the ground, prompting the others to do the same.

Suddenly Mystic Four screamed a barrage of curses and ran off. His body was swallowed up by night, disappearing around a corner, back toward the entrance. The other three stiffened at once. The soldiers shouldered their guns and turned to follow him.

"Here, let me in front," ordered Mystic One.

All three walked in dread, seeming to fight through a sense of menace even thicker than the darkness. They turned the corner.

Mystic Four was nowhere in sight. They picked up the pace, anxiety spurring them on.

"Oh no . . ."

Mystic One had switched on his flashlight, and its bright beam had found a heap lying in the dirt ahead.

Jon's heart slipped into an even higher gear. The heap had not been there five minutes ago.

Another curse echoed in the tunnel. Jon caught up with Mystic Three and looked down on the cause of his dismay.

It was Mystic Four, his eyes wide, staring straight ahead. In the soldier's hand was a nine-inch knife, dripping red. Blood covered his neck, his chest. Four seemed to be smiling, despite having shattered his external radio gear, then nearly decapitated himself with his very own knife.

CHAPTER
_6

A moan broke the nocturnal calm of Jerusalem's Old City, a low cry which rose from the rooftop terrace of the Church of the Holy Sepulchre. The sound wafted past rows of round huts and the shadowed skyline of the Christian Quarter. It seemed to penetrate each of the Old City's two hundred twenty-five tightly packed acres.

Instantly a door to one of the terrace huts clacked open. A thin Coptic monk scrambled out, eyes wildly scanning the expanse before him.

The source of the moaning lay only thirty feet away, at the roof's edge, where he knew Sister Rulaz always sat. She was there, still wrapped in the shawl she habitually wore as her only concession to the evening chill. Her torso bobbed rhythmically.

The monk reached her in seconds and wrapped his arms around her bony frame. Her demeanor frightened even him, for in twenty-seven years he had rarely seen her in such a state.

"Sister! Sister!" he panted. "Please calm yourself! Please do not tax yourself like this!"

Her brown eyes lay wide open and fixed somewhere far away.

"I must speak to her," she muttered, "and warn her. He has breached one of the principalities. He is not prepared for that much evil. That much malice . . ."

"I will help you, Sister," he whispered, "but you must calm yourself. Remember your health. You are in no condition for such a disturbance."

"I *must* speak to her!" she repeated more forcefully. "I must warn her now, before it is provoked!"

"I will bring the phone, but only if you settle yourself."

She took a deep breath and stilled her breathing. The monk ran off to another, larger shack and quickly returned bearing a leather satchel, clutched high in his fingertips. With fumbling hands he opened it and pulled out an oversized cordless telephone.

He held it out before him and shuddered in surprise when she snatched it from him and began to dial frantically.

SANTA MONICA—THAT SAME MOMENT

The young woman still sat upright in her bed, eyes still shut, the Book still clasped against her chest. Her lips were now moving in silent prayer. Her phone rang, yet she was too immersed in her experience to even notice.

However, she did shudder and open her eyes at the shock of seeing her mother appear in the doorway, bleary-eyed in her gown.

The woman's presence had not been the cause of her awakening, which meant the two women had arisen together.

Simultaneously. Mutually provoked. Not a good sign.

"He's in trouble, Mama," she mumbled. "Big trouble."

"I know, sweetheart. It woke me too. What's the phone call?"

She glanced to the side, almost oblivious to its noise, even though its ring was quite loud. Its caller ID screen was jammed with the thirteen digits of an international call. Starting with 972.

Jerusalem.

Her body stiffened and she grabbed the receiver.

"Thank God you've called!" she exclaimed.

"Are you seeing it too?" came the voice on the other end of the line, weak both in signal and physical vitality. "Sister, please tell me you see the horrible place he is in."

"I just awoke with this terrible sense of foreboding. You probably see more clearly, as always. What do you see?"

"A place of outer darkness. You must know, that is no idle phrase. Outer darkness is a state supposed to exist only in hell. Yet some believe it might also exist in a few cursed places on earth, inside the earthly dwelling places of the enemy's generals. The principalities."

Remembering the famous verse, she shuddered at the sound of that word. *Principalities and powers . . .*

"I have no idea where he is, Sister. Do you see anything specific?"

"Two words. *Mystic. Sender.*"

"Something's coming to me now, but it makes no sense. The number nine."

"He is in some kind of cave, or tunnel."

"He is with other men. Soldiers. They are all moments away from—oh, please, can you reach him? Can you do something?"

"Sister Rulaz, I have no idea where he is! Tell me, do you think he's ready? Do you think he's equipped to handle something like this?"

"He has the Sight, of course. But he also has a rebellious streak. He lacks the spiritual maturity and strength. If he's out of fellowship, and he isn't covered in prayer . . . Do you have all our sisters praying?"

"No, I just woke up. I haven't done a thing but pray myself, then talk to you and my mother."

"What about email?"

"I suppose I can—"

"Then start now. Don't waste a moment. That place, and the beings inside it, could destroy him. Not his soul, of course, but every other part of him. His physical body and his mind. Mortal danger. My dear, I have never felt such a darkness in all my life."

FORT MEADE, MARYLAND, NSA HEADQUARTERS

Mystic Sender.
Number nine.
Cave.
Soldiers.

That combination of words, plucked from the airwaves by hypersensitive antennae at a hidden base in Britain's Yorkshire Moors, provoked a top-secret National Security Agency database to issue a Capture Alert. The order instantly caused the recording and encrypting of the entire conversation, along with several dozen lines of code delineating the phone call's origin and destination, its satellite carrier, and its level of suspiciousness—or what agency staffers nicknamed its "heat index."

Five seconds later, the conversation was replayed in its entirety straight into the headphones of an intelligence officer in the agency's massive complex at Fort Meade.

A side program soon calculated the odds of someone uttering the words *Mystic Sender*, a term housed in a massive buffer list constantly being refreshed, alongside the words *nine*, *cave*, and *soldiers* without possessing active knowledge of a particular off-the-books military operation currently in progress.

The odds were listed as exceeding 250,000 to one.

Anything beyond a hundred to one the agency automatically designated as beyond the parameters of ordinary chance. To make matters worse, the fact that the call had been placed in the Middle East, specifically Jerusalem, raised its heat index fifteenfold.

The identity of the caller was impossible to ascertain. The identity of the domestic recipient, however, was child's play for the agency's supercomputers. An exact ID and street address took less than eight seconds to appear on the staffer's monitor.

His arm flew out to snatch up an encrypted desktop phone.

CHAPTER
_7

TUNNEL 9, TORA BORA, AFGHANISTAN

Another flurry of motion drew Jon's eyes to the corpse, despite his very human impulse to look away.

Jon gasped loudly and stepped back. A stench more foul than anything the corpse could emit had crept into his lungs. He could not take a full breath; his chest only expanded halfway, then ran out of capacity. He wanted to run, but for a moment couldn't even remember which way to turn. The next second plunged him into pure terror. Disorientation set his head spinning and he thought he might fall. He knelt and felt the ground with his hands, suddenly grateful for the cave floor. Then he spotted the source of the awful smell and his overpowering sense of repulsion.

Like a column of fleeing rats, vile creatures were spitting forth from the dead soldier's open mouth. Each form was transparent yet loathsome, each a distinct vision of grotesquery and evil. The flow must have numbered in the hundreds.

"What is it, Three?" Mystic asked again, an edge to his voice.

"You mean you can't see them?" Jon Ferrugia replied.

"See what?"

Jon went over to where his squad leader stood and went nose to nose with him. "I'm ready now. But if you want to hear the truth, you have to promise to listen with an open mind. Because I'm not gonna mince words."

"Out with it," said Mystic One.

"What I'm seeing is a demonic stronghold."

The man's face recoiled in a combination of surprise and distaste. "Go on."

"This place is filled with evil spirits. No strongmen or leaders, at least so far, but hundreds of spirits of the air. They're not usually that powerful, except when they attack in force. And I've never seen such numbers of them. They just poured out of Mystic Four. We need to get out of here before they regroup and attack again."

The squad leader maintained his fierce gaze into Jon's eyes for a moment as though unsure of how to respond, how to process such a bizarre report. Finally he sighed and broke eye contact, looking back down at the body.

"No, you're gonna do better than that, tactics man," he said. " 'Cause if you think I'm gonna put that in a report, you're even crazier than you sound."

"Remember all our briefings?" Jon countered frantically. "All the warnings about how strange, how unconventional this mission is?"

"Unconventional maybe. But whacked-out? I'm not going there."

Jon turned abruptly toward Mystic Two and froze. Unconsciously his right hand reached out to graze Mystic One's forearm as a silent warning. The fingers of his left hand sought out his machine gun's trigger guard.

The vile creatures were creeping up Two's body. They were disappearing inside his gaping mouth.

Jon felt a sensation not unlike that of a thousand insect legs crawling up his arm. Then another sensation—his insides filling up with ice water. The feeling ran down his legs to his feet, causing them to seem rooted to the ground. Even though his years of training and experience returned, instinctively relaxing his muscles, fine-tuning them for what lay ahead, he found he could not move.

Do something! he screamed inwardly. *Seize the initiative!* But the feeling of coolness had frozen into sheer dread. Terror was taking control of his limbs. Even a blink of the eyes required a jolt of determination. Summoning every ounce of will inside him, he forced his lips to move.

"Mystic Two?" He tried to keep his voice calm and unthreatening.

The man looked his way with a cold gleam in his eyes.

"Do me a favor and let me check your weapon."

Mystic One stared at him. Clearly he did not like having his authority undermined. This was an order for *him* to give. "Three, what in the world are you doing?"

"I'm tactics, remember?" Jon answered. "Well, now's the time to trust my battle sense. Mystic Two, lower your—"

In a fraction of a second, Jon's eyes took in the briefest of warnings: a rapid double blink of Two's eyelashes, the tiniest flex in his upper forearm, an anticipatory quiver across the shoulders . . .

It was enough and Jon did not hesitate. He dropped into a crouch, then spun around with a roundhouse kick that struck the soldier behind the knees and sent the man flying. The soldier's gun, still grasped in a falling hand, shattered the darkness with a thunder of fire and whining ricochets.

Beside him, Mystic One froze with his machine gun in one arm, his face slack in disbelief. For a moment he seemed unsure who the real villain was—Jon or the other soldier. That is, until Mystic Two rolled upright and leveled his gun barrel straight at the squad leader's head.

"Run!" Jon screamed at him. Rather than wait for Mystic One to obey, Jon pushed him out of the chamber, away from Mystic Two. A barrage of gunfire followed them. A blinding flash chipped the rock beside Jon's head with a pinging sound.

The gunfire was so deafening that Jon didn't hear Mystic One moaning until they had gotten some distance between themselves and Mystic Two. Then he saw that his squad leader had been hit, his upper back and shoulder smeared with blood. Instead of pausing, Jon helped his leader keep moving, forcing himself to run even faster.

From behind them came the sound he had feared beyond anything else. Its vibration rumbled the pit of his stomach before his ears had processed the noise. It struck him as deeper and more savage and more powerful than before, as though sheer rage had somehow found a way to incarnate itself in throbbing waves of terror.

The roar.

Getting closer . . .

"What's that?" Mystic One shouted from his place at Jon's side.

"You hear it now? That's Mystic Two. A major demonic spirit just took him over. The strongman I told you about. A being we don't want to mess with!"

Bearing up his wounded leader with one arm and holding a flashlight in the other hand, Jon continued into the mountain until he felt as if the outside world were an abstraction, a fantasyland. His legs and arms burned so mercilessly that he could carry the weight no longer. Finally, heaving raspy lungfuls of stale air, he fell to his knees and, as gently as he could manage, cradled his squad leader into a resting position against the rock wall. The flashlight was beginning to dim. He positioned it facing upward for maximum illumination.

"Is he following us?" Mystic One whispered.

"Probably," Jon muttered. "But for now, there's no external sign of him. How are you holding up?"

Mystic One pressed a hand to his wounded shoulder and grimaced. "Hurts like crazy. I've lost a lot of blood, but I'll live."

Once he'd found the first-aid kit and cleaned and dressed the wound, Jon stepped over to an outcropping of rock and pulled down the SAW's tripod to stabilize his firing position. He checked his magazine and ammo, then turned back to his companion.

"How do we call for help?" Jon asked.

"Remember, our comm guy was Mystic Four. He destroyed our main link to the outside before killing himself. But we have this emergency transmitter." He pointed to a small green box mounted on his belt.

"Well, let's turn it on."

"Looks like you were right," said Mystic One as he pushed the box's glowing red button. "But how did you see all those things? And know what they were?"

"Experience," Jon replied.

"What possible kind of experience could that be?"

Jon gave him a sharp look. "Remember the big Abby Sherman story last year?"

The man nodded. "Yeah, sure. The girl who had all those weird visions, got attacked on the *Mara McQueen Show* and then disappeared, kept popping up all over the globe."

"Do you remember the final story that came out? About the black-ops assassin assigned to kill her, who instead became her friend and then her protector?"

"Yeah, but I didn't believe it, along with half of America. She couldn't even produce the guy, or give anyone a real name."

"Well, it was true. That guy was *me*."

There was a long, shocked silence. Mystic One stared at his companion as if he were an alien.

"She did have my real name, but the rest of the world couldn't confirm it because I use about six of them. And besides, Uncle Sam would never acknowledge my existence. So Jon Ferrugia is not my name. That's just an old cover identity. My real name's Dylan Hatfield."

CHAPTER
_8

"I remember the name Dylan Hatfield," Mystic One interjected. "I don't get it, Dylan. What are you doing on this mission?"

"Long story. Abby and I had a parting of ways. I guess I wanted to see some action again. Do what I do best. Then I got a phone call out of nowhere, and at the time it seemed like the perfect solution. Except this mission's brought me right back to the very same things I learned with her."

"Things like what?"

"I'm not sure it's worth trying to explain. I had a hard time with it, at first."

"Try me."

"All right. First of all—"

"And, Dylan," the squad leader interrupted, "call me Mike. We're beyond rank or protocol now."

"Okay. So, Mike, do you believe?"

"Believe what?"

"You know. God. Well, more than that. The whole package. The supernatural. The existence of angels and demons. Spiritual warfare."

"*Spiritual* warfare? Never heard of it," Mike replied with a shrug. "But I go to church every once in a while and believe in God. Good and evil. I've always figured He's up there somewhere doing His thing while we're pretty much stuck down here trying to clean up our own mess."

"You've been to War College, right? Remember the name they had for all those Cold War fights we used to pick with Communist puppet regimes?"

"Proxy wars?"

"That's it," Dylan said. "Proxy wars meant fighting stand-ins for the true threat, a single power we didn't want to mess with head-on. Vietnam. Korea. Afghanistan. Grenada. Angola. Yet the common enemy was Communism, either the Soviet Union or China. We fought proxy wars in lieu of jumping feet first into the big one."

"You got that right."

"Well, in a way, mankind's conflicts have been proxies too—of another, hidden war that's been going on since the beginning of history. These days we think we're fighting terror, but that's not the whole truth. We're fighting the powers that *fuel* terrorism. And those powers aren't physical; they're spiritual. They're the same powers that live in this place. And that's who we've got to destroy before they trigger the *real* war to end all wars. That's spiritual warfare."

"So you're talking about"—Mike's voice turned incredulous—"Satan? The devil?"

"Well, not him so much as his armies. The legions of demons who occupy this world."

"How do you explain that you see them, when I can't?"

"It's like a gift. Or a curse, depending on your perspective. Most people have to take this stuff completely on faith. Apparently I'm the first man to belong to the Watchers, this ancient spiritual family line that carries the ability, like an odd recessive gene. The ability to see beyond. The other side."

Mike leaned back and sighed into the darkness. "Well, Watcher or not, you're still my tactics man. What do we do now?"

"You want a tactic?" Jon said, staring hard into his eyes. "Pray. Pray like crazy. And not some namby-pamby, thank-you-God-for-the-food kind of prayer either."

"Pray for what exactly?" asked Mike.

"For faith, first of all. That's your shield. And your weapon, that's the Spirit."

"What in the world does *that* mean?"

"All I know is, just start talking to God—sincerely, from the heart—and beg Him for more faith, and for protection and strength. And while you're at it, ask Him to send a few warrior angels. That's one of the scary things about this place, now that I think about it. I haven't seen an angel since I got here."

"You see angels too?"

"I do, and they're one of my major consolations. But I'm not seeing them right now."

"You mean we're on our own right now?"

"Well, no. God's presence is everywhere. But the absence of angels, if I remember what they taught me, means this is some kind of hellhole. And I don't mean that as slang. I mean literally."

"Then how about taking some action?" Mike urged in an agitated tone. "As in getting out of here! The way I see it, we'll both die in this cave if we don't find another exit. I'm liable to bleed to death and you'll run into that monster who used to be Mystic Two and go down in another firefight. Either way, we're both sitting ducks unless we keep moving."

"You up for it?"

Mike groaned as he rose to his feet. "I don't know. But I'm not gonna sit here and wait to die."

Just as Mike was reaching for his flashlight, its last glow blinked out completely. Sheer darkness seemed to collapse upon them.

The speed and severity of its fall took Dylan's breath away. He felt himself swaying, his balance compromised by a lack of visual reference. Then he stumbled sideways as panic rose within him, seizing his heart, stomping down on his lungs. He began to wonder which way was up and which way down.

He was lost. Lost forever, never to find his way out again to open sky and clear sight lines and the coolness of fresh air in his lungs.

"Got a glowstick?" came Mike's voice through the gloom.

Dylan shook his head, chuckling at himself for forgetting. Mission planners had stuck one into their side pockets for marking and emergency illumination. He reached down to his pant leg, pulled one out, and bent it in half. Its welcome lime green glow caused him to sigh with relief.

"Who would have thought," he said, "that with a half million bucks' worth of gear on our bodies, and a half billion's worth waiting for us outside, we'd be thanking our lucky stars for a fifty-cent glowstick!"

When Mike's glowstick had flickered to life, Dylan ducked under the man's shoulder, supporting him from his uninjured side while holding up his own stick. Then the two began walking, the glowsticks' light barely reaching their feet.

They hadn't taken ten steps when the unmistakable echoes of distant gunfire reached their ears. A short volley, fully automatic, maybe a dozen rounds.

Dylan stopped, waiting for more.

Mike started to form a question, but Dylan was first to speak.

"They've taken Mystic Two. They know they'll never have us. Not our souls, at least. So they decided to harvest him, or to make him harvest *himself*."

It felt to Dylan like two hours later when it happened. In truth it had been just over fifteen minutes of walking alongside half-glimpsed shapes of revolting and bloodcurdling beings. And drawings—etchings of huge heads devouring tiny human forms. Of mutilation and torture. He had thought of Dante's *Inferno*—"*abandon all hope, ye who enter here*"—and told himself that whether this place was hell or not, it certainly deserved that sort of billing.

Dylan had decided not to look at the monstrosities portrayed around him, for his first glance had instantly turned his stomach. Then he felt something hard and smooth graze the top of his head. Feeling it too, Mike let out a cry. Dylan raised his gun barrel, and both men held up their glowsticks at the same second and gasped. Mike uttered a retching sound. Dylan groaned in disgust.

Skeletons. Everywhere.

They had been hung upside down, hundreds of them. The two men immediately noticed something else. They were headless.

"What's with the missing skulls?" Mike whispered.

"You really want to know?"

"I think so . . ."

"They were sacrificed."

Dylan turned toward the wall beside him. Mike followed suit, letting out a sharp cry.

The glowsticks' scarce light revealed a large heap of skulls, neatly stacked like so many cans of soup. Empty eye sockets lined up in dozens of rows leveled cold, ghastly stares into their own. Both men took a step back, for they could feel each one like a chilled exhaling upon their faces.

For the second time that day, Dylan was having difficulty drawing a full breath. That was because he could see more than Mike did. He saw the ratlike demons curling in and out of the skulls' empty cavities.

Muttering to himself, he scattered them with a waving motion of his right hand. Then he looked down as though in prayer.

"Mike, did you notice the size of those skulls?" he said, still facing downward.

"They're small, aren't they?"

"They're the skulls of . . ." But Dylan couldn't make himself form the word.

He swallowed hard and turned away.

CHAPTER

_9

Good morning, everybody!

I'm sorry it's been so long since I wrote you all. I won't bore you with the reasons that have prevented me from communicating like I needed to. Besides, there's no time. This is an official alarm, a full-blown crisis.

Dylan's in trouble. I don't know exactly how, or even where, and yet it's definitely happening and it's very serious. Sister Rulaz and my mother and I have all received the very same warnings in the Spirit.

So why don't I know where Dylan is? The short answer is that we had a disagreement. Let's just say it was a combination of emotional and relationship stuff, combined with disagreement about the future direction of our lives and the Watchers. Then shortly afterward, Dylan disappeared. Just like that, he left.

You remember Dylan's background, of course. He'd made that clear after joining our side. Before meeting me, and more importantly, before meeting God, Dylan was one of the most skilled soldiers in our government's secret-ops arsenal. He traveled the world on solo missions, going after those people whose death was considered to be in the interests of America. Ethnic cleansers, renegade generals, terrorists, traitors, drug lords, you name it. And he took pride in doing his job carefully, secretly, and efficiently.

So in the normal course of such a career, there would be nothing unusual about his taking off without warning. He's just never had anyone concerned about him during such absences before. Dylan has a very large, extended family now, even if it's a family of the Spirit.

If he'd been harmed or killed, I'm sure I would have found out about it right away, and so would many of you. I just assumed all this time that he was stepping back and taking some kind of break to think about things and get his head together.

Now I think it's something darker than that.

So fellow Watchers, I have two things to ask of you.

First, if your gifting has shown you anything of Dylan, anything at all, please contact me right away. Second, it's time to bombard him and his surroundings with the most aggressive forms of prayer. We can't just be watchers now. We have to be warriors as well.

I know that you guys don't know Dylan like I do, like you should have been allowed to. That's my fault. And I know many of you are still wrestling with the idea of a male Watcher, since our family tree has been female for two thousand years. But I've seen a wounded and tender side to this man. I know he's surrendered his life and will to our Lord.

And I know beyond all doubt that this morning he's fighting for his life.

Please pray!

—Abby

TUNNEL 9, TORA BORA, AFGHANISTAN

The global intelligence team overseeing Operation Mystic Sender—everyone from forward air controllers keeping their eye on the cave from nearby cliff tops, to AWACS pilots thousands of feet overhead, to satellite analysts across the planet in Fort Meade, Maryland, and Colorado Springs, Colorado, to watch commanders at the National Counterterrorism Center in McLean, Virginia—had already become quite nervous.

Three hours had passed with no communication back from the squad. Inquiring signal pings to their communication man's receivers had gone unanswered. The only tangible bit of intelligence had been a smattering of machine-gun fire echoed from the mouth of the cave, picked up by microphones roughly thirty minutes into the operation.

Worse yet, all sensors monitoring the site had fluttered wildly and without ceasing, almost to the point of damaging their systems' sensitive tolerances. All of the disquieting signs that had brought Mystic Sender here in the first place had just doubled in their intensity.

Then suddenly, reports emerged that the satellite had acquired an emergency signal, incredibly faint.

The brass at the operation's highest echelons had little choice in the matter. The squad had been chosen for its skill and experience precisely because there would be no backups. Once at the cave's entrance, they would be plucked from the spot in seconds, but making it back out to that point was entirely up to them. That had been clearly understood.

A rescue team was on standby, but the brass was loath to pull the trigger on that operation, labeled Orkutz Rescue. The generals reasoned that if this crew couldn't safely navigate the place, sending another team after them sounded like a waste of perfectly good soldiers. Nevertheless, it was a possibility not only planned for but now actively considered.

Soon, however, their carefully delineated action window would expire. Shortly after dawn, the time frame for their carefully constructed alibis, cover stories, and outright silence would pass, and the entire ring of secrecy erected around the mission would begin to crumble.

Whatever they did, they had to finish it before then.

And when that happened, the once-prized freelancers would have become liabilities.

That is, if any of them survived.

DEEP INSIDE TUNNEL 9—TWO HOURS LATER

The end came at the final hour before dawn. Such a comparison, however, would have meant little to Mystic Sender's remaining pair. Daylight, open air, or even a hope of seeing the sun again, lay an eternity away. Their universe had shrunk down to the sound of their own breathing, the stifling mouthfuls of vengeful air, the agony of their trudging limbs, and the foot or so of light on either side of their barely surviving glowsticks. The faint, intermittent flashes of light seemed to mirror the two men's waning strength, not to mention the faltering hope within them.

In fact, their steps became so forced and strained that Dylan almost stepped over the edge of a void before even realizing he'd reached its edge. His awareness came more from the currents of air swirling against his face than any other clue. He pulled back his foot just in time, though the momentum of Mike close behind him nearly sent them both over. Dylan gritted his teeth, pulling himself and Mike back toward safety.

"Some kind of pit," Dylan whispered.

"This may be the end of the road," said Mike. "Unless we can find a way to take a look down there."

"Got a match?"

"I have a lighter," Mike replied, pulling it out and handing it to Dylan.

"Good. I'll light something and toss it down."

Dylan tore off the sleeve of his shirt and held it above the lighter's flame. When the cloth caught fire, Dylan dropped it into the pit. An initial gust of air nearly blew it out, yet the fire revived as the cloth fluttered into its descent.

Dylan frowned and leaned forward. Some seconds later the still-burning rag finally struck bottom. It had fallen much farther than either man would have dreamed possible.

"What is that down there?" Mike asked, prevented by his injury from leaning over the pit.

"I can't tell. Some kind of junk pile."

Just then their glowsticks gave out completely, both at the same time.

In the next instant they heard a loud *whoosh,* and as if determined to punish their intrusion, flames rushed toward them with a deafening crackle. Mike fell back, but Dylan was so entranced by what the fire revealed that he remained where he stood, the front of his body lit up by the glow.

He then dropped to his knees and, near the edge of the pit, bowed his head.

Before him, more than a hundred feet down, a latent pool of methane had ignited into a firestorm. The gas must have floated there for decades, gathered from layers of decomposing human bodies.

Now the eruption of fire and superheated air caused the cadavers to rise and contort in a macabre ballet, even as they were consumed.

Mike stared down at the horror, and in an instant his face seemed to melt, to slacken and lose the shape that made him who he was. He screamed and yet the voice was not his own.

In that moment, he lost his sanity.

In the midst of his horror, Dylan realized something. Even after urging Mike to pray as though his life depended on it, he had failed to do so himself. He hadn't prayed! He was virtually defenseless!

And surely neither had Mike. If Dylan was now helpless, how much more his naïve friend!

The answer came immediately. Before Dylan could do anything, Mike raised himself up with a grimace on his face, bent his knees, and leaped.

Screaming after him, almost losing his balance in a futile attempt to stop him, Dylan watched Mike dive into the inferno. Weeping tears that the superheated air whipped from his face, Dylan did not turn away as his companion struck the pile of burning bones and burst into flame.

Alone in the flickering shadows, he watched and wept like a child.

A moment later, Dylan saw the pit's center open just enough to reveal a stone structure. It was stained red.

An altar.

He heard the roar again, close now, directly beneath him, bellowing up at him so fiercely that it filled his ears and blew through his hair. He saw the one from whose throat it had come, raging from its altar, its throne. Dylan saw . . .

His brain refused to process the image.

Shutting his eyes against the sight, he stepped back from the edge of the pit. His thinking began to twist, to warp. It came to him that without a doubt he'd just peered over the rim of Hades.

The notion caused his head to swim and the whole scene to launch into a fiercely spinning maelstrom of despair and horror. He felt himself fall, powerless to stop it. His head struck something cold and unyielding.

Then his world went dark. Silent.

CHAPTER
_10

GADZHIYEVO NAVAL BASE, SKALISTYY CLOSED ADMINISTRATIVE
DISTRICT, MURMANSK OBLAST, RUSSIA

Fog was a familiar sight here in the bays of Russia's far north, a sight commonly associated with spring, when the sea grew warmer and the coming of daylight offered greater contrasts in humidity and temperature. And when the presence of sunlight allowed the fog to be seen.

Yet no human eyes witnessed this particular wisp of fog, alone and oddly whisked along by a freezing offshore wind. It seemed to catch the faintest of light from the nearby shore and the crystalline gleams from harbor quays, ships, and security beacons, then amplify them like some vaporous prism.

Had a human being by some coincidence been able to pull alongside it in a boat, he or she would have been struck first by a sense of frost creeping through their innermost parts. They would have found themselves grimacing the way people do in a sewer. Then wincing at a sense of evil so pungent and searing that they would never forget it as long as they lived.

The ancient, hateful presence dislodged from Tora Bora in 2001 had spent the years since then gaining strength to carry out its objective, hovering all over the globe, gathering bloodthirsty demons to take part in its upcoming war.

It was now ready to take its first human host in pursuit of its vengeance.

Steering his skiff through a stout northerly wind and the white-caps of Sayda Bay, Sergei Yastrebov found himself, for the first time in his life, grateful for his home's annual spell of continual darkness. Without the endless night, he would not have had a cover for his theft or such a plausible reason for being abroad in these conditions.

Bracing himself against brutal seaborne gusts, the thirty-year-old welder allowed the serendipity to warm his spirit. It was the perfect alibi: the fact that up here at the farthest reaches of the Russian arctic, everybody conducted their business in darkness. With two months of gloom, nobody could afford to wait for spring to take care of important matters.

As a result, skulking around in the so-called dead of night here in the far north did not arouse the suspicions it might have provoked in Moscow. His presence, alone in a godforsaken and uninviting part of the bay, was at least explainable enough to avoid arrest. He had been out on a routine bay crossing when the winds had pushed him off course, taxing his small engine's ability to compensate. It was within the realm of possibility . . .

That was, assuming no one looked under the blanket at his feet.

Regardless of any safety net, simple caution had compelled Sergei to hug the bay's countless inlets and rocky promontories to avoid encountering any unforeseen patrols. He knew the regular harbor guards and was quite confident that the night's gift of vodka would have certainly by now produced the desired result. There would be no patrols tonight.

However, with the steel hulk of Russia's largest submarine graveyard lying on the opposite shoreline, one never knew for certain. The commanders at Gadzhiyevo were notoriously skittish, even more so given their current project, which involved the most sensitive, dangerous, and politically charged in the base's history. Their complex had for over a year now been defueling the ruined *Kursk*, the Russian submarine that had sunk several years before and killed all one hundred nineteen of its sailors.

The *Kursk* incident had emerged as one of modern Russia's most embarrassing debacles—especially, as Sergei remembered with a sneer, when the Moscow fools had out of stupid pride declined Western help and thereby sealed its crewmen's deaths.

His cousin's death.

Sergei's hometown, had his bosses bothered to check, was Severomorsk, the nearby home port of Russia's Northern Fleet and of the *Kursk* itself. A city devastated by the deaths, where hardly a family had been spared a needlessly bitter grief.

His cousin Anton had been on board. A handsome, bright-minded young man, sacrificed to the Russian leader's ego. The very thought of his cousin's life being thrown away made Sergei shake with rage.

That was the reason for the bundle under the blanket. The reason why, two months earlier, he had failed to report the discovery of a nuclear weapon no one had thought to account for. A device which did not appear on the schematics or manifests, precisely because its presence was kept secret even from the *Kursk* crew, known only to the captain and the ship's political officer. The very existence of such devices was not even officially acknowledged by the Kremlin.

They called it a "scuttle bomb."

A small nuclear device, no bigger than a rugby ball and weighing about fifty pounds, but powerful enough to vaporize the *Kursk* in case of imminent capture by enemy forces. It was made to be detonated by the pushing of a hidden button inside the captain's quarters, the submarine equivalent of a poison pill.

Sergei had found it by accident, detached from its hiding place in a dark corner of the ship's bulkhead. A spot near impossible for anybody to find, except for a welder, who crawled in and around the tightest of spaces to do his work. Sergei hadn't even known what the thing was until closer inspection had shown him the universal symbol for an atomic bomb.

He'd known that, much like his cousin's, his life would be drastically cut short by the encounter. The radioactive device wasn't supposed to be there. He had been assured by his superiors that the room was clean, that his work on its periphery was entirely safe.

Typical bureaucratic incompetence, he snarled to himself. Now he was making them pay. And his new clients would pay in the most obvious of currencies—enough to leave his family secure for life. The nation which had betrayed him would pay by suffering a firsthand encounter with his discovery.

It wasn't the most powerful bomb in the world's inventory, but it was ready. No scientists needed, no expensive infrastructure or years of fiddling in a laboratory. And it was many times more deadly than any other bomb of its size and weight. Placed in just the right spot, it was powerful enough to kill thousands of people. Maybe more, if its location was leveraged perfectly. He smiled just thinking of all the commotion he alone, old Sergei from Sayda Bay, would soon ignite around the world.

Smuggling out the device had proven far easier for someone unconcerned about exposure. But he would die a famous man, that was for certain.

Sergei peered ahead and cursed under his breath. A fierce fog was rolling in. Meeting his rendezvous would now be doubly challenging. He pulled back on the engine's throttle and steered straight toward open water.

Just then a strangely isolated trail of fog overcame his boat, closed its gap with his head, and vanished whole inside Sergei's body. The young man reared back violently, then bent forward coughing, nearly capsizing the craft. At last he stood up ramrod straight, held out his arms at his sides, gazing dead ahead into the night sky as though drinking in the darkness.

Before he had a chance to end the strange posture and regain his seat, the weather suddenly changed. In less than twenty seconds the wind redoubled its strength and the waves tripled in size. Suddenly surviving every wave was a challenge. He lowered his head and regretted not having insisted on a safer method of exchange. Three minutes overboard in these waters and he would be dead. Still, it was the only means his contact had been able to arrange.

Running lights blinked on, merely fifty yards to port.

He closed his eyes in relief and thanked Allah under his breath.

He pulled alongside the small fishing vessel, which at great risk had entered the secluded bay in total darkness, all its lights extinguished. Two pairs of arms reached down to take his tie line and the thick ropes attached to the box beneath the blanket.

"Salaam!" came the greeting from overhead.

They were Chechnyans. The best-paying, most troublesome customers Sergei had been able to find with his limited contacts. And fellow Muslims.

"Salaam!" he said in reply. But then he frowned, for when the payload was pulled up, his skiff's tie line was tossed back at his feet.

"What's happening?" he shouted.

The answer came with silenced bullets, shattering his skull and plunging the rest of his world into darkness. The last sensation he felt was the frigid water, rising up to embrace his falling body.

The Chechnyans noticed a strange fog wafting up toward them from the point of the body's impact.

By the time they had turned around and traced a course for the quickest way out of there, the two men had made eye contact, and each saw in the other an eerie, cold fire smoldering there.

Instead of jihad, their brains now burned with a whole new creed, a whole different murderous devotion.

JERUSALEM, CHURCH OF THE HOLY SEPULCHRE

Sister Rulaz rolled off her old reed mat onto the tarpaper of the church rooftop. She began to shudder. Her eyes remained open, calm, and unblinking despite her body's trembling. But

Brother Jiwobu knew this was no ordinary symptom. He had seen her dehydrated, seen her weakened to the point of losing a pulse, seen her so transported by waves of joy that an outside observer would have deemed her an epileptic.

Yet he hadn't seen this. He had never seen foam fleck her lips. He had never seen such a distressing shade of blue splotch her skin.

He picked up the sister's cell phone and began to dial 101, Israel's universal emergency number for medical assistance.

SANTA MONICA, CALIFORNIA—MINUTES LATER

The black Suburbans pulled up to a two-story condominium belonging to Abigail R. Sherman, disgorging a half dozen identically black-clad men. The squadron stormed her front door, banged on it loudly three times, then kicked it in and entered with laser-sighted machine guns drawn.

They found the living spaces empty and clean, the garage vacant, and the aquarium containing a long-feeding tablet used by people away on extended travel.

They were too late.

At that moment Abby and her mother were eleven miles away boarding a 747 at the LAX International Terminal, bound for Amsterdam with a booked connection to Israel's David Ben Gurion Airport. The tickets had been paid for in cash, purchased at the airport counter.

Jerusalem.

The warning to detain Ms. Sherman arrived to Homeland Security staff just as the jumbo jet's wheels left the runway.

CHAPTER

_11

Twelve hours into their flight, squirming in her business-section seat, Abby had but one thought. *Lord, please let me make it in time!*

She turned to her mother. "Should we try again?"

"Honey, you *will* speak to her before she dies. We've both gotten assurance of that. Please stop worrying."

Abby frowned, shaking her head while staring at the in-flight phone turning over and over in her fingers. The receiver had not been returned to its cradle in the opposite seatback since shortly after takeoff.

If the monk's frantic phone calls were true, then one of the women she treasured most in the world, a frail Ethiopian Coptic nun known worldwide as the Sentinel of Jerusalem, now lay dying in a hospital bed on Jerusalem's Mount Scopus. Abby could hardly believe it. Yes, Sister Rulaz was physically frail and seemed always on the verge of some illness or other. But her overpowering personality and spiritual vibrancy made it impossible to picture her succumbing to anything short of the apocalypse.

The reports said otherwise. Something had frightened the woman so terribly that it had jarred loose her tenuous hold on earthly existence. There were medical names, of course, which related to her heart. Names such as arrhythmia and infarction. And yet Abby knew better. Something truly earthshaking was under way. Sister Rulaz had things to say, Abby had been told, things she would say only to her.

The thought tormenting Abby the most was not Rulaz' death itself, but the idea of missing her friend's parting gift of those vitally important words.

Abby took her thousandth deep breath of the trip and re-minded herself to remain calm. *Think of something else.*

She forced herself to bask in the peace of the cabin at mid-flight, lights dimmed to a soothing glow, the engines' hum her only audible distraction. She glanced beside her, at her mother's outwardly serene demeanor. Reaching out, she patted her hand. "Thanks for coming, Mom," she said softly. "I'm so proud of you for making this trip."

Her mother smiled, seemingly unfazed by the role reversal inherent in those words.

Abby Sherman might have been a name known across the world, but not because she had wanted her life to turn out that way. She'd been a typical young college student when fame had found her, unsure of her future yet anchored by a few certainties in life: her nurturing father, her love of the beach, and most of all, her passion for God. Everything beyond that had come unbidden. The murder of her beloved housekeeper had led to repeated attempts on her life and an unfolding plot to keep her from exploring the meaning of the Sight—an ability to see spiritual manifestations that had suddenly begun to startle and intimidate her.

None of this, even the adventure's amazing outcome, had prepared Abby to become a shepherd of sorts to her own mother. Abby thought back to the cruel way in which her mother had been wrongly committed to an asylum for much of her adulthood. Her gifting had been mistaken for insanity, then later exploited by family. Heavily drugged, gradually enslaved by a combination of lies and the inevitable effects of her imprisonment, Abby's mother had emerged years later as a frail, childlike woman.

Abby looked into her mother's kind eyes and thought of how far she had come. Time alone with her long-lost daughter, who had grown up believing her dead, had already sparked a remarkable recovery. The Suzanne Sherman of today was unrecognizable in every respect from the stooping, bleary-eyed wraith that Abby and Dylan had spirited out of the high-security wing of St. Stephen's Home for Mental Health and Recovery so many months ago.

Despite all the encouraging signs, however, Abby had worried that the long flight and what awaited them in Jerusalem might prove a daunting prospect for her mom. As it turned out, it was the mother who was bearing up the daughter, the so-called strong one. Abby had grown more distraught and dependent with every somber report from the hospital and every prayer returning the same verdict. *Rulaz doesn't have much time left.*

In fact, the Watchers shared far more than a spiritual lineage or even a common gifting. They were also connected by a bond of kinship that allowed them to share in each other's emotional and spiritual life. That bond, even more than medical opinions, fed Abby's growing concern that she would not make it in time.

She could actually *feel* Sister Rulaz slipping away, like an inner throb beginning to fade.

Suzanne smiled, leaned toward Abby, and whispered, "It's God—He's the one who has made it possible for me to come with you. Thank goodness He's seen fit to take away my gifting right now. I don't think I could bear it otherwise."

"I know," Abby agreed. "I think He's done the same for me. The last time I made this trip, it was so frightening to see dominions constantly fighting each other around me. And it doesn't get any easier once you get to Jerusalem, believe me. The place is one giant, nonstop spiritual battleground."

"I'm sure that's not the only change we're going to see."

"No, it's not. This is such a different flight from last time," she whispered to her mother, gladly settling for the new train of thought. "I was coming from London, and Dylan was with me. I think London was the place where my feelings for Dylan started. There was this huge cloud of suspense over whether we would make it through Israeli customs. And yet things seemed a lot clearer. Fresher. It seemed everything was ahead of me. Whereas now, for some reason, it feels like I'm rehashing old ruts in a sad kind of way."

"You miss him, Abby. There's nothing wrong with that."

"Maybe. Or maybe it's just that he should be here. He loves Sister Rulaz very much. He'd want to know. He'd be on this flight in a heartbeat, if only . . ."

"You didn't leave, honey. Remember that. Dylan's the one who walked away."

"I know, Mom. But I keep thinking if I'd kept my mouth shut, or at least phrased things a little more kindly, maybe it all wouldn't have happened like it did."

Despite her best efforts, Abby's mind whisked her back to their final conversation, replayed in her imagination over and over again.

The dispute had taken place on the sidewalk outside her condo, just as the sun was setting over San Pedro Bay. It had been the same old fight, the same tired disagreement, only lately it had escalated to a critical level—Abby's unwillingness to confront a faction of the Watchers, a group of bloggers who had started questioning whether Dylan belonged among them.

"Dylan, these women don't have anything against you," she had argued. "It's just that the Watchers has been a family of African women for centuries. It's who they are, spiritually and physically—descendants of this ancient family tree. Then *we* come along and ask them to accept a white sister, then two, and now a man. It's too much, all at once."

"You're patronizing them," he snapped. "They can figure out the logic of how their family has expanded beyond a single demographic. They're not stupid."

"Then think about *this*," she countered. "You're not only a man but a former government assassin and special-ops soldier. You gained my trust under false pretenses in order to win my confidence and then murder me."

"But I didn't, did I? Kill you, that is."

"No. Thank God you turned away from your mission and from the men who sent you, then risked your life to save us. But you've got to see how that kind of background could cast doubt on your character, and on your intentions. It's not exactly the best first impression a person could hope for, Dylan. These are women who think of the term *soldier*, let alone *assassin*, as having terrifying associations. And word got out that you can be reckless and argumentative, that you don't always listen to the counsel of others."

"Yeah, and sometimes the things I insisted on wound up saving our lives. Spiritual baby or not, I have things to offer in a tactical situation—even a spiritual one."

"Dylan," she said, her anger rising, "nobody said otherwise. But the fact is, you've been a stubborn student. You've been slow to accept things you couldn't understand. That has nothing to do with your being a man, or even a soldier. It has to do with your unwillingness to surrender your fallen nature!"

"Hah! There's the problem!" Dylan shouted. "You and your sisters are so arrogant, so convinced you know it all, that you cast any disagreement as a rebellion against God himself!"

"And *you* cast any request to lay down your pride as a bunch of old mother hens trying to emasculate you!"

"Bottom line? You could have defended me. You could have ended all this debate by going on record that you stood behind me. And you didn't."

"You're right, Dylan. That's because I didn't disagree with a lot of their concerns. Surrendering your pride is a much bigger issue than a little grumbling among the sisters."

"You know what," he said, shaking his head darkly. "Maybe I agree with them. Maybe there isn't room in the Watchers for a man. I'm not going to fight them. But you, Abby, need to consider this question: Did God create men with their innate aggressiveness for a reason? Because maybe we have something to add to your moth-eaten old traditions, something that would help the Watchers be more effective. You ever think about that?"

Now in retrospect, Abby could see that it had been a valid, even a good point. But at the time, she'd been in no mood to concede it.

"But that isn't the issue, Dylan! The issue is total surrender! *That's* what the Christian life is all about!" She was shouting at this point. "We've all surrendered our old selves, our sinful natures, and laid them at the cross!"

"No," he said. "You surrendered your sin. Your guilt, your shame. But not the best parts of yourself. Not your strengths, not the gifts He gave you. Those are blessings to be shared, not tossed away. You have something to offer, and so do I. I have something to offer the Watchers. And"—his voice suddenly lowered—"I have something to offer *you*. Or at least, I thought I did."

So there it was, finally, the underlying force driving this argument—romantic feelings between them. Emotions that had simmered below the chaos of all their previous adventures and now demanded to be dealt with in the relative calm of present day.

Yet something about his presumption had galled her. He had swerved into this most delicate of issues far too boldly for her taste, and she was not about to go along.

"Please," she had replied with all the coldness a woman of her temperament could muster. "Stop insisting on being my knight in shining armor, Dylan. I already have one."

"Yeah," Dylan said, his face muscles gripped by anger. "Well, you and he—go have a nice life."

With that, he had whirled around and stormed off toward his car. Standing by the door, he turned back to face her.

"I liked you a lot better *before* you were a Watcher," he said, his anger tinged by sadness. He then disappeared inside his car, started the engine, and sped away.

And Abby had not seen Dylan since that day.

CHAPTER

_12

ISRAEL, DAVID BEN GURION AIRPORT

It all seemed so different from the first time.

Abby walked into the gilded, soaring hall of Terminal 3, one of the most dramatic rooms in all of Israel, yet even though the whole experience returned to flow over her at once—the templelike columns of pale Jerusalem stone, the same rock which made up the Wailing Wall, the echo of a public-address announcer reading off foreign names, beams of sunlight pouring through oversized windows—most of the previous thrill had vanished.

She knew why, of course. This time she was here for reasons she dreaded, and there was no time to waste. A dear friend of hers was dying.

"I'm sorry I'm not being a better travel companion," she said to her mother as they stepped onto a people mover and were swiftly carried forward. "It's just that—"

"There's no need to explain," Suzanne interrupted. "I understand."

"Maybe later on, we can spend some time looking around, take in some of the sights. Right now all I can think about is getting through customs and making it to Sister Rulaz before it's too late."

"We'll both know when Rulaz passes away, or even starts to come close. You know that." Her mother laid a comforting hand on Abby's shoulder.

The touch of a mother's hand was something she had learned to live without over the years. But then she'd realized its presence had the calming power of a hundred massages. She smiled at the thought.

They arrived at the long, crowded Passport and Security hall. Abby sighed in resignation when she saw the lines crammed with weary travelers, snaking toward the back of the room.

Her mother's grip on Abby's arm tightened, causing Abby to turn and ask what was wrong.

Suzanne's eyes were alit with a faraway look.

That was when it struck her. Her view of the airport swooned and she sensed life—someone's life, not her own—begin to disengage, to flutter off-center like a movie slipping from its frame. Her world was briefly replaced with a flicker of bright hospital lamps framed by faces staring down, worried, weeping, one of them with a clerical collar at the neck.

It took another second for the meaning of it all to reach her conscious mind.

Rulaz was about to die!

The moment was upon them, and here they stood ninth in line, not to mention a fifteen-mile cab ride away.

"Do you feel it too?" Abby asked her mother in a trembling whisper.

"You mean *them*?"

Abby followed her mother's gaze, then quickly realized she had been watching something else altogether. She engaged her spiritual eyes, willing them forward, seeking, probing, and shuddered despite herself. No matter how many times she sensed such visitors, and how many times she combated them, their ugliness never failed to send an involuntary shiver down her spine.

She took a deep breath, straightened her back, and faced ahead. The back wall of the airport lobby was lined with a hideous gauntlet of evil spirits. They stood unnaturally still as though poised for battle, their cold and leering eyes fixed hard upon the two of them.

Worse than her shudder of revulsion was the realization that these beings were not there just to harass her and Suzanne. They were there for a bigger purpose—to hinder them from leaving the airport. They knew full well which archenemy of theirs lay nearby, awaiting Abby's arrival.

Abby felt her knees buckle and her breath rattle in her chest.

She wasn't going to make it . . .

Suddenly another realization burst into her understanding. *They don't own this ground.* Those beasts are not unopposed!

Ignoring any attention she might draw to herself, Abby dropped to one knee, closed her eyes, and lowered her head. Abby knew

God wanted her there. He wanted her to see Rulaz. So it was little more than a matter of asking Him.

She heard a rustling beside her, her mother joining her in prayer. Both women now knelt as one.

After a few moments she looked up, expecting to feel the eyes of waiting travelers staring at her. To her surprise, nobody was watching. She chuckled to herself, remembering this was Jerusalem, where visitors were constantly making shows of reverence and great emotion.

She stood, then helped her mother to her feet. The two women looked around them.

Abby tried her hardest to sense the arrival of any friendly spiritual entities. Praying constantly, she scanned the room and saw nothing. There were only the demons, aligned as a solid barrier to her progress.

A commotion beside her seized her attention—a dark-skinned man in an equally dark suit was rushing toward her, holding a black briefcase and breathing heavily from exertion.

"Miss Sherman?" he inquired between pants, having reached her side.

"Yes?" she said warily.

"I am a diplomatic attaché from the Ethiopian Embassy, and I have been instructed to escort you through customs on an emergency basis. You are entering Israel under covering of our embassy, on a humanitarian mission to one of our most prominent citizens in Israel, are you not?"

"Well, yes . . ." she stammered.

"Then please, you and your party, come with me. Hurry!"

The man turned on his heels and began swiftly heading for the room's exit. Abby shot her mother a glance of amazement mixed with gratitude as she picked up their bags to follow him.

Both women kept their eyes focused down on the floor just ahead, not wishing to observe the demons' rage as they painlessly bypassed the intended ambush. The line that had loomed minutes ago like an endless gauntlet of doom now whizzed past in a happy blur. The interview partitions flowed by, and even the outermost gate to freedom, guarded by a pair of well-armed soldiers, proved no match for their abrupt rise in status. One soldier took a sheath of documents from the attaché, read for several seconds, and waved them all through without hesitation. Abby's heart filled with wonder at the change a few moments could bring.

They swerved toward a side door, which their guide quickly opened, and all at once they were climbing down metal stairs to the tarmac level. A black Lincoln awaited them, engine running, doors already open. Abby offered an arm to her mother, who stepped inside the car and took a seat, Abby close behind her. Soon they were reclining on warm leather and feeling the surge of a powerful engine pulling them forward.

"Thank you," Abby mouthed to the guide, who had taken a front seat next to the driver.

"You are most welcome," the man replied, his English including an accent she could not quite place. "Sister Rulaz has many friends. I am very happy to assist you today. Let us pray we make it in time."

Abby took that as a cue, bowed her head, and begged for a smooth ride into Jerusalem.

As it turned out, fast was no problem, but smooth proved another matter altogether. From the airport's manicured citrus grove and landscaped grounds to Highway 1, the main roadway from Tel Aviv to Jerusalem, and on into the city itself, their chauffeur proved to be a dexterous driver. Vehicles and landscape alike rushed past their windows in a swerving, stomach-churning circus ride of a journey.

Abby once again felt her mother's hand squeeze hers, hard this time, looked over and saw her with eyes clenched tight, mumbling furiously. Wondering if she was praying for Rulaz' health or merely begging for survival, Abby looked down again at their hands. For her, "white knuckle" had become far more than an idle catchphrase.

The car, with its horn blaring and headlights blinking continuously, hardly slowed down as it entered Jerusalem's outer suburbs. Abby felt a fleeting urge to point out the distant hulk of the Knesset building and the rise of Mount Scopus, but her mother insisted on keeping her eyes shut. Sightseeing would have to come later.

CHAPTER
_13

With a desperate acceleration up a long stretch of highway, followed by a sharp turn to their right, the Lincoln's brakes eased them to a stop and they were there. A humble five-story brick building, its true purpose betrayed only by an ambulance at the curb and a telltale red cross. The door flew open, and Abby felt her mother's hands at her back, pushing her out.

"Don't worry about me," her mother urged. "Just go as fast as you can, and I'll catch up!"

Abby did as she was told. Her guide's hand found hers and pulled her forward, and soon they were pushing through the crowd in the hospital lobby and down a narrow hallway, then up a flight of stairs.

At the landing they turned to face another crammed hallway, but this time Abby recognized the faces and the spiritual light of the Sisterhood. The women were Rulaz' fellow Ethiopian

Watchers, who maintained a fierce loyalty and affection for Rulaz, the Sentinel of Jerusalem.

Immediately a sea of outstretched palms rose up to stop them, followed by a clamor of women's voices.

"You cannot go, sir! No one allowed inside!"

But Abby's guide lifted up his badge and said, "This is Sister Abby!"

A hush fell over the crowd as hands lowered and revealed dozens of staring, expectant faces. The wall of obstructing bodies parted immediately.

A young sister near her reached out a hand and grazed Abby's. "Forgive us. Please, come in. She awaits you."

A strange sense of beckoning seemed to draw Abby onward, into the narrow corridor between their bodies. The door at the far end now appeared to grow out of proportion. She stepped forward, and the sensation of their presence nearby made Abby feel immersed in a large and sacred family. A tingle lit up her insides, and her eyes filled with tears.

Then, just as quickly, she was inside Rulaz' room, small yet filled with a palpable peace. Abby moved to the bed where Rulaz lay. The only spot of color in a frame of white sheets was the old woman's face. Thin, brown, skin drawn tight, eyes closed, a face that did not seem to inhabit her world.

"Abigail" came a light, breathy whisper.

"Oh, Sister, I came as fast as I could," Abby replied. "What did you need to tell me?"

"Listen, for I am near to . . . I have seen a wave of death strike your eastern shores. A giant wave of destruction beyond any that has come before it. It must be stopped. And it . . . it can be."

Her voice was weakening. Abby quickly lowered herself closer to Rulaz' ear. "How, Sister? The Watchers?"

Those rheumy brown eyes then opened and fixed themselves upon Abby's. "Turn away from the Watchers, Abigail. A great evil is on the move, even now. You need to release the Watchers and look beyond. They are not enough. A greater army, a deeper force awaits. You must summon the warriors now."

"Warriors?" she said, shocked at what Rulaz had just told her to do.

Rulaz' cheek muscles quivered in response. She seemed faintly dismayed at the question, that Abby did not understand her reference.

"Call them out. I see a summons etched in stone. And I see you finding it. But find it soon. There is little time. When you do, they will listen to you. They will awaken."

"Dylan? Do you see him?" Abby asked, nearly pleading in her overwhelming awareness of how few seconds she had left. She felt a presence behind her right shoulder, then realized in a flash that it was her mother, arrived and now at her side. Rulaz smiled at Suzanne and continued to speak in an ever-weakening voice.

"No, Dylan has passed beyond our sight. He was in one of the enemy's darkest pits. He may lie beyond our help. If you can, find him, and heed his ways, before it's too late."

"Too late for what?"

Rulaz did not answer, but paused and merely lowered her eyelids. At length, she answered.

The last word was accompanied by a long exhaling.

"Please, find it where, this summons?"

But then Rulaz' face fell utterly still.

Abby held her breath and suddenly became aware of the many faces crowded around her. Each of them, including her mother's, holding their breath as well.

And then something remarkable happened. Abby heard a rustling sound. She straightened and turned just as all of the sisters stepped aside. At first, her focus on their movement left her unable to see what was really taking place. But then she looked ahead, and saw them.

Her mouth fell open.

She had seen angels before, but she had usually been alone in seeing them, and seeing alone was a different experience. She was unaccustomed to being in a roomful of women who could *all* see, who each stepped back in unison, at the perfect moment. Who all saw what she saw . . .

A pair of luminescent beings stepping through: tall, beautiful male figures filling the room with an incandescence that seemed to pour forth from right behind them, just behind their broad shoulders. Some light-filled hall from which they had just walked.

The pair moved slowly toward the bed. Abby immediately felt a compulsion to turn aside and give them room, even though as spiritual beings they could obviously move straight through her physical form. She turned away, nearly bumping into her mother's side, just as the nearest angel reached Rulaz' bed. The sheer proximity filled Abby with a sensation of love and caring so rich and vibrant that the difference between this and her former notion of those words was like that between feeling a raindrop on your shoulder and being immersed in a mountain lake on a warm summer day.

The angels bent over Rulaz and a surge of brilliance poured out from the point of convergence. What was happening was so intimate and precious that Abby could hardly look at it. She averted her eyes and only saw the glow, intensifying and shimmering in her peripheral vision.

She knew without a doubt that something which once had been Rulaz had left her body. Abby had never given much thought to what an actual spirit might look like on its own, outside of its human home. And now a desire for reverence kept her from looking straight in its direction. The passage of this soul felt too precious a thing to simply gawk at.

The angels slowly moved from their sight, bearing the glow which blended into a greater light and faded from view.

"Thank you for allowing me this time with her," she said softly to the others nearby.

A young sister who struck Abby as vaguely familiar, as though she'd encountered her in a dream or vision, approached her with an inquisitive expression.

"Are you our leader now?"

Abby had not known how she would answer such a question until just that moment. But at that instant, the words poured out.

"The Watchers are without an earthly leader right now. And I will not be the next one. The Lord will surely raise one up in time, but I will leave that to you. Each of you are desperately needed. It appears I am needed elsewhere."

She paused, and found she could not go on. Another syllable and Abby knew she would have erupted in tears. And something told her Rulaz would have wanted anything but tears to mark her passing.

It seemed as though a veil of shock swept over the women's faces at Abby's words. Smiling as best she could and holding her mother's hand almost for physical support, she slowly walked from the room.

They reached the street outside, both of them in a daze. Blinking in the sunshine, they saw that the Ethiopian Embassy car, along with their helpful guide, was nowhere to be seen.

Two brown sedans hurtled forward from out of nowhere and stopped with loud screeches of rubber on pavement. Abby felt her muscles clench in an immediate fight-or-flight response, but there was no time. The cars' front doors were already open, and darkly trousered legs already extending outward, seeking the sidewalk. Caucasian men in sunglasses jumped out and strode to her side.

"Abigail Sherman, please come with us." The speaker of those words looked sharply at her mother. "You too, ma'am. You are now in the custody of the United States government."

CHAPTER
_14

The streets of Jerusalem, which an hour before had swept past in a rush of fatigue and overstimulation, now shot by in blurred panic.

"What is this about?" she heard herself ask. She had said it so many times in the last several minutes that it felt more like an attempt to soothe herself than a genuine question to which she expected an answer. She looked at her mother as she said it and stiffened in alarm. Suzanne was pale, wide-eyed, and staring straight ahead. Abby sighed and took her mother's hand. "Are you all right?" she asked softly.

She received the hint of a smile in reply. Abby realized that her mom was in crisis mode and simply trying her best to live through it.

"Look," Abby said to the front seat in the most commanding voice she could produce, "I'll be glad to cooperate with you. But my mother is quite fragile, and she's in the middle of an anxiety attack. Please, you have no right to inflict this kind of suffering on her."

The agent turned in his seat and said, "Our sympathies to the both of you, Miss Sherman. You will be given the chance to express your concerns when we reach our destination. Until then, there's nothing that can be done."

"Fine," Abby said. "But if any harm comes to my mother as a result of this trauma, I *will* be taking action. You ever heard of the *Mara McQueen Show*? Well, I've been on her show twice. And I'll go on again and speak of nothing but you and your indifference toward a suffering woman you detained for no good reason."

"I assure you, Miss Sherman, there is a very good reason for this."

"A good reason to talk with *me*, maybe. But a reason for dragging us off the street in a time of grief? No way. I would have been glad to talk with you without having to be treated like some terrorist."

"You are not being considered a terrorist," said the man. "But if you fail to cooperate with us, that could change very rapidly."

"And if my mother's needs are not taken into consideration, your career and that of whoever cooked up this little escapade are over. Do you hear me?"

"You do what you have to, Miss Sherman. You are still an American citizen, and you certainly have rights. But you should know this"—he raised a sleek-looking pistol—"right now your status means those rights have been lifted. All the legal rights you've been brought up to expect are temporarily suspended. So until that changes, none of your threats have any impact on me or my colleagues whatsoever. But then again, I am only a courier. Save your arguments for the interrogation officer."

U.S. EMBASSY IN TEL AVIV, ISRAEL—ONE HOUR LATER

The man walked into the room carrying a folder and several attached sheets of paper. His eyes were fixed on the sheets as though reading them was far more important than making eye contact with the young woman who had waited on him for the last forty minutes. And he maintained that stare all through the motions of sitting at the table before her and dropping the folder onto its surface with a loud slap.

He then made a small jerking motion with his shoulders to straighten himself inside his smartly tailored suit jacket, doing the same with his wrists and sleeves.

Finally he looked up, his gaze wary. "Hello, Miss Sherman. I am Ron Guillian of the United States Department of Homeland Security. I need to ask you a few questions. The degree of helpfulness and truthfulness you exhibit during these next few minutes will determine whether this is a relatively short and painless interview or the worst experience of your life."

"Sir, am I under arrest for something?"

"You see, that's not the kind of question that's going to lead to our desired result."

"Nevertheless, it's what I require in order to even start cooperating with you. Please, am I under arrest?"

"Miss, you are under what's known as interrogative custody, which means you are being detained for questioning. You are not under arrest. Yet you are not free to go."

"Thank you, Mr. Guillian. I'm ready to talk to you now. But I'm going to bring up the first topic."

He made a small wave in the air. "If this is about your mother, let me set your mind at rest. Your mother is resting comfortably in one of our embassy guest rooms. She has been offered food and drink and a sedative, and is at last report feeling much better."

"Is *she* free to go?"

"Not exactly, no. But it's far from an eight-by-twelve cell, I assure you. How long she spends in the comfortable room is now up to you. Now we need to discuss a telephone conversation you recently engaged in. A call you received three nights ago from Andolo Rulaz, right here in Jerusalem."

She stared at him in disbelief. "You people intercepted a cell phone call?"

"I'm asking the questions here, Miss Sherman," he said with a sudden sharpness. "During this conversation, you and Ms. Rulaz exchanged descriptive terms regarding someone for whom you were deeply concerned. First of all, can you name this individual who was the subject of the conversation?"

Abby shrugged, debating her options. It struck her that she had nothing to hide and therefore in a situation this serious should choose forthrightness. After all, if the truth was on her side, why not employ that to her benefit?

"Sure," she said. "His name has been publicly linked with mine. It's Dylan Hatfield."

Guillian stared at her for a long time.

"You spoke words like *mystic sender*," he finally resumed, "and described a cave. And soldiers. How did you come across that information, Miss Sherman?"

She chuckled. "That, Mr. Guillian, is going to be a very interesting answer."

"All I need is the absolute truth."

"Oh, and that's what you're going to get. Whether you're ready to accept it is another matter entirely."

"Please just answer the question. Where did you get the information?"

"All right, then. I received that information through divine revelation."

"Explain what you mean by 'divine revelation.'"

"I and Sister Rulaz and many thousands of women like us all around the world share a common spiritual gift. Part of it is seeing beyond the veil that separates the physical world from the spiritual one. We see spiritual beings of every sort. But another part is that we often receive visions and revelations from the Holy Spirit."

"You mean . . . the Holy Spirit in the Bible?"

"Yes," she said, trying hard to conceal her amusement at his incredulous expression. "That's the one."

"So you claim that your discussion about 'mystic sender' or 'number nine' was not inspired or prompted in any way by any *earthly* preknowledge or communication?"

"Not from anybody human, it wasn't."

He exhaled a breath and stared back at his folder on the table, seemingly in search of his next question. "Miss Sherman, I am under no obligation to tell you—although I will—that it is no longer necessary to hook up the subject of an interrogation to a polygraph machine in order to determine if she is telling the truth. Concealed video cameras can now make that assessment quite accurately, analyzing a variety of physical reactions known as biometrics."

Abby leaned forward in her chair, looking him in the eye. "Are you suggesting I'm lying?"

"No," the man said. "I'm merely informing you. Just in case."

"Then why don't you leave the room and go verify what those biometric machines are telling your colleagues about me. You might be surprised."

"I will in due time, Miss Sherman. Believe me. Until I do, however, let me inform you that the context of our conversation is of the utmost seriousness. Even if you haven't done anything to threaten the United States, any dishonesty in your responses can, and will, expose you to a level of criminal prosecution that would make your head spin in an ordinary domestic context."

"Would you care to translate that?" said Abby.

Now it was Mr. Guillian who leaned forward, his face only inches from hers. "If you decide to fudge anything you're telling me, even if you're not trying to cover up anything, lying even for a reason like simple embarrassment, you could spend the next decade behind bars. Is that clear enough?"

CHAPTER

_15

OUTSIDE THE U.S. EMBASSY, TEL AVIV—MINUTES LATER

Due to the obvious sensitivity of its location, the U.S. Embassy in Tel Aviv was monitored by an even higher than usual number of video cameras. No fewer than thirty-one lenses, both obvious and concealed, scanned the compound's periphery twenty-four hours a day. It was only the outermost layer of a security array that employed a formidable series of systems, beginning with visual surveillance and ending with the business end of an M-16.

However, none of the cameras, or the marines monitoring them from a secure room deep within the compound, noticed the unobtrusive figures trickling into the plaza just beyond its gates.

They did not notice the eyes fixed on their walls from behind the thick black robes.

Or know anything of the intensity behind those stares.

Or of the intent gathering strength right before them.

U.S. EMBASSY INTERROGATION ROOM

"By the way," Abby pointed out, "if you think I'm cooking up this whole version of things, then maybe you should do a little more homework. You might be aware that some time back, my life became the focus of considerable media attention."

He nodded. "Yes, I'm well aware of that, Miss Sherman."

"I'm not trying to puff myself up; I'm only mentioning it because these beliefs of mine are common knowledge. I even wrote a book about my experience and the nature of the Watchers. So whether you believe me or not, you can at least rest assured I'm not making all this up, or 'fudging,' as you put it earlier."

"Thank you," he replied, his voice thick with sarcasm. "That was most helpful."

"It would probably be even more helpful if you'd read the book."

He stifled an outburst of exasperation and read another question from his open folder. "Miss Sherman, what was the last contact of any kind you exchanged with the man you know as Dylan Hatfield?"

"It was a little over three weeks ago, the twenty-fourth. I remember it well, because we had a fight."

"What was the nature of your relationship with Mr. Hatfield?"

She sighed. "Well, you could say *that* was the reason for the fight. We were friends. Good friends. Backing up a little further, Dylan was once assigned to kill me, but you probably know his line of work better than I do. Only he didn't. Kill me, I mean. Instead, after spending time with me in preparation for his mission, he wound up becoming my protector in Africa. He saved my life more times than I can count. So he first entered my life as my knight in shining armor, and seemed to be transitioning into my Prince Charming. But then things got a little complicated. I bungled a few of the steps in between, and so did he."

"A romantic dispute, then?"

"More like a near-romantic dispute. Believe me, it's not worth exploring beyond that."

"And when he left, did Mr. Hatfield tell you where he was going?"

"No. He just disappeared. No postcard, no forwarding address."

"And yet you told Miss Rulaz that you thought he was in a cave."

"Again, Mr. Guillian, that was a revelation. A spiritual sight."

"Describe these . . . spiritual sights."

Abby shook her head. "They're usually just a flash of something, like a snapshot going off in my head. Often, as in this case, it comes with no accompanying knowledge or commentary on what I'm seeing. That's why I was so eager to compare notes, as it were, with my spiritual sister in Jerusalem."

"Yes. Miss Rulaz." His eyes darted back to the folder. "From whom do you believe *she* gets her information?"

"From the same source I do, only on a deeper level. Sister Rulaz, who passed on right before your men snatched me up, was the leader of the Watchers family. Here in Israel, though, she was known as—"

"The Sentinel of Jerusalem," he interrupted. "Yes, I know. She was in fact an Ethiopian citizen, correct?"

"That's right."

"Has Miss Rulaz ever conveyed to you any strong political opinions? Such as her views on matters like Arab-Israeli relations, or the fate of Jerusalem, or the War on Terror?"

"No, Mr. Guillian. She saw the world on a much broader and more strategic level than that."

"Did Miss Rulaz share any information to you during your final meeting that could shed some light on our conversation?"

"Not about Dylan, specifically," said Abby, trying to remember exactly. "She said something about his passing beyond our sight, speaking of the Watchers. And that has me very concerned."

"What are," he asked, reading the word from his notes, *"principalities?"*

"I'm not an expert, but I do know it's mentioned in the Bible. Ephesians. 'For we wrestle not against flesh and blood, but against principalities, against powers, against the rulers of the darkness of this world.' Essentially it means a stronghold of evil."

"Do you mean a physical stronghold, as in a specific place, or something more . . . metaphysical?"

"Good question. I'm pretty sure most Christians consider it something without form. But Sister Rulaz seemed to suggest something more. Actual places on the earth."

Guillian straightened up and shot a casual glance toward the back wall. The spot had elicited several such looks from him already.

"Speaking of which," Abby went on, "the last thing she told me was a warning. Something about a wave of death about to strike our 'eastern shores.' America . . ."

Behind the opaque surface of the room's back wall, a seated computer operator pointed to his screen and leaned back to make sure his supervisor could view the precise location of his index finger.

"We have a match on that phrase *wave of death*. A classified memo from somewhere in Sigint."

His supervisor's eyebrows darted upward as he quickly wheeled his office chair over to the operator's side with a squeal of metal against wood.

Signal Intelligence, or Sigint, was another politically correct way to refer to the National Security Agency, a government organization still so secretive that even decades after admitting it existed, some within the organization jokingly continued to spell out its acronym, NSA, as *No Such Agency*. Signal Intelligence referred to the millions of electronic signals bouncing through earth's atmosphere, which the agency tracked, apprehended, and analyzed every single day. It was a massive task, but one of the most crucial in the War on Terror.

In this case, the phrase *wave of death* had been apprehended from an electronic signal somewhere around the world. And if this computer operator was correct, the words had been assigned a high degree of importance.

"Can you find me any more on that?"

The operator's fingers flew across the keys with a rapid clatter. "Looks like there's all kinds of eyes on that memo right now. Pentagon, CIA, FBI, National Security Council, you name it. Somebody seems to think it's very serious."

Wave of death.

Abby had no clue how many minds across the planet had been pondering those words during the precise moment she spoke them. In those three words, Abby had unwittingly escalated the level of attention on her interview by a factor of a thousand.

CHAPTER
_16

TUNNEL 9, TORA BORA, AFGHANISTAN

The Black Hawk pilot's first sign of mission's end was an eruption of green flashes in the night sky—the marines' handheld laser bouncing across cliff faces like sparks from an eerie lightning storm. Sitting high above it all in a hovering Black Hawk helicopter, he flipped down his infrared goggles and spotted dark silhouettes crouched at the entrance to Tunnel 9. Shouts suddenly crackled in his earphones.

"Big Bird One, this is Orkutz Rescue! We have six teammates, one evac. Request immediate transport!"

"Roger that. Inbound, ETA three minutes."

The pilot eased forward on the cyclic control, tensing his body as he anticipated one of the most challenging landings he would ever execute: a rapid nighttime descent with no spotlight or visual references onto a narrow mountainside.

Despite the rigors of the task, the message's implications hung stubbornly at the edges of his mind. Operation Orkutz Rescue appeared to be a limited success. Although all six of its members were returning safely, the news from his headphones meant that three seasoned and highly trained commandos were probably dead and their bodies would likely never leave the granite hulk now tilting beyond his windshield. The mission's objective—rescuing the four missing members of an earlier mission, Mystic Sender— seemed a near washout.

He forced the dismal thought from his mind and doubled his concentration, for the hazardous landing zone now swayed before him. One slip of his wrist would send rotor blades smashing into the mountainside, likely killing him, his crew, and shredding everyone awaiting him below. Gritting his teeth, he picked his spot, focused on the small patch of ground, and began his final descent. A dull *thump* beneath him, accompanied a half second later by a blinking light on the instrument panel, told him his front wheels had made contact. Immediately the doors opened and shouting soldiers poured inside.

He felt bodies heave onto the metal floor behind him and waited for his crewman's tap on the shoulder, signaling for him to lift off again. This was supposed to be a short hop.

The signal never came.

The pilot finally turned and saw the crewman staring blankly at the soldiers. He then glanced back at what it was that had spooked the man. He furrowed his eyebrows, cocked his head, and fought to suppress a gasp.

The soldiers who had just thrown themselves into his helicopter were not the same men who had jumped out of it six hours earlier. Although he didn't make it a practice to memorize the faces of those he dropped off and picked up, he now realized that some form of image must have adhered to his mind, because that image did not match the faces he was seeing now.

Oddly, the features before him were not dramatically different from what he remembered. Just different enough. In fact, in the right light . . .

Get a grip on yourself, he grunted inwardly. *Are these the same men or not?*

He squinted for a better look and began to doubt himself completely. And yet . . . A shudder ran down his spine, a chill that seemed to seep through his uniform, clear to his spirit. He didn't like the feeling one bit. It didn't help that a foul smell, like that of struck matches, seemed to have followed the soldiers into the helicopter. But the foulness went further than his nostrils. He shuddered again, then felt a sense of recoiling, of revulsion. The sensation came from behind him, as clear as a slap on the head.

The inner warning was now too powerful to ignore. He wrenched around in his seat to openly peruse his passengers. Three of them faced forward and glared back at him with hostile features.

Then, after taking a closer look, the pilot saw that these were indeed the same men he had dropped off earlier. Yet something was deeply, powerfully different about them, something impossible to describe in words. He thought he detected a strange movement and shifting of dark shadows among them. Or perhaps he was just being paranoid, or worse, losing it entirely.

"What? What is it?" barked the squad leader.

The pilot glanced at his crewman, then shook his head. "Everything go all right?"

The squad leader's glare doubled its intensity. "We're ready to go," he shouted again, louder this time, ignoring the pilot's question.

The pilot shrugged, turned back around, and began preparing for takeoff.

U.S. EMBASSY, TEL AVIV

Back inside the interrogation room, Abby's conversation with the man from Homeland Security had taken a turn for the worse.

"Look, Mr. Guillian," she said, "just because your work takes place purely in the natural realm, and just because it doesn't allow you to delve into matters of the spirit, doesn't mean those things don't exist."

"They effectively don't exist for me," he said, "and for the very reasons you stated. I'm not sanctioned to venture into such matters."

"Well, until you do, you're not going to make any headway into understanding how I came up with these phrases. You can explore my contacts and my phone and email records until you're blue in the face, and you won't come up with a thing. Because I'm telling you the truth."

"In my business, Miss Sherman, nothing is the truth until something or someone puts a stamp on it stating that it is."

"Why don't you be that someone? Why don't *you* take the first step? Think about this," she continued. "How many of your technologies are based on discoveries that would have been considered pie in the sky or even magical years ago? Everything from radio waves to space flight to wireless Internet? How seriously would you have taken me back in the fifties if I'd told you that we'd sit here someday having my honesty measured by tiny lasers scanning my face with hidden beams, controlled by a computer that could also, using its leftover power, invisibly access ninety-nine percent of the world's information in less than half a second?"

"So you're saying these spiritual matters of yours are scientific facts? On the order of computer science or the electromagnetic spectrum?"

"No," she conceded, "not facts in the same sense of something that's proven. But yes, I believe they're bodies of knowledge the human race just hasn't been able to explore yet. And probably never will. I believe there are dimensions beyond the three in which we exist. By the way, many scientists would agree with me on that point. I just believe that while human beings exist on both the physical and spiritual levels, many more life forms exist only on the spiritual. And the one who created us exists on every dimension at once. He is beyond them all."

"Let me get you straight. From that vantage point, God sends you messages about the fates of other people, all around the world?"

She shook her head at the unbelieving way he'd phrased his question.

"Sometimes. Sometimes, though, it's a matter of this strange gift I and many others were given. Also, let's face it—human beings are strange, complex creatures, and like I said, we exist on both sides of a great divide. It's no wonder aberrations take place. It's only a wonder they don't happen more often."

Abby closed her eyes and smiled. She looked like someone who had just received an inner confirmation of something.

"Tell you what, Mr. Guillian. If you doubt me, then go to the nearest window, look out, and tell me what you see."

They stared at each other.

"I mean it. Go look, and then come back."

He shrugged and left the room. When he returned a few moments later, the color of his face had altered, turned ashen.

"They're called Watchers, Mr. Guillian, because they see things. They have come to show their support for me, but more importantly to protect me through their presence. Their prayers. Don't worry, they're not spies, and their presence outside the embassy poses no threat to Homeland Security."

He stared at Abby, seeming to be at a loss for words.

"They're not here because they followed anyone either," she continued as she rose from her chair. "Or because there's a leak within your organization. You know better than I do how secure your operations are. They're here because they could see where I was taken. So I'm telling you the truth. Can I please go now?"

He nodded and closed his folder.

"But before I go, I have one last question for you," she said, as though she'd been leading the interrogation all along. "Where is Dylan, and what has happened to him?"

Guillian's eyelids fluttered. He looked down, and there was a long pause before he spoke. Finally he replied, "A rescue operation found Mr. Hatfield alone after the failure of a classified mission of which he was a member. His fellow soldiers were all killed in action. Mr. Hatfield was airlifted from the site and given intensive emergency care. Regretfully, Mr. Hatfield did not recover from his injuries."

CHAPTER

_17

Four thousand miles away, deep in the second level of the White House's multilayered basement, David Ashman sat on his desk, arms crossed, and watched the conversation unfold on a wall-mounted plasma screen. Beside him, standing stiffly, were his boss, National Security Advisor Melvin Watkins, and CIA liaison Rachel Waddell.

At that moment, however, Ashman felt as though he were the only witness to what was unfolding. He felt rooted to his seat, unable to move, incapable of forcing his muscles to raise his body and get himself facing his desk, where he desperately needed to check one of the several red-tagged folders lying there.

The video screen was displaying a fascinating, if not morbid, human drama—the face of a young woman who had just been given news of the death of the man she loved.

Ashman had launched his career as a Philadelphia police detective, and had never forgotten the familiarity with human responses that job had seared within him. At first, Abby Sherman's reactions had been fairly predictable. Ashman had noted the backward recoil in her posture, accompanied by a visible stiffening, as though she had been struck by a blunt object. Then her eyes and face began to pick up the story. He had discerned pure shock, followed by a surge of grief as tears threatened to force themselves from her eyes. Then came denial, held together with a brittle courage he found himself admiring. She was refusing to show her questioner just how deeply his disclosure had pierced her.

Finally, he saw something in her eyes that he had not expected.

Disbelief. Not the sort of disbelief signifying denial, the unwillingness to accept something one knows to be inevitable. No, it was something else. Something far more subtle, indefinable.

Waddell then broke the silence, turning to the others.

"Did she say 'wave of death'?"

Ashman nodded, and finally found the will to move. Taking the chair facing his desk, he picked up the topmost folder and opened it—to the words *Wave of Death*, in boldface, underlined type.

The paragraphs that followed contained the usual elaborations of intelligence officers trying a little too hard to justify their existence. Rambling attempts to analyze and deconstruct the expression's meaning. Lists of the expression's past occurrences in terrorist rhetoric. Lists of people known to have used it. Linguistic translations and idiomatic etymologies.

When he had first perused the words hours ago, Ashman had found nothing remarkable in their usage, only in the context during which they had just emerged. That had been the case for everyone reading the same report that morning. *Wave of death* was fairly standard jihadist hyperbole: a boastful metaphor depicting the legions of young men, women, and even children who were willing to sacrifice their lives in the destruction of their enemies. Infidels.

But what gave the words significance was the infamous bearded mouth of Sheikh Omar Nirubi, al-Qaeda's new mouthpiece, who had uttered the words on a battered video just delivered to Al Jazeera's Islamabad news bureau. The usage, when combined with the detected movements and communications chatter of suspected terrorist networks across Europe and the Arabian subcontinent, produced a remarkable discovery.

It turned out the phrase *wave of death* and its individual component words had popped up sixteen times in the last twenty-four hours. That not only made the specific phrase topic one in the intel community, but raised the general level of paranoia throughout the ranks of Homeland Security. There was talk of raising the terrorism threat level by one color, and even of arranging for a pseudo-inadvertent leak of "grave concern" by a high-ranking White House official.

And now came the strange coincidence of a young woman using the very same term, only hours later, during an interrogation that had taken, to put it mildly, some highly unusual turns.

"Quite a coincidence, wouldn't you say?" Ashman said.

"Back at Langley, you could be fired for saying that word," Waddell replied. "You might say the very notion of a coincidence is antithetical to our whole culture."

Ashman peered at the screen. Across its bottom ran a strip containing the biometrical analysis of her reactions—skin temperature, eye movements, pupil dilation, muscle tension, vocal stress, and more.

"Coincidences do happen, Rachel," he retorted, obviously a little bothered by her reply, "but I'd bet against it here."

Watkins turned to him now. "You're saying you believe Sherman?"

"I believe she's sincere, which is almost as important. Guys, the biometrics have been flatlined ever since she opened her mouth. Zero deception. And my experience tells me the same thing. She hasn't shown any lying or even evasiveness. Whether she's right or not, she believes what she's saying one hundred percent."

"Well, I can't do anything with divine visions and spiritual revelations. This isn't the Vatican."

"I know. But we can't avoid the facts either. Those women from her group, these Watchers, just showing up right outside the embassy window . . . they had no way of following her there. Or of knowing which room she was in, even though our cameras show them pointing to the exact window outside the interrogation suite. They're calling out the officer's name like it was on a billboard somewhere. Not to mention those spoken words that clearly identify Operation Mystic Sender. That leaves us with two facts we can't, or won't, reconcile. One, she and these Watchers know things they shouldn't possibly be able to know about matters of national security. And two, she's absolutely not lying about where she believes the information came from. Until we come up with a plausible explanation for those two facts, I think we need her to cooperate as fully as possible. And the best way to do that is to quit treating her like a suspect. Utilize her to figure out what it's all about."

"For what, precisely?"

"To make connections. She's the first person to suggest a link between Mystic Sender and the wave-of-death threat. Her past experience shows she's a self-starter—"

"More like a loose cannon," Waddell interrupted.

"Maybe so. But she's tough, and determined. And we know she's a good guy."

Watkins pointed at Ashman's chest. "Fine. Bring her in. But if this thing blows up and I get called down, it'll be your job."

BALTIMORE, USA, "THE PROJECTS"—DAWN

When the gunfire started, Luci Holliman walked over to the window, as always. She flipped open the latch, raised the sash and reached her shaky right hand out into the world, as though forbidding the bullets to enter her apartment. Far below, explosions punched big holes through the peace of night. She could hear tires screech too, and young male voices growl in rage. Her eyes shut and her eyelids fluttered for a long moment.

Despite the task at hand, she could not keep from making the usual mental assessments. *Not automatic. Large caliber, though. Big handguns, yes sir. Could be police. Could be those crip patrols too . . .*

Yet her every instinct told her this wasn't the event she was waiting for. She stood there because she had to rule it out, her thin old body swaying against the precarious angle of her pose, her every sense groaning for confirmation. She had not been told when the real threat would come. She never thought it would be the gangs or the violence; she always considered that just a side-show. But she never knew for sure.

In either case, she had to verify. She had to make sure.

Luci knew it was her calling to stand guard. So she stood and waited until the shots died away and the tires peeled off into the distance.

She smiled faintly, for her instinct had been right. This was not what she had been called to wait for.

Reaching for the window, her hands hesitated as a tiny tremble passed through her fingers. After a moment the gnarled digits stilled themselves. She shut the window with a clatter and turned the latch, locking it. Old tendons flexed, their thin cords so sharply outlined under parchment-thin skin that they reminded her of corpses under a shroud.

Like those three gangbangers last year, she thought. The swagger and menace all shot out of those lanky bodies lying so still under the police lights and the folds of that single bloodstained sheet. And the boys' mommas, barely into their thirties, standing off to the side and howling into the night.

The fingers shivered again, as though purging themselves of the thought. Crossing the room, they reached out to touch the piano keys, as much for reassurance as for balance. Always the broken old middle C. Then to straighten the old lace doily beneath the lamp, even though it never needed it anymore. Not since the boys . . . not since her own boys were . . .

She let the thought go unfinished.

Making her way to the old recliner, whose seat cushion bore two worn spots, formed not by the weight of her body but by her forearms leaning forward as she kneeled, she bent over with a grunt, gripped the chair's sides, and watched her knuckles turn white while that old body of hers began to sway toward the floor. Finally her knees touched the carpet and her forearms found their way into their familiar channels. Her fingers wove themselves together. Her eyelids closed.

And then a quavering voice filled the room.

"Lord, what're you doin'? I don't understand.

"I've grown tired to death of this. Sitting up here all alone, waiting for whatever it is you asked me to look out for. I know I heard you right those ten years ago, and I obeyed. Lord, I've stayed here in the shadow of death and watched, and waited, and listened. I've sat and watched the men who killed my boys grow rich and fat and I've borne the sound of them laughing at the sight of me. I've sat and fought the rats and shut my ears against the guns, night after night. I've gotten lonely, Lord. Felt myself turning into an old recluse. And that's not me. I love people, you know that.

"Yes, I've felt you with me, Lord. I can't deny that I've felt your presence here beside me. But I'm an old woman, and I can't wait much longer.

"I know you kept me here to be a lookout, and I ain't about to quit, Lord. But would you bring it soon, this thing I'm here to look out for, whatever it is? And would you bring me someone to hear my alarm? I mean, what's the use of my standing guard if there's no one to warn?

"Lord, you know I ain't mad at you. I could never be sore at you. But I need for this vigil to end. Soon, 'cause I ain't got forever. All right . . . ?"

She paused and then gave a low moan of satisfaction. Her hands started to rise, palms open, into the air. Her smile found its way back onto her lips.

"Oh yes, Lord. Yes, yes . . . thank you. I hear you. I'll wait a little bit longer. I'll watch for it, I will. I believe it's coming soon . . ."

Just as quickly, her smile disappeared. Luci frowned and stood, quite nimbly this time, walked back to the window, unlocked it, and threw it open.

The eastern sky was just beginning to blush with that first rosy glow of dawn, a time she usually cherished, or at least when it had been safe and simple for her to venture outside. But this morning, the sight did not return a smile to her face. Her frown deepened, accentuating the wrinkles already traversing her face.

Luci was not seeing light. She was seeing trails of darkness, filling the sky like those old photos of airplanes dropping paratroopers in World War II, the ones her beloved Harold had shown her after returning from Europe. She shook her head. These things she saw were dark but not black, numerous yet not visible. Not to her earthly eyes, at least.

Something inside of her, upon seeing this sight, wanted to die. Wanted to crumple up and wither and leave this earth, or at least any part of it within proximity of those . . . those things, those beings. Wanted to crawl up into the Lord's bosom and be sheltered from the kind of bristling hatred she could feel radiating from whatever they were. Malice like a blistering wind. A silent hurricane.

"O Lord," she whispered, and this time it was neither adoration nor praise. It was a plea for solace.

She turned away, remembering something. She had watched, and now she had witnessed. It was time to tell someone.

Where was that email address her niece had sent her?

That *Watchers'* website?

BLACK SEA—THAT NIGHT

After its commandeering by Chechnyan rebels near the mouth of Sayda Bay, the Russian fishing trawler *FV Kirgov* had traced a long and deliberately circuitous route to the Black Sea.

In the Barents Sea, where its journey had begun, winter ice pack had forced the *Kirgov* to follow the cleared Northern Sea Route as it bypassed the region's maze of icebound peninsulas and inlets.

Once in the North Sea, however, it had left crowded shipping lanes and maintained a time-consuming yet low-profile itinerary, hugging nautical boundaries like an everyday domestic fish-seeking modern vessel. On the several occasions when it had come within sight of land or other boats, the trawler's pilot and one-man crew had awkwardly deployed its nets and made a bumbling pretense of working about the deck, despite having no clue how to fish.

Once having threaded its way through Scandinavia, the *Kirgov* had skirted through the English Channel, distantly flanked the western coast of France and the Iberian Peninsula containing Spain and Portugal, then sneaked through the Straits of Gibraltar in the dead of night. It had sailed the length of the northern Mediterranean Sea Route and crossed Istanbul at three o'clock one morning.

Praising Allah for their good fortune, the amateur sailors had continued on toward the northwestern fringes of the Black Sea, where their lethal cargo would be off-loaded and smuggled deep into Chechnya to strike a fierce blow against the hated Russians.

Within two miles of their intended port of call, a much smaller and fast-moving ship, flying a crescent flag, came speeding over the horizon. Assuming a mere change of off-loading strategy, the *Kirgov*'s two passengers waved at the newcomers and helped them board.

Once on deck, however, the four darker-skinned men merely reenacted what the original two had done at Sayda Bay. They pulled out pistols and emptied them into the two erstwhile sailors. With practiced efficiency they dumped the corpses, located the scuttle bomb, unloaded it into their hold, and with a pair of tossed grenades, sank the luckless *Kirgov* in thirty fathoms of water. The smaller craft sped away as though it had never even slowed down.

The wave of death had just acquired its fuel. Not a soul around witnessed the takeover.

Thankfully, the ocean surface was not the only vantage point from which watchful eyes could peer down upon the scene.

CHAPTER _18

Abby barely waited for her questioner to shut the door behind him, returning from an abrupt trip out of the interrogation room, before barking out her demand.

"Tell me he's dead."

"Excuse me?"

"Tell me that Dylan Hatfield is dead. You used some kind of weasel words to phrase it earlier. Something about 'did not recover' . . ."

He shot her a look that defied interpretation, a totally inscrutable expression.

"You can't answer," she persisted, "because he's not actually dead, is he? Everything inside me screams that he's in big trouble, but not gone."

Guillian sat down, took a deep breath, examined his fingernails. "You're right. He's not deceased, nor did I say he was."

"Where do you have him?"

"I'm not at liberty—"

She almost launched herself out of her chair, causing him to stiffen visibly and begin to eye the back wall again.

"Tell me!" she shouted. "What kind of trouble is he in?"

Guillian hesitated, just long enough to ponder the conversation he'd had in the hallway outside moments ago. A message from Washington telling him to "bring her in." Let her cooperate in any way possible.

"All right," he said. "I will. Settle down, and I'll tell you."

Abby scooted her chair back up under her, all the while staring at him.

"Dylan Hatfield is in a conscious but unresponsive state diagnosed as semicatatonia. His vital signs are strong. His physical functions are good. His pupils respond to stimulus and movement. But other than that, he has not spoken or made any facial expression since his discovery two days ago. He could emerge from this state at any time, although that is statistically less than likely. Odds are he will remain catatonic for the rest of his life."

Abby sat back in her chair, her knuckles wrapped tightly around the armrests. Here was the truth, she could tell. And the truth was far from a comfort.

"Are you people interested in having him recover?" she asked.

The man made a disappointed face. "Of course we are. First of all, we care about our soldiers and what happens to them. Second, there are many things we would like to find out from Mr. Hatfield. His was a very dangerous and important mission."

"Where was he?"

The face went blank. "I'm not at liberty—"

"Yeah, yeah," she interrupted. She leaned forward as far as she could. "Well, if you and the United States government have any desire to see Dylan recover, then here's what I propose. You get me and my mother out of here, on a plane, and you take me to him. Because you and your doctors have clearly closed the book on his treatment. And my prayers, along with those of Watchers around the world, are the best hope you've got of seeing him make it."

He did not budge a muscle; only his eyes moved. At last, he nodded. "Okay. I believe you."

"Where is he?"

"Ramstein Air Base. Germany."

LANDSTUHL REGIONAL MEDICAL CENTER, RAMSTEIN AIR BASE COMPLEX, LANDSTUHL, GERMANY

For the first time in days, Dylan became aware of a *surface*.

That is, he realized for the first time that a surface existed—somewhere far above him, within him, around him, someplace—not the surface of some body of water but a boundary, an edge. An end to his smothering immersion, this eternal thrashing in a dim emotional mire. *Surface*, as in a spot where he could burst forth from his confinement into open air, and freedom. A place where he could gulp in a lungful of coolness and relief and solace.

No, he hadn't been drowning, exactly. He hadn't even been swimming, exactly, although the sensations of his stupor had given him an almost physical feeling of waving desperately around, grasping for some kind of hold, for something against which he could push and gain traction and propel himself forward and get out of there. Wherever *there* was . . .

It wasn't even water surrounding him, threatening to overcome him and suffocate his will to live. It was thicker, more like a gel, only its substance felt far more odd and disquieting than that. Because it wasn't physical, he vaguely knew. It was emotional and psychic and inward. It was a soup of disorientation mixed with trauma and diffused emotion and diluted memories and large, floating clumps of terror.

Yes, terror. Another thing he sensed clearly, and began to sense more sharply with every growing minute, was that something unspeakable had propelled him into this dim lostness. Something quite specific: an event, a memory, a fright. Something he could neither look at nor remember.

He had almost, just barely, in the haziest kind of way, started to feel this surface before, the growing reality of some end to this experience. But each time prior, his mind had bumped up against something hard and cold and bright: a memory of fear. A flash of something horrific would blind his thoughts and he would find himself, rather than moving slowly out of there, careening back into the muck. The protective, almost maternal thickness.

Yes, he wanted out. But he also felt that this haze had protected him from something too raw and terrible to endure. And that evil awaited him out there, out in the world of consciousness and wakefulness.

Finally, his thoughts became clear and coherent enough for him to realize that he didn't care. Whatever heinous thing awaited him was not worth staying here, in this state of suspended animation. He was a man of action, of movement, of life.

And then he became aware of a bright whiteness. A piercing patch of light had entered the depths. It threw out beams that dispelled every shadow, every murky depth. He could almost, but not quite, recognize its shape. A rounded square fringed on top by long, thin protrusions that each moved of their own accord.

Of course, *a hand.*

And this hand was touching him. Grazing . . .

. . . his face. His forehead, he sensed. He hadn't even been focused enough to remember he *had* a face, until now. Now he knew that he in fact did possess a head, and a face, which was in contact with the hand of someone else. A person of great spiritual power—the thought came to him unbidden. Pure insight.

Now he felt—*windows?*—opening up before him, allowing in the world to which he so desperately wanted to return.

"Look. He's opening his eyes. Isn't that a good sign?"

The voice was soft and gentle. Female.

Light and color, no longer imaginary but quite vivid and real, flooded his world. He'd opened these windows before, he suddenly realized, but hadn't been strong enough to see anything through them.

That was far from the case now. Now he saw eyes, large and close, peering at him. A nose, cheeks, hair.

Someone. Someone from whom he felt a warm honeylike affection pouring his way, and the twang of fear turned to joy.

"Dylan" came that voice again. "It's me. Abby."

The sound of that name, those two syllables, yanked him upward with a pull that was both powerful and gentle. He could feel an almost palpable sense of the murk and the lostness and all those clumps of trauma slither past his body as he ascended.

And then he was there . . .

. . . *free!* Indeed, gasping for breath like a man bursting forth from the most brackish and murky of waters, surging into the bracing sharpness of cool reality, the waking world striking his innermost being.

"Abby."

The voice was now his. He recognized it: low, smooth, and male.

CHAPTER

_19

LANDSTUHL REGIONAL MEDICAL CENTER, RAMSTEIN AIR BASE

And now sight returned in all its fullness—brightness and color and the outlines of a living world. Dylan found himself lying in a narrow hospital bed. One wall contained a large window with sunlight filtering through parted curtains. From the room's low ceiling flowed electric light, turned down low, subdued.

Faces surrounded his bed. He recognized, even before identities, the faces' expressions: *Love. Joy. Concern.*

Abby. Her mother. A nurse in a military-style uniform.

"We've been here praying for you, Mother and I." It was Abby's voice, without a doubt. "For three straight hours. Most of the Watchers on earth were praying too."

"Where am I?"

"Ramstein. Landstuhl hospital."

He nodded, glancing out the window at a thick green fringe of forest. "I thought it looked familiar. I was here before, back in the old days."

"Do you remember where you've been?" she asked.

"I'm not sure. I was about to ask *you* that question."

He sent his thoughts in search of an answer and quickly realized that he was unprotected, out here in the brave new world of the conscious. His awareness felt jostled, then battered, by a series of chills and dark presences. He frowned and tried to focus his gaze.

Then he saw . . . the physical objects in the room were awash in a writhing film of apparitions and half-visible spirits. Some of them were blindingly bright, beaming from some unseen source. Others, with whom they grappled, seemed like dark pits of swallowed light, outlines defined more by lack of color, by emptiness. And yet as they moved, as they rioted murderously against each other, he could also see faces. Some of them beautiful and grim, and others terrifying and animalistic, boiling with rage.

The scene filled him with wonder and dread.

Then he remembered the images that had afflicted him, and the horror was still too much. His chest threw itself forward, then stopped as if struck by some invisible barrier. His head snapped still. His throat retched, spewing a bellyful of bitter liquid from his mouth and onto the blue quilt over his legs. The nurse jumped to his side, a towel suddenly produced in her hands. She started dabbing at his mouth, holding his torso from behind, but Dylan would not be touched. He waved her away with wild sweeps of his arm.

Abby was right behind the nurse, dodging her movements and his swings.

"Dylan! Dylan! What is it? What are you seeing?"

His eyes were wild with terror now.

"I see everything! I see it all! I remember it all!"

From the bed's opposite side, another hand crept forward and grasped Dylan's in full motion. A low and soothing voice began to speak.

"Dear God, surround us with your Spirit and calm . . ."

It was Abby's mother. The serenity in her words, combined with her own peaceful nature, cast an immediate balm across the room and its occupants. Dylan stared at the older woman as though he'd never seen her before that instant.

". . . and fill this room with your angels, I ask you. Bring a hedge of protection around this bed and your servants beside it . . ."

Another male voice sounded out from the back of the room near the doorway.

"What do we have going on in here?"

Abby's mother spoke a few more words, then drifted off and turned toward the door along with the other two.

A man in full army uniform stood perfectly straight, his expression taut and stern.

"I'm Colonel Alan Cook," he said in a voice that seemed to expand and fill every inch of the room. "Dylan's commanding officer." He walked to the bed, bent over Dylan, and took his free hand.

"You seem familiar," Dylan said weakly. "But I don't remember reenlisting."

"Do you remember Mystic Sender?" the man asked. "The mission. The cave."

At the sound of those words, Abby shot a wide-eyed glance at her mother.

The officer turned to Abby and her mother. "Ladies, necessity requires that I attempt an immediate debriefing here. I'm very sorry, but I must ask you to please return later. Perhaps in a few hours."

"Colonel," Dylan interrupted, "their presence is the only reason I'm able to speak to you right now. They're going to stay. If you want me to say word one to you, then I need them with me."

Cook turned and looked at the two women. Clearly nothing he saw caused him to immediately change his mind, for his disdainful expression remained unaltered.

"You know we're cleared," Abby broke in. "Captain Guillian filled us in on the flight over. We know about the mission in Afghanistan, although we didn't learn its exact name until just now. We know about the alert situation and the suspect phrases. There's nothing we can't hear."

Dylan's back stiffened in his bed; it seemed the frightful battle scene in front of him had not paused with the officer's entrance.

"Look, the mission is over," Dylan said. "So you have no authority over me. There's no way I'm saying a word without the two of them at my side."

The colonel shrugged, the first time his upper body had moved at all since his entrance. "Fine, Hatfield. But I'm only agreeing because of orders from higher up. You should know that."

"Oh, you made that perfectly clear," Abby interjected.

The officer pulled forward a nearby chair and sat down awkwardly. "For today we'll just cover a few basics. The preliminaries."

Dylan grasped Abby's hand, unashamed. "Fire away."

"Hatfield, what happened to the others? Why did they do what they did? What did they say?"

Dylan closed his eyes slowly and leaned back. He spoke without opening them, in a voice almost too faint to hear.

"We provoked something. Something too evil and horrible to even talk about."

"Well, you're going to have to talk about it," the colonel interrupted. "Three men died in there, and you're the only survivor. You've got to clear the record. Give their families closure, at least. The mission's not over until you talk."

"All right, Colonel. I fought this battle the whole mission long, and I guess I'll fight it again. I'm going to tell you the truth, and you can hook me up to a machine if you want to verify it. But I'm going to tell you once, and I'm going to tell it straight. And if you want closure on this thing, you're going to believe me. We walked straight into one of the . . ."

His voice lost its strength, and his lips stopped moving. Then, finally, he fixed an icy stare at the man. "No. I'm not going to tell you. You won't believe me. And even if by some miracle you did, you wouldn't be able to do anything with it. It wouldn't be deemed actionable intelligence."

"You leave that kind of assessment to me, Hatfield," the colonel answered, his tone rising. "I deserve—your *country* deserves—a report from that mission. Wouldn't you agree?"

"Yes. You do. America does. The world does. But you're not ready to hear it. Or maybe I'm not ready to tell. Who knows. I'll tell you this. Remember all those warnings, all those disclaimers you gave us during that initial briefing? All about how odd and speculative and strange the mission parameters were? All those weird reports and sensor readings?"

"Yes, Soldier. I remember."

"Well, they were nothing. Nothing compared to the truth of it. Take your wildest imaginings, Colonel, and multiply them times a hundred."

"Tell me, then."

"Colonel, if I tell you, before the day's out I'll be behind that locked door upstairs with straps around my arms and a Thorazine drip going into my veins. Tell me this. Who found me? And how did *they* get out alive?"

The officer paused for a moment, breathing in and out slowly. It clearly galled him to answer such questions in front of the two women.

"We sent in a rescue squad," replied the colonel finally. "A whole different mission: Operation Orkutz Rescue. They went in with new rules of engagement. It was a search-and-rescue mission only, and they went in force with twelve men. Full conventional lighting. Real-time, landline radio contact. We were taking no new chances. Even then, it took four hours to find you on that ledge."

"And are those men okay?" Dylan asked.

"No, they were pretty shook up by what they saw," the officer conceded. "Everything about that place. The bodies of your squad mates, the grotesque carvings, the skeletons, everything. I almost threw up just looking over the photographs. They're being given some counseling. In fact, they're only about three doors down, in this very same ward. Getting help."

Dylan's pupils darted around the room, thinking, assessing, plotting.

"I'd like to see them," he said at last, "to express my thanks."

The colonel nodded. "They've asked to see you as well, if you ever regained consciousness. I'll call for them right now. Might do them some good."

He nodded to a young woman in army fatigues standing in the doorway. Her figure disappeared.

"Colonel, I have just one more question for you right now. Did the rescue team stop and examine the wall drawings when they approached the tunnel core?"

"Yes. They were scanned and analyzed."

"I'll bet they created quite a stir back at Langley, and . . . elsewhere," Dylan offered. "What's the conclusion?"

"That's on a need to know—" The colonel stopped himself. He appeared to be reminding himself of something. Orders he had received? He sighed and continued. "We had them looked at by archaeologists. It doesn't make much sense; some of them are thousands of years old. But they seem to depict a huge massacre. And some of the imagery is very recent. It suggests that the target is the modern United States."

"A wave of death," Abby said.

The colonel turned to her with a stare. "Miss, I don't pretend to understand any of this, or why I'm even saying these things in front of you. But you're absolutely right. Our entire Homeland Security force is braced for a nuclear attack against the United States sometime during the next several days. And the chatter we've been monitoring around the world speaks of a *wave of death*. So while I may not be allowed to compel you to answer this, I'm asking you outright. How did you know that?"

He was greeted by silence.

"I'll ask you again. How did you come across those words?"

The man's intensity cast a chill over everyone listening.

"I don't mind telling you the kinds of things Dylan won't," Abby finally answered. "A spiritual sentinel was given those words. By . . . well, by God himself."

The officer glanced back and forth, gauging the reactions of the other listeners. He seemed even more confused to see that not one of them rolled their eyes or showed other signs of disbelief. He then shook his head and smiled faintly. "You know, as crazy as it sounds, that's not the wildest thing I've heard in this whole mess. And something tells me it won't be the last."

"No. *Here's* the last," Dylan broke in. "The threats are real. Don't ask me how I know. Just, please, listen to me. The hatred gathering against us is deeper and stronger and older than any threat assessment the CIA ever conjured up in its worst nightmares."

"Colonel?"

The voice belonged to the woman in fatigues who had stepped away a few moments earlier. He raised his eyebrows in response.

"The men are here to see him. Orkutz Rescue?"

The colonel nodded and waved them in. A group of muscular young men filed into the room. Before they had even fully entered, Dylan's whole upper body tensed into one great coil.

As though pulled along invisible strings, Abby and her mother turned slowly around, their eyes widening. Their hands trembled despite themselves. Abby successfully disguised a gasp of shock and revulsion, but her mother was not as successful. She reeled backward, her skin pale, staring wildly at the men.

They'd carried in with them a mob of large and small, terrifying and revolting demonic beings. The men were being devoured, even as they stood smiling gamely and appearing physically healthy.

Abby nodded at Dylan.

These soldiers had come for an entirely different purpose than to pay their respects.

CHAPTER
_20

LANDSTUHL REGIONAL MEDICAL CENTER, PSYCHIATRIC WING

What happened next seemed to last for an eternity, at least the way it was remembered by those who survived it, especially Abby.

She saw Dylan—whose initial concern about his rescuers had obviously predicted the problem at hand—motion for his commander to come closer as though he had a secret to whisper in his ear. While the colonel bent over and cocked his head, Dylan's fingers reached over to the man's waist and unbuckled the holster at his side.

"Is your sidearm loaded?" she barely heard Dylan whisper.

The colonel gave a start and turned to look him full in the face, just as the revolver slid out.

Grimacing from the sudden flex of his underused muscles, Dylan shot up onto his knees, leaned away from the officer, and waved the gun wildly before him.

"Down! Right now! On your knees!" he shouted at the men.

Colonel Cook, still the closest man to Dylan, held up his hands but glared at him, his face reddening. "Hatfield! What's the meaning of this?"

"Colonel, back up and I'll tell you."

The officer took three steps backward.

"Tell me you don't feel it!" Dylan began, panting heavily. "You want an answer to what I encountered back there. Well, it's here. Right now. Don't you feel the darkness, the evil that just entered this room?"

The officer's eyes darted sideways, a dubious look betraying the tiniest hint that yes, he was sensing something quite palpable and disturbing.

"Men, why don't you put your hands up," Cook said slowly, unconvincingly, "and show Dylan here that he's overreacting."

The men slowly raised their hands. But the third man from the right, a lanky young man with light brown skin and a broad grin on his face, pulled out a revolver from somewhere behind him and fired a single bullet through the colonel's head. Even before the officer's body had struck the tile floor or the echo of Suzanne's scream had faded from their ears, he trained the weapon straight at Dylan's face.

Just as swiftly and almost simultaneously, Dylan's body launched into a flurry of action. From his crouch he aimed his weapon upward and shot out the room's light, casting them all into deep shadow, then wrenched his shoulders sideways. With a sound halfway between a scream and a grunt, he heaved up a large oxygen tank standing beside the headboard, ripping it from its tether of tubes and wires.

The gunman adjusted his aim and fired at him, but instead of Dylan's dimly lit forehead, he shot into the upraised gleam of a metal cylinder. The large-caliber bullet pierced the metal and, half a second later, the tank exploded with a thin plume of fire shooting out in a direct line right back at the shooter, who stood by the other men against the wall.

The gunman shouted and lifted his arm to shield his head, falling back against his comrades, his face and hair in flames. The tank kept on throwing fire at them, setting several of them aflame at once.

Dylan jumped to his feet and shouted, "Follow me!" He grabbed Abby's hand, who then grabbed her mother's hand, and yanked the two women through the door and into the hallway. The hospital room, now a maddening blur of screams and terror, fell away behind them.

Once in the hall, Suzanne stopped dead in her tracks, her eyes fixed on what lay beyond—the longest hospital corridor in Europe, curving endlessly ahead. "I can't do this, honey!" she pleaded.

Overcome with the knowledge that they must escape, *must* put distance between themselves and that spot, Abby felt on the verge of full-blown panic. Just then, Dylan seized an empty gurney nearby and quickly helped Suzanne onto its cushion. Pushing the gurney ahead of him, he stepped behind it and began running down the corridor, shouting warnings, the bed wheels slipping and careening sideways through a parting crowd of stunned white-coated doctors and other medical staffers.

Abby ran alongside, her mind reeling, aware of little more than the blood pounding in her head, her heart thumping wildly to keep her moving forward.

A volley of shouts and more gunfire erupted from behind them. A bullet whined past her head. Another struck the gurney's side with a metallic *plink*! Abby's mother reared back, a bright red spray misting the air above her right shoulder. A scream of agony echoed dully in her ears.

Dylan glanced over at Abby and yelled, "Switch!"

She knew just what to do. Dylan gave the gurney another shove forward, then threw himself rolling across the floor. She jumped over his flying limbs and grabbed the bed's push handles, taking his place.

The crowd of medical staff filling the massive hallway, frozen in place by all the shouting and commotion, fell to the floor as Dylan began firing back at the door from which they'd emerged. Abby cried out as a line of bullets crossed a wall of windows beside her and exploded its surface into a rain of flying glass.

Lying prone on the floor, Dylan continued firing. Seventy-five yards away the gunman flew backward. Another who stepped into his spot next squeezed off two shots before shuddering under a stream of bullets. A third hunched forward and then fell with a thud.

Two loud clicks announced that Dylan was out of ammunition. He tossed the gun aside and turned for the gurney. Abby was now oblivious to the madness all around her. She was bent over her mother, whose injured body still lay on the gurney.

Suzanne reached up and cradled her daughter's cheek.

"Let me go," she said in a labored breath. "Leave me."

Abby felt a wave of fear wash over her. "Are you crazy? Never!"

"I'm in a hospital. I'll be all right. Besides, I can't keep up with you! You've got to get out of here!" Suzanne gripped Abby's arm and pulled her close. "You go find that summons, the one Sister Rulaz talked about! The message of awakening. I'll be waiting for you. Praying you find it in time."

"No way, Mom. I'm not leaving you."

"It's the only way! Now hurry on. I'll see you soon."

Dylan's hand grasped her shoulder, confirming her mother's decision.

With a dazed shake of her head and a brief kiss on the cheek, Abby nodded as she wiped away tears. She reached for Dylan's hand, and the two continued sprinting down the corridor.

Within seconds, a trio of armed guards in fatigues ran up, M-16s in hand. Apparently confused in the heat of the moment, they paused at the sight of Dylan's flushed face and the sound of frantic breathing.

"It's that way!" shouted Dylan, feigning panic. "We're just escaping! The action's back there!"

Without waiting for a reply, Dylan pulled Abby onward, down the hallway again. Twenty-five yards later, they slid to a halt before the hospital's front entrance. Abby shot one final glance back toward her mother and saw medical staffers already crowded around the gurney. She turned away with relief, just in time to see Dylan punch through the doors.

CHAPTER
_21

The two ran out into cool, pine-scented German air, glancing around at a parking lot filled with cars, medical vans, and ambulances.

A blue school bus sat idling at the curb, its windows lined with soldiers' faces. Dylan rushed to the front passenger door and leaped up the few steps, with Abby following close behind him. "We need to drive out of here right now!" he shouted. "There's been a shooting in the hospital and a fire's broken out. They've ordered an immediate evacuation. Please, let's go, now!"

The driver eyed Dylan's blue patient scrubs with a suspicious look, but after hearing a fire alarm in the distance and seeing panic-stricken people pouring from the hospital building, she nodded her agreement. She reached up and pulled the door shut, wrenching the gearshift into position. The bus growled ahead.

"Where do I go?" the young woman asked.

"Back through town," said Dylan. "They're going to close up the entire hospital perimeter, and you don't want to be caught inside. It'll be a nightmare. Just take us back to the Ramstein processing center—that's the default assembly point."

The woman nodded, looking impressed by his official-sounding jargon, and pushed the accelerator to the floor. The bus lurched forward with a bump and a hard swaying to the right and left, and soon the parking lot gave way to thick woods on both sides of a steeply descending mountain road. Dylan and Abby stood at the front, grasping a metal handrail for support.

Suddenly Dylan spun around and said in a booming voice, "Men, I have a favor to ask. I'm going to be debriefed in a few minutes, but I had to run out of my room before I could change. Do any of you have a spare set of clothes? I'll pay fifty bucks for the trouble. And an extra twenty for size twelve shoes, no matter how smelly."

Half a dozen men stood and yanked duffel bags from the overhead compartment. Within seconds everything he needed— blue jeans, shirt, socks, even a pair of shoes—had been lofted his way.

"Thanks, men!" Dylan called back.

Abby started pulling out bills to pay, but her outstretched cash was met by good-natured dismissals and waves of the hand. She turned forward again, then glanced out the window to avoid the sight of Dylan pantless, balanced on one foot. Outside, the ancient streets of Landstuhl rushed past in a colorful array of narrow lanes and ornate red-roofed houses. The bus turned, and a picture-perfect postcard of small-town Rheinland filled the windshield—a rich, green hillside bisected by a medieval church steeple.

"Stop!" Dylan shouted to the driver.

The driver stomped on the brakes and the bus shuddered to a halt.

"I'm sorry," Dylan said, "but I'm about to be sick. Please let us out here and keep going. We'll catch another ride later on."

The driver shrugged, then swung open the door. Dylan and Abby waved good-bye to the men and stepped from the bus. The door closed behind them, and the bus continued on down the road toward Ramstein.

"Why did we leave like that?" Abby asked.

Instead of answering, he took her by the elbow and led her away from the street curb, finding a secluded spot near an old stone wall, away from other pedestrians.

"Because we need time to talk," he explained, "and figure out what's what. I mean, are these guys gonna keep coming after us? Are we on the run again? Like before?"

She sank to a crouch against the wall, thinking. "I don't know. How many of those men did you kill?"

"Three, I think. And I badly injured another two."

"But there were eight of them, right?"

"Yeah, and all eight were possessed."

Neither of them wanted to speak any more words than necessary to describe the poor soldiers' enslavement. And neither wanted to conjure up the images of the creatures feeding on their souls.

"They'll come after us," she said, nodding with certainty. "You know what's driving them. And that's not all. Uncle Sam's desperate to debrief you. They brought me here to see if I could help bring you out of your . . . the state you were in. They sure didn't do it out of kindness. They want your story—a lot more of your story than you told them just now."

"Why don't we just go in and give it to them?" he said.

"Because it'll give those soldiers another shot at killing us. Besides, we don't have time to deal with them. You know better than I do—going through their wringer will cost us a week. By that time, it'll be too late. America will have been attacked."

"This . . . wave of death?"

"Exactly," she replied. "I'll explain later. Look, I don't know where we're going yet, but for now we just have to get out of here and trust that God's going to lead the way."

Dylan raised his chin to indicate a business across the road. "That's the reason I got off the bus right here."

Abby turned. A large white sign read, *Used Mercedes-Benz*.

"How much money do you have?" he asked.

"Luckily, I still have everything I brought to Israel still on me."

"Israel?"

"It's a long story, Dylan. We have a lot of catching up to do. For now, I have three thousand in traveler's checks and a couple of credit cards, right here in my pants pocket. I heeded all those warnings not to keep cash in my purse. Otherwise it'd still be in your hospital room."

"Great," he said, placing a hand on her shoulder as they hurried across the road. "That'll be perfect. These kinds of dealerships cater to American servicemen without a lot of dough. Good old reliable Mercedes. Cash on the barrelhead."

CHAPTER

_22

Less than an hour later, the pair drove out of Landstuhl in a twenty-year-old Mercedes sedan with a dented rear bumper, a full tank of gas, and a map of Germany in its glove compartment. Abby had managed to make the purchase in her own name, merely signing over her traveler's checks and flashing her passport.

Abby swerved onto Autobahn 6 and drove west toward Mannheim, slowly inching up to the customary 90 kilometers per hour—within an acceptable range of Germany's posted limit of 80 kilometers per hour.

"Why did you want me to drive?" Abby asked.

"I'm not ready," said Dylan, leaning back against the seat. "My head's still swimming. I mean, here I was in Afghanistan, living through the most horrible experience of my life, and then the next thing I know, I'm waking up all groggy in a hospital bed, looking straight into your face."

"Is that so bad?" she asked with a smile.

"It was wonderful. But my point is, it was jarring. Too much, too soon. And twenty minutes later I'm in the middle of a tactical situation, a shootout, having to bring back every skill and instinct my training ever gave me. It's all been a little much, and I'm just now starting to come down off the adrenaline high. I'm crashing, in fact."

She glanced over at him. He still looked every bit the man of strength she had come to admire on their last adventure in Africa. He had not lost the lean physique, the graceful motions, the air of calm, and those steel blue eyes brimming with wariness and ultimate competence. He was still one of his nation's most resourceful soldiers, a covert ops veteran who could kill an attacker with his bare hands, repel every remaining threat, comfort a panicked companion, and formulate a multipronged plan of escape in the same instant.

And yes, those same qualities had awakened in her, ever so gradually, an unlikely attraction she had been even slower to admit.

Yet something was different about him. She could sense the faintest hint of fear in him, a fear she'd not glimpsed before. Somewhere under the surface of his professional demeanor lay a barely detectable erosion of confidence, a heightened vigilance.

"Okay, you convinced me," she said. "So where do we head first?"

"Before anything else, we have to reach one of my old money caches. Probably the only good thing left from my former life."

"It's not the only thing left," she said. "If you hadn't had those special skills of yours, we'd all be dead by now."

"Thanks, but don't go too far. You don't want to concede all those points from our last argument. According to you, my special skills were beneath a true spiritual warrior, if you care to remember."

"Dylan, please, let's not start *that* again."

"Hey, I'll be glad to drop that line of reasoning if you will. But I think the point is well taken, if I do say so myself."

"Touché," she said. "Your earthly skills have their place, okay? Although I still say they're nothing compared to the powers God gave us. Now, can you tell me exactly where this cache of yours is located?"

"Nearest one is Switzerland," he replied. "Which is not as far as it sounds. In a few minutes we'll take the number five south to Basel. It won't take more than a couple of hours."

"Where did you go? And why?" Abby asked after they had safely bypassed Mannheim and were speeding south on Bundes-autobahn 5. "I mean, we had this fight, and I know it was a bad one. I've had a lot of time to regret how I said things back then. But never in my wildest dreams did I think my words would drive you away."

"You didn't, Abby, and neither did your words. It was a co-incidence really."

She smiled. "Oh, still believe in coincidences, do we?"

"Good point. Whatever it was, it seemed to come out of the blue. I was home, licking my wounds after our fight, when I got a phone call. It was someone from my black-ops days, asking me if I wanted to sign up for an incredibly sensitive, government-sanctioned mission. Lately I'd be inclined to refuse an offer like that, but something kept urging me to take it. At the time I would have said it was just my anger at you and the whole Watchers thing and my sorry place in the whole scheme of things. So, almost on impulse, I said yes. I'd be glad to go. However far away it is, it can't be far enough."

"Thanks. It's nice to know what a repellent I am."

"It was never *you*," he assured her. "You know what it was. All of it—the media attention, the questions, the criticism. People angry at me for suggesting that only members of some select spiritual family could change the world. Something I never said, or even believed."

"But I'm still hearing that my diplomatic way with words had something to do with your decision to join the mission," she said with mild sarcasm.

He smiled. "Maybe. Anyway, *far enough* turned out to be Afghanistan. It was a recon to investigate what they called 'paranormal phenomena' in the al-Qaeda caves of the White Mountains."

"Paranormal?"

"You got it. A better word would have been *spiritual* phenomena. Or more accurate still, *demonic*. The place was a . . ." He paused, unable to complete the sentence.

"A principality," Abby offered at last. "Sister Rulaz called me from Jerusalem, completely agitated. She saw it."

"What?" said Dylan. "She saw it? You mean the cave, the whole thing?"

"I was shown a little of it myself," she answered, nodding. "As much as God knew I could handle."

"What did she say?"

"She talked less about any physical description than the darkness of it, the evil. That it was so deep and so strong she feared for your survival."

He stared ahead, narrowing his eyes as if in pain. "She was right to fear."

"Dylan, I don't know how to tell you this." She took a deep breath. "What she saw frightened and . . . disturbed her . . . so greatly, I think it played a part in her death."

He visibly recoiled. "Her death? Sister Rulaz is dead?"

Abby winced as she realized he'd not heard the awful news. Nodding, she blinked away tears and stared even harder at the road ahead. "I'm not saying it's your fault," she added. "You know that she was very old and in poor health. And spending year after year out in the elements on that church rooftop, those poor monks lived in fear of her death practically every day."

"Yeah, but you and I both know there was another strength to her . . ." His voice trembled and faded.

"That's why my mom and I went to Israel. Sister Rulaz fell very ill and then called me, begging me to come and be with her before the end came. It was like she had something to say that was so dark and foreboding, she wouldn't even trust it to the phone lines."

"What was it?"

"She seemed to think that some evil force had been unleashed from the place you explored. Not by your mission, necessarily. Maybe beforehand, I'm not sure. But she was convinced that a great threat, a wave of death, was aimed at America's eastern shore. Right now, this very minute." She reached over and placed a hand on his forearm. "What did you see there, Dylan?"

He shook his head as stubbornness took hold of his features. "No."

"Please," she said. "You know you can tell me."

"I know you're up to hearing it. I just don't know if . . ." The sentence trailed off into an agonizing pause.

"Was it worse than the beings we saw in Africa?" she asked. "Everything we've already been through together?"

He nodded an emphatic yes. "I can't talk about it. Not yet."

"You know what the good part is?" she said in a comforting voice. "God's love and power is a million times stronger than whatever it is you saw. That's the part we need to dwell on."

His hand found hers, and any animosity left between them instantly melted away.

CHAPTER

_23

THE WHITE HOUSE BASEMENT, OFFICES OF THE NATIONAL
SECURITY COUNCIL—THAT SAME MOMENT

"One more body through that door," David Ashman smirked inwardly, "and it's officially a turf war." From his seat at the conference table's far end, he watched yet another starched uniform follow yet another black power suit through the room's glass doors.

His boss, the national security adviser, hadn't left his seat in over an hour, which was rare. Ashman chuckled derisively at the thought. Usually the man could interrupt even the most sensitive meeting for at least three trips to the bathroom, the coffee table, or some urgent cell phone call.

Waddell, the CIA liaison, had now been replaced in the meeting by a full-blown director and three section chiefs, who even now eyed Ashman with the brooding stares of conspirators just waiting to take over the agenda and put him in his place. A deputy director of Homeland Security sat directly across from him, glaring in his direction.

He sighed, glanced back over his notes. He hated these kinds of meetings, watching a half dozen factions step all over each other and hardly pretend to care about the other groups' interests. The only things created in these meetings, he told himself, were impasses.

"Can we start?" he heard himself say, in a tone that barely masked his contempt.

"Sure," said the CIA director, even though it wasn't his meeting to run.

Ashman opened his folder as if to telegraph the notion that he had far too many facts at his disposal to indulge in niceties like winging his speech or trying to recite from memory.

"Before I begin, can we recap the latest on the wave of death?" Even as he said it, Ashman marveled at how quickly the three words had evolved from a terrorist's threat to a common phrase tossed around between them.

The faces around the table stared at him with blank expressions. Apparently nobody wanted to start; nobody wanted to show their cards first. Again Ashman sighed. Typical bureaucratic cowardice.

"All right, then. I'll start, and I'm sure one of you will kindly supplement my meager knowledge on the matter. 'Wave of death' first popped up on my radar from an NSA finding and was added to the threat matrix and conveyed to the president five days ago. It started out as al-Qaeda cell phone chatter picked up over the Afghan-Pakistani border, exact identities unknown. It was later confirmed by a deep-cover human source in Balochistan. Since then, it's reoccurred in Cairo, Amman, and Beirut, all of them reliable sources. Does anyone have anything helpful to add?"

"Yes," said the CIA director, holding up a sheet of paper. "The wave-of-death threat is now officially linked with the theft of a detonation-ready nuclear device from Sayda Bay in Russia."

Whispers broke out among those gathered around the conference table, each of the men displaying a look of shock.

"Wasn't that supposedly headed to the Chechnyans?" asked the man from Homeland Security.

"We thought so too. But the shipment was commandeered in the Black Sea. We lost it right after it went through the Bosporus. And now it's officially linked. I'm not at liberty to disclose how."

"So the wave of death is now a nuclear threat?" asked the Homeland Security official.

"That is correct," muttered the CIA director.

"Great," Ashman said. "As if this thing needed escalating. So back to today's agenda. 'Wave of death' also occurred in a satellite phone call placed from Jerusalem by an Ethiopian Coptic mystic of some sort."

"Yes," broke in one of the CIA section chiefs, "and if that wasn't bad enough, the conversation you're referring to contained key words indicating knowledge of an ongoing secret-ops mission."

"Have we had this woman worked up?" asked the Homeland Security official.

"Well, she's dead, for one thing. But her contacts are completely clean."

"What's the explanation for her knowing this?" asked Ashman's boss, the National Security chief.

"No explanation, sir. The term in her file is 'uncorroborated psychic knowledge.'"

"Never heard of that designation."

"It's left over from our work with remote viewers and psychics in the seventies," replied the CIA director. "A random term to describe someone who has classified information without a necessary suspicion of espionage."

"Sounds like some fuzzy intel work to me," grumbled Ashman's boss.

"Well, these things happen," added the CIA director. "All the time. Our files are full of hints and monitored phrases from people's dreams and night visions and even prayers."

"What I want to know," interrupted the deputy director, "is why in the world the recipient of this call, this Abby Sherman person, was flown by our government to the side of the mission's only survivor."

"It was my idea," Ashman said. "All of our observations concluded that she was being truthful with us. She was known to be close with Hatfield, and he was catatonic, with any meaningful recovery too unlikely to measure. We'd given up trying to communicate with him. So I deemed it a good idea to bring the two back together. Try to spark something."

"Oh, you sparked something all right," his boss chimed in. "Our best European hospital has been shot up, and this *spark* is now loose in Europe somewhere, while the rest of us are about to go up in flames."

"Isn't that overstating things just a bit?" Ashman asserted.

"I don't mean our careers, David," snapped the national security adviser. "I mean it literally. If that bomb is successfully delivered to our shores, 'up in flames' will no longer be a metaphor. It'll be what's known as an understatement."

"And now that Hatfield has revived," said the Homeland Security official, "he's on the loose? Who do we have to thank for that bit of genius?"

"Depends," Ashman replied. "You might thank the thug from the army's extraction team, Orkutz Rescue, who took a shot at him."

"Any motive for that?"

"None whatsoever. The survivors from the shootout are so ticked off, they've checked out of the hospital. Disappeared."

"Any idea what Hatfield and Sherman are up to?" the CIA director asked, his voice quickly rising in rage. "Did Hatfield give anything up before leaving the hospital? For that matter, did any of these kooks associated with this affair say anything that's of any interest or relevance to our job of protecting America from its worst nuclear threat in decades?"

"Not really," Ashman answered. "Like before, it's pretty strange, quasi-religious stuff. We're interested because these people knew things they shouldn't have, couldn't have known. We're going to find out why."

Watkins leaned over and spoke again. "Mr. Director, is it your opinion that this Hatfield and Sherman ought to be apprehended and brought in, or just closely monitored?"

The director chewed on the curved end of his glasses for a moment. "I consider Hatfield a rogue agent on the run, for now, so I'd favor bringing him in just on principle. I'm not sure what connection there is between his mission and the wave of death, other than his association with Sherman and Rulaz. And I'm not going to take some dead Ethiopian woman's word for it either. But you know something? The last time Sherman went dark, she wound up pulling in a whole genocidal group against her and bringing them down. With the wave of death now a nuclear threat, and her record as an accidental provocateur, I say we dangle her and Hatfield."

A dozen faces turned as one toward the director, eyebrows raised. *Dangle* was the term used to describe an operation that placed, or left, unwitting individuals in the path of an enemy in hopes of exposing that enemy.

"She's a civilian. Can she survive being dangled?"

One of the dark-suited men raised a hand. "Everybody, Bruce Cochran, CIA. I know Dylan Hatfield. Worked with him years ago, and ran him on some of his toughest missions. He's one of the most self-reliant and accomplished black-ops men America ever fielded. And tougher still because he believes in what he's doing. He had such a strong moral code that we only sent him on righteous ops, the best red, white, and blue work on the dirtiest targets. The world's worst scum. He's going to be hard to follow, especially once he's accessed one of his caches."

"Do you know where his caches are?"

"Switzerland would probably be the closest."

"How will he get in?"

"Oh, he'll find a way. Hatfield is one of the best evasion men I've ever known. For now, just put all eyes and ears on that border, and pray he's gotten rusty."

Watkins nodded, then turned to a man in a navy uniform. "Admiral, may we have NSA help with this?"

Only half of those assembled even saw the man nod, his motion was so imperceptible. However, they all saw him stand abruptly and briskly walk out of the room.

CHAPTER
_24

Within thirty minutes the triangular region encompassing the juncture of France, Germany, and Switzerland had fallen under the magnifying lens of what American intelligence insiders jokingly called a "snoop in a can"—a hurriedly improvised, yet massively scaled surveillance operation.

CIA assets were deployed from Zurich and Frankfurt to watch all three borders—a total of twenty-two agents equipped with high-powered scopes, earpieces playing wiretapped feeds of local law-enforcement comm chatter, satellite phones, and sniper rifles.

But that was far from all. An AWACS plane lifted off from Ramstein Air Base, its roof-mounted radar dish already rotating to coordinate radar and communications traffic. Out in space, two keyhole satellites, one officially tasked to the National Security Agency and the other to the National Reconnaissance Office, adjusted their synthetic-radar-aperture antennae to provide opposing angle aerial footage of every square foot in the region.

Most quietly of all, the three surviving soldiers from Operation Orkutz Rescue and the Landstuhl Medical Center shootout vanished from their rooms at the hospital's psychiatric ward. Soon after their disappearance, a Huey helicopter was commandeered from Ramstein Air Base. Its transponders were rendered inoperative and failed to report the craft's position to controllers on the ground and in the air.

It was seen, however, following the Autobahn 5 heading south—toward the A5 border crossing into Switzerland at Weil am Rhein.

Abby and Dylan's only advantage was the fact that none of these groups had any idea what sort of automobile they were traveling in. But if the pair presented themselves at the Weil am Rhein border crossing, that fact would not help them for an instant. Their faces would have been recognized before their brakes had even brought them to a complete stop.

BUNDESAUTOBAHN 5, SOUTHERN GERMANY

Looking out toward the thickly wooded foothills of the Black Forest, Abby felt a strange chill of anticipation pass through her neck and back. To the south and east, the distance grew jagged and rocky, promising the coming of the Alps. To the west, the Rhine Valley's broad swells tantalized her with occasional glimpses of the river itself, shining in the afternoon sun. For the first time in a young life spent along the Pacific coastline, the sight of mountains and woods surpassed that of a hazy blue ocean horizon. She wondered why as she rested her head against the doorframe, allowing Dylan to drive for the first time. Her emotions seemed to be playing tricks on her.

"I'm exhausted," she told him. "We flew straight from L.A. to Jerusalem within an hour of hearing from Sister Rulaz, and then after being detained we flew straight over to Germany without a break. I should have slept then, since Mom and I and this government guy had a private jet to ourselves. I could have had a row of seats to myself, but I was so keyed up over what Sister Rulaz had told me that I didn't shut my eyes even for a second."

"You were frightened by her descriptions of my mission?" said Dylan.

"No. There's something else I haven't told you yet. She gave me a mission of my own. She started by saying something . . ." Abby paused, chuckling at the thought of it. "You're going to love this, Dylan. After what we fought about. She told me to set aside the Watchers, to basically forget about them for a while."

Dylan shook his head and stared at her, his eyes bright with surprise. "You got me there, Abby. Of all the things I would have guessed you'd say, that would have been last on the list. The leader of the Watchers tells you to forget about them?"

"Yeah. On her deathbed, no less."

"Amazing. Was there a reason for this?"

"She said I needed more, that I needed to go beyond the Watchers. She made it sound like the threat ahead was so dark, I had to gather a force way larger and stronger than the Watchers had ever dreamed of being. I needed them too, of course, but their ranks were only the beginning. I needed to awaken 'the Warriors.'"

"Warriors. I like the sound of that. A little more my style, wouldn't you agree?"

She lightly punched his arm. "Maybe. What I like is that it sounds more inclusive. Something any believer can join."

"It's another organized group?"

Abby shook her head. "No idea. I couldn't tell if this was some official title or just a description. But now that I think of it, it sounded like something dormant. Something that needs to be awakened."

"And did she bother with giving you some instructions for accomplishing this awakening?"

"She mentioned something called a 'summons.' A summons etched in stone somewhere. She said she'd had a vision of me finding it, and calling out these Warriors to face the threat."

"Where did she see you finding it?"

"That's the problem. Just as I was about to ask her, she breathed her last. It was basically the final thing to ever come out of her mouth."

Dylan slammed the steering wheel in frustration. "Great. Sounds like one of those wild-goose chases that could yank us all over the place for nothing. Not a whole lot to go on, wouldn't you say?"

"Yeah, but somehow I don't think it will be. The important thing is that we stay spiritually on target with everything. If we're deliberate and prayerful about each step we take, I think we'll find that the way is already prepared."

"I don't know," he muttered. "I loved her too. But still, the lives of half of America is an awful lot to put on the line based on the vision of a dying old woman."

Abby turned in her seat to face her companion. "Dylan, what's the matter with you? Is your problem that this knowledge came to us through prayer? Through nothing more solid than people on their knees?"

"Hey, I value prayer as much as you. I'm just saying it's pretty flimsy stuff to go on. You're talking about scouring the world based on some statement you know little about. You don't even know whether this summons thing actually exists."

"Dylan, you've got to show more faith, or we're done for. So far, God's ordered our steps in pretty remarkable ways. I mean, look at how I was able to find you. Or look at you—thinking you were accepting some random mission to the ends of the earth, when actually you were being taken right to the heart of the threat."

Just then, Dylan looked out at a sign announcing their imminent stop at the Swiss border. He took a sharp intake of breath. "Speaking of the ends of the earth, I just remembered something."

Instead of elaborating, he swerved rapidly onto a wide freeway exit marked *France, EuroAirport, Saint-Louis.*

"What is it?" Abby asked, gripping her armrest with whitened knuckles. "Why did you leave the freeway?"

"Because I can't get into Switzerland. At least without a detour."

CHAPTER
_25

As they raced across the Rhine and into the nearby French village of Huningue, Dylan explained his dilemma. Several years back, the European Union had made it effortless to travel between its member, or *Schengen* countries, without papers or checkpoints. But the continent's lone EU holdout, Switzerland, had by contrast beefed up its border checks and its passport requirements. Dylan had considered relocating his cache of emergency funds, but his dependence on Switzerland's unshakable secrecy laws motivated him to solve the problem in another manner, the easiest way he could think of.

"Since the whole point of a cache is to have resources waiting just in case—presumably a crisis in which I don't have a passport on hand—I've done the next best thing." He brought the car to a halt along a sidewalk and switched off the engine. "I've hidden one of my drops near the border."

He jerked his head sideways, toward the awning just beyond a window, swaying in the afternoon breeze. It read, *Musée
Militaire.*

"A museum," he said. He stepped out, then turned back toward
Abby. "No need to come with me. You'll be perfectly safe. Try to
get some sleep, and I'll be back before you know it."

Abby hardly needed any prodding. Before Dylan had even
disappeared through the museum's old wooden doors, her eyes
were already closed, her mouth partly open, and she was spiritually
far, far away . . . stumbling through a landscape of death . . .

*Not merely the death of people, although there were hundreds of
them lying motionless everywhere, both young and old, but the death
of everything else as well.*

Birds. Animals. Trees. Grass. Homes. Neighborhoods . . .

*Essentially anything that at one time had life or order was now
destroyed. The land lay knee-deep in debris—a nauseating stew of sew-
age, trash, black smoke, and human remains. The wreckage stretched
on and on, as far as the eye could see.*

Inside her dream, her heart broke.

*Somewhere within hearing, someone was laughing. Celebrating.
Chanting. Singing. Throwing up screams and shouts of joy.*

She heard words in the song. Jihad! Fatwa! Sharia! Islam!

Then she knew. It was the wave.

The wave had struck.

And this was much more than a dream . . .

She woke up panting, her heart thumping in her chest. It took
her a long moment to remember where she was—in a car, a foreign
country, on the run and taking a respite from a desperate quest.

HUNINGUE, FRANCE, MUSÉE MILITAIRE

Although the Musée Militaire was the perfect site for one of his caches—filled with artifacts, dimly lit, and uncrowded—Dylan had to admit he'd indulged some of his own private interests in making his choice. He loved military history. And Huningue, which for centuries had been a fortress town along the Rhine, whetted his appetite for battle lore. After buying his ticket and casually walking inside, he had no trouble locating his favorite display: a lithograph of an ancient siege scene featuring the duke of Savoy's men, depicting Huningue's defenders continuing to fight in the throes of an ignominious defeat.

Checking to see that the room contained no obvious video cameras and that he was alone, he lifted the dusty frame from the wall and quickly stripped away an envelope taped to its back. Two seconds later the envelope was safely tucked away inside his shirt and he was ambling out, giving the docent the pained grin of a less-than-thrilled visitor.

Abby was sitting wide awake with a strange, distant look on her face when he entered the car and slid into the front seat. He started the engine and made a quick U-turn before asking, "What's the matter? Has your Sight started up again?"

"Not exactly. At least not in the usual way of seeing spiritual beings. I fell asleep when you went inside, and I had this dream. A dream, I think, of what's ahead. What's bound to happen if we fail."

"Do I want to know?" he asked in an apprehensive tone.

"No. It's horrible. I don't want to talk about it. I don't even want to *think* about it. All I can tell you is we have to find this summons. We must find a way to stop what the enemy has in store for us."

"But what you saw—did it provide any details about what had happened? Or how?"

She stared ahead for a moment, frowning, clearly pained by the act of revisiting the experience. Finally, she shook her head. "Total destruction . . . consistent with a nuclear explosion. Please don't ask me any more. Just tell me it doesn't have to happen just because I saw it."

"I'm not certain, but aren't prophecies, visions, and dreams like that given as warnings from God? Images of what *could* happen if we don't take Him seriously? Not things that *have* to happen."

"Thanks." She sighed. "Whether you're right or not, it sounds good. Now, please. Tell me how we plan to stay alive for the next twenty-four hours."

"Well, the odd thing is," he explained, "all three countries share an airport a few miles from here. It serves Basel as well as Mulhouse, France, and Freiburg, Germany. It's called EuroAirport because, although it's on French soil, it's under three different jurisdictions. The Swiss have a fenced-off, duty-free road that leads straight from the airport to their border. It's a less obvious way to enter the country, and that's how we're going to do it."

"That's where we're headed?" Abby asked with a frown. "I mean, isn't that a fairly major crossing into Switzerland?"

"It's far less major than the autobahn, but yes, it's the only route from the airport. Why?"

"I don't know. I'm getting a very strong feeling that we're being hunted a lot more intensely than we think."

Just then, Dylan looked up at the sound of a helicopter flying through the sky just ahead of them. At the same moment a police car whizzed past them at twice their speed.

The pair looked at each other.

"Fine," Dylan said flatly. "Let's take the scenic route."

BENGHAZI, LIBYA

Ibrahim de Soud waited for the drop of sweat to gather, to gain critical mass as he liked to call it, then slowly separate from the skin at the tip of his nose, and fall.

He watched the liquid sphere strike the leather gloves encasing his hands and did not worry. The device was ready. No way would a single drop of salty water manage to reach through the thick leather gloves or the even thicker glass window and do any harm to what lay beyond.

Only four more screws and he was done.

He blinked in amazement, still in awe that he, a modest science teacher from Beirut, could have played such a part in crafting the destiny of the Islamic Revolution. *What an honor!* he marveled to himself. If only he was at liberty to tell his family back home, or even his wife, who believed him to be a simple, unremarkable high school teacher incapable of making a living in his home country, and most of all his children, whom he had not seen in over a year. How they would beam with pride, and how he would bask in the glow of their adulation, if they only knew he had played such a part in bringing the Great Satan to its knees!

He finished with the last screw while mumbling a prayer. He pulled out his hands and mopped his forehead at last.

The wave of death was ready, ahead of schedule. He had labored without ceasing, straight through three days and two nights to complete his task. He laughed softly to himself, picturing the destruction that would come as a result of his own work here today. The Americans would never stop it, he was certain. They would never pierce the cunning genius of this attack, handed down from the creativity of his brethren.

Ibrahim had been told that the enemy knew the device's name. He had also been informed that the enemy had mistakenly concluded *the wave* referred to a combined attack from multiple sources, all targeting American soil.

The irony of it made him laugh out loud, straight into a clear blue sky.

CHAPTER
_26

FRENCH-SWISS BORDER CROSSING, NEAR
NEUWILLER, FRANCE

Gazing out her window at a field of green grass practically glowing in honeyed sunshine, Abby took in the beauty of the landscape. She focused on a farm with its stone barn, a tranquil pond, and a fringe of forest climbing up into the foothills. She wistfully thought that had the situation been less fraught with danger and stress, she might have been having the time of her life.

Dylan was navigating less by map now than by instinct and a keen eye on the countryside, veering continually toward the mountains.

Abby's spirits lifted as the road led them through a meadow toward the heart of a valley thick with trees and the distant promise of a high mountain ridge.

Within minutes the country around them had turned alpine, the road steeper. A grove of hardwoods gave way to pine forest and a brook, which had begun as a watering strip for cows but had now narrowed into a vigorous mountain stream.

Abby lowered her window and found herself revived by the sound of running water and the kiss of cool, pine-scented air across her cheeks.

"Can't we just stay here?" she said.

Dylan looked at her and grinned. "I wish we could. But we won't be safe really until we're in Switzerland. And we're not going anywhere until we reach my cache in Basel."

The road took them up the ridge, marked by ribbons of switch-backs, soon ushering them out of the trees, across a grassy summit overlooking a valley of rolling hills and thick forest. In the distance they could glimpse the Rhine and a geometric outline of Basel's suburbs.

By the time Abby had finished raising her window against the new chill, they were traveling on a hard-packed dirt road and approaching a barricade flanked by a small building.

"Here's our border crossing. Start praying," whispered Dylan.

He slowed to a stop, and a young man in a thick uniform sweater walked out to their side. Dylan had already opened his window and held out both of their passports.

The border guard flipped through their pages, looking back up at their faces to check against the photos.

"Where from in America?" the guard asked, peering over at Abby.

"Los Angeles," she answered.

"Ah. Tinseltown."

"Yes."

The exchange fell flat as the guard continued to stare at their passports.

"You only here to visit . . . Mr. Weirgard?"

"Huh?" Abby said. But a quick glance from Dylan brought her back to her senses. Weirgard was the name on Dylan's passport.

"Yes," answered Dylan.

"How long is your visit?" the guard asked.

Dylan smiled at the man. "Very short. Over to Basel for dinner and back out again."

"Anything to declare?"

"No, just ourselves," Dylan replied.

A bitingly cold wind kicked up. The guard winced and shrugged his shoulders for warmth. Thankfully the discomfort seemed to cause him to hand back their passports. "Welcome to Switzerland," he said, then quickly turned and strode toward the guardhouse.

Dylan started to inch the car toward the red-and-white barrier when a shout came from inside the guardhouse.

"Wait!"

Dylan tried to stifle his disappointment as he applied the brakes.

"Just a minute!" the guard called from the doorway. "There's a bulletin coming through. I cannot raise the barrier until I see what it is."

Abby kept praying, yet she felt herself on the brink of total panic as she watched Dylan's muscles tense, his eyes dart back and forth, and heard his breathing change. His whole body seemed to ready itself for conflict.

"What can I do?" she whispered.

"Get ready to take the wheel," he answered through his teeth.

Seconds crawled by, with the increasingly cold wind blowing through Dylan's open window.

Finally the guard emerged again and stepped up to their window. His demeanor seemed remarkably calm. "I am sorry," he said in his accented English. "There are always transmission problems when thunderstorms are moving up the valley. I cannot receive the broadcast."

"Could you let us go through anyway?" Abby asked in her most girlish voice, surprised by her own brashness.

The guard shook his head. "This is a high-priority message. No one is allowed through during the reception."

Dylan stared straight ahead through the windshield. "We'll wait," he said.

Returning to his guardhouse, the man stepped inside to check the computer.

"He's in no hurry," Abby remarked.

Dylan nodded his reply. His body language told her that he was readying himself to take action. Again, Abby prayed desperately. Her answer came as another gust of wind, two bright flashes announcing the arrival of lightning, and the sound of a thunderclap directly above them.

A revving noise from the engine betrayed Dylan's impatience. The guard looked their way and held out an outstretched hand in warning.

"Dylan . . ." said Abby, placing a hand on his arm to calm him.

"I'm gonna go," he growled.

"Don't you dare!"

A blinding flash filled the car, followed by a crash of thunder that seemed to tear apart the sky. They opened their eyes and saw that lightning had struck the guardhouse roof. In that instant a loud drumming sound hit their ears, rain pelting the car.

Dylan began raising his window when he heard the guard calling to them over the tumult.

"Go!" he was yelling. Then suddenly the man's face was at their window again. "Go ahead! My computer is dead! Go and be careful!"

So after they'd thanked the guard and he had manually raised the barrier for them, Dylan pulled the car forward through the mud and into Switzerland.

They turned away from the ravine stretching off toward their left and exchanged looks of amazement and dazed shakes of the head.

"Take a deep breath," she said, laughing softly.

CHAPTER

_27

Ashman settled into his hard-fought corner of the NCTC's conference table and looked out over the expanse of the team's new digs—sprawling, dimly lit, with multilevel walkways of smoked glass reflecting the glow of large, suspended video screens. In fact, rumor had it the center had been designed with the help of Disney Imagineers, the better to orchestrate its interplay of light and shadow, openness and isolation, instant communication and dazzling cutting-edge technology.

Impatient, Ashman checked his watch, tapped his pen on burnished walnut. Over the adamant objections of the CIA and NSA contingent, coordination of the Sherman-Hatfield *dangle* operation had been moved here to the NCTC in McLean—an unmarked, seemingly nondescript office complex occupying the juncture of the Capital Beltway and the Dulles Airport Access Road.

Actually it made sense. The greater intel community had developed some highly coordinated communications centers, but this place was truly state-of-the-art: hard-wired to satellite arrays, supercomputers, instant video replay, and enhancement capability. Not to mention that the situation at hand fell under the jurisdiction of Homeland Security and of this, its counterterrorism arm. Everyone knew the move was the best choice and yet a bothersome one, Ashman told himself. The wave-of-death threat had escalated into a race, a race with the potential survival of America at stake. Combination manhunt, border control, terrorism prevention, disaster preparedness, even contingency plans for all-out war.

He drained his second cup of coffee of the morning and checked his watch again: 7:00. It was one aspect of his work he hated most—accounting for time differences in the rest of the world. In Switzerland it was afternoon.

A loud curse came from a far corner, from an agent who sat staring at a computer monitor. Instantly three analysts converged on the man, crowding around his desk and peering furiously at his screen.

More curses filled the air.

"They slipped through," called out one of the analysts. "Found a poorly manned mountain crossing that was late getting the bulletin."

Ashman rolled his eyes and looked over at Cochran. "You think we can reacquire them?"

"The Swiss have helped us about as much as they're going to," the operations man replied. "But we'll shift our eyes to all the banks in Basel. It's going to be a footrace. If Hatfield finds his cache before our assets can get in place, I'd say we won't be dangling him anymore. He'll be dangling us."

BASEL, SWITZERLAND

Cursing the rain, Lance Corporal Bryan Armacost, survivor of Operation Orkutz Rescue, the Landstuhl hospital shootout, and currently absent without leave, sat in his rented Range Rover, as he had for the previous five hours, and stewed.

It didn't take much effort for Bryan to find provocation. Even without the obvious, he could right now list about fifty reasons for his being in a murderously foul mood today. He had never been good at surveillance, or for that matter, any of the extended waiting periods associated with being a soldier. He was at his best when moving, tracking, stalking his prey. If he'd wanted to be a warm body sitting in a car on a rainy day, he told himself, he would have joined his local police department.

Then there was the dull throbbing headache that had been his constant companion since returning from Afghanistan. He'd taken every medicine known to man at overdose levels, but nothing had helped. He found himself grinding his teeth at every distraction.

He caught himself grinding them again.

Armacost had often felt that a small gray cloud was following him, sadistically raining on his parade. It had been one of his life's sour little mantras. But since escaping Tunnel 9 that cold morning and collapsing on the ground within sight of his evac chopper, he'd felt something else. Something stronger. More alive. More hate-filled than anything, or anyone, he'd ever encountered. And since that moment it had always been with him, along with the stinking headache.

Somehow, he felt, this *something* was growing closer by the minute. Had it been something visible, he would have sworn it was crawling into his head, inexorably burrowing into his mind like some alien worm.

Strangely, beneath it all was a gnawing desire to unite with it, to get the process over with and become the instrument of justice and revenge he had sworn himself to become.

And strongly connected with this desire was a bubbling, overflowing hatred seething inside of him against this Dylan Hatfield, the so-called soldier who'd failed in his mission and then had to be bailed out, and whose idea of gratitude was to savagely mow down Bryan's buddies, the very men who had risked their lives to retrieve the loser's sorry little behind.

His watch beeped. Five minutes—time to rotate to another bank. They had been promised that the creep would show up at one of them. If Basel hadn't been crammed full of banks, it would have been a far simpler task. But they knew what they were doing. Pooling your numbers in exactly this way would give them an overwhelming chance to spot the guy.

At that moment Bryan's whole body tensed up, thrown into a seizure by a power outside himself. The presence hovering just outside his body for days now had suddenly entered him entirely. Had Bryan been in his right mind, he would have found this presence foul and monstrous beyond description. He would have resented its invasion. But all he felt at this point, worn down by days of slow infiltration, was a surrender to hatred. An embrace of the killing urge.

If Hatfield didn't show up soon, he was going to have to kill someone, anyone. Just to release all this *stuff* burning up inside him.

SCHRIFTBANK, BASEL—SEVERAL HOURS LATER

It was nearly closing time when Dylan and Abby drove up to the entrance of the Schriftbank—a massive five-story stone structure, a monument to the permanence and limitless resources of Swiss banking.

Abby, who was driving, watched as Dylan threw open his door and hurried toward the bank's front doors. She then made a wide circle, entered the adjacent lot, and parked the Mercedes at its far end.

Once inside, Dylan went through the process necessary to access his safe-deposit box with the rote, sullen motions of a veteran. The first thing required was his signature. Then, after writing down the name Jean-Paul Weirgard, he underwent eye-scan identification. Next was the elevator ride down to the bank's basement, where a man in an impeccable pinstriped suit awaited him. The employee escorted him to a curtained stall. Inside the stall he could access the steel box, which had been placed on a table for him.

Tense and wary, anticipating an attack at any second, Dylan wasted no time emptying the box's contents into the overpriced backpack he'd brought in with him. Thirty thousand dollars in cash, plus thirty thousand euros. A pair of rubber license plates, one for France, the other for Italy, magnetized for instant installation. Two Glock handguns and four loaded clips. Three passports—American, British, and Swiss. An untraceable cell phone.

He almost audibly sighed in relief at the sight, then felt guilty. Indeed, these were the instruments of his old self-reliance, his talent for melting in and out of the visible world to accomplish his country's dirty work. But he needed to resist that notion. He should have seen them for what they were: mere tools.

He knew now that his reliance on God and his purity of heart were far greater assets for the kind of fight he was presently in. But years of conditioned response had proven hard to quench. He found it difficult to suppress the thrill as he zipped up the backpack and slung it over his shoulder, feeling the weight of world-class contraband and technology at his disposal.

Pushing the perennial debate from his thoughts, he emerged into the outer basement. There, the bank employee smiled and dutifully ushered Dylan back to the elevator.

Outside in the parking lot, Abby was beginning to worry, wondering what could be taking so long.

CHAPTER
_28

Dylan emerged from the bank at full stride, remembering the old days when a skilled operative would have already been cruising alongside him, ready to throw open the door and take off again without his even needing to break stride before jumping inside. Actually, for an amateur Abby wasn't too far off. Dylan had only to walk a little ways down the sidewalk before he was reaching for the door handle. Tossing the backpack in first, he climbed into the car, questioning whether he should take over now with the task of driving.

He never had the chance to ask Abby her preference.

A dark metallic shape engulfed the rear window of the Mercedes, quickly followed by a deafening *crunch* that flung them and the car sideways.

As if they needed confirmation of a deliberate attack, the vehicle that struck them didn't stop as with a normal accident.

Instead, its driver kept accelerating, revving its engine and plowing even farther into the back of the Mercedes.

Abby looked over to the passenger seat, expecting to see Dylan. She saw instead only the backpack, the sight of the bank jerking up and down through the side window, and heard the screech of wrenching metal. She realized then that Dylan hadn't finished shutting his door when their attacker had hit them. Dylan was gone, and more than likely that was a good thing.

The only thing better would have been his holding on to the backpack. Dylan was free, but he was also unarmed.

Which burned one thing into her brain. *I have to get out of here!*

She was still moving forward, still being shoved ahead by the homicidal maniac behind her.

Then the jerking stopped, and she heard shouting coming from behind her. Her instinct told her that Dylan was dealing with the attacker. She reached over, grabbed the backpack and scrambled out of the Mercedes.

But the pavement struck her feet with a dizzying, head-spinning unsteadiness. The bank spun wildly overhead. Her right foot buckled beneath her. All around was chaos—cars speeding past, doppelganger crescendos of car horns, screeching of tires, and crunching of metal against metal.

Blazing through her disorientation, however, was one over-powering thought—*I have the guns! I have to help!*

She forced herself to turn around and face the vehicle that had plowed into them. It was a big SUV, a Range Rover. Dylan had apparently gone after the driver and dragged him outside. The two were now circling each other on the sidewalk, both looking battered. The other man was huge, Abby noted immediately. He lunged at

Dylan, who barely ducked in time, then came back with a swift kick that slammed into the man's jaw with a sickening *crunch*.

The attacker reared back, cupped his chin with a hand, and spit blood onto the pavement.

Tearing her gaze away, Abby forced herself to open the backpack and dig inside. She pulled out one of the handguns, but it felt strangely light in her hand. She turned the gun over and saw it was missing the part that held the bullets. She frantically searched the backpack until she found something rectangular and metallic. Remembering how she'd seen it done in the movies, she snatched it up and tried shoving the rectangular thing into the bottom of the gun. Seeing she was inserting it the wrong way, she quickly flipped it over and tried again. Finally the thing slid into the gun perfectly with a ratchet-like click.

Shaking now, she looked up and struggled to aim the gun. A chorus of voices and angry calls surrounded her, and she became aware of a ring of frightened spectators and bank employees yelling at the two men fighting. She heard sirens in the distance.

She tightened her grip on the gun, moved her finger to its trigger, and leveled the barrel on the attacker, who had just connected with a blood-spurting punch that sent Dylan crashing into the side of the SUV. The attacker then prepared to finish off Dylan with a knockout blow.

Abby brought her free hand up for support, aimed low, and squeezed the trigger.

Her fists rocketed backward, and her ears rang from the blast. Smoke hung in the air before her. As it floated off, she saw what she'd done. The attacker lay on the pavement, grasping his left thigh, groaning loudly.

Her grip on the gun loosened. Feeling as though she might faint, Abby saw Dylan's hand reaching out toward her, motioning for the weapon. She dropped it in his hand, glad to rid herself of its frightening power.

Scooping up the backpack, Dylan guided her to the Range Rover's passenger door. She felt Dylan's hands help her inside, and her body seemed to melt into the seat's leather softness. He shut the door, ran around the vehicle, and climbed in behind the steering wheel. With the sirens' whining growing louder now, Dylan shoved the SUV into reverse and stomped on the accelerator. They shot backward, up onto the sidewalk, and collided with a light pole. Dylan shifted into drive and sped forward around the ruined Mercedes. Abby winced, grabbing for her seat belt as they raced toward the boulevard, where a few seconds later Dylan jerked the Range Rover to the right, the opposite direction of the fast-approaching police.

Just when Abby thought they had escaped, out of nowhere came another vehicle heading straight for them. Sure enough, it smashed into them with a loud bang, pushing them violently to the side. Dylan shouted for her to hang on as he yanked the wheel to the left, pressing up against the new attacker. It turned out it was another Range Rover, identical in color and make to the one they were driving.

Dylan floored the accelerator, and the boulevard ahead became a blur. Weaving around cars, he approached an intersection whose light glowed red. With a deep breath and a glance to his left and right, Dylan stiffened his arms and drove straight through. A small pickup darted in front of them. They clipped his rear bumper with a jarring crash, but Dylan straightened their course and kept on driving.

Abby turned in her seat and saw their pursuer was gaining ground, also speeding through the last intersection and sparing no risk to catch them. She screamed as they were suddenly skidding sideways, thrown almost off their wheels. Dylan was aiming for a narrow side street. They corrected just in time to avoid hitting the corner of a brick building. As they shot down the cobblestone street, she noticed their pursuer right behind them.

They followed the street around a sharp curve that began sloping upward. Just beyond it, Dylan turned to Abby. "Start opening your door!" he said. "I'm going to stop, and when I do, I want you to jump out and hide behind that dumpster up there!"

She looked ahead and spotted the dumpster. "Okay . . ." Her fingers found the handle, popped the door open. The wind and the straining engine filled her ears. Another few seconds passed and Dylan slammed on the brakes, throwing her forward against her seat belt. "Now! Go!" he shouted.

She clicked off her belt and leaped out, running as fast as she could to get herself behind the dumpster.

At the same moment, Dylan jumped out and stood next to the idling SUV, his gun on the ready, aimed at the oncoming Rover's tires.

Three shots rang out in rapid succession. With the first, the pursuer's windshield shattered and the vehicle swerved wildly to the side. With the second and third, the front tires exploded and the SUV smashed into theirs without even slowing down.

"Follow me!" Dylan called out to Abby as he reached in to grab the backpack.

They began sprinting away from the crumpled Rovers. They hadn't gone far when from behind came a terrible blast, hurtling them forward onto the street.

Dylan was the first to his feet. "Are you all right?" he panted, extending his hand to help her up.

"I think so . . ." she said. "Shook up mostly."

They both looked back in unison. The two Range Rovers were now dark spots amidst an orange ball of flame.

"C'mon, let's go," said Dylan. "We've no time to lose."

Just minutes later they were hurrying down steps two at a time. A cloud seemed to dissipate as Abby recognized the turnstiles, tiled walls, and yellow light of a subway station just ahead.

"Dylan, we have to stop," she said, examining his face more closely. "You're a bloody mess. It's going to attract attention."

He looked at her blankly, as though he couldn't recall the cause of his condition. Finally he nodded. "Oh yeah. Right," he said while touching his lacerated cheek.

Reaching the bottom step, Abby pointed to a nearby men's restroom, where he quickly disappeared inside. Grateful for the break, Abby took a seat on a bench not far from the entrance, leaned back and closed her eyes in exhaustion.

But before she knew it, Dylan had returned. She sighed. *So much for getting a little shut-eye*, she thought. She stood and looked him in the face, then crinkled her nose and moved in closer to better inspect his features. Dylan was staring at her impatiently, waiting for her verdict. The blood had cleaned off well, but his cheekbone wore a deep bruise and his left eye socket had turned a purplish hue.

"It's a lot better," she said, "but still not great. I hate to tell you this, but as soon as we can get to a store, you may have your first encounter with makeup."

He laughed. "Sorry, girl," he said as they started walking toward the turnstile, "but if you knew how many times I've worn a disguise and had to camouflage my face—"

"Oops. Forgot."

CHAPTER
_29

The pair stepped onto a Basel subway train and soon were savoring the growing distance between them and the chaos they'd just left behind.

In the skies above them, however, billion-dollar specimens of humanity's most sophisticated technology—spy satellites and remote sensors and high-flying aircraft—were working hard to maintain a grasp on their whereabouts.

The collision and shooting in front of Schriftbank had been easy to monitor through the agency's clandestine taps into Basel police and communications feeds: traffic tie-ups along two of the city's main thoroughfares, cell phone chatter among civilian onlookers, frantic police traffic. A Predator drone from Aviano Air Base in Italy had quickly acquired the dueling Range Rovers as they left the scene and had broadcast their street chase in live video across the planet. The eventual explosion had been recorded from space as closely and vividly as if the cameras had been mounted on streetlamps mere yards away.

And yet the technology's human counterparts had not been so swift on the draw. The CIA manhunt had gone essentially underground when its prey had moved inside Switzerland. As usual, the Swiss were highly reluctant participants in any incursion into their territory, and the American authorities were loath to reveal themselves unless absolutely necessary. That covertness came at a price. The pursuit agents moving into Switzerland had been forced to cross the border using diplomatic cover, which burned up time concealing their surveillance gear and weapons in sealed pouches bearing the State Department seal.

By the time the first CIA asset arrived at the explosion scene, the two Rovers were nothing but charred steel frames, with Swiss police poring over what little evidence remained.

BASEL SUBWAY TRAIN

For the first few minutes Abby and Dylan sat silently, basking in the calm and relative quiet, drinking in the clacking of the wheels and the gentle pitching of the train from side to side.

Abby was the first to break the silence.

"Dylan," she whispered, "we have to take a break. You're beat up, and we're both exhausted. In this state we're liable to make a mistake and get caught. I say we find a place to hide out for a while, get showers and something decent to eat, then get some rest."

Sitting opposite, he leaned forward and went face-to-face with her. "Good idea. But hold on just a bit longer. We've got to get farther away before we can pause for even a minute."

She nodded, then asked, "How many of those men do you think are left?"

"Of the original men in the squad, I think only one is left, at least uninjured."

"Do you think they're acting on their own?"

"You mean, on their own, *humanly* speaking?"

"I guess so, yes."

"Well, there's no way Uncle Sam wants us murdered. Captured, maybe. But not killed the way these guys are going at it. No, I think these men are under the control of our real enemies."

"The spirits out of that principality in Afghanistan?"

"Yeah. My guess is these men were spiritually attacked and possessed by demons even before they left the cave carrying me. It's the only reason they survived. *Physically* survived, that is. The demons wanted them kept alive."

"But if they were already possessed, why did they continue with the mission? Why not just kill you and leave you there in that cave?"

He shrugged. "Maybe killing me isn't their mission. Maybe they wanted to kill you, or both of us together."

Abby looked away, a cold chill traveling down her spine. "So this last soldier who's after us—if he's possessed, then he's never going to stop until either he's killed us or been killed himself."

"I'm afraid you're right," he agreed. "And that's why you need someone like me on your team. You always have."

"I *do* need someone like you. I've never denied that."

"You're someone like that yourself," he said in a low voice, leaning toward her with a smile. "Did you forget what you did today?"

"Please, don't remind me. I've been trying to put it out of my mind." Then she put a hand to her mouth and whispered, "Dylan,

I shot a man! I can't believe it. I never thought I would . . ." She paused as tears began pressing their way to the surface.

Dylan reached over and squeezed her hand. "For whatever it's worth, you saved my life. Thank you, Abby. Thank you for your courage."

"There was no courage to it. I don't even remember deciding to pick up the gun. I just saw that you were in trouble, and the next thing I knew, I was aiming the thing at the guy and he was falling down in front of me."

"Well, believe me," said Dylan, "just because you acted on instinct doesn't mean you weren't brave. It means your courage was strong enough to take over and act on autopilot. It shows that you—"

"Cared?" she interrupted.

He nodded.

"Don't flatter yourself," she said with a little grin. "It was mostly survival. How long do you think I'd last alone, with no resources, in the middle of Europe, with all these men trying to kill me?"

"Something tells me you'd do just fine," he replied.

"Still, Dylan. I shot a man. I feel terrible. I don't know what I believe anymore . . ."

"He was a murderer who was about to kill me, then you."

She sat with a dark expression, mentally trying on Dylan's rationalization like some garment too small to fit right.

Dylan stood and walked over to an adjoining seat, where he picked up an abandoned newspaper and returned to his spot facing Abby.

"Interested in the local news?" Abby asked, mildly curious as he shuffled open the pages.

He smiled while scanning the columns. "No, not exactly." He lowered the paper. Its headline was recognizable in many languages. "Automobiles."

She nodded her understanding, then watched him reach into his backpack and pull out a cell phone. He dialed what seemed to Abby like a hundred numbers, after which she realized he was activating the unit for the first time.

"Hello, do you speak English? . . . Good. I'm calling about your advertisement. I take it you'll accept American dollars? Cash? . . . And can you meet me at the Münsterplatz in, oh, fifteen minutes? I'll throw in an extra hundred dollars over your asking price . . . Great. I'll look for the car."

He slapped the phone shut. "Things are a lot simpler when you have cash."

"What are we getting this time?" she asked.

"This time we're buying function over form. A good old, beat-up American Jeep."

CHAPTER
_30

LANDSTUHL REGIONAL MEDICAL CENTER, GERMANY

The CIA agent in charge of Abby's mother thought the men posted outside her door were sufficiently disguised—wearing civilian clothes and sitting around casually—to keep Suzanne from realizing she was under close guard.

He was wrong.

He knew the woman was in a delicate emotional state, and his files told him that she had spent many years unjustly committed to a mental institution. So being the careful judge of human character that his profession demanded he remain, and knowing that Langley was frantic for any actionable intelligence she might provide, he had gone to great pains to keep her comfortable, well-fed, and amply cared for.

His indulgences, however, did not spare him the verbal darts of a thwarted mother when he met with her and attempted to interview the woman.

"Mrs. Sherman," he began, then without waiting for a reply switched to her first name. "Suzanne, if I may call you that."

"You may not. Not until you remove those guards and stop treating me like some kind of a suspect."

"Mrs. Sherman, then, those guards are there as much for your protection as for any other purpose."

"Then why was I denied a walk outside for fresh air, just an hour ago?"

"Same reason. Your protection. Remember, the men who attacked your daughter and Mr. Hatfield are still on the loose."

"They're miles from here, sir. I would smell their foul slave masters anywhere within a ten-mile radius."

"You're referring to these . . . spirits you spoke of earlier?"

Suzanne shook her head. "I'm sorry I mentioned them. What I said seems to have made me a lunatic in everyone's eyes."

"Not at all."

"Don't lie to me, young man. Deception is far easier to spot than any sort of spirit."

"Fine. Then I'll level with you. You and your daughter know things you shouldn't. And your explanations are simply not acceptable to me and the people I work for."

"Sorry, but I'm not going to lie simply to accommodate your lack of faith. Look, you can keep trying to assign some dark, sinister motive to my daughter and me, or just accept the truth. Abigail is a wonderful all-American girl with strong values. She has no hidden or harmful allegiances. She loves God, me, and the beach, in that order. And her fellow Watchers. She was a little unsure of her future, at least until all this started happening. But nothing worse than that. Then last year she woke up one morning in the middle of a strange international firestorm. But none of it was her doing. Or my doing either."

"Well, she must have a knack for setting off these global firestorms," he muttered. "Because it looks like she's just sparked another one."

"No, she didn't," insisted Suzanne, her face reddening. "It found *her*. God has great things in store for Abby, I'm sure. But none of this is of her own making. She would just as soon be lying out on the sand than running for her life out there right now."

"What is she doing? Why is she running?"

"If I tell you, will you believe me? Will you accept what I tell you?"

He shrugged. "Until I'm given reason not to."

"She's following the last request of her friend in Jerusalem. She's trying to find an ancient document that will help awaken a dormant army, which in turn will take up arms to help stop a bloodbath."

The agent paused as if needing to take a moment to digest her words before continuing.

"Okay, then," he said at last. "Tell me—who is this army?"

Suzanne smiled. "Ordinary people, many of whom don't even know yet who they are. They would never think of themselves as warriors. People like me. And like whoever's praying for your own soul, Agent Krantzler."

He turned to her with a sharp, alarmed look. "What are you talking about?"

"I'm looking at your guardian angels right now. You have two very powerful-looking guardians on either side of you this very second. And yet I can also see that you're spiritually, if I may say so, in a state of arrested childhood. So there's someone else interceding on your behalf. I would bet a mother or father, maybe a grandparent, but someone out there who is praying for you every day."

Appearing thoroughly agitated now, the agent said, "Please, Mrs. Sherman, do not try to turn the tables of this conversation. This discussion is about you, and your daughter, and why the two of you should not be taken into federal custody for interference with the security of our homeland."

"Is *that* what this is about?" she snapped. "The wave of death? I don't want it to happen any more than you do. So all right, then. Let's get started. What do you want to know?"

"Everything you know or believe you know about this matter, Mrs. Sherman. My superiors want to hear everything you have to reveal. So what do your . . . contacts tell you about this threat?"

"I had a dream about it on the plane over here from Jerusalem. Abby had the same sort of dream. I saw the Washington Mall surrounded by stagnant water, filled with floating bodies, thousands of them. I smelled death so strongly that in the dream I got sick and doubled over with retching. Nothing moved except for vultures and rats and the tiniest ripple of breeze across the water. It wasn't a city. It was a graveyard."

"So the buildings were intact?"

"I suppose so. The trees were destroyed, but the Capitol was still there, although it was stained somehow, across its base. The Lincoln Memorial was standing, and most of what I recognized as the Smithsonian buildings."

"How did the sky look? Was the weather normal?"

Suzanne looked up, thinking. "It was a beautiful day. A few clouds."

"Any smoke in the air?"

"Nothing but humidity and the smell of rotting flesh."

"And you believe this is really going to happen?"

"Mr. Krantzler, I didn't imagine this or conjure it up. I saw it as a reality. And it's happening soon."

"Anything else you can give me?"

"Yes. When I awoke, I had these words on my lips. *Ancient peak.* Look for the attack to come from an ancient peak."

"Is that symbolic, or crypto-language, or what?"

She shook her head, resignation in her features. "I have no idea. It could be any of those."

NATIONAL COUNTERTERRORISM CENTER, VIRGINIA

In one of the several dozen communications rooms monitoring their conversation that very moment across the world by video, a CIA section chief leaned forward in his black leather executive chair and turned to a young assistant.

"Let's run a search on that term, Mike," he said, his face still flickering under the image of Suzanne Sherman blown up to three times her normal size in brilliant high definition. "Look at all domestic geography with an emphasis on the East Coast, and any reference to old or weathered or revered mountaintops. You got that?"

The assistant nodded and rolled away on his chair to a nearby computer monitor. Seconds later his keyboard was clacking away quietly as silent digits began flowing throughout the vast intelligence complex.

CHAPTER
_31

The sun was finally beginning to drop through a thin layer of clouds over Basel when Dylan and Abby emerged from the subway station and out onto Münsterplatz, the city's largest and most historic square. Abby, whose fatigue was beginning to overwhelm her, raised her face to the cool breeze while taking in their new surroundings of centuries-old buildings and the twin spires of a towering cathedral.

"You know, Dylan," she said in a weary voice, "I'm going to have to come back here someday. A day when I can fully appreciate the beauty of this place."

"I know," he said. "I feel the same way. Right now, though, all I can think about is watching the cars and looking for our contact. Thank goodness Jeeps aren't common in Switzerland. Ah! Look—there he is."

Abby followed his gaze and, sure enough, there alongside the cathedral's far wall sat an older model Jeep Wrangler with fat tires. By the time her eyes had processed the sight, Dylan was halfway there.

As Dylan spoke with the owner, a middle-aged bearded man, she hung back and waited. At one point she looked away, scanning the crowded plaza, and nearly screamed out loud.

Her Sight was back, and in full force! Her view of well-dressed Europeans strolling about the beautiful plaza now included glowing white warriors grappling with pools of black, which, when her eye could settle on their writhing forms, resolved into hideous imitations of human and animal forms. She heard angelic shouts, deep and powerful, and demonic growls that seemed to rumble through her insides like an earthquake. She saw a black body strike the ground and dissolve into the earth. Then another. Then, in a blaze of light, an angel tossed high into the air by an unusually large strongman.

"No . . . please, God," she whispered, closing her eyes. "Take this from me. Please let me get my strength back." Then it occurred to her that she might be praying wrongly. She started again. "Please give me the strength for this, if it's your will . . ."

She opened her eyes and looked around again. She saw Dylan climb into the Jeep and heard the engine start. While revving the motor, Dylan poked his head out the window and waved for her to come. The seller was walking away now, stuffing a wad of bills into his shirt pocket.

And that was when she noticed it. The path between them was lined with angels standing shoulder to shoulder, smiling at her. The love and assurance emanating from their features caused her to fight back tears as she dashed toward Dylan.

"It's got some age, but it's in good shape," he told her as she climbed inside. "Perfect for us."

She sighed, leaning back against the headrest. "Dylan, I need to get some sleep," she said softly.

"Sure," he said while speeding away. "I'm going to drive us as far from all this attention as I can. There's not much of a back seat, but you might be able to curl up back there, if you want."

She crawled back and, although it was cramped, found a halfway comfortable position. And despite the sharp turns and the bumps of cobblestone streets, she was soon soothed into a deep slumber.

NATIONAL COUNTERTERRORISM CENTER, MCLEAN, VIRGINIA—
ONE HOUR LATER

The Deputy Director of Operations stood after a long huddle with his analysts, scratching his head and frowning at nobody in particular.

"Looks like we lost them for now," he announced. "Basel police are investigating the Schriftbank shooting. We lost them at the subway. They're on the run somewhere in Switzerland. It's going to be a tough job reacquiring them, I can tell you that."

Ashman slammed his folder shut and rubbed his eyes. Typical. He looked up and caught an I-told-you-so look from Cochran, the CIA man who'd bragged so shamelessly about Hatfield's talents, and fought a strong urge to cuss out the agent in front of everyone.

Watch it, he told himself. *You're getting punch-drunk. Go home and get some sleep before you seriously damage your career.*

GRINDELWALD, SWISS ALPS—NEXT MORNING

Abby was awakened by a wedge of golden sunshine creeping across her face, though its progress was too gradual for her to know precisely what had ended her sleep. The light simply inched over her eyes, and they slowly fluttered open. Feeling rested, she flew awake at once, trying to assess where she was.

The first thing to greet her eyes was a high ceiling of pale wood. She looked over and realized she was lying on a thick mattress covered with a quilt festooned with squares of purple, sunflower yellow, and green. The room was lined with windows and filled with the glow of natural light on blond timber beams.

An open French door beckoned her, ushering in a cool breeze. She stood up and walked toward it. Gazing out at the landscape beyond the room's balcony, she breathed in deeply for several long minutes.

Directly before her hung a fringe of leaves glowing brightly in the sunlight. But beyond that lay the true wonder. A jagged stone horizon flung snow-clad teeth into a sky so blue it seemed almost purple, its gleaming towers of granite thrust heavenward from a canopy of emerald forests and lime green meadows.

She smiled at the sight, stretching herself with a joy she hadn't felt in a long time, and breathed in the refreshing current of mountain air. Immediately her nostrils were filled with the scent of pine and dewy grass and wildflowers. Filtered through the leaves above, sunshine danced across her cheeks and traced a path of warmth on her skin.

Below her, the lawn of the alpine chalet in which she stood stretched farther down to a village sidewalk and a blue stream running through a stony bed. She felt as if she were floating, captivated by a country so beautiful and sublime that she wasn't sure she would ever return to reality.

"Quite a view, isn't it?" came Dylan's voice from the balcony adjacent to hers.

Startled, she glanced over and realized he'd been sitting there silently the whole time, cradling an oversized mug in both hands. "I had no clue you were there." She laughed.

"Sorry. Didn't mean to scare you. But I had the same reaction when I first walked out. You should have seen it at first light. That peak on the right is the Eiger. Remember that old movie *The Eiger Sanction*? The one on the right is the Jungfrau."

"I'm impressed."

"I went down and got a map."

"You've been up for a while."

"I can't sleep during daylight," he admitted. "A curse of my profession."

She leaned forward against the railing, drinking in all the detail of distant cliff faces, pastures, and almost blinding patches of snow and ice. "So where are we?"

"Southern Switzerland, not far from the Italian border. A little village I picked at random and whose name I won't even dare try to pronounce until I've had more coffee."

"Wow. You drove a long time last night."

He chuckled. "And you slept a long time last night. No complaints, though. It's exactly what we both needed. A clean getaway, a long drive, and a good rest. C'mon. Let's go down and grab some breakfast while they're still serving it."

A few minutes later they were sitting together in the chalet's dining room, where Abby ordered a *café au lait* and warm biscuits slathered in butter, with plenty of jelly and cream cheese.

"You seem in better spirits than last night," he said at last, after she'd devoured most of the food.

She nodded. "It's amazing how some sleep, a hearty meal, and an incredible view can change your outlook." She glanced through a nearby window, out at tourists who walked by with an odd slowness in the bright mountain air. "Can we stay here forever? Just hole up in a chalet and forget the world?"

"If the world agreed to forget us, I might be tempted," he replied, his expression dimming a little. "But I doubt very much that's gonna happen. I'd say we have a few hours before it all comes crashing down on us again. Not much more than that."

She sighed, conceding the wisdom of his words. "Well, then, can we just enjoy it as much as possible while the calm lasts? I've never seen anything so majestic."

He nodded with a smile that matched her own—one she had scarcely seen before. "Sure, Abby. Let's hop in the Jeep and go for a little ride."

Abby felt like a schoolgirl just let out on summer vacation, leaving the breakfast table and spontaneously striding across the lawn to their waiting Jeep. As Dylan pulled out, he warned her, "I'm not sure how far these roads will go. The Swiss aren't as enamored with driving as we Americans are. We're liable to wind up at a trailhead and need to get out for a long hike."

"That's fine with me. In fact," she said, patting her stomach, "it might be a good thing after that big breakfast!"

CHAPTER

_32

They followed the creek upstream for a while, quickly leaving behind the village, which was little more than a dozen or so large chalet-style buildings. The pavement ended, the incline started to rise, and soon the Jeep was laboring to climb a rugged mountain road. And yet Abby's elation persisted. With every bump and lurch of its wheels, the Jeep offered her breathtaking views of valleys both near and far, making her want to stop and spend days exploring each one.

"So are we just out here having fun," Dylan asked after several minutes had gone by, "or are we testing your proposition that God would lead us to this summons wherever we find ourselves?"

Her bliss punctured at last, Abby blew out a long breath. "Well, you got me on that one," she confessed. "I've been having such a good time this morning that I seem to have forgotten the reason we're on this little adventure."

"That's what I'm asking you."

"And I have no clue," she replied. "Maybe we should ask Him. Wanna pull over?"

With that, Dylan stopped the Jeep at a precipitously inconvenient place on the road.

"Dear God," Abby began, "we can see how you've ordered every one of our steps so far, and now we're asking for more of your direction. We don't want to waste time, even though your creation is breathtaking. So could you please let us know soon, and quite definitely, whether we're still on the right path or not? We ask you in Jesus' name. Amen."

She looked up at Dylan and smiled. "Well, I'm not sensing that we should turn around and leave yet, are you?"

"No, and if I did, I might have had some doubts. I'm not sure it's humanly possible to turn around where we are. Not until we reach a wider spot in the road."

"Then let's keep going," said Abby.

So they kept clambering upward, soon breaking out onto a level and open cirque valley, fringed in thick fir trees and a bracing aroma of pine. Not only did it offer turnaround space for the Jeep, but the road ended soon after, in a trailhead bordered by a wooden fence.

"Turn around or hike?" he asked, idling for a moment.

"I want to hike a little," she said.

The trail began as the road had earlier—as a well-paved surface flanked by evergreens and, hidden somewhere to their right, the gurgling sound and drifting coolness of a mountain stream. The paving ended just as the forest began to thin out into a stretch of alpine meadow overhung by sheer rock faces.

They had walked a few dozen paces, both of them too entranced to say a word, when Abby suddenly stopped and frowned.

She pointed ahead, at the base of a cliff, and stumbled backward. "Dylan, do you see that?" she asked in a suddenly pained voice.

He peered in the direction she'd indicated, shaking his head. "No. I see nothing but trees and rock."

But Abby was not consoled. Her mouth hung partly open, her index finger raised stiffly forward. Then her knees buckled and she nearly fell, catching herself on Dylan's arm at the last second.

"Bodies . . ." she said.

In her field of view, the cliff's base was piled with the shattered corpses of nearly fifty women and young girls. Limbs protruded at unnatural angles from torsos tangled with ragged dresses and filthy blouses. The shock and horror of it was too much, too sudden. She backed up, stumbled once, and then glanced up toward the cliff's summit.

A scream ripped from her mouth, echoing through the valley.

There, plummeting through the pure alpine air, a tiny body was falling, its clothing fluttering in the wind. Abby looked away yet could not prevent her ears from hearing the sound of impact, whose horror twisted her face in a pained wince.

Now she fell to her knees.

"What is it?" Dylan asked, crouching at her side.

"God, what are you showing me?" she wailed, oblivious to Dylan.

"Please tell me," Dylan pleaded.

"It's too terrible," she panted, looking away. Then their eyes met, and she knew she had to put it into words. "Little children, girls, being thrown over this cliff. Their bodies lying there in a pile."

Too bewildered to do anything else, Dylan began leading her away, back toward the Jeep. But just as they reversed course, Abby once again froze in her tracks and stared, her lips quivering.

"What do you see now?"

"Two men, dressed in old, medieval clothes. They're looking up at the massacre with these awful tortured expressions, moaning and weeping. Their faces are bloody. They've been beaten. And they've got . . ." She paused and coughed twice, in a way that informed Dylan she was about to lose her breakfast. "They've got children's heads, decapitated, strung around their necks."

Abby flung her head back and her body simply crumpled. Close by her side, Dylan caught her by the shoulders and swept her into his grasp. He began to run the rest of the way, holding her as tightly as he could. Anything to whisk her from this awful place.

She was not unconscious, but moaned in his arms the entire way back to the Jeep. "There's a priest standing behind them," she muttered. "And some man in robes. A bishop or something . . ."

Dylan knew nothing more but to get away from there, to throw the Jeep into gear and race back down the mountain, holding Abby's limp form in the front seat with only the pressure of his outstretched arm.

It seemed like mere seconds before they were back on pavement, then speeding back into the village. Dylan led her to her room, helping her to the bed. The whole time she continued to groan about sickening murders and mutilations.

"Dylan, I don't just see them," she whispered. "I feel their despair, their horror. It's their own children they're seeing massacred. O God . . . what is this! What happened here?"

The question pierced Dylan just as powerfully. "Abby, let me get this straight. You're saying these things, these events you're seeing, happened right there, in that very same spot?"

"Yes. I can't say when, but I'd guess it was a very long time ago. But absolutely, they happened right there. Oh, Dylan, I've changed my mind. I want to go. I want to get away, as far from here as I possibly can!"

"Now, there's where I think you're wrong," he said. "Don't you see, this is the confirmation you asked God for! I think this is exactly where we need to be."

"Yes, but I'm in agony!"

It seemed to Abby as though she were in the throes of child-birth, rolling and flexing her muscles in spasms of very real physical suffering.

LANDSTUHL REGIONAL MEDICAL CENTER

Suzanne Sherman's screams drove both of the undercover CIA guards outside the woman's secured room straight from their chairs to her door, peering in to see if their charge was being attacked by some assailant.

Her nurse was ahead of them, however. She punched the door open and was at Suzanne's side before the men could even exchange a glance. Amazingly, only the two women were inside. Suzanne had been alone, in bed, when she had issued her first cry.

"What is it, honey?" the nurse asked, taking her pulse with one hand, staring in sheer bewilderment at her patient's bloodless, asymptomatic state of pain. Yet this was a psychiatric ward, and the nurse knew better than anyone how anguish could arise from purely emotional sources.

"It's Abby," the older woman moaned. "I'm feeling Abby's pains. She's deep in a vision, and she's witnessing the most horrible things! Those poor people, those wretched children! Please, God . . ."

The nurse had read the file. She knew that, in addition to the shoulder injury, which was healing quite well, the patient believed herself to be part of some mystical, spiritual family that shared each other's visions of the supernatural and some kind of unusual mental bond. She also knew that, in a rare breach of standard treatment procedures, the hospital was not treating these beliefs as delusional per se.

In fact, the file was riddled with strange ribbons and flags she hadn't seen before, most of them prohibiting the usual psychiatric care. Some outside force, which she assumed to be somehow related to the disguised agents posted outside the room, was twisting the ward's arm into an unorthodox method of treatment, if you could even call it treatment.

"Can I give you something, Mrs. Sherman?" asked the nurse, running down her list of approved suggestions. "I can calm things down a bit, maybe take this pain away."

"No, no," the woman blurted. "I have to experience this. I have to help her survive it."

"Can you tell me what *it* is?"

"It's genocide, that's what it is! The most sadistic, cruel genocide of innocent people!"

"You see this happening somewhere? Right now?"

"No! It was almost a thousand years ago. But it's afflicting my Abby right this very second! It's literally tearing her up inside!"

CHAPTER
_33

GRINDELWALD, SWITZERLAND

Dylan, for only the second time in his life—the first having taken place in Tunnel 9 a mere week ago—had simply no idea what to do. He could not decide whether to find medicine for Abby, or to seek medical treatment, or to just stay by her side and hold her hand. One thing he did know was that his traveling companion was in serious and prolonged anguish.

But as much as he wanted to seek help, he knew he could not—at least not until he was certain that Abby's survival was at risk. So, driven nearly frantic with indecision, he made an impromptu trip downstairs to the front desk.

Trying desperately to mask his agitation, he rested his elbows on the large wooden desk and faced the chalet's manager, a plump woman in her forties.

"Mind if I ask you a rather strange question?" he said.

Her eyebrows shot up. "That depends on your meaning of *strange*," she replied in accented English.

"I was just wondering if by any chance some kind of mass murder or massacre took place in this area."

She cocked her head. "You mean in the war? The Germans?"

"Well, I'm not sure. But I think it might have been something earlier, maybe much earlier than that. Even centuries ago."

She nodded. "You're referring to the Waldenses. Les Vaudois."

"Excuse me?"

"You call them Waldensians. Early Protestants, if you will." She then made a gesture of passing her index finger across her neck, the universal sign for getting one's head chopped off.

"Is there a museum here that covers this history?" he asked. "Somewhere I could go to find out more about what happened?"

She shook her head. "No, not this side of the border. Most of it happened in Italy."

A male head appeared in the doorway behind her. She spun around to speak to the person, and several sentences of rapid French followed. The woman turned back to Dylan and hit herself playfully on the side of the head.

"What was I thinking? You, you are American, right?"

"Yes. I am."

"Well, you are in luck. There has been in town an American scholar who is studying this, the Waldenses history, for many months now. And he is going to present a lecture two nights from now in our church. Saint Martin."

"He is here? In town?" Dylan pressed, his face brightening.

"Yes. In two nights you can learn everything."

"Forgive me, but I can't wait that long. I have an urgent need to learn more about this in the next few hours, before leaving. Is there any way I could find this scholar myself, right now?"

The woman turned back to the man. *"Tu sais où il habite? L'Américain?"*

Dylan could neither hear nor comprehend the reply, except that it prompted her to turn with a nod. *"Hôtel du Chemin Haut,"* she said. "Just five doors down on your right. His name is Skinhead."

Dylan stared. "Skinhead? Are you sure?"

Another burst of irritated French came from the man behind. The woman rolled her eyes and struck herself again, only harder. "Skinhead, what was I thinking? The name is *Skinner*!"

The hotel's host shrugged when Dylan asked for the American named Skinner, merely pointing outside. *"Il est parti,"* he said, which Dylan understood. His quarry had just left the premises.

So Dylan walked out into the sunshine and scanned the flow of pedestrians. Immediately a man caught his attention. He was standing on the edge of the street, looking around as though lost, his hands on his hips.

Dylan decided to approach him. "Excuse me, but you wouldn't happen to be Dr. Skinner, would you?"

The man turned. For a moment he did not reply but peered into Dylan's eyes with a scrutiny that initially felt intrusive.

"Are you?" Dylan asked again.

"I am," the man said, still staring at him with a peculiar, inquisitive expression.

"I've been looking for you," said Dylan with a friendly tone.

"Well, it seems I've been looking for *you*," replied Skinner.

"You're kidding."

"You're a follower of Christ, aren't you?" Skinner asked sharply.

Dylan drew back, startled at the man's directness and the odd nature of the question. "Yes, I am. And it's quite possible that He's brought us together."

"It certainly looks that way. Is there someplace we can go? Someplace private?"

"As a matter of fact, yes," said Dylan. "It's a bit unusual, but it's also somewhat of an emergency, something I need your help with. It's a woman's hotel room."

Skinner shot him a questioning look, but then followed him anyway.

Moments later Dylan stood outside Abby's room, knocking on her door, with Skinner close beside him.

"Come in," she called. "It's open."

The two of them stepped inside. Abby lay just as Dylan had left her—on the bed, clutching her stomach, grimacing.

With Skinner remaining by the door, Dylan went over and kneeled down by the bed. "Are you feeling any better?" he asked.

"No, Dylan," she moaned. "It's worse. It's horrible. I'm seeing hundreds of people hiding inside a cave and being burned alive by a whole army on horseback."

Immediately Skinner moved forward. "Excuse me, but what did she say?" he whispered to Dylan.

Dylan rose and said, "Abby, I have someone here who may be able to help us—help us understand all this, at least. He's a scholar in . . . well, some of the things you've been seeing." He stepped aside then so Abby could get a better view of the man. "This is Dr.

Peter Skinner." To Dr. Skinner he said, "When we drove up the valley this morning, when we were out hiking, she began to . . . to see things, and to feel things. Images of medieval families being slaughtered. Children being thrown from a cliff."

"The *Rocher du Sang*," Skinner muttered, almost to himself. And then he stared closer at Abby's face. "Loosely translated, Boulder of Blood. Wait a minute," he said. "You . . . you have an amazing resemblance to that young woman who was in the news so much last year. Abigail Sherman."

Abby straightened her back, turned, and looked him full in the eyes. "Yes, I'm that woman."

Neither broke eye contact, and something profound passed between them.

"Do you know our story?" she asked finally.

"Well, I know the story everyone else heard, because I followed it quite closely. But I have no idea what's brought you here."

"No," she said, "you certainly don't. Dylan, would you mind filling in our new friend?"

Dylan nodded and led Skinner over to the room's divan, where they could sit and talk. There he spent several minutes giving Skinner the full story of all the events that had brought them there.

Skinner's eyes seemed to grow wider by the minute. He obviously was struggling to absorb all that he was hearing. When Dylan was nearly finished, as he recounted their drive that morning up the valley and the specifics of what Abby had described, Skinner turned to stare at her and did not look away.

Then, without waiting for Dylan to complete his last sentence, Skinner got up and walked to Abby's bedside. "I should have known why your story last year captivated me the way it did," he said softly. "I know all about the Watchers. And as fantastic as this sounds, it doesn't surprise me one bit that you would react this way to the events that took place here." Suddenly his voice rose in authority and volume. "Miss Sherman, may I call you Abby?"

She nodded, her hands still clutching her stomach.

"Abby, you're absolutely right about what happened in this valley, and elsewhere throughout these mountains. Some of humanity's most heinous crimes were perpetrated by so-called spiritual leaders against the Waldensians, an early Christian rebellion against the Catholic Church, during the late Middle Ages. I've spent the last five years researching a book on the subject, and I've discovered traces of massacres that were thought to have taken place elsewhere in the Alps."

"I need to know," she said, gritting her teeth. "God put Dylan and me onto this search, and we have to learn. Not only will our learning possibly end this strange affliction, but it may help us find what we've been sent for." She turned away, her eyes on Dylan now. "Did you tell Dr. Skinner about the summons?"

"No. I didn't feel clear enough about it. Do you think you could describe it for him?"

"I'll try," she replied, looking back to Skinner. "The Sentinel of Jerusalem, the leader of the Watchers, told me as she was dying about some kind of document I needed to find, which would call forth the Warriors in the body of Christ. And finding it would entitle me to issue the call."

"Yes, of course," Skinner said, nodding. "The Summons to War."

Abby shot straight up in her bed, and she and Dylan exchanged glances. "What? You *know* about this?" she said.

"Well, it's a fairly well-known, well-documented prophecy. It's been around even longer than the Waldensians themselves, although it exceeds their provenance."

"Meaning?"

"Meaning it's not unique to them. The summons is a legend that's floated around Christian literature across Europe and Christian mission fields since the Middle Ages."

"And where can we find it?" Dylan asked.

Skinner laughed at Dylan's presumption. "The document itself? First of all, liberal scholars would tell you it doesn't physically exist. They would call it the very first Christian urban myth, an extrabiblical legend cooked up by Templar sympathizers and overzealous military types. In fact, most modern scholarship has written it off as a metaphor and that's all. You're looking at one of the few academics left in the world who believes in the document's existence."

Dylan took a step closer to Skinner. "In that case, Dr. Skinner, I'll repeat my question," he said. "Where do you think it's at?"

Still amused by Dylan's brashness, the scholar replied, "I don't know. I do think it was the work of an early Christian warrior, someone who knew quite a bit about earthly soldiering."

"Could you narrow that down a bit?" Dylan asked.

"Well, given the time frame involved, I probably can. Ancient groups fitting that profile would include the Albigensians, various Huguenot groups in France as well as the Camisards of Provence, Knights Templar, and the Waldensians."

"How much territory are we talking about?"

"Oh, man. The Waldensians, nearly all of the European Alps, huge swaths of northern Italy and southern France. The Knights Templar traveled across most of Western Europe and the Middle

East. The Albigensians are your easiest bet, covering southernmost France and the Pyrenees."

Dylan rubbed his eyes in dismay. "There's no way we can search all that ground. We don't have time—"

"But we're not being asked to," Abby interrupted, her voice suddenly stronger. "God's clearly been at work, leading us here, then bringing Dr. Skinner to us. He'll show us the way. We just have to stay on course."

"Yeah, but our course has been random, unplanned," Dylan protested.

She flashed him a defiant grin. "In *your* eyes, maybe."

CHAPTER
_34

GRINDELWALD, SWITZERLAND

The notice at Grindelwald City Hall announcing a lecture entitled Grindelwald's Page in Waldensian History became suddenly, unexpectedly, adorned with the blunt word *canceled*. The man who had thus defaced the poster, in fact the same man pictured in its grainy black-and-white photograph, was seen jumping into a Jeep and racing away with a young American couple, who had swept into town the day before.

So learned the tall, muscular American who drove into town only an hour after their departure and wasted no time asking questions, a man wearing the uniform of a U.S. Marine. He soon found out that the people he sought were gone—carried away by a vehicle he ought to know well: an American Jeep. After all, there weren't too many of those in Switzerland.

SWISS HIGHWAY F-8, HEADED SOUTH

Abby sat bunched up in the Jeep's back seat, feeling stronger than she had in several hours.

"You know what we've failed to do?" she asked the two men in front of her. "It's so easy, I forget all the time. We're in combat right now. We need to ask for cover, to stay hidden from the enemy. We have a killer after us who is possessed. If any evil spirit has seen us, then tracking our movements will be child's play for them."

After leading them in a long, detailed plea for spiritual concealment, she pulled herself between the front seats to join their conversation.

"Dylan," said Dr. Skinner, "do you know why I was standing in the middle of the street when you found me, looking around like a fool?"

"I just figured you couldn't quite choose which way to take your morning walk."

"No. I was standing there because I was certain a voice inside was telling me to go outside and find my destiny."

"Whoa." Both Dylan and Abby uttered the same reaction.

"And you both should know that even though I study global movements in spiritual warfare, unlike you and your Watchers, I don't hear God's voice like that, ever. So I'm here to tell you— you guys are up to something incredibly powerful and anointed, something I've never encountered in my entire life."

"Since it's so obvious God led us together," said Abby, "will you stay with us? To the end?"

"Yes," he said emphatically. "I certainly will."

"Welcome aboard," Abby said with a grin, touching his shoulder. " 'Cause believe me, we have no more of an idea where this will end than you do."

Dr. Skinner laughed. "Does that mean you don't know where we're headed? Maybe I should have asked you that first."

"Wherever God leads," Abby said.

"Yeah, well, for right now that's not a direction I can physically steer in," Dylan said. "I mean, not to be blasphemous, but is that north, south, east, or west?"

"You'll do just as well to head toward Italy, then," Skinner cut in. "Toward the heart of Waldensian country. Do I take it you'd just as soon avoid border crossings?"

"Oh, we don't like border crossings," Dylan shot back.

"Well, you're in luck, as the faithless say," said Skinner. "I've been crossing these mountains back and forth dozens of times a month in my research, and I've learned all the hidden back roads through mountain passes. Good thing you have a Jeep."

"Just warn me before we go off-road," Abby said, "because I'm not back to my old self just yet."

"Roger," Skinner replied. "So tell me, how is finding the lost summons going to save America from some horrible attack?"

"I know it sounds a bit strange, phrased that way," Abby conceded. "But this attack, like all of the terrorist campaigns against us, is fueled by something much deeper and darker than just human hatred."

"That doesn't surprise me," said Skinner.

"Yeah, except in our case we've learned the source and nature of the powers involved. And the Holy Spirit has given us glimpses of what they have planned. It's an attack designed to wipe out our entire eastern seaboard. Every city, every man, woman, and child. We don't know how, but we've been shown the aftermath. And it's the kind of operation that won't be stopped by human intelligence alone. It'll take everything our government can muster, plus every spiritual warrior we can persuade to step in. So, according to Sister Rulaz, if I find that summons and issue the call, we have a fighting chance to stop this thing before it's too late."

"So you think this attack is definitely going to happen, without some drastic turnaround?"

"Yes, I do," Abby replied. "But that doesn't mean it can't be reversed. There's plenty of cases in the Bible where God had determined to let a nation get wiped out. But when the people got on their knees and prayed, God seemed to change His mind. At the very least, He reversed course. He allowed the onslaught to be stopped."

"God flat-out changing His mind," Skinner said thoughtfully. "I have to admit, I had never considered it that explicitly before. But you're right. I'm thinking of a verse in Jeremiah—"

"Jeremiah eighteen," Abby interrupted. "'If at any time I announce that a nation or kingdom is to be uprooted, torn down and destroyed, and if that nation I warned repents of its evil, then I will relent and not inflict on it the disaster I had planned.'"

"Yes, that's it," said Skinner.

"Brace yourself," said Dylan, "'cause we're coming up on a mighty big dip."

Abby crouched lower and gripped the seats on either side for support, but still found her head grazing the Jeep's hardtop when it lurched across a wide pothole in the road.

"Where are we going again?" Dylan asked in a dubious tone.

"Italy," Skinner answered. "The Waldensian valleys."

CHAPTER
_35

BREGA, LIBYA—THE NEXT MORNING

The *Medina*'s cargo manifest listed a load of bananas, figs, goats, and lambs, all headed for the Canary Islands. She was a small boat, only thirty-five feet in length, but large enough to handle the route ahead as well as the brisk traffic along the northern coast of Africa. And large enough to carry a fifty-pound nuclear bomb deep in its cargo hold, in the secret compartment usually reserved for guns and ammunition and the occasional shipment of hashish when money ran tight.

This particular shipment had placed ten times more than the usual bribe into the pocket of Captain Yahmin Ranmeb. The captain had welcomed the extra money, even though he didn't know the exact makeup of the cargo, and even though it had placed an unwelcome stranger on board his boat. This brooding man brought with him no sailing skills but only silent, menacing stares. The one who arranged the job had insisted this stranger accompany the shipment and be added to the craft's books as an engineer. The stranger bolted to his feet and insisted on watching any time a member of Ranmeb's crew, which consisted of his teenage sons Musab and Mahib, so much as approached the cargo hold. Suspicious bulges in his ample robes suggested he was carrying the means to keep the shipment safe.

Despite Ranmeb's ignorance about the nature of the cargo, he had been around the Mediterranean long enough to know that it was serious. He had been chosen precisely for his discretion on previous jaunts up and down the coast, so he knew when and how to avoid government patrols and pirate attacks alike. He was a good shot and an unerring navigator of the coast's innumerable inlets and escape routes.

Neither Ranmeb nor his sons had any idea of the hideous and invisible beings who had followed their strange passenger onto their boat. They only noticed the unusual reaction of the harbor dogs, which had launched into a vicious and prolonged fit of barking when the man had stepped aboard. Though the *Medina* was hardly a boat smelling of fresh-cut flowers, even so, all three had noticed a disturbing, vile stench and spent two hours searching in vain for some rat carcass or other vermin source. They had found nothing.

They pulled out on a bright Tuesday morning, and Ranmeb, despite the trip's unsettling aspects, proved unable to contain his exuberant love of the sea. Calling out his traditional sailor's prayer in a booming voice, he glanced over at the stranger leaning against the railing. The man had a sneer plastered on his face, staring at him with vacant eyes. He leaned over the side and spit, then resumed his staring.

The captain had quickly looked away, fighting off a cascade of shivers rippling down his spine. The man was positively evil. Whatever this shipment was about, it was far darker than mere narcotics.

THE WHITE HOUSE OVAL OFFICE—ONE HOUR LATER

The document was handed over by the Secretary of Homeland Security, although the Chairman of the Joint Chiefs of Staff, sitting beside him, and the Director of Intelligence, on his other side, looked as though they might have clawed his eyes out for the privilege.

The President of the United States slipped on his reading glasses, the ones he'd argued about with his handlers to let him use on-camera sometime, as his wife had always told him they appeared to add twenty points to his IQ.

Let's see this puppy, he told himself. *With all three of these jokers here to give it to me, it must be a doozy . . .*

PRESIDENT'S DAILY BRIEF

Item One: Terrorist chatter has increased fivefold in the last 36 hours. Much of it originates from the western Pakistani provinces, where the heart of the terrorist network is generally believed to be housed. The nature of these communications raises grave concerns. Much of it consists of pronouncements of victory and praise for the upcoming decimation of the Great Satan, i.e., the United States. It seems to presume that the attack is a foregone conclusion, along with its success. It also seems to presume that its execution is imminent. Prediction based on past uses of the term in its native language: *imminent* means 72 hours or less.

Item Two: Three of the identified domestic recipients of this terrorist traffic are cells under federal surveillance in the Eastern U.S. One communiqué warned the occupants to leave their city immediately and move west. The individuals complied within the hour. The other two were successfully encrypted, but the recipients immediately evacuated their areas upon receipt of the email messages.

Item Three: Intelligence assets of the United States and our allies are tracking the route of a low-yield nuclear device smuggled from the salvage of the Russian submarine Kursk at Sayda Bay. Last report places the device in Libya, but without official government sanction.

Item Four: Domestic Evacuation Plan Delta Bravo is now ready for real-time execution. Airborne and underground egress sites are fully operational. All protectees have been informed and have pledged utmost cooperation.

Item Five: Homeland Security will deliver an eight-point disaster management plan by day's end. Lead scenario for the attack: the detonation of a low-yield nuclear device in an eastern metropolitan area (Washington, New York, Boston, Baltimore, Philadelphia), accompanied by mass, coordinated conventional suicide bombings.

Item Six: DCI has identified three American persons of interest in the investigation: Abigail Sherman, 25, of Santa Monica, California; her mother, Suzanne Sherman, 58, also of Santa Monica; and Dylan Hatfield, 34, primary residence unknown, retired U.S. Army lieutenant, former classified foreign operative of joint CIA/NSA/Special Ops Command missions worldwide, most recently a participant in Operation Mystic Sender, a reconnaissance mission in Tora Bora.

The three are linked, primarily as high-interest media profiles resulting from a globally publicized disappearance and manhunt last year. All three have recently shared information with each other regarding classified deep-cover data unknowable through civilian sources, specifically data germane to the wave-of-death threat. Suzanne Sherman is in federal care in Ramstein, Germany, under debrief. Younger Sherman and Hatfield are being tracked in Switzerland as potential targets of terrorist reprisal.

The president lowered the brief and the reading glasses in twin sweeping gestures of both hands. "What's this gibberish about Abby Sherman and unknowable data?"

The Secretary of Homeland Security shrugged and shot a barely perceptible glance toward his two companions. "Sir, there's been considerable debate about even including that item on the brief. However, as strange as this item is, we feel it's germane enough to report. Somehow, these women have learned and seen things that are of great significance. We have no overriding recommendation, sir. No actionable perspective on the matter. That's why I was reluctant to include it."

"However," interrupted the Chairman of the Joint Chiefs, "I'd have to concede that their . . . revelations, however bizarre and out of place they may be, are not only startling because of their classified nature. They are, if proven true, of potentially enormous help to our efforts. They have seen things that are both confirmed and quite specific."

"Well, John. You ever heard of prayer?"

"Of course, sir. There's no need to be—"

"I'm not being anything. I know where you go to church. That's why I'm surprised to see you so perplexed by all this."

"But, sir, in this context—"

"Forget context," interrupted the president. "Jamie closely followed the whole Abby Sherman story last year. I know all about that young lady. She's a deeply committed believer who's been given a gift for seeing things. A gift, I might add, which doesn't seem to discriminate between items of huge spiritual importance and those with national security ramifications."

"Yes, sir, but we're not tasked to . . . even address issues of this sort, Mr. President," said the Director of Intelligence.

"Look, the people didn't elect me to dance around what the intelligence community can't or won't talk about. They put me here to keep them safe. And if keeping them safe means wading into some murky waters—well, it wouldn't be the first time."

"What are you proposing, sir?"

"Ah, Harold, I'm not proposing anything. Yet. It's just that everyone knows about my faith. I mean, it's one of the things that put me here. Bottom line, I'm on record as believing in God, the Bible, prayer, the whole spiritual realm for that matter. That may not compute in some CIA database, but it's a fact. It's who I am, and I'm not going to leave it by the roadside just because it may be hard to explain.

"So here's what I want. Let's use every asset at our disposal. First of all, stop dangling the poor girl. Don't look at me that way; I know what 'potential target of reprisal' means. You're dangling her, and I want it to stop. I want you to bring her in and treat her like a national security asset of the highest order. I want you to treat everything that's already come from her mouth, and her mother's, as human intel. And don't you dare let this thing leak."

"Yes, sir," said the Director of Intelligence.

"Come to think of it, I want Miss Sherman here. In my office. ASAP."

CHAPTER
_36

"Isabella! Where are you? Don't you know you're late for Vespers?"

Sister Rosalia cracked open the door to the girl's room much more quietly than she would have any of the other novices' doors. No one would blame her, at least not within these walls. Every nun in the convent knew what a remarkable follower of Christ was their Isabella. Most of the sisters already thought of the girl as the next Mother Superior. She was a full three years younger than the traditional age for the novitiate, yet approved by the Archbishop of Coimbra himself after the amazing acts of piety, her mastery of Scripture, and supernatural knowledge she'd displayed.

Indeed, if Isabella ever strayed one bit from the convent rules, had arrived late for even the most casual of observances, it was usually because she was found in her room so deep in prayer, earnestly and spontaneously kneeling on that hard stone floor, that she was never scolded. In fact, Rosalia chided herself, she was probably being a little too harsh right now. She lowered her voice, pushed open the door a little farther, and whispered, "Isabella, are you in here?"

Yes, Isabella was kneeling in the center of her room again, leaned back and facing up at the sky through her open window as always. This time, though, she seemed different. Rather than leaving, Rosalia sensed something and stayed. She peered around the side of the girl's figure, the thin back turned to her. Isabella's arms were not raised to her chest in prayer as usual. They lay outstretched beside her, palms facing up.

Rosalia looked around far enough to see her face. She gasped.

The girl's eyes were wide open, unblinking, her features frozen in a mask of distress.

Rosalia was not trained in the handling of the human psyche, so she immediately panicked. Should she move the girl from her posture? Try to talk with her? Get her to bed? Go for help?

"Sister Rosalia?" It was the girl's voice, soft and weak, barely audible.

"Yes, my dear girl. What is the matter? Are you ill?"

"Perhaps, my sister. But do you see them?"

"See who?"

"The spirits. They're everywhere. They're dark, evil. They hate me. What did I do to them?"

"You follow Christ, my dear. You labor to bring His light to the world."

"But why are they coming here, and in such numbers? They're covering the sky, Sister Rosalia. They cover the trees. The world is turning black with their coming."

The elder nun looked outside, then back again. "I see nothing."

"But they're everywhere . . ."

SOUTHERN SWITZERLAND

Abby got to the point where she had to avert her eyes from the sheer physical beauty all around her. The long drive along the Swiss-Italian border had revealed an unending procession of lush green valleys and vast sun-drenched mountain ridges—so awe-inspiring and stimulating as to tax her capacity for wonder.

"Do you think we're being unrealistic," she asked Skinner, anxious to focus on a new subject, "to be combing through all this history to find what we need?"

"Not if you're really looking for the summons," he replied. "If it's real, then it was left by someone who knew about spiritual warfare. And, I imagine, earthly warfare to boot. And if the legends are true, then the time frame is fairly specific. It couldn't have been left by any of the Welsh revivalists, for example, who achieved prominence in the late nineteenth and early twentieth centuries. They knew all about spiritual warfare, but they couldn't have been the source of a legend that's been around for at least half a millennium."

"Who are the Welsh revivalists?" Abby asked, feeling sheepish.

"The Welsh Revival was a huge turning to God that swept through Wales in 1904," Skinner began. "One hundred thousand people became born again in the span of a few months. But the person I find most interesting was someone who didn't lead the revival but was a product of it. He was a coal miner named Rees Howells, who insisted on taking God's word about intercession literally. His favorite verse was in Second Corinthians ten, the one that says, 'The weapons of our warfare are not carnal, but mighty through God to the pulling down of strongholds.'"

"Strongholds. I like the sound of that," interjected Dylan. "Sounds like the sort of place I visited recently."

"Although Sister Rulaz did call it a *principality*," Abby added.

Skinner turned to her with a look of amazement. "She used the word *principality* to describe a real place?"

Abby nodded.

Skinner whistled softly. "Most Christians are content to quote the phrase 'principalities and powers' with a kind of hazy, symbolic meaning. But there's a movement of intercessors around the world who look to Rees Howells as one of their pioneers, who take such words far more literally. It's fascinating." He turned in his seat to face Abby. "You know, Abby, you're at the forefront of something that God's been brewing among His people for a long time."

"I'm just starting to get a sense of that," she said breathlessly. "It's a little scary, and humbling."

"Don't worry," Skinner said with a reassuring nod. "If He chose you, then it's just a matter of trusting—"

"Looks like we've got company," interrupted Dylan, looking up into his rearview mirror. "There's someone behind us, been on our tail for the last couple of miles, and I think he's about to have a close encounter with our rear bumper."

"You need to give him the slip?" Skinner asked. "Because the turnoff for the Italian border is coming up soon."

Dylan nodded. "Let's do it."

Skinner reached down and cinched his seat belt with a tug. "Better hang on tight," he said to Abby with a boyish grin. "It's going to be a rough ride!" He held out an index finger, looking through the windshield at the pine forest as they hugged a long, left-leaning curve. "It's coming up . . . right NOW!"

Dylan yanked the wheel hard to the left. They left the pavement in a moment of flight, landing on a bed of craggy earth. The impact launched Abby's head into the Jeep's hardtop. She winced as she grabbed hold of the roll bar for support.

They lost momentum for an instant while Dylan fiddled with the four-wheel drive control, but a second later the gear kicked in and they shot up a steep loose-dirt embankment.

"Did we lose him?" Skinner yelled above the commotion.

Abby dared a look behind her. The angle and altitude below them made her face blanch and her stomach turn queasy. Then she spotted it—a Volvo sedan, its headlights peering through a veil of dust, following them with a doggedness that made her shake her head in mock admiration. "He's still back there!"

CHAPTER

_37

After glancing up at the rearview mirror, Dylan slapped the Jeep's steering wheel. He leaned forward and gunned the engine, determined to evade their pursuer, focusing on the wild weavings of the road ahead. For the next hundred yards it was all uphill—a tire-grinding, stomach-churning climb. They slipped and fell a few feet, then regained traction and roared ahead all over again.

"No way is that car following us up *this*!" Dylan shouted.

Skinner turned and looked behind them. "He's tearing up his car, and he may not live through it, but we haven't shaken him yet!"

"Man!" Dylan muttered. "Must be the last of those guys from the hospital. Want to talk about principalities?" he said to Skinner. "That guy back there is possessed by a demon from the principality I told you about. The deepest, darkest, most evil tunnel in all of Afghanistan. The one where bin Laden disappeared."

"You know what some missionaries say about those disappearances?" Skinner called out over the motor's roar. "They say it's a common practice among certain adepts to call on spirits to transport them. Whisk them away."

"Do you mean whisk them to *hell*?" Abby asked.

"No, you don't understand! Shoot them across hundreds of miles of earthly landscape in just a few seconds. It's been reported all over the world. Haiti, Central Africa, and parts of the Middle East."

Dylan gave Skinner a rueful shake of the head. They shot up onto a plateau, a deeply rutted stretch that was more streambed than roadbed. "I don't know about this, Doc! You're blowing my mind here. I've never even considered stuff like that in my wildest dreams!"

"Oh, you wouldn't believe all I've seen and heard in my time," Skinner said. "A professor of ancient history and comparative religions gets told all sorts of strange things when conducting research in the field and interviewing folks about their experiences."

Dylan scowled as he tried to make out the trail ahead. "What about this Rees Howells? What happened to him?"

"Ah yes—I wasn't finished! He developed this habit of deciding that God wanted something to take place, then praying for hours, even days, until he was certain the Lord had granted him his request. Then he'd tell the world God had heard him and would make it all come true."

"That's gutsy," Dylan said.

"It was, except for one thing! Time and time again, it *did* come true. Later on, he started a college in Wales, during World War II. He started praying about the outcome of specific battles. Ever hear of Dunkirk?"

"Sure," Dylan replied. "Studied it in army training."

"Remember its nickname?"

"The Miracle of Dunkirk?"

"Bingo. Howells and his students prayed straight through the night for the weather to calm and the British Army to get away safely. I'll give you another doozy—what was strange about the invasion at Salerno?"

"Nothing, unless you count the German artillery halting on the stroke of midnight."

"You're good!" said Skinner. "On the stroke of midnight Rees told his men to stop praying for the invasion because God had answered their prayer. That very second the German shelling, which was destroying the Allied beachhead, suddenly stopped until morning. For no apparent reason."

"They didn't teach that part in my army training!" Dylan said.

Abby chimed in. "Nobody had a problem with his praying for one-sided military operations like that? Turning prayer into a biased Allied weapon?"

"Why would they? It was clear which side was the evil side. I mean, our side did some awful things too, but you'd be crazy to say that World War II was morally ambiguous. Think of Auschwitz, for goodness' sake!"

"I see your point," said Abby. "I ask because . . . well, I'll tell you later."

"Better believe it!" Dylan said with renewed alarm. "This guy's still on us!"

"He won't be for long." Skinner leaned forward. "Hang on, and let off the gas just a bit."

Abby looked ahead through the windshield and saw that the trail was coming to an end. All she could see ahead was pale blue sky and the peaks of the Apennine Alps.

Suddenly there was no ground beneath them—only air filled with the engine's racing, the spinning of tires, and the flinging of dirt clods down a dizzying height. Through nearly shut eyelids and an odd soaring sensation, Abby caught a frightening glimpse of a hill rising up to meet them. She covered her head with both hands for protection and huddled as far down as she could.

Actually, they struck the earth with far less of a bang than expected. Granted, they bounced three times, high enough to clear the ground all over again. And when they regained traction, they were headed about ten degrees off course. Dylan corrected his steering with a whoop of joy, Skinner grinning at him like a man vindicated, and somehow the Jeep stayed upright.

Then a loud clanging shook the hillside behind them. Abby turned. One of the Volvo's front tires had blown out from the impact, its front bumper torn off, yet the car was still running, still moving, still in pursuit!

"No way!" Dylan shouted. "Don't tell me!"

"I can't believe it!" Skinner exclaimed.

They turned to the right and soon were hugging the face of a cliff along a narrow road. Abby took one look over the edge and turned pale.

"All right, this is the hairy part," Skinner warned.

Dylan glanced at him. "No kidding!"

"If you're not careful, you could go over the edge. And then it's all over."

"Unclip the hardtop," Dylan ordered.

"What?" said Abby and Skinner in unison.

"See those chrome clips there? They hold on the top. Unclip them! Hurry!"

Abby and Skinner did as they were told, both of them reaching up and releasing the front and back clips that held the Jeep's hardtop in place.

"On a count of three," shouted Dylan, "push up on the top with both your hands! Ready—one, two, three . . ."

In a burst of energy, Abby and Skinner stood in their seats and with hands above their heads, struck the hardtop and sent it hurtling into the air.

Abby twirled around in time to see the heavy fiberglass roof fly backward and hit the Volvo's windshield head-on. She caught a glimpse of a man's face, twisted by rage, through the shattered windshield. The driver attempted to ignore the obstruction blocking his path, but the roof's bulkiness proved too much. A corner disappeared under the car's right front wheel well, and the sudden barrier flipped the Volvo violently sideways, then upside down. A split second later the car catapulted over the edge of the cliff, down through a rush of mountain air, ending in a loud crash and then an explosion that echoed up to the ears of the three in the Jeep, which Dylan had pulled to a stop along the narrow road.

Skinner said to Dylan, "I've taken this road before, but at one-fifth that speed! Congratulations on surviving."

Dylan blew out a breath. "Thanks, Doc."

Skinner then turned to Abby. "Welcome to Italy."

CHAPTER

_38

"I've got an explosive heat bloom right above Schieranco, Italy!" an analyst announced loudly. "Abandoned mountain pass, basically a goat trail, which makes a fossil fuel explosion even more out of place, don't you think?"

Instead of turning toward him, the heads of the other analysts remained with their eyes fixed on their oversized monitors, furiously typing on their keyboards. The screens closest to him flashed wildly with a montage of images of the Italian mountainside, one of them a thermal view of the area, the other an eerie infrared perspective.

"Thermal shows a vehicle leaving the scene, same trail, half a mile south. Anyone pick it up on a visual?"

"Got it!" came a shout from across the room.

"Can we ID the make?" asked the lead analyst, standing in the center of the space with his hands on his hips.

"I'm seeing heads—three, to be exact. They seem to be going topless!"

The supervisor turned to the speaker. "What?"

"Their vehicle has no roof, sir," the analyst replied amidst a chorus of snickers. "I see a woman in the back, two men in front. They seem to have picked up some local help."

"Can anyone get me the make of the vehicle and a license plate number?"

"Negative. Angle's bad, they're going too fast, and it's a bumpy road. Can't get resolution."

"What's this shiny metallic shape across the top?"

"Appears to be a roll bar, sir. If this was America, I'd say that makes it a Jeep Wrangler."

"I'd say it has to be. Don't they have those in Europe?"

"I'll check on it."

"Do we have any assets close by?"

"Not really. Unless you want to bring in the Italians."

"Can't do it. Our new marching orders say involving the locals is off-limits. Since this search for Sherman and Hatfield is now based on the president's orders, ground rules are out of our hands. How far is Aviano?"

A man raised his chin to acknowledge the request. "Aviano Air Base, an hour and forty minutes by air. But no pertinent assistance capability."

"Aviano doesn't even have a chopper?"

"Negative. Not standing by or remotely prepared, that is."

"All right. I want all NSA, NRO, Homeland Security—everyone participating in this op to receive our updated data within the next three minutes. Let's re-task those northbound birds, move those ground assets out of Germany and Switzerland to—"

"Turin's the best staging city, sir. Almost all the highways and other transportation routes run through there."

"Okay. Turin it is. Everybody relocates there, headlining a topless Jeep with two men and one woman. Guys, we've gotta close this gap. The threat level is going off the charts, and whether we understand it or not, these folks are key players."

TURIN, ITALY—FOUR HOURS LATER

By the time the three had reached Turin, Dylan had turned silent and begun to brood, a contemplative state of mind that Abby had come to know well. "What are you plotting?" she asked him.

"Just trying to figure out what kind of trail we've left for Uncle Sam to ID. Abby, you're becoming a warrior; it's time you worked on your craft a little. Why don't you tell me."

"I'm trying to be a spiritual warrior, not a CIA agent, Dylan."

"Nevertheless, this applies. The strategies you learn from me, you'll be able to take over to the spiritual side. You were praying for angels to hide us from the enemy earlier. Well, here's more ways to stay hidden."

"What do I do?"

"Tell me the two main ways we gave ourselves away today."

She gazed out the window at the approaching wall of mountainside. "We left a burning car high up in the mountains, I suppose."

"I *suppose?*" he said, chuckling. "No need to suppose, Abby. Assuming Uncle Sam knew we'd gone into Switzerland and was combing the Alps for anything suspicious, they would have detected that heat signature in seconds."

"But was there any way to prevent it?"

"No. Nothing to be done, except be aware of it. What's our second?"

"No idea."

He reached over into his backpack and tossed Dr. Skinner his untraceable cell phone. "Doc, best as I can tell, you left your room back in Grindelwald without settling up. And you left your car there. Without those things, our meeting you would have been completely untraceable. So call the hotel and settle up by phone, tell them you had to attend to some urgent business that came up, and you'll be glad to pick up the car within a couple days. Offer to pay a parking fee, and make sure they know it's no big deal. If they file a police report or any kind of inquiry about your whereabouts, then you're blown."

Skinner nodded, pulled out a small card from his pants pocket, and began to dial.

"I'm also getting a little jumpy about our wheels," Dylan continued to Abby. "Driving a Jeep was bad enough. But one with no top, across hundreds of miles of highway, is just calling attention to ourselves."

"I have a buddy in Torre Pellice," Skinner broke in, his hand over the cell phone, "who I think would trade us his old Mazda for a novelty like this one."

Dylan's face brightened. "Is that on our way?"

Skinner nodded, returning to his phone call.

"Then let's not waste a second."

By the time they passed Turin and headed southwest into the Piedmont region of the Alps, Abby was taken in all over again by the beauty surrounding the open Jeep. The Italian version unfolded with a magnificence all its own. Thriving vineyards lined hillsides beside a river that grew wider and rushed faster with every passing mile. They passed stone manors, colorful villas, and quaint towns that took her breath away. While the earlier sights of chalets had unmistakably said *Switzerland*, these vineyards and high-perched buildings appeared as Italian as spaghetti and olive oil. The peaks ahead, although not as majestically carved by ice and wind as their northern counterparts, gave Abby a sense of wonder, altogether different from the ones she'd just left.

She sighed, slid forward in her seat. "Do you think we've got a good chance of finding the summons up here?" she asked Dr. Skinner.

"I do," he answered. "The Waldensians are one of the most notable, if overlooked, examples of spiritual warriors in all of church history. And their valleys, just ahead, are filled with museums, monuments, and relics where we might well expect to find a stone sculpture just like what you described."

"Why haven't I heard of them before?"

"One of the reasons is that for years their oppressors wrote their history and succeeded in painting them as weird heretics. The truth was, the Waldensians were humble sheepherders and grape farmers who grew disenchanted with the excesses of the Mother Church. You have to understand, back in the Middle Ages, the clergy lived high off the hog, demanding huge bribes to let dead relatives into heaven, keeping mistresses and whole families as slaves, indulging in drunkenness and debauchery. And on top of all that, insisting they alone spoke for God, and that no one but they could get close to Him in any personal way."

They passed a sign that read *Pinerolo*, pointing toward the south. Skinner motioned for Dylan to turn that way. As they drove through a valley of nondescript industrial development, the professor used the downtime to brief them on the story surrounding their destination.

CHAPTER
_39

"All that the Waldensians did to earn the rage of Rome," said Dr. Skinner, "was loosely translate popular-language versions of the Scriptures, take vows of poverty and charity, and start their own forms of worship without the corrupt priests."

"That's it? That's what made Rome so angry?"

"Basically. And it's hard to even talk about how savagely they were treated. Besides whole families being slaughtered and parents being forced to watch the rape of their own children, the reports of sadistic torture simply boggle the mind. Back in Turin, history books say one man had his insides yanked out for belonging to the movement. Another, in a town just ahead, was tortured a step beyond: a crazed cat was crammed into his empty stomach cavity to torture him even further. One was slashed with sabers and his wounds filled with lime powder to burn the rest of him. One had his tongue torn out just for praising God. Another had matches stuck in every open place of his body and lit afire for the same offense. And one Waldensian, every time he refused to recant his faith, had another part of his body sliced away, starting with his fingers, then his hands, feet, arms and legs. The women weren't spared either."

"I think I've heard enough," Abby said, her face pale. "Any more and I'll be sick."

"No wonder they took up arms," Dylan said softly.

"Exactly. They tried everything else beforehand. First, they retreated higher and higher into these hills. They ventured so far and were so skilled at melting into the caves and mountainsides that they became like ghosts—a hidden, mythical group invisible to the rest of the world. But the Church knew they were there, and they started driving armies up into the mountains, sealing up whole caverns and setting their entrances on fire to kill hundreds at a time."

Abby let out a breathy groan. "Please. I don't know if I can take this. I'm starting to feel it in my bones. These valleys, they still seem to . . . resonate somehow with all the suffering."

"I'm sorry," Skinner offered. "It's small wonder, though, that you're feeling it so strongly. We're approaching Torre Pellice, the heart of the Waldensian homeland. I think we need to visit a museum and library here. Will you be able to handle it?"

"I'll have to," she replied. "I'm sure I'll be given the strength."

"First, let's meet my friend Paolo and see if we can trade cars," Skinner said.

Several minutes later they entered an ancient-looking village overlooked by steep slopes, its narrow lanes presided over by the tall bell tower of a church. Skinner directed them to a side street, where he hopped out and knocked on the door of a narrow two-story house. The door opened quickly, and a young man in his twenties peeked out. After an enthusiastic conversation with Dr. Skinner, he looked out at the Jeep and nodded with a smile.

Soon they had made a new friend and acquired a different vehicle—a Fiat SUV. It was more compact and worn than the Jeep, but roadworthy nevertheless. Dylan slid onto the driver's seat, looking relieved to have left the Jeep behind.

After a rushed dinner of fresh pasta and vegetables at a nearby trattoria, Skinner checked them in under his name for two rooms at a bed-and-breakfast along a secluded, steeply pitched street with spectacular mountain views. Abby wasted no time in finding her room. Hardly pausing for her usual bedtime routine, she curled up on her bed and slept for ten hours.

SANTA CRUZ, LA PALMA ISLAND, CONVENT OF LA MADRE—
MINUTES LATER

The nuns found Isabella the following morning still kneel-ing on her floor, facing her open window, her bed unmade, her mumbling lips bluish from the overnight chill.

Sister Rosalia tiptoed in behind her, not wishing to startle the teenage novice, and gently placed a hand on her shoulder. Nothing happened. The rocking of her small torso and the softly muttered prayer continued unabated.

Rosalia squeezed just a little harder. Nothing.

Now she spoke. "Isabella."

Still no response. Clearly the girl was in a delicate state. Word of her dark forebodings had swept through the convent within minutes of Isabella speaking them the day before.

Three other nuns stepped into the room from behind Rosalia and approached the girl. "Isabella, it is disobedient for you to refuse acknowledging us!" scolded Sister Muriella—a pale, thin-faced older nun.

The girl's bobbing and mumbling only grew stronger.

Rosalia gave her elder a stern look. She turned to her other companion, novice Laura, who was Isabella's close friend.

Laura crept forward, found a place beside Isabella, and knelt next to her. Closing her eyes and bowing her head, she started to rock in unison with her friend. And she listened.

"Dear Jesus," Laura overheard her friend whisper, "please stop its coming. Stop its going out. Stop its work. Please make it leave. Please make *them* leave . . ."

Over and over again, the same combination of phrases, in the same rhythm, the same imploring tone of voice.

Laura began to repeat the words, also in unison. Then, on the fifth time, she ended with an amen and reached out and took her friend's hand. It felt like that of a corpse.

Isabella finally stopped her mumbling, lowered her head, and allowed a tear to flow down her left cheek.

She turned to Laura with anguished eyes. "It has come, my sister. Death is upon us."

A MOUNTAIN RANGE NEAR THE ATLANTIC—ONE HOUR LATER

He appeared to be just another hiker traversing the national park's high places—a young, fit European wearing unassuming western clothes. He sported long black hair, a loose-fitting T-shirt, cargo shorts, and a pair of Nike hiking boots. However, the man's backpack seemed excessively full, too bulky and heavy for a mere day trip.

Despite the backpack, the hiker moved with a swiftness and certainty of direction that belied his lack of a map or familiarity with the terrain. He quickly left behind the park and its throngs of hikers, marching onward to reach the summit of its famous volcano. The surrounding forests of laurel pine, studded with a half dozen towering waterfalls, seemed to hold no interest for him, for he didn't even pause at their feet. Instead, he maintained a steady and relentless pace.

By early afternoon he had left the mountains behind and was trekking into a barren grassland six thousand feet in elevation. A brisk, cold wind began to lash at his limbs, and clouds formed around him, a gray shroud through which he occasionally could have caught fleeting views of coastline and distant ocean—that is, if he'd been looking. For he was still maintaining the same manic gait as he had since the trailhead.

He made it to the ridgeline bisecting the very top of the wilderness at nearly three o'clock, the time when most hikers were scrambling downslope to avoid midafternoon thunderstorms and post-sunset arrivals. Yet this hiker was unconcerned with weather or time. He appeared to speed up when he reached the narrow spine of rocky, volcanic soil. His only concession to the location was to reach behind him, for the first time, and unclip a handheld GPS monitor from his pack. He never broke stride as he punched several buttons and held out its screen before him.

He hiked on for several more hours. The sun was starting to graze the ocean horizon when he finally reached his destination, where he stopped, carefully shrugged off the bulging backpack, and took a long drink from a water bottle. Then he extracted a collapsible plastic shovel and began to dig frantically in the loose soil.

Forty-five minutes later he had created a narrow circular hole several feet deep. He turned to his backpack and, with the care and concentration of a surgeon, pulled out a metallic cylinder. Turning the object sideways, he found a small LCD display glued to its side and began pressing its digits.

With a glance skyward and a stab of his outstretched finger, he punched home a red button in the corner of the display. It gave out a beep and the hiker smiled. He cradled the cylinder in both hands, moved forward on his knees, and lowered it slowly into the hole until it was resting at the bottom.

It took him only minutes to fill the hole back in with dirt. Soon he was hiking again, his backpack relieved of its burden, walking away from the clock that now ticked toward the doom of America.

Twenty-three hours and counting . . .

CHAPTER

_40

The three visitors walked through the Waldensian Museum, scanning every row, every aisle of artifacts from the distant past of the movement's existence. After twenty minutes of brisk examination, Dylan stopped and looked toward Abby. She had also come to a stop, her hand resting on a glass case containing one of the group's earliest songbooks.

"Find something?" he asked.

She shook her head, a confused expression on her face.

Dylan approached her and asked, "What's wrong?"

"How do I put it?" she said, grimacing. "I feel like I'm in pain yet also like I'm right on the verge of God's purpose in all this. That's as exhilarating as it is painful."

"I'm not sure I understand," Dylan said as Skinner came and joined them.

She breathed deeply and spoke in a halting tone. "I feel something, at least a sense of something, as though there's a whole new person being given life inside me. God's shaping something new and strong. It hurts like crazy, but it's also exhilarating somehow—feeling the force of creation at work inside of me. I think maybe it's the Warrior. The soul of a Warrior, growing fast and about to hit the ground running."

Skinner leaned forward. "You know, I've heard some believers talk of entering a state like that. They used the same comparisons to describe it. They called it 'birthing in the spirit,' and it can be an incredibly agonizing experience. However, it also can signal the start of rather huge changes in a person's life. Sometimes it can signal death too. Other times it can take the biblical phrase of God 'doing a good work inside' to a whole new level. Either way, it's a sign of something enormous coming to pass."

"So," said Dylan, "do you think these feelings have anything to do with locating the summons? I mean, do you think it's anywhere around here, or are we wasting our time? After all, that is our objective."

Abby shook her head. "No, Dylan, we're not wasting our time. Although I don't think the summons is here, still, this museum has taught us things we needed to know."

"You know what's strange?" Dylan said. "I think my senses are growing too. And I agree with you—as interesting as this place is, the summons isn't here."

"Fine," said Dr. Skinner. "Then let's get out of here. We've got plenty of other places to look."

Outside the museum, on their way to the Fiat, Skinner caught sight of a nearby newsstand. Clipped to its awning hung copies of the newspaper *La Stampa*. He walked over, grabbed a copy, fished some coins from his pocket, and handed them to the stand's owner.

"What is it?" asked Dylan, drawing closer to the professor.

"Headline from America," Skinner answered. "Let's get in the car and then I'll tell you."

All three climbed in, and Skinner instructed Dylan to take the main road north, following signs marked *Angrogna*. Afterward he began to explain.

"The headline reads 'America in State of Terror.' Apparently word has leaked of an anticipated terrorist attack against the eastern seaboard of the United States. Nobody in government will talk about it on the record, either to deny or confirm, which makes the story all the more believable to the public. Border security is tightening. Harbors are being shut down. Airport personnel are openly profiling people of Arabic descent. But off the record, sources are saying the government's convinced that within the next day or so, America will be hit by some kind of undefined 'wave of death.'"

Abby's hand flew to her mouth.

LANDSTUHL REGIONAL MEDICAL CENTER, GERMANY—
HALF HOUR LATER

Had her vital signs not been displayed on the monitor above her bed, Suzanne Sherman would have appeared to the visiting psychologist as a cadaver waiting to be carried away. Her face was ashen, her body motionless, and her eyes so tightly shut it seemed they would never open again.

The psychologist, however, did not even glance at her before sitting down at her side, his clipboard in hand. He'd been down this road before. He understood the drill.

He touched her forearm and leaned over. "Mrs. Sherman," he whispered, "I'm here to talk when you're through praying."

The psychologist accepted the act of praying at face value, as a soothing way for believers to slough off anxiety and stress. He found no reason to argue over whether prayer actually reached anybody *upstairs*, or whether God really was a being with whom one could communicate. Such questions interested him far less than the therapeutic value of believing one way or the other. And the psychology of the day was clear—prayer worked, inasmuch as it carried a therapeutic benefit to those who practiced and believed in it.

At last, Suzanne's eyes slowly opened. "Hello, Doctor."

"Hello, Suzanne. Are you ready to talk with me?"

"Not about how I feel. How I feel can be fixed quite easily—by Uncle Sam releasing me from custody. I haven't done anything illegal, just as I hadn't when I was wrongfully locked up for over thirty years."

The psychologist nodded. He knew her story, and knew that Suzanne had a legitimate grievance. He was also aware that her continued "protective custody" in this place, however benignly it was being presented to her, was starting to reawaken old issues: emotions of confinement and mistreatment. Unfortunately, the reasons for her being kept here were far beyond his control. His job was to manage her fears, not grant her wishes.

"I know you haven't," he said in a soothing voice, "and I'm sorry for your situation. Your gunshot wound still needs some time to heal. And we feel that given the attacks against you and your loved ones, this is the safest place for you to be right now."

She fixed him with an angry stare. "I'm sorry you've been ordered to feed me those lies, Doctor, but I'm not a fool and you don't have to talk to me in that tone. You don't just lock up American citizens because they're facing some kind of danger. If you did, you'd be locking up half the country. Civil liberties don't work that way."

"Mrs. Sherman, our nation is facing a serious terrorist threat right now, and you're somehow a direct target. I think that qualifies as a slightly different kind of risk than what most citizens face."

"Granted. But given the fact that I was almost murdered in the hallway of this very hospital, I think I'm entitled to believe I'm safer on my own. I can get a doctor back home to treat my shoulder. Besides, if I survive this thing, it'll be God's doing. Not my doing, not Uncle Sam's, and certainly not yours."

"Maybe God would like to protect you through the able efforts of America's finest."

"Oh, stop it. That's not the point. You people aren't being candid with me. And I can tell. That's what matters."

"What matters to me, Suzanne, is your well-being."

"Well, my well-being isn't feeling very happy right now."

She stopped and gave him a rueful grin, hands folded in her lap. Then she took a deep breath and spoke with a new purpose. "Doctor, your family doesn't live here in Ramstein, do they?"

"No, they don't."

"They live in America, right? On Maryland's eastern shore."

The psychologist felt his spine stiffen. "I'm not sure I want to bring them into this conversation."

"Well, they've been brought into my dreams. Would you like to know what I saw?"

A frostiness crept into his voice. "Mrs. Sherman, is this new topic a retaliation for the displeasure you expressed before?"

"It is *not*," she said emphatically. "I genuinely care about Linda and Trenton and little Emma. In my dream, I practically fell in love with them. And I'd like for them to live."

"Suzanne, I don't know where you received information about their names, but I don't appreciate—"

"Please," she interrupted. "I want you to be warned. You've been fair with me, my anger notwithstanding. I want you to know."

"Know *what*?" He inwardly kicked himself for asking, giving in to her tactic, as soon as the words left his mouth.

"The wave of death. It's going to touch them. I saw them last night being carried out of a large white house. I saw you rushing up to the coroner's truck, trying to unzip the bags. They wouldn't let you. There were too many, they said. Too many casualties to allow it. And you were muttering something I overheard. Something like, if only I'd taken them inland. If only I'd sent them off to the mountains like Suzanne told me. If only I'd listened to that old woman. You fell to the ground when the truck pulled away, and you were weeping like a little boy."

The psychologist fanned his palms out across his clipboard's top page, not once but twice, as though smoothing out a table linen. He stared ahead, breathed in and out in a deliberate manner. Then he stood up, his eyes never meeting Suzanne's. "We're through for today, Suzanne," he said. His voice sounded cold, mechanical. "I will see you tomorrow, if you're up to it."

With that, the psychologist turned and left the room.

CHAPTER
_41

The satanic warning signal went out through media both technological and spiritual, on the Internet and cell phone networks, but also by way of messenger demons speeding through the air above the Atlantic coast. Physical channels were almost immediately intercepted by agencies of the U.S. government, most notably the National Security Agency, whose outsized technological ears could detect most of the world's communications. In this case, fifteen different iterations of the same message were captured by antennae at the agency's headquarters in Fort Meade, Maryland.

Within minutes their occurrence and the words they contained had been forwarded to both Langley and McLean, Virginia, and a series of command centers assembled to manage response to the wave-of-death threat.

However, the signal's spiritual emanations were also monitored by human intercessors already spurred to a state of alarm by a pervasive shock wave that had been pulsing through the heavens for hours.

In her small Baltimore apartment, Luci Holliman looked out her window again and immediately saw the frantic crisscrossing of evil spirits in the sky. She had been in a constant state of prayer for days now, prompted by a sense that something dark, something truly awful, had descended on the shores of her native country. But now a feeling that was merely physical and emotional became visual as well, for she could spot the frenetic pathways of demonic couriers ferrying the warning to their millions of human lackeys.

The old woman stood before her open window, trembling with an odd combination of fear, awe, and exhilaration, her hands extended high above her.

Truly, she now knew, the time had come. Her gifting, which she had alternately cherished and resented at various points of her long life, was now at a fever pitch, at a level of sensitivity she'd never experienced before.

Which was why, within a very short time, the words of this warning came to her. Prompted by an undeniable urging, she picked up a pen, grabbed her grocery pad from the refrigerator door, and watched her right hand begin to write. And as soon as she saw ink touch paper she knew it was the exact text of the message being delivered to every follower of evil within a hundred miles.

Get out. Seek higher ground. Don't attract attention, but make it look like a casual trip. Gather up all you consider most precious and

make your way without hesitation to at least twenty miles inland.
Even better, get to the mountains.

ANGROGNA VALLEY, NORTHWESTERN ITALY

As they drove higher into the Italian Alps, Abby felt a distinct sensation of moving backward in time. She became increasingly aware that the peaks here exuded a majesty all their own. In some ways they were not as picture-perfect as Switzerland. Their summits didn't gleam with the same crystalline beauty, or their forests stand as perfectly on high-flung terraces and plateaus. No, these peaks seemed more wild, rugged, and forbidding. And somehow those qualities struck a chord within her that resonated more powerfully the closer she drew near to them.

"There were three great Waldensian valleys," Skinner explained. "First was Luserna, the Valley of Light. Next was Rora, the Valley of Dews. But their greatest refuge was Angrogna, the Valley of Groans. The heart of the valleys, they called it. If we're going to discover the summons anywhere in Waldensian country, it'll be up here. Look—do you see that outcropping there?" He pointed up to his right. Abby leaned, craning her neck to see. "That's Rocchamaneout, where two hundred women and children were thrown from the cliff, and where husbands and fathers later took their revenge."

Abby's eyelids quivered. She grasped the sides of her head like someone feeling the onset of a migraine. "What we're looking for is not there," she said. "I can feel it."

So they kept on driving for several minutes more.

"Did you know," Skinner continued, "that the slaughter of these people elicited so much sympathy across Europe that Milton himself wrote a sonnet on their behalf? It begins, 'Avenge, O Lord, thy slaughter'd saints, whose bones lie scatter'd on the Alpine mountains cold . . . in thy book record their groans who were thy sheep, and in their ancient fold slain by the bloody Piedmontese that roll'd Mother with infant down the rocks.' Dylan, pull up right here, would you?"

They exited the Fiat, and Skinner led them up a trail toward the mountainside. A few turns up, they came upon a small cave opening, nearly obscured by granite boulders.

"This is the *Guieiza de la Tana*, the Stone Church. One of many secret sanctuaries up and down this valley and also the most beloved."

Abby stepped inside, running her hand along the cave wall. Dylan followed her, turning back to tell Skinner, "I wish we'd thought to get a flashlight." Before Skinner could respond, however, he and Dylan were both compelled to stop in their tracks. Abby had returned already and was facing them, shaking her head, tears running down her cheeks.

"Right now I'd give anything to be able to travel back in time and meet these people," she said. "I can sense their courage, their faith. It seems to just drip from these stones. It's so sad that I could have gone my whole life without having learned of these dear people."

"Do you sense anything . . . I mean, do you believe the summons is near?" Skinner asked.

She shook her head again, then wiped her cheeks with the back of her hand.

Leaving paved road for a dirt one, they continued in the Fiat up the valley. Sitting in the back seat, Abby was struggling with overwhelming emotions. After several miles, they stopped in front of a meadow at the far end of which stood a tapered stone monument bearing a sculpture of an open Bible.

"Look, there's your stone sculpture," Skinner said.

The three hurried over to the monument, propelled by a sudden surge of enthusiasm. Abby began praying for discernment and revelation before even reaching the monolith.

"This is Chanforan," Skinner said. "It's where the Waldensian leaders voted to join the Protestant Reformation. Abby, do you sense anything special here?"

She was now kneeling before the monument. After finishing her prayer, she faced him. "Nothing. But I'm trusting that God is going to make it very clear when we reach the right place."

"I'm feeling some of these things too," Dylan told her, placing a hand on her shoulder as she stood. "And I'm with you. This isn't the place. C'mon, let's keep moving."

CHAPTER

_42

The slope continued to rise sharply as the vehicle forged its way upward, the road growing rougher with every mile, the weight of history enveloping the three like a shroud. They fell into a deep, contemplative silence, brought on by Abby's inner turbulence.

"So the people who took up arms," she asked Skinner at last, "who resorted to earthly warfare, did they just lose heart? Were they of lesser faith?"

"Ah, here goes," Dylan interjected from his spot in the driver's seat. "Our old argument, raising its head."

"Well, if we can't settle it here, Dylan, where will we? Isn't this the right place to ask?"

"I'll grant you that. I'd love to settle the issue here and now."

"What is this debate between you two?" Skinner asked.

"First, Dylan," Abby suggested, "why don't you tell Dr. Skinner what you used to do for a living?"

Staring hard at the rocky road ahead and gripping the wheel intently, Dylan sighed.

"No need," Skinner said. "I followed your story quite closely. You were some kind of special operative for the government, as I recall."

"Actually, I was a government assassin," Dylan broke in. "I killed a lot of men. But ever since meeting Christ, I've been on a crash course in a different kind of warfare. I think I've learned a lot, yet the one thing I haven't been able to figure out is whether there's a place for the kinds of skills and tactics I once practiced. Abby thinks I'm holding on to my old life and refusing to submit to God's ways. Me, I just don't know . . ."

"I'm sorry but I find it hard to reconcile earthly warfare with the spiritual kind," said Abby. "I mean, do the two work together? Can earthly warfare serve a heavenly purpose? And can spiritual warfare address matters that seem carnal, even partisan?"

"Funny you used that word *partisan*," Skinner said, "because it points to something that could perhaps answer your question, at least in part. It turns out that centuries after taking up arms, the twentieth-century descendants of the Waldensian warriors were the very first to form a resistance against the Third Reich. Right here in the very same valleys where their ancestors had fought. They used the same strategies, the same knowledge of the mountains and their layout, even some of the same crude tactics. And guess what? They were nicknamed *partisans*."

"You're kidding . . . I guess I see your point," said Abby. She reached up and patted Dylan on the shoulder, after which he nodded. "And what you've shown us today, Dr. Skinner, is that the atrocities inflicted all those years ago on these people were every bit as cruel and sadistic as what the Nazis committed."

"I think that's a fair claim," said Skinner. "The papal generals may not have been as prolific in their killing as the Nazis, but they were just as cruel. Dylan," he said, pointing, "pull over there, next to those rocks."

They stopped and got out. It looked as if an army of giants had amused themselves by tossing down hundreds of boulders into the valley, trying their best to block the way up. Some of the stones appeared to be suspended in midair, poised to tumble down onto their heads.

The stream they'd followed up the mountain now fell in a torrent and crashed against the rocks in a spray of white water. Ahead of them, the path crossed a narrow, old stone bridge.

"I take it they lived up in these rocks?" Dylan asked.

"You got it," answered Skinner, grinning at the implausibility of it. "You see that clump of boulders over there? They stacked those by hand. In case of attack, they could push the right one and send the whole bunch down onto their enemies. This is the *Roccliagie*, the historic stone gate to the *Pra del Torno*, which may be our final stop. It's where we'll find the College of the Barbe. From here, the going *really* gets tough."

CHAPTER
_43

REDHOUSE, MARYLAND

Pastor Wally Landers was a hearty man, whose health gave him cause to lament his love of church potlucks and the celebratory feasts of the faith, making him no stranger to the sensation of heartburn. So when he awoke that morning, he soon realized he was experiencing one of his life's worst attacks of stomach acid.

He was not a young man either, now finding himself in the company of the "semi-retired," a dubious term that meant his church paid him less but by no means demanded less in regard to his duty to the congregation. His old age was the reason it took several minutes for his mental faculties to clear out the cobwebs. Slowly, through a throbbing sense of darkness, of danger, he came to understand that something serious lay at hand, something of an otherworldly nature.

He found his wife, Mary, already up and reading her Bible at their small dining room table, its pages flipped open to a passage about turning away from fear and trusting in God's strength.

He sat down and asked her to read out loud. As she read, he gazed out the window at the thick hardwood forest and the view of distant valleys surrounding their Maryland home. This was the Eastern Continental Divide, with Hoye Crest, the highest point in the state, only a few miles north of them.

The mountain views and wooded landscape had been one of the leading factors in their choosing this community for his later ministry. Wally was a man who loved to walk among nature, especially the forest. He had explored most of the woodlands here through the years and found that sermon inspirations and personal edification had flowed from the practice.

But this morning, the sight held no joy for him. He frowned, for it was the first time his spirits had failed to lift after looking out his window. In fact, not only did the outdoors seem stripped of joy and meaning, but it seemed impregnated with a foreboding, a brooding presence and even hostility his spirit found alarming.

"Honey, why did you choose that particular passage?" he asked when Mary had closed her Bible.

"Because I seem to really appreciate those words this morning," she answered. "Why do you ask?"

"Do you feel . . . anything?" he asked tentatively. "Anything that would motivate you to go to that passage of Scripture?"

She looked at him and squinted, her mental gears clearly spinning. "I suppose," she admitted. "I guess I thought it was just me and my moods. You know how I get sometimes."

He reached out and squeezed her hand. "Maybe your moods are catching," he said, "because I seem to be feeling it too this morning. There's something going on, something not right. How about we take a walk together, see if we can't shake it? Or else find out what it is that's troubling us."

But Mary didn't feel up to walking, so it was Wally alone who shrugged on a jacket and ambled across their front porch, past his church next door, and disappeared among the hardwood trees. An experienced woodsman, he stepped through the forest as quietly and expertly as a fox.

About half a mile up the trail, Wally was shocked when he saw a bright flash of color through the trees. A few steps later he saw what it was—a gathering of vehicles. He quietly edged up to a big maple tree, keeping himself hidden behind its trunk. From this vantage point he was able to observe the goings-on.

As he watched, he soon realized it was not mere curiosity motivating him to spy on these newcomers. The sense of menace and darkness that had seemed to lift during the opening moments of his jaunt now assaulted him fivefold. In fact, he suddenly felt light-headed, clutching the bark of the tree to stay on his feet and remain focused on the strangers ahead.

Three of the six parked cars appeared to contain folks of Middle Eastern descent, while exiting the other three cars were Caucasian types. What they all had in common, however, was an air of malicious triumph that seemed to float over from their gathering like a gas cloud. He saw twisted smiles, heard peals of sadistic laughter.

Pastor Landers leaned over for his longest look yet, and gasped so loudly he feared he might have given himself away. Two of the open car trunks were now being unloaded of guns—not just a shotgun or two, but armfuls of black automatic weapons. He saw faces turn his way and realized their holders were scanning the surrounding forest with renewed vigilance.

Another motion caught his eye from nearby—the sight of two young men unveiling a black banner, festooned with bright red Arabic letters. The image reminded him of those hostage photos from Iraq, the ones overhanging haggard captives with only minutes to live.

He took a deep breath and found that his lungs were heaving and refusing to take in oxygen. His heart was racing madly, and his feet no longer anchored him with much confidence.

But he had to leave. He simply had to get home and think about his next step. He prayed for help, for some way of getting out of there undetected.

A growl rose in the distance and grew louder. He recognized it as a Harley Davidson motorcycle, then knew with a surge of hope that it was approaching the gathering. In seconds, all eyes would turn toward the biker and Wally would have his diversion.

The motorcycle did indeed roar into the intruders' midst, and when it did, Wally was fortunate to have already been a dozen yards away, rushing on his way back to the house. He was not only fortunate for his own safe getaway, but because the cloud of darkness hanging over the group had deepened in power and intensity when the biker arrived.

Wally knew it was not their love of mountain vistas that had drawn these people to the area. This was no casually planned outing. He understood now the full weight of what he had been feeling. Some unthinkable evil was afoot.

CHAPTER

_44

ANGROGNA VALLEY, ITALY

After another hour of laborious four-wheeling, the group finally reached the site of Dr. Skinner's greatest hope for discovery, the College of the Barbe. The three exited the Fiat in the raw chilly air of a high mountain valley, its timberline only yards away. Snowcapped peaks rose high above them, with a veil of mist not far from their heads.

What had sounded like some medieval campus turned out to be a single, precariously preserved stone hut, set on three levels against a steep hillside. Walking inside, the trio climbed to its middle floor. They found a single room under a smoke-stained wooden ceiling. The interior was bare except for a fireplace and a large stone-slab table.

Dylan turned to Dr. Skinner, eyebrows raised.

"I know it doesn't look like much," Skinner said, "but believe it or not, this was the training ground for Waldensian pastors and missionaries for over a hundred years. People went out from here and then to all of Italy, France, Switzerland, Germany. They were taught around that very stone tabletop, which has been there for seven hundred years."

"What's the matter, Abby?" Dylan asked, looking at her closely.

"I'm starting to panic," she said. "This is our last chance, and I feel the same as I did before. I sense the great soul of these people. Their faithfulness and bravery seem to just drift from the walls of these places . . . but that's all. I don't know where to look, what to touch."

Dylan said nothing, but instead began a search of his own, running his hands along the table's underside. He walked along every inch of wall, looking for clues of something hidden, something unusual or out of place. "You're sure it's a stone sculpture?" he asked. "Not some other kind of writing?"

"No, I'm sure it was sculpture. I saw it again in a vision last night."

Dylan turned around, surprised. "What did you see?"

"The author was holding something small and hard. He was tall, very thin. He seemed to be wearing soldier's clothes."

"What makes you think that?" Skinner asked.

"I don't know. They just appeared to have a medieval military design to them."

Skinner exhaled loudly. "Then I don't think it's from here. Waldensians didn't wear uniforms. Even when they took up arms."

Abby stood and stared at him. Her head lowered, her chest caved in slightly, and an invisible yet obvious energy seemed to leave her. Without a word she made for the stairs and left the hut. Dylan and Skinner exchanged a glance and followed her.

When they emerged outside, they looked up to see a cold front beginning to blow in from the north. Abby was crouched in the grass, gazing moodily out at the valley below.

Dylan walked over, sat down beside her, and began rubbing his temples with both hands.

"Dylan, are you all right?"

"I feel like I've just run out."

"Run out of what?"

He sighed. "You remember when I acknowledged Christ as Savior, back in Africa? We were in that canoe, drifting down a stream, and the monsoon opened up and there you were, looking so beautiful and singing praises to God in the middle of this drenching rain. I saw you, and my soul just ripped open. I started to see other things, half-visible singers all around you. It seemed like all of creation, even the spirit world itself, was just lit up with God's presence on every side of us."

"I remember . . ." Abby said in a low voice.

"Well, now I feel none of that. All I feel, all I seem to see, is darkness. On every side. The enemy seems so much more real right now than anyone else. And I hate it."

"I'm sorry," she said as her hand reached out to touch his forearm. "And I'm sorry I'm not much of an encouragement to you right now. I feel defeated too. There may be only hours left before this attack, and I've invested all my time into obeying an order from Sister Rulaz that—"

"Don't blame her, Abby," Dylan interrupted. "She was telling you the truth as she knew it."

"Yeah, but everything she saw, and everything I saw, and my mother and you, has turned out to be true! There *is* a bomb! There *is* an attack coming against our country! And there is something the body of Warriors can do to stop it, if only I can summon them in time!"

"I'm sorry, Abby." All the fire had just left his voice. "I was just trying—"

"Do you feel like telling me now?"

Dylan looked at her. "Tell you what?"

"The thing you haven't been able to tell me yet." She looked intensely into his eyes. "What you saw in that cave."

He sighed, turning to face the valley again, then closed his eyes and breathed in sharply. "I'm only going to say this once, okay?"

"Okay."

"I looked straight into the face . . . right into the eyes of something. I don't even know what it was. But it was more than just some demon. This was a strongman, like a general. I don't know but maybe the devil himself. It's hard to describe . . . It was filled with more hate, more concentrated evil than I've ever imagined existed. I didn't think I'd survive it, and I'm not talking just physically. I'm talking about my soul. Because, in that moment, I lost all faith. I despaired of God himself, I think because it suddenly didn't seem possible that He could ever be stronger than this . . . this thing."

"And yet He is," Abby assured him. "That's the awesome part. He's way stronger." Then she turned her eyes to the heavens and said, "God, what do you want us to do? We thought we were following your leading. We thought we were on target. What now? Please tell us! Please, don't just leave us here!"

"Are there any other places we should look?" Dylan asked Skinner anxiously.

Skinner, who had been standing patiently behind the pair, shrugged. "There are other museums, but they're nothing compared to what I've shown you. We can go canvassing every inch of these valleys if we care to and have the time."

"But that's just it—we're running out of time," said Dylan.

"Still, we need to keep searching," Abby cut in.

"You talked about some other warrior groups elsewhere," Dylan prompted Skinner.

"Yes, there are. In southern France. Almost a day's drive from here."

"Can we spare that much time?" Dylan asked.

"If it's where we're supposed to go," said Abby, "then yes, no question about it." She faced the sky again, her eyes shut against a soft misting rain that had begun to fall. "God, can you give us some clue? Can you let us know if France is the place?"

A long pause followed, filled only with the sounds of the gentle rain and the cold wind ruffling the treetops. Despair seemed to surround them, and it appeared as though they'd reached the end of their journey.

"I know you're used to hearing powerfully from God," Skinner said, "but I know from my own experience that a lot of times, responding to Him means just turning away from the wall I've been beating my head against and stepping out in faith. With no obvious response to guide me. Sometimes that's the greatest faith of all. To just take one unsure step after another, with no strong leading, and yet trust that He'll still guide the way."

"So we just head for France?"

"If it's all we know to do next, then I say why not?"

Groaning from the strain on her knees, Abby rose to her feet. "France it is, then."

CHAPTER
_45

Having sold off its modest cargo at ports along the northern and eastern coasts of Africa, the Libyan boat *Medina* sailed homeward through the afternoon shadow of the fourteen-hundred-foot rock wedge once known to Moroccans as the *Gibel Tariq*, or today, to its British occupiers, simply as Gibraltar—gateway to the Mediterranean Sea.

Navigating the wakes of two cruise ships and an imposing British cruiser, Captain Yahmin Ranmeb felt more than his usual share of relief at seeing the rock's massive profile and knowing he had returned to within sight of Muslim shores.

He took a deep breath and steeled himself for the mind-numbing ritual to follow. Soon he would leave Moroccan territorial waters and enter those of Spain. Moments later, however, the absurdly drawn fan shape of Spain's sovereignty would end and make way for the most dangerous zone of all to men like him. The lanes immediately south of British-Gibraltar Territorial Waters were officially designated as *high seas* yet notoriously subject to inspection and boarding by ships of the Rooke, England's Royal Navy Base.

Soon his well-honed internal watch told him it was time. He was now in the high seas, the area where he was most vulnerable to Western harassment.

Always on guard for problems to come, Ranmeb casually scrutinized the Rooke from his wheelhouse perch. He frowned. Its usually busy quays lay empty, which meant only one thing: the British boats were out in the Mediterranean all at once, and such a concentrated presence was never good news for a sailor of his ilk. He tightened his grip around the wheel and vowed to reach Moroccan waters in record time.

Suddenly he heard his two sons cry out, and from out of nowhere three rubber Zodiac boats pulled up alongside the *Medina*. A voice boomed across the waves at him in Arabic of all things, telling him to throttle down and prepare to be boarded. Then came the source of the order: the same British cruiser from before, racing up to him now at high speed. Ranmeb noticed the angle of the ship's on-deck machine guns. He could see almost straight into their barrels.

The captain debated whether he should try to make a run for it, but his deliberations ended abruptly as his two sons made the decision for him. Shouting anti-Western curses, the teenage brothers ran to the foredeck with two of the *Medina*'s four rifles in their hands. Mahib, always the better shot and quicker athlete, had his weapon shouldered and squeezed off a shot that knocked one of the Zodiac's occupants into the water. What followed in retaliation would effectively end his father's life as a thinking human being. A half dozen machine guns immediately opened fire on the young man. The windows of Ranmeb's wheelhouse were abruptly splattered by something that made him turn away in horror. The captain let out a piercing cry, then ducked as his other son uttered a scream just as quickly drowned out by a thunder of exploding gunpowder and lead.

Ranmeb reached down and shut off his engines almost by reflex, then stepped out with his arms held high.

The men standing on his boat, their boots slipping in the blood of his sons, were anything but white-clad British sailors. He recognized their uniforms from the cable TV shows his sons were so fond of watching, even as they pelted the actors with anti-Bush and pro-jihad slogans.

These are American commandos, he thought as his chest slammed hard onto the fiberglass deck and his feet were trussed up behind him with plastic ties. He noted the nationality and make of the M-16 barrels aimed at his face. Ranmeb knew his weapons.

Definitely American.

FORT MEADE, MARYLAND, NSA HEADQUARTERS—LATER THAT HOUR

The National Security Agency, whose surveillance tentacles reached down to the very heart of the Internet's central core, was the first to intercept the emailed video file. Before it even reached its intended recipient at Al Jazeera Television, it was being watched by a roomful of analysts in the National Security Operations Center, the communications hub of the agency's vast complex.

First, the video file showed a black banner bearing Arabic characters that read, *The Great Satan Is Dead!*

Then the bearded, hooded face of the most hated man in America came on-screen. "Yes, the Great Satan is dead," he said in Arabic, which was immediately translated by analysts sitting in the room. "It is as good as done. The wave of death will sweep over your shores at exactly two o'clock local time. Heed our warning and turn to Allah before it is too late. All who survive will live under the blessing of sharia law and the fading memory of the abomination which was once the United States."

He finished with a smattering of religious expressions and the video was over.

"That's just great!" exploded the NSA director in charge. "So now we have a ticking clock . . . !"

THE WHITE HOUSE OVAL OFFICE—TWO HOURS LATER

The president's vocabulary—cabinet officials and media alike had long since noticed—tended to become far less Southern and colloquial with each added measure of stress and suppressed frustration a situation presented. That was why the Director of Intelligence, standing before a pedestal bearing several mounted placards, now found his questioner far less loquacious and charming than the day before.

"The *Medina*, Mr. President, had the unmistakable radiation signature of the bomb carrier. It was strong, fresh, and pervasive, meaning the device had been on board for at least four days. The boat's books showed it off-loading at El-Jazair, Oran, Dar-el-Beida, and Laayoune in the Western Sahara, just across from the Canaries. But of course he could have met someone on the high seas and transferred the weapon any time he pleased."

"Well?" said the chief executive. "What's the greatest army in the world doing about it?"

The director nodded to a navy admiral standing to his left.

"Sir," the admiral began, "every ship in our navy is steaming full speed ahead toward the area. Our search planes and boats in the Azores are already deployed. Whoever it is has a substantial head start on us, but they're going to run right into our teeth as soon as they approach the American coastline. Makes you wonder what in the world they're thinking, sir."

"Admiral, until this is resolved, I'd rather you do a lot more than wonder about it! Are we or are we not still going on the supposition that a bomb is being smuggled into America during the next twelve hours?"

A half dozen heads nodded their reluctant assent.

"But we're not yet sure about the *Medina*," said the admiral. "Sure, it looks suspicious. But the bomb you're referring to could just as well have come in overland in the last month from Canada, Mexico, or for that matter, even in a shipping container of Manolo Blahnik shoes sailing into Baltimore Harbor."

The heads were even more reluctant to nod on that point.

"Understood," said the president. "Now on to this mess about our domestic front."

The Director of the FBI stood and said, "Sir, five hours ago we intercepted a mass-deployed message from diffused sources across the Middle East and suspect sites in Europe, to several hundred sites across the eastern U.S. The message said, and I read, 'Get out. Seek higher ground. Don't attract attention, but make it look like a casual trip. Gather up all you consider most precious and make your way without hesitation to at least twenty miles inland. Even better, get to the mountains.' At last count, two thousand individuals on our domestic watch lists both received and obeyed the contents of that communiqué. The high points twenty miles inland and farther from the Atlantic have witnessed five times the usual automobile traffic in the last four hours."

The president suddenly appeared deflated. "So am I to un-derstand that despite the lack of intel, the consensus in this room is high confidence in the potency of this threat?"

There was a long, completely motionless pause.

"Come on, men! The only thing fatal right now is a lack of candor."

Slowly, one by one, the men nodded their agreement.

"Glad to hear something definite," replied the president. "And now—and I don't care who hears this—I want to know why Abby Sherman is not in that outer office waiting to see me!"

CHAPTER
_46

Over the next four hours, the Fiat SUV, now with French plates, wound its way south and west. First it looped around the impassible massif of the Italian Piedmont, then down across the French border—no passport check required between EU members—and into the rolling foothills known as the Maritime Alps, so called less for their mountainous topography than for their relative proximity to the Mediterranean.

Once again, Abby began to suffer an almost unbearable tension between, on the one hand, wonder at the beauty around her, and on the other, an inability to process anything except the crisis she was facing. The bulk of her emotional energy was almost entirely invested in trying to wrestle with God's leading and the question of whether this journey into France was a responsible stab at victory or mere self-indulgence.

So when a bit of unspeakable beauty presented itself through her window, she felt a disconnected part of her demand some sort of response—wonder, gratitude, awe—yet felt herself unable, or unwilling, to react appropriately.

It didn't help matters that the map they were using called for them to trace a route along the coast itself. Descending through a gradually flattening sea of rolling pine-covered hills, they weaved through the well-preserved villages of Haute-Provence. There, nestled perfectly atop green ridges and ledges, sat a string of hamlets consisting of little more than a dozen or so narrow steep-roofed houses, the requisite parish church, and a rustic fountain in a square, where old men sat playing the ancient game of boules.

The sun had just begun to sink against the horizon and bathe the countryside in a vibrant golden light when they reached a straight stretch in the highway. Abby glanced to her left, made a small cry, and motioned for Dylan to pull over.

The color enchanted her first—row after row of bright purple stalks quivering in a fragrant breeze. Except their shade was a bit more pale and subtle than purple, she realized.

Lavender.

She stepped out and leaned against the Fiat, raising her face to breathe in the intoxicating scent. Her exhale sounded more like ecstasy than respiration. She looked out over the field of lavender, thinking it was too good to be true, complete with a honey-hued manor at its far end. This was what she'd needed to help ease her out of her onset of panic, replacing it with peace. Smiling, she climbed back in the car.

By late afternoon they had reached the coast at Nice, a bustling metropolis of over a million people. After fighting their way through a traffic jam, they sped along a beachfront highway called La Provençale, with the unbroken beach on their left and a wall of mountains to their right.

As they were driving, Dylan resumed the conversation they'd abandoned back in Italy.

"So when the Waldensians became warriors," he asked Dr. Skinner, "did they do so after a lot of prayer and thought?"

"Oh, definitely," replied Skinner. "They wrestled long and hard with the depth of their anger. Let me quote you what one of their own carried in a letter to the other Protestants of Europe. 'Our tears are no longer of water; they are of blood. They do not merely obscure our sight; they choke our very hearts. Our hands tremble and our heads ache by the many blows we have received. We cannot frame an epistle answerable to the intent of our minds, and the strangeness of our desolations.' Clearly, they didn't know what to do, or how to respond. Finally they decided as one that they could no longer watch their loved ones being mutilated and killed."

"I don't know if I would have done any different," Dylan offered.

"Are you kidding?" Abby joked. "You would have wiped out the enemy single-handed."

Dylan laughed. "Abby thinks I jump too quickly into combat mode," he said to Skinner. "She forgets that it's my years of military training at work. I was brought up to believe the best way to keep someone from hitting you is to hit him first."

"I just want him to think about the weapons of the Spirit before going to other kinds of warfare."

"I *do* think about the weapons of the Spirit. I think about how to wield them. Abby, once you've awakened this force of Warriors, have you given any thought to what you're going to do with them? How you're going to deploy them? To maximize your assets?"

She seemed at a loss. "No, I just figured God would lead . . ." Her voice drifted to a close.

"And I'm sure He will," said Dylan. "He might just lead you to listen to someone next to you, someone with years of military experience. You might learn how to deploy your Warriors for maximum effect. How to gain intel on your enemy. How to defend your perimeter. How to survive a frontal battle. And how to go on the offensive. All in the Spirit."

"Are you saying, then," Abby asked with a frown, "that earthly tactics are on a par with God's ways?"

"Not at all," Skinner interjected. "He's talking about making the best of everything God gave us. Look, when the children of Israel surrounded Jericho, they were badly outmanned to beat such a large enemy. So what did He tell them to do? Use their voices and instruments, of all things, to make the walls come down using principles of physics they never would have understood at the time. But still, they used what they had. The Word's full of examples of spiritual warfare blended with earthly combat, using the tactics of the day."

"If you listened to me, and we did this," Dylan said, his voice rising with excitement, "we could field a fighting force more powerful than anything the world has ever seen!"

Abby shook her head. "See my problem?" she said to Skinner, a hint of a smile playing on her lips.

"Look," Skinner continued, "Jesus said that those who came after Him would do even greater things than He did. Do you think that's ever happened? Probably not. So perhaps there's a revolutionary step that God's people have yet to take. And why not now when we're being threatened with such an enemy? The book of Joel says, 'Like dawn spreading across the mountains a large and mighty army comes, such as never was of old nor ever will be in ages to come.' There's a lot of disagreement over who that army truly was, but what if it was meant to describe *us*?"

"I like the sound of that," said Dylan.

"What about you, Abby?" Skinner asked.

"I don't know. How about you let me get through these next twelve hours before I take a position?"

"Yes, but here's the rub," Skinner added. "What if this topic is exactly what you have to get clear in your mind *before* being entrusted with the summons? What if working through this issue is the preparation God has in store for you—even more than my crash course on the Waldensians?"

She exhaled loudly. "All right. You're a mighty persuasive guy. Again, I see your point."

"It's mind-blowing when you think about it," he said. "You may be calling forth a warrior, but a kind of warrior the likes of which our world has never seen before."

Their excitement lasted well into dinner, which they ate in the university town of Aix-en-Provence. They dined along the city's famed *Cours Mirabeau*, a wide boulevard lined with ancient plane trees, fountains, and cafés that fronted the crowded sidewalks. There, over a bouillabaisse fragrant with stewed mussels, monkfish, mullet, and eel, with the traditional combination of Provençal cheese and herb bread, they discussed tomorrow's search.

"Much like the Waldensian saga," said Dr. Skinner, "the story of the Huguenots in France stretches out over centuries. The long wars of Reformation led to a truce, the Edict of Nantes, which guaranteed Protestants freedom of religion. But after the Huguenot

king died, the edict was revoked and another bloodthirsty repres-
sion started. Huguenots scattered to the winds, including a large
number who came down to the valleys and forests of a mountain
range called the Cevennes. They would become the Camisards,
a hardy and God-loving population. When the Catholics came
after them, imprisoning their prophets and threatening to take
their children off to state-run orphanages, they rebelled and took
up arms. And so started the Camisard War."

"So they were warriors as well?" asked Abby.

"Oh yes. They were arms-bearing soldiers. Just to defend the
privilege of meeting together and worshiping God, they waged bloody
campaigns where hundreds of them died by the sword. Against a
threat of death just for assembling, they met in large crowds in secret
meadows and outdoor fields. They would nickname these places
'The Desert' in reference to a verse in Ezekiel about a woman being
sustained by God for forty days in a barren wilderness."

Dylan nodded. "And what did they believe?"

"Well, unlike the Waldensians, the Huguenots were ordinary
Protestants with no question about any of their beliefs. By today's
theological standards they were squeaky clean. The Camisard
branch did have many spectacular prophets, both men and women,
and there's been some debate about their authenticity. But as to
the group's common beliefs, not a blemish. Just like in Italy, there
were many stories of incredible bravery and heroism."

"And you've got a particular spot picked out for us to visit?"

"Just inside a French national park there's a museum com-
memorating the whole movement. It's called *Le Musée du Désert*.
The Museum of the Desert, or to English-speaking visitors, the
Museum of the Protestant Struggle. It's the only central collection
that I know of. And if they don't have the summons somewhere
on their property, they'd surely know where else to look."

CHAPTER

_47

The three visitors were standing at the entrance when the museum opened. They'd risen well before dawn, then driven through Provence's exquisite countryside, including the old Roman towns of Arles and Nimes. By the time they'd reached the hills of the Cevennes, Abby had already become a veteran of sun-drenched vineyards, sleepy roadside chateaus, and rustic villages still awakening under the shade of their café parasols and courtyard plane trees.

The museum was quite an impressive compound: an immaculate stone villa in the Provençal manner, leading into a series of rooms, their design taken from the Camisard style and period. However authentic the artifacts and furnishings, though, Abby and Dylan had matured by now into a highly efficient team whose only purpose was the discovery of a certain stone sculpture.

While Dr. Skinner attempted to follow them with a running monologue on Camisard history and the facts surrounding this or that object, the younger pair essentially ignored him. They moved swiftly through each room and every individual row of artifacts. Abby often stopped in place and closed her eyes, her lips moving in a fashion that might have looked a bit strange had there been other visitors to witness it. Every so often, her eyes would catch Skinner's, and she would shake her head. *Nothing. Not yet.*

In a little under an hour she and Dylan had walked through a dozen or more rooms detailing every nuance of Camisard life, and they had only one more to go. By now Dr. Skinner had given up on his commentary and stood off to the side, asking the docent whether she'd heard of the Summons to War—after which the docent had replied with a definite yes—when Abby called out from the adjoining room.

Something about the urgency in her tone made both Skinner and Dylan rush to her side.

"What is it?" both men asked her at once. Abby was standing before a framed print depicting the face of a serene-looking young woman. One of Abby's fingers was suspended in midair, indicating the portrait before her. Her expression was filled with wonder, her eyes wide.

"Who is this person?" she asked.

From behind them, the docent answered, "That is Marie Durand, one of the great heroines of the Camisard struggle."

Abby turned. "Why is she famous?"

"She was taken prisoner by the king's men, simply for being the daughter of a prominent Camisard pastor, when she was only sixteen years old. She was thrown into the dungeon at Constance, along with several other women, and kept there for over fifty years. Yet her faith never wavered. She kept up her companions' morale and resistance, refusing to recant her beliefs, and helped the others remember Scripture verses and great hymns. She left behind a stirring memento, which endures to this day: the word *Resist!* carved in the stone with her own fingernails."

Abby stared at the docent. "She sculpted it in the stone?"

"Well, yes. One word, with her finger."

"Was there ever a soldier in there with her?"

"Oh no, madame. The women were segregated from the men at all times."

Abby frowned.

"What kind of soldier, Abby?" Skinner asked.

"He wore a white tunic with a large red cross."

"Oh, you mean a Templar," the docent said.

Time seemed to hiccup for a moment. All three glanced at each other, taken aback by the docent's words. Then Skinner's eyes closed as he inwardly chided himself for not having elicited this information from Abby much sooner. "Of course," he muttered to himself.

The docent continued speaking, and then the final piece settled into place.

"Constance was a prison for many, many years before then. And it's recently been discovered that it housed a group of men reputed to have been some of the very last Knights Templar remaining alive."

Even though Abby stood facing Dr. Skinner and Dylan, her next question was directed at the docent. "Could you please tell us where we might find this Constance prison?"

THE CAMARGUE, PROVENCE, FRANCE

They drove across the landscape with a speed and certainty that felt, oddly, as though they were passing through thick clouds of destiny and time. The route led them due south toward the sea, down through Nimes, then in another direction, toward a vast and strangely beautiful swampland. Abby could not place where she had seen this scene before, until she spotted a herd of dappled white horses running wild through shallow waters. The sight of their gray manes waving in the salt breeze and the brackish water flying out from under their beating hooves struck a chord deep within her.

Then her brow furrowed, for she hadn't known this place really existed. She had thought the pale saline bogs and reed-covered sandbars overrun by wild mustangs had perhaps been a staged set for the perfume companies in whose commercials she'd seen this place. It seemed lifted all too perfectly straight from the core of her romantic imagination.

"This is the Camargue," Dr. Skinner explained in a wonder-filled voice. One of the last wild places of such beauty left on earth. The largest river delta in Europe, nearly four hundred square miles across. Home to over four hundred species of birds, including a rare type of flamingo, and a breed of pale white horses native to its boundaries for almost a thousand years.

Next, Skinner briefed them on the Templar.

"They called themselves warrior priests," he said. "The Templar were the first to explore the notion of mixing religion and warfare. They were also the first to discover its pitfalls. After guarding pilgrims and soldiers alike during the Crusades, they started building power, both financial and military, all across Europe. They were the first to pioneer banking. They built garrisons throughout France and the Middle East. They developed all sorts of secret codes and passwords. As a result, some of their leaders grew arrogant. The European kings had become threatened by them, and they exploited the arrogance to attack them. Trumping up a whole host of worthless charges, they rounded up every single Templar in Europe and slaughtered them by the thousands. Ever since then, legends have swirled around their allegedly possessing the Holy Grail or some other great secret. For a time, the rumored Summons to War was thought to be that secret. We may be on the verge of finding out the truth."

A town lay just ahead, marked by a grouping of rooftops and the castlelike walls of a medieval battlement. They passed a sign that read *Aigues-Mortes*. A shudder of delight ran down Abby's spine, and an involuntary smile creased her face. Something was afoot. She could feel it.

CHAPTER
_48

AIGUES-MORTES, PROVENCE, FRANCE

They saw the Tower's rounded shape rise above the medieval walls even before entering the town itself. The structure's white stone, because of age, had turned a pale gray and seemed to match the mustangs grazing beyond, together with the clouds hovering just above it.

Dylan parked at the foot of the structure, and they exited the car in silence. After paying a fee at the gate, they climbed to the top of the fortification and approached the Tower's arched entrance. For Abby, every step resonated powerfully within her.

While Dylan and Dr. Skinner walked inside without hesitating, Abby herself was held back by something. A senseless fear began to whisper inside her, telling her that she may not come out again. Finally, when she forced herself to take a couple of tentative steps inside the Tower, with its walls twenty feet thick, the gloom beyond confirmed her oppressive feeling. After walking in, she looked up and realized the only light penetrating the dank prison came from a single narrow window, an open slit halfway up the staircase's first turn.

Pushing aside her uneasiness, she began to climb, and as she moved upward her senses were awakened, all of them at once. First came a swelling up of primal fear, an ancient defiance mixed with dread and sadness. It reminded her of how she once felt when at a cemetery and approaching the grave of a distant relative. Indeed, this place was in every way like a tomb, and as she climbed its steps, her limbs cried out that, yes, this was in fact a prison. Sane people did not enter such places willingly; the person whose presence she now sensed certainly hadn't come here of her own accord.

Reaching the first level, Abby's Sight suddenly awakened, and she began noticing the presence of spirits, though she couldn't tell which type they were. It was as if the gloom of the place had extended into that realm as well, obscuring everything close to it.

The three made it to the second level and walked into a large room, dimly lit by a hole at its apex and two narrow slits along its walls.

Abby could hardly breathe.

Was this simply due to the exertion of the climb? she wondered. She hadn't breathed deeply or steadily during the way up, and the damp, salty air now seemed to have a will all its own. But then, as she continued to pant, she realized the problem had another cause.

Abby, who had experienced strange spiritual sensations of every sort during the previous few days, now felt her very soul crushed by an entirely new feeling: an overpowering weight of resignation and misery, as though every one of the thousands of prisoners who had inhabited this room over the last millennium had left a residue of themselves behind. The walls seemed to speak the fact, the air pungent with those spirits that had languished, those who had suffered here so long ago.

She felt the rising terror of a condemned man. The depression of a woman imprisoned here for decades. The fear of one who had just realized he would die here, never to see his family again. She prayed, then glimpsed an angel approaching her. The angel touched her forehead, which sent her soaring in elation.

She felt the triumph of someone who had overcome, of one filled with the Holy Spirit despite facing a life sentence in this awful place. Surely, it was the heart of Marie Durand herself. Then Abby felt a masculine heart beating in her chest, also pulsing with elation and hope . . .

Dylan and Skinner, who at first had walked all around the room, now hurried to her side.

"Are you okay?" asked Dylan, genuine worry in his voice.

She shook her head and took his outstretched arm.

"Here. Let me help you sit down so you can rest a minute."

Glancing down at her side, she accepted his offer and let him slowly lower her to the floor. She reached out to steady herself as she crossed her legs. Touching the floor for support, she felt . . .

A flash of unearthly light!

Images danced, a ghostly human figure kneeled, the world lurched wildly on its axis. She withdrew her hand, gasping even harder for air. The normal world returned.

"What's the matter?" Dylan said, crouching beside her.

"The floor," she muttered. "I touched the floor and . . ."

He touched the floor himself and recoiled, as though he had just touched a hot iron. "Whoa. Did you see that?"

"Dylan, I don't know what you mean by *that*, but yes, I think we both just saw the same thing."

"This guy—"

"A soldier," she corrected. "He's the soldier I've seen before."

She ran her hand across the floor, winced at the blinding reaction but was ready for it this time, keeping her hand steady. "Dylan," she said between breaths, "I need to ask you a favor. We need a video camera."

"Shouldn't be a problem," replied Dylan. "I have the money back in the car."

"A good digital model, the kind we can download easily."

He nodded, stood, and disappeared down the stairs.

"Would you help me up?" she asked Dr. Skinner.

He pulled Abby to her feet, and she began walking slowly around the room. At one point she closed her eyes, trying to recall where it was exactly that the soldier in her vision had been kneeling.

She crouched down and touched the stone again, and recoiled. Skinner came quickly over and gripped her arm to support her. But instead of rising, she stayed there and pressed down with her hand, not removing it from the spot . . .

The condemned man was kneeling before a shallow hole in the floor, digging into the removed piece of limestone. Scratching it with a tiny object gripped in his right hand.

He could hear a hammer striking loudly from outside.

Then the sound stopped.

CHAPTER

_49

The first sign of the video's discovery was from an NCTC computer operator surfing the wired world for clues to the ongoing threat. To his co-workers he called, "Hey, I'm sending you all a URL. Check it out."

The room's main monitor, a screen over seventy inches across, suddenly brightened with the garish, animated VideoCorner logo. A face came on-screen, ten times life-size. It was Abby Sherman.

"Pause that," a man cried out, "while we get the suits in here!" It was Ashman, clearly a suit himself, yet hands down the most sympathetic in the staffers' eyes. He was the one who stayed behind when the other muckety-mucks had dispersed throughout the complex or even gone home with varied excuses, requiring them to be called away every time something went haywire in their investigation. Unfortunately, Ashman was now requesting that very thing—that everything be stopped while the wayward executives were rounded up. But at least he'd been there in the first place.

"Ah, forget it," he said, changing his mind. "Play it anyway. It's not like we have to rewind anything."

Abby's face came to life again, her voice filling the air.

"Hey, everybody. It's Abby Sherman. I'm sorry—seems like I've developed a habit of disappearing and popping up again in some unusual places. I hope I haven't worried anybody. But I've got something incredibly important to talk about, with anybody who sees this and is willing to listen."

The camera lens pulled back to reveal her surroundings—a large, empty room, stone walls, and very little light.

"I'm in an old medieval tower on the southern coast of France. And I wanted to record what's about to happen because I need everyone to know I'm not faking anything. I believe that God has led me to an ancient stone carving that's of grave importance to our country right now. I'll explain more in a minute. You see, this carving hasn't seen the light of day in over seven hundred years. For all that time it's been right here, undisturbed . . ." The camera shook and aimed downward while she knelt along with it, the frame now capturing a slice of her face and a floor stone at her fingertips.

"Dylan, would you zoom in and make sure it's clear that this stone hasn't been touched or messed with in any way?" The view rushed forward awkwardly, but then clearly showed a ring of grayish dirt around the stone like a seal of very old mortar identical to those surrounding it. Unless the re-creation job had been unbelievably cunning, the stone in question hadn't been removed in centuries.

"I hope this makes it quite obvious. I walked in here today for the first time in my life, along with two friends of mine, and we're convinced that seven centuries ago a soldier of the Knights of Solomon, a Knight Templar, carved a message on the bottom of this stone just before he was executed. Rumors of this lost manifesto have floated around the church all these many years, and now I think I've been shown where it is—right here. Please bear with me, because with a little help I'm going to dig it out now. I'd rather not cut away from this shot, so you'll know nothing was doctored."

She pulled out a small knife and started to dig into the dirt ring cementing the stone in place. Another pair of hands joined hers, masculine fingers, both peeling away at the age-old seal. It took several tedious minutes, but eventually the rock was free enough that they were able to loosen it within its spot in the floor.

Abby turned to face the camera again, her expression tense. "I guess this is the moment of truth. If I'm not crazy or misled, there's going to be writing on the underside of this stone. I don't know how visible it will be, or in what condition, but I'm convinced it'll be worth the wait. Okay, here we go . . ."

The camera lowered once more as Abby's hands started pushing and pulling in earnest. "Man, it's really heavy," Abby said.

Finally the male fingers started to raise the stone a bit. A man's grunt was heard. Suddenly the rock was lifted several inches, enough for Abby to get her hand under it to ease the stone from its place in the floor with the assistance of the other pair of hands. The stone's sides were nearly four inches thick, stained brown.

Abby now took it and slowly turned the stone over.

The camera zoomed in again. All that filled the lens was a solid square, also stained a deep brown from its contact with underlying dirt.

"Is there anything there?" Abby's voice now sounded worried as she swept her fingers over the surface of the stone. "I'm not sure." Then her fingers stopped moving. "Wait. Maybe there is . . . Yes! There's something here! I was fooled for a second because they're so tiny . . . but there's definitely something written here!" Her voice started to shake with emotion. "I'm sorry . . . I promised I wouldn't get all teary-eyed, but we've been searching for this for what seems like forever now . . ."

"Tell you what" came a man's voice. "Why don't we take a quick break, clean off the stone, and do a rubbing, then maybe we'll be able to read something."

The camera shifted back to Abby's face. "Good idea. I'll be back in a minute," she announced. The screen went black, then flickered back on again with a different shot. The stone was now substantially cleaner, and a piece of paper drifted in and out of the frame, filled with rows of very small, raggedly formed letters.

"Well, the rubbing went well," Abby said. "Dr. Peter Skinner, who's here with me, is an archaeologist. He not only pulled off the writing that appears to be in an ancient form of French, but he can translate it as well. Dr. Skinner, you're on."

The face of a middle-aged man—a face everyone at the Langley command post knew quite well, as he'd already been identified as Abby's second traveling companion, whose passport photo stared at them from every wall—now came on-screen. Skinner looked down, reading from a sheet of paper.

"Thank you, Abby," he said. "I'm amazed at how much writing the carver managed to fit onto the stone's surface. The words are tiny, but I'm confident I can decipher them anyway. So here it is. Title: 'A Call to War.'"

CHAPTER

_50

A CALL TO WAR

"'The stillness and solitude of this place have sharpened my sight and allowed me a wondrous revelation. I have been shown things of which most mortals know but a glimpse. I have beheld the battlefronts of a vast and ancient war.

"'I may be called a soldier, yet in the face of this war I know nothing. I am less than a spectator. This is a war beyond all things, beyond all conflicts, beyond time itself.

"'Do not be deceived, for although my words may bear the ring of legend, they describe truth of a supreme order. Truth so monumental that by comparison the reality of our present travails, the urgency of our earthly Crusades, are as trifling as the grains of salt upon these nearby shores. Truth of such magnitude that it could alter the course of a conflict which has engulfed heaven and earth since before the dawn of history.'" Skinner's voice stopped while he squinted at the next line.

"'Here is what I witnessed,'" the voice continued.

"'I saw, long ago, so far in the past that it happened before the first human being, the birth of the blackest betrayal in the annals of divine history. A breach so grievous that the Word itself speaks of it only in the most fleeting of sidelong glances; brief, almost abashed references seemingly reluctant to stray too near their subject. A treachery so monumental that I could somehow sense its aftermath continuing to echo across the millennia, resounding like a frightful echo into eternity.

"'I saw a greatly different age altogether. A time when the veils between dimensions seemed more transparent and porous than today. An era whose citizens moved freely between the realms of flesh and spirit.

"'The inhabitants of this distant past lived in a state of joy unknown by any created being before or since, for they served Yahweh, the great I Am, the divine Creator of all that is. I saw them, surround His throne in gatherings wider than the broadest ocean, a sea of spirits quivering before His love like banners in a coastal gale. I heard Him laugh with pleasure. I heard His thunderous voice call them angels, even then.

"'And I beheld their leader: a being so luminous and beautiful that even in my vision I found it difficult to gaze upon his face.

"'I spied the day the Archangel gazed upon his own beauty and something foul birthed deep within him. A tiny warp formed in the fabric of emotion. He swooned at his flawless form and a spark of pride ignited. I watched it flame into ambition, then jealousy. The angel forgot the source of his beauty and light, and began to covet the very throne of Yahweh.

"'In one instant, evil was born and given form in this being, the angel Lucifer. Yahweh's favorite remade himself into His scheming enemy. I saw a shadow creep into a kingdom of pure light and begin to spread. A rebellion grew where once only bliss and harmony had reigned.'" Dr. Skinner paused again and looked briefly into the camera, obviously moved, then lowered his head over the text.

"'Whole legions of angels joined Lucifer's revolt; that much I saw. I almost turned away from the wretched sight of angels twisting into demons as they relinquished their angelic bodies and embraced the foulness of Lucifer's hate. Why they sided with a created being, one of their own, over the supreme power of the Almighty may never be known. But they took up spiritual combat against their brethren with the intention of overthrowing the Most High.

"'We humans were not told enough to describe the ensuing war in any detail. I myself was shown battlefields stretching from one edge of the sky to the other, filled with whole legions grappling in the most desperate and vicious combat I have ever witnessed. But like any man, I know little of its true history, only that it was a war more terrible than any afflicting this earth. I know that it raged through the heavens for vast swaths of time and consumed countless numbers in its wake.

"'And I do know its ending, or at least that of its first phase. Lucifer and his fellow conspirators were defeated. I watched them plummet through space with their growls of rage echoing across the heavens, ejected from the sight of Yahweh and banished from His presence forever to an exile here on earth.

"'All this took place before human history ever began. It is vital to remember this, for from our own finite perspectives we

humans tend to cast ourselves as the central players on the stage
of history. The truth is that our race's current travails comprise
at best Act III of this sweeping, celestial drama. A saga which is
less about us than about God and a war which has not yet ended,
although its outcome has been won at a great price.

"'And the period I just described was merely Act I.

"'Act II we know well from the Word, for it concerns the great
sacrifice Yahweh made to cleanse our race of the enemy's stain.
He made himself one of us, then in that Person paid the supreme
penalty to reconcile us to himself.

"'But here is the wondrous fact I learned about Act III. Even
though victory is assured, humanity rises to play a breathtaking
part in its winning.

"'I saw a black day dawn, many long years after this one, a day
of immense threat and shadow when the deepest of evils forces
God's people to rise above their ignorance and shallow faith. A
day when they unite to hone the gifts and powers with which God
has endowed them. A day of warfare and victory.

"'I saw human Warriors become a fighting force for Yahweh
the likes of which the world has never witnessed. On that day I
saw men and women alike wage war with not merely the carnal
weapons of steel and wood, but those of the Spirit, wielding arma-
ments of prayer and supplication, of submission and love.

"'I saw these fighters soar beyond any notion of valor and glory
ever known in my benighted age. I saw God pour out upon them a
power unknown since those very first acts of the early apostles.

"'Mark my words. This was not prophecy. It was vision. I
saw it as bright as daylight, as clear as the walls that surround
me now.

"'I only pray that God will preserve these words for the day when eyes worthy of their import are led to find them. So to the finder of this stone, and the next beholder of these words, I commend thee into the service of the Almighty. I pray for you even these many years hence, and I charge you to keep watch for that day of unbearable evil. For if you are reading these words, that horrid day must be either nigh or already upon you, and you must be one of those anointed to gather these Warriors together.

"'So hurry from this place and beg the Lord to form you and His people into Warriors worthy of the fight!'"

Dr. Skinner's head did not lift from the words on the stone for a long moment.

Abby's tearstained face returned on-screen. "Sorry, again, for my emotions, but I just heard that for the first time along with you. So you've seen it, virtually live. This is exactly what I'd hoped and prayed the sculpture we've been looking for would reveal. For you religious scholars, what you just heard was the long-rumored and prophesied Summons to War, left here in the 1350s by the last Templar burned alive."

CHAPTER
_51

Pastor Wally Landers rarely spent more than a moment of his precious time on the Internet, but that afternoon he'd received two calls from parishioners, both urging him in the strongest terms to access VideoCorner.com and watch the new posting there from Abigail Sherman.

So now Abby's labored explanation flickered across his aging laptop, just as it did that moment across tens of thousands more all over the world.

"What's the big deal, you ask? Let me explain. First of all, remember that my whole crazy time in the spotlight started when I posted a seemingly innocent update on my blog, asking if anyone had experienced a dream like mine. The rest is Internet history. So I feel it's only natural that today I would send out a second message, even more important than the first, only this time on a video site. You've now heard the summons, and I'm honored and humbled to be the person allowed to find it. So I'd like to direct that summons to every follower of Christ who's watching this and hearing these words right now."

On-screen, Abby stood and began stretching her back, recovering from the tension of the previous minutes.

"You may also know that my last adventure led to the uncovering of an ancient spiritual family, the Watchers, who possess a remarkable spiritual gift. When I got home, I heard from a lot of you who didn't belong to that family tree and you were quite unhappy with me, saying this was unfair because those not born into the Watchers, spiritually speaking, were basically left out. This upset me greatly, and I had no idea what to do about it. I had never wanted to exclude anyone; I just wanted to introduce this amazing heritage to the world . . ."

THE WHITE HOUSE SITUATION ROOM—SECONDS LATER

President Burrell never liked being upstaged, but at the moment he didn't care. Disregarding the Situation Room's seating protocol, he stood leaning against the conference table's east end with his arms folded and his face bearing the expression of a man who couldn't believe what he was watching.

The room was lined with televisions and computer monitors, each of them showing the same feed, a visual overkill usually reserved for breaking news of the highest priority. In this case, the image was that of Abby Sherman's face, quivering in the low-resolution of Internet video.

"Well now, here's our chance to lay all that aside," she said on-screen. "Because no matter what your gifts, if you've ever wanted to do more, to go deeper, to take action and make a difference on a wider level than you ever thought possible, then this is your summons, this is your time. If you've ever wanted to take up arms in the Spirit and wage a real war on behalf of causes that matter for all eternity, but you felt held back by fear, by inertia, by weakness, by the emergencies of life, then this is your wake-up call. You're one of the number who will awaken upon receiving the summons meant for this day. You're one of the Warriors who will step forward and help win the victory today."

The president looked away and caught the eye of his National Security Director. "I'm the leader of the free world," he called out with a wry look on his face, "and even I can't get this girl to come talk to me! Turns out she's got more important things to do!"

THE PEOPLE'S INTERNET PROJECT, BALTIMORE, MARYLAND

The room was lined with eighteen perfectly identical computer screens, each designed for an altogether unique and diverse low-income citizen. But at that moment, all eighteen displayed only one image: the face of Abby Sherman. The video replays were not all synchronized, however, which made for a brain-twisting cacophony of brief and not-so-brief delays piled on top of each other.

Closest to the door was an elderly woman who had never been there before. She called herself "Luci with an *i*."

Luci Holliman.

She had come by bus to report something via email, something she refused to divulge to anyone. The senior citizen had known nothing whatsoever of computers or logging on, and was halfway through her learning curve when the first user had started playing VideoCorner. Like the arms of fans doing the wave at a boring ball game, Abby Sherman's face had cascaded across the rows, one screen at a time. And as soon as Abby had come on-screen, Luci had sat riveted to the show before her.

"I don't know exactly what form all this should take," Abby continued. "I don't have an organized response prepared. As you can see, I'm not even in the country right now. In fact, until a few minutes ago, I didn't even know for certain if the summons was here. But all I can say is now's the day to take action. Not tomorrow. Not later. Now. A terrible threat is planned to invade our country, this very minute. And I need Warriors who will take up station along our shores to repel this threat in the only way they know how."

Luci punched the desk with a fist. "That girl's right!" she cried to no one in particular. "Let's hurry up and send this email thing. I've got someplace better to be, and I need to get there *now*."

LANDSTUHL REGIONAL MEDICAL CENTER, GERMANY

The nurse who entered Suzanne Sherman's room to check her vitals had no idea whose face was on the television screen, much less what relation the owner of that face shared with the patient in her care. All she knew was that nearly every patient she'd seen that hour had been watching the same feed being replayed on its cable news channels.

The same attractive young woman, filmed by some amateur videographer, saying something that seemed important, except the nurse could never quite make it out. She was growing a bit tired of it. So tired that at last she determined to do something about it. Suzanne Sherman had been drifting in and out of sleep, so surely she wouldn't notice.

But when the nurse reached over to change the channel, the remote control went flying across the room and struck the wall just inches from her head. "What on earth are you doing?" said Suzanne, her voice suddenly strong and bright. "That's my girl!"

The video replay continued.

"You know the threat we're under," Abby said to the camera. "The darkest evil our country has ever seen is poised to commit an act of mass murder. And only prayer can stop it. Maybe you think I'm being dramatic. But I assure you, without your prayers and spiritual warfare, the brave men and women trying to protect us will not succeed. They need spiritual reinforcements."

Suzanne closed her eyes and formed a smile. She breathed out slowly, peacefully. For the last three days she'd fought like a tigress to leave this place, driven as much by her own emotional trauma as by her stated wish to go and somehow help her daughter.

Now, slipping out of her bed, she realized she could help Abby, and her people, right here from her room. She knelt down on the cold terrazzo floor, leaned into the bed rail, and closed her eyes.

CHAPTER

_52

Once more, Isabella was missing from Matins. And yet again, Sister Rosalia was sent to those places where Isabella had been found before, usually praying alone, indulging this growing fervency that seemed to have gripped the girl in the last twenty-some-odd hours.

Rosalia checked Isabella's room, the veranda, the prayer room—all of the secluded alcoves where nuns were known to pray privately. The troubled young novice was in none of them.

At last, almost by accident, while walking through the vestibule, she shot a glance into the convent's front office. Sister Rosalia stopped abruptly, planted her fists at her waist, and glowered. For once, she'd found Isabella in an incriminating place.

At the office computer, fiddling on the keyboard.

Rosalia walked in and approached the computer desk. "Isabella, I've been looking for you everywhere! Have you given up any pretense of following our daily schedule?"

The girl looked up at her with a look so intense that her elder took a half step backward in alarm.

"She's talking about *me*," Isabella said quietly. "She's talking about what I've been feeling."

Rosalia turned and reluctantly began to watch the face speaking on-screen.

"Maybe you can lead a prayer-walk around an important place," Abby was saying, still in the Tower. "Or maybe a vigil along some boundary that matters, and pray for protection."

"You see?" Isabella said, turning to Rosalia. "Something is happening."

"Maybe you can keep watch," Abby continued. "Maybe you can report something nobody else would have ever seen. I don't know all the ways—but I'm sure God will guide you. Because He guided me here. Thanks for listening, and for heeding the summons. Now, please, don't ignore the voice you hear inside you."

TOWER OF CONSTANCE, AIGUES-MORTES, PROVENCE, FRANCE

Feeling both overwhelmed and physically drained, Abby, Dylan, and Dr. Skinner had stumbled down the stairs of the Tower after finishing their video. They had accomplished their purpose; all that remained was to find an Internet outlet and upload their work. Each one of them was shocked to realize how much strength they'd expended in the final stretches of their mission.

It took only a matter of minutes to find an Internet café, even in a small medieval village. Apparently the French took wi-fi quite seriously, Dylan noted with a grin as he clattered away before a computer monitor, a cup of espresso steaming beside him.

Fifteen minutes later he stepped out onto the sidewalk, where Abby and Skinner awaited him, sitting silently at a bistro table. The pair straightened when they saw him, making way for Dylan to take a seat at the table.

"So what now?" asked Skinner.

Abby let out a sigh. "Good question. I guess now we should go home and then see what comes next." She turned to Skinner. "I can't thank you enough for dropping everything you were doing and helping us like this. Without you, we never would have found the summons. You were a true answer to prayer."

He smiled. "Just being involved in this search has been the highlight of my career. Believe me, the privilege is all mine."

"You guys really think we've done all we can?" Dylan asked.

"Our part in it," said Abby. "We found the summons, and issued it to the four winds. What else are we called to do?"

Dylan gave her a disapproving stare. "How about obeying the summons ourselves? You didn't think that having found it, you were now excused, did you?"

Abby shook her head and laughed. "You know, Dylan, somehow that never occurred to me. Okay, let's talk about our next step, but first, can we find a place to rest a while? I'm bone-tired . . ."

Then she suddenly hugged her midsection and grimaced.

"Abby, what's the matter?" said Dylan.

"It's that birthing sort of sensation again. I don't know. It's not terribly painful this time, but more of a cloud moving in my body. Something intense is kicking in. It's . . . somehow I sense it's the summons. Something really deep is going on."

Dylan jumped to his feet. "C'mon. Let's get out of here."

In the age of lightning-fast Internet communications, Abby Sherman's striking challenge had taken only minutes to cross the globe and reach a vast number of people. The tens of thousands who already counted her as a MyCorner.com friend and belonged to her blog now text-messaged and emailed her video's online address to dozens of additional friends apiece. Pastors and Christian leaders felt compelled to send alerts to their bulging contact lists. The websites monitoring other websites to rank the most talked about items immediately named Abby's story as number one.

Because of its inherent newsworthiness, not to mention its relevance to the national alarm over a potential attack, the message had been instantly catapulted into being the lead item on all of the cable news networks. This helped to drive a massive amount of traffic to the video website.

Before long, videographers were being interviewed about the odds of the stone's removal being forged. At first, most concluded that it was authentic. Archaeologists and theologians went on record about the truth of persistent rumors regarding a Summons to War. The fact that Abby had made her find at the Tower of Constance was generally viewed as evidence of her claim's accuracy, as the site had always been a lightning rod, though obscure, for historical and religious intrigue.

For a time, the VideoCorner.com server shut down, inundated with the deluge of visitors. That by itself became a lead story for about forty-five minutes, until an emergency redirecting of the network's resources solved the problem. Nevertheless, the summons had traveled at the speed of light across the various channels of earthly communications.

All the high-volume clamor raised by the media was dwarfed, however, by the spiritual shock wave now flowing through the global kinship known as the body of Christ. The pleas of believers who hadn't uttered an earnest prayer in years now rang like a bell through the heavens. In high places of the Spirit realm, whole armies of angelic hosts raised their vigilance and readiness for battle. The Spirit of God stirred like a great body of water surging from beneath.

And back on earth, that stirring in turn awakened army upon army of dormant, disheartened souls.

Human debaters have yet to explain the link between passionate intercessory prayer and corresponding responses from the Almighty. Whether prayer and supplication empower His response, or change His mind, or simply intensify His attention is not known. All humans know for certain is that prayer can create change, that somehow prayer can move God on humanity's behalf. And when that movement is brought about by the prayers of huge numbers of people, the impact can magnify beyond anything ever witnessed before.

On this day, the effect was multiplied in countless ways as one by one scores of ordinary believers rose from their chairs, their beds, and their confining walls, left their homes and places of employment, and began to seek out the front lines of an imminent attack.

CHAPTER

_53

Coast Guard spotters on their patrol boats and satellite analysts at Langley, Fort Meade, and McLean quickly took note of several thousand people who, seemingly deployed by the same simultaneous impulse, had walked out onto the dark beaches and bluffs along the Atlantic Ocean and, dressed in their street clothes, knelt to the ground. And stayed there, with hardly a break for food or rest.

Alarmed, authorities dispatched scouts to furtively photograph and identify the individuals—to ascertain whether this was some unanticipated facet of the terrorist plot. In every case, the reports catalogued citizens of zero-suspicion level, harmless people with no criminal backgrounds. Hardworking, churchgoing family people.

The first one spotted was an elderly woman named Luci Holliman, who led a group toward the beach of Ocean City, Maryland. The respected widow had been reported missing from her apartment in the Baltimore projects simply because, in her neighbors' recent memory, she had never once left her apartment for more than a few hours at a time.

Shuffling slowly toward the water, the old woman seemed impervious to the stiff off-shore breeze, the cold spray against her face and body, and the discomfort of walking across the unsteady surface. In fact, she appeared joyful. Sinking to her knees in the sand just yards away from the plunging surf, she looked beside her and smiled at a young mother who knelt with her daughter. The old woman reached out and took the mother's hand in her own. With her eyes shut, her lips began to move.

At New York's JFK Airport, as well as the terminals at Newark and Washington/Reagan and Baltimore, security personnel began to notice visitors with no apparent baggage kneeling along the edges of security perimeters, lowering their heads and remaining still for prolonged periods of time. At first, police and Homeland Security staffers had accosted a few of them, demanding that they move. The officers had cited regulations and strict guidelines, threatening arrest if not obeyed.

Suddenly a strongly worded order filtered down from the Homeland Security leadership that these people were to be left alone. In fact, their presence was to be protected. They were to be accorded every courtesy possible. Violation of this order would be met with strong punitive action.

In Washington, the Minority Leader of the House of Representatives stood before his thirty-five party cohorts, introducing a resolution to decry the sudden ratcheting of high-security measures by the U.S. intelligence and Homeland Security establishments. In mid-rant he stopped speaking, looked up toward the gallery, and cocked his head in bewilderment.

Five minutes earlier, only a pair of reporters had occupied seats in the upper balcony. It was midmorning on a weekday.

Now, however, the gallery was nearly full.

Every single one of several hundred newcomers was hunched forward in his or her seat, eyes shut, head lowered and resting against upheld hands. A dozen or so held their hands high in the air in a nonthreatening yet somehow unsettling gesture never before seen in the stately chamber.

In each of the gallery doorways, confused Capitol police officers stood looking around with wide eyes, poised to respond should any of these people so much as budge too quickly.

The Minority Leader tried to continue, but his words shook and drifted off, as though he was having a difficult time reading. The confident timbre in his voice had all but disappeared.

His cohorts began to turn around in their seats. The provocation was their leader's strange pause, but also something else.

A presence—or many presences—were gradually filling the room. Every one of them could feel it, like a foreign scent. Like the stares of an unseen crowd against their backs.

THE ATLANTIC

Several miles out to sea a brooding evil floated across the waves, virtually invisible to ships of the naval armada furiously closing a blockade across the U.S. coastline.

All but the most mature spiritual warrior would have seen little more than an oddly formed mist upon the waters. Someone with gifted vision, however, would have seen something capable of eliciting an almost violent reaction. The observer would have reeled back at the sight and done almost anything to protect the eyes from a second look.

Then, with the summons hanging in the ethereal breeze like a banner of high calling, this gifted observer would surely have clung to prayer.

The bestial presence floated with the waves and wind—waiting, watching. It craved more than anything to simply waft ashore and work its way inland, finding a place to wait in anticipation of the bloodbath to come.

Every bit of its demonic essence was poised to come ashore, except for one impediment. An equally invisible, impassable barrier of angelic resistance now stretched across the shores of America like a high and unclimbable stone wall. The evil being could not enter. It must have taken thousands of pleas to call forth protection of this magnitude, its warped mind grudgingly conceded.

Curse these sniveling peons and their wretched babbling to him. When the attack begins, they'll be the first ones destroyed, the first to wash away under the wave . . .

CHAPTER
_54

THE CAMARGUE, PROVENCE, FRANCE

The Fiat sped along a back road, a shortcut to Marseilles, the nearest large city. On either side of them, the reed clumps and marshlands of the Camargue stretched unbroken to the horizon.

In the vehicle's back seat, however, Abby continued to slip back into the unexplainable labor that had been afflicting her since Switzerland. Glancing back at her through the rearview mirror, Dylan struggled to keep his eyes on the road.

Once again, he was forced into the horns of a dilemma. Part of him wanted to hop on a plane for America and let Abby tough it out until they reached home. More than likely, this thing would fade away of its own accord, as it had before. Another part of him, the part that loved her, cried out for immediate help. Dylan was so preoccupied with monitoring Abby's pains that he failed to anticipate the right turn just ahead. So he was totally unprepared for the sight of two minivans blocking the way, parked across the road nose to nose.

A second too late he threw the Fiat into a sideways skid. Its tires screeched in protest as Dylan shouted a warning to the others to brace themselves. He yanked the steering wheel hard to the right, trying to mitigate the impact, but the tight flexing of his facial muscles told the truth.

They crashed. Metal screamed as vicious g-forces hurled them forward in their seats.

"Is everyone okay?" Dylan yelled.

"I think so . . ." said Abby.

Dylan glanced over at Dr. Skinner, who was nodding at him. "I'm all right," Skinner said, patting his seat belt. "Just shook up a bit."

Satisfied, Dylan grabbed his backpack and reached inside. He then kicked open his door and jumped out with a gun in his fist. In an instant he closed the gap between the crumpled side of the Fiat and the two men in suits standing off to the side.

His voice filled the air, raging like a wild animal. "Down on the ground! Now! Get down!"

One man obeyed immediately, launching himself onto the pavement. The other held his outstretched hands even higher and shouted, "U.S. government, Dylan! We're here to help! Here to help—"

"Friendlies don't blockade highways!" Dylan shot back. "Who are you?"

The still-standing man now paid for his disobedience. The barrel of a Glock handgun shoved into the flesh of his cheek, and he was thrown into the side of his van.

"I said, who are you?"

"Mr. Hatfield," the man groaned, "I'm Special Agent Norman Grady from Central Intelligence. Please desist. You're not considered fugitives. You're not being detained."

Dylan gave him a push and stepped back. "Then what's this about? Why the barricade out here in the middle of nowhere?"

"Because we're avoiding the French authorities every bit as much as you avoided us. We've been ordered to escort you back to America. The president has conveyed an urgent request for both you and Abigail Sherman to meet with him. We have a plane waiting for you at Salon."

"Salon?"

"A French air base, twenty-five miles east of here. We have permission for takeoff and landing, but nothing more. If you resist, I cannot and will not stop you. But think about it, Dylan. There's no reason to run anymore. You've completed what you wanted to accomplish. Please, come with us and help your country prepare for what might be her darkest hour."

SALON-DE-PROVENCE, FRANCE—HALF HOUR LATER

The Gulfstream V, pride of the American civil aeronautics fleet, was plain white, utterly unmarked except for a token blue stripe across its middle. Dylan noticed an absence of tail numbers as they drove up, but understanding secret ops, he dismissed it.

In official government circles, the forty-million-dollar Gulfstream was deployed for two objectives only. First, escorting political prisoners from the countries of their capture to highly classified locations, usually in a country legally approving of torture. And second was the transportation of high-profile individuals. Dylan didn't realize it was a plane like this one that had flown Abby and her mother to Ramstein, Germany.

He and Dr. Skinner half carried Abby into the aircraft, the two agents following close behind them. As they all took their seats and buckled themselves in, the engines revved up for take-off. Immediately Dylan noticed thick cords and a length of chain lying coiled on the floor of the plane, along with handcuffs and leg shackles.

Agent Grady and the other, now-humiliated agent sat on either side of the cockpit door with dark, expressionless faces. Dylan glowered back, as they had demanded that he give up his gun before boarding, Due to the strict regulation about firearms on aircraft, he knew he had no choice and had grudgingly complied.

A few minutes later they were airborne, with Provence little more than a tilting green flatness receding in their windows.

CHAPTER _55

The navy admiral stormed through the conference room's glass doors like a man with nothing but bad news to deliver. And like a man who couldn't wait to rid himself of it. Before even reaching his seat, he bellowed, "Not a stinking thing on a single vessel! Not even a miserable rad on the Geiger counter!"

Around the table, a dozen chests reared back in disappointed shock. Ashman buried his face in his hands and cursed to himself. He no longer had the strength for disguising his emotions, nor did he care.

It was truly a blow. The U.S. Navy and its numerous support agencies had spent millions and moved proverbial heaven and earth to arrange a security cordon across the Atlantic Ocean.

Three aircraft carriers and over two hundred naval vessels had been directed to the mission, and crowded Atlantic shipping lanes had been brought to a standstill. Video footage of ships clogging up the ports of Rotterdam, Hamburg, and Marseilles filled the cable-news hours.

Not to mention that the president's administration had expended considerable political capital to get a pass on the bruise this operation had delivered to international relations and domestic civil liberties alike. "Nobody likes a blockade," they'd been warned. Not unless the blockade produces the desired result.

And the admiral's fresh news meant exactly the opposite.

"I'm sick and tired of heeding every harebrained idea floated by these civilian nut-jobs," the CIA operations director hissed out. "We've got to act on hard evidence alone, assuming there's any out there. Either that or shut this whole thing down."

"That's not your call, Norm," countered the Homeland Security liaison. "Besides, the ship's already sailed on that option. I mean, word's out across the world. At this point, we need something blown up or there's gonna be heads rolling."

"What if this is good news?" said another CIA staffer. "What if this just means our response scared them off?"

"Sounds good enough for CNN," the admiral responded. "Personally, I wouldn't believe a word of it. These people are crazy. Getting caught doesn't scare them in the least."

"So does this mean," Ashman began, "that none of the warnings are true? What about this 'ancient peak' tip we got from Jerusalem? Is water the only way to deliver a nuclear device to the East Coast? What about mountaintops? What about a land incursion from Canada or Mexico? Let's face it, we aren't done yet!"

"Here's a rich one," broke in the junior CIA analyst. "This Suzanne Sherman, the mother to Abby, has made numerous pronouncements that the wave of death means what it says. That a tsunami will sweep across the East Coast of the U.S."

A round of snorts let loose around the table. "Looney tunes," scoffed Ashman. "How does she say Sheikh Nirubi proposes to control the movements of the ocean, let alone plate tectonics?"

Those around him shrugged and rolled their eyes.

"In all fairness," said the Homeland Security liaison, "I think we're all comfortable with the probability that it's a bomb, not some contrived natural event."

"Of course," added the admiral. "Now, can we stop wasting our time? According to Nirubi's deadline on the video, we only have three hours left. Let's get to work!"

ABOARD THE CIA GULFSTREAM V

Abby's pains didn't begin to subside until two hours into the flight. By then, the aircraft had already flown them south, halfway around Spain's Mediterranean coast toward Gibraltar. Regardless of where they'd landed to pick up their "cargo," standard operating procedure for a prisoner rendition flight was to avoid overflying any NATO country. While secretly acknowledged by most nations, prisoner renditions were bad PR, and the U.S. strove to give its allies as much *plausible deniability* as possible.

In their case, however, plausible deniability meant a flight made longer by almost ninety minutes.

Abby opened her eyes, without anguish this time. She straightened herself somewhat on the couch where she'd been resting and gave Dylan a long overdue smile. "So we're on our way home," she said, relishing the thought.

"It appears that way," Dylan said with a bit more caution in his voice.

She looked around at the cabin. Dr. Skinner sat in a chair, sound asleep. The two other men were gone. "Where did our CIA chaperones go?"

"I think there's some berths up by the cockpit. They're probably sleeping too."

Abby frowned. The atmosphere in the cabin seemed more conflicted than she would have liked. Near the front passageway, a hazy pocket of swirling darkness hovered. She didn't want to focus her gift and search for faces or demonic influences. She was still too raw from her bout of spiritual birth pangs.

She straightened up the rest of the way and yawned. "I wish there was a way to get the news," she said, "and see what's been going on in the world."

Dylan glanced around the cabin. "Look. There's a laptop on that corner desk."

"Let's try it," said Abby. "I'll bet this plane has wi-fi."

She walked over and opened the laptop. The screen lit up, and the computer's programs popped into view, including the icon for a popular Internet browser. Moving her finger to the touchpad, she clicked on it.

The browser not only came on-screen instantly but showed a strong signal. She looked at Dylan and shrugged.

"Try CNN.com," he suggested. She typed it in and began to read. The lead headline said, "Countdown to Terror."

"What's it say?" asked Dylan, who was a little too far away to comfortably read the text of the article.

"It says al-Qaeda vowed the wave of death would happen at exactly two o'clock local time, and the whole country, the whole world even, is on pins and needles. Every ship in the mid-Atlantic has been scanned for radiation and searched. All major urban areas are under curfew, although that's become a mess with roadways clogged by motorists trying to escape. There's been looting in Newark and Baltimore. Basically, everyone's holding their breath," she finished as she straightened up from the screen.

He leaned forward. The next headline said, "Abby Sherman Sparks National Response."

"It says my broadcast from France has become the most watched video clip in the history of the Internet. And with no other way to take action against the threat, people have started to respond. Prayer warriors are showing up at key spots all over the country. Whole churches and families are taking up the challenge. Beaches across the coast are lined with people!"

Abby's expression was lit up as she looked back at Dylan.

CHAPTER
_56

"Yes!" Abby shouted. "Thank you, God!" She turned and gave Dylan an exultant high-five.

The noise awakened Dr. Skinner, who shook his head and almost fell from his seat. "What is it?" he said.

"The summons has traveled the world over, and believers are taking up battle stations—thousands of them!"

Skinner stared with a mixture of delight and pure shock. "Has it produced any results yet?"

"Good question," Dylan interjected. "We'll know in about . . . an hour, if I'm calculating right. Hey, Abby, what about checking your email?"

"That might take a while," she said. "I haven't checked my email since before leaving home for Israel. There's bound to be thousands of messages by now."

"You could at least make a search for something from your mom."

"That's very thoughtful, Dylan. And a great idea." She entered her provider's website address and clicked on WebMail. After typing in her password and search terms, she pointed to a cascading list and smiled. "There she is.

" 'Dear Abby, I hope this reaches you soon. I realize how busy you've been. I just saw your video on TV. It's leading every newscast, right up there with the wave of death. Which, besides giving you a big online hug, is the reason I'm writing this. Honey, I've had a major eureka. Ever since you left I've been seeing standing water in my visions. Drowned and bloated bodies everywhere. All this time I've assumed the water imagery was just that, imagery. A metaphor. But now God has shown me the truth. It wasn't symbolic. It's a real tidal wave, a tsunami. I don't know how, because I'm well aware that tsunamis happen on their own sweet time, not on a terrorist's schedule. But I'm as convinced of this as I was about your following Sister Rulaz' last request. See if you can make sense of it. Love, Mom.' "

"Please step away from the computer."

All three turned around abruptly, for the voice that spoke those words was deeper and older and came from behind them. It was Agent Grady, returned from his berth.

"Excuse me?" said Abby.

"That computer is a dedicated government communications terminal—"

"No, it isn't," Dylan interrupted. "It's just an ordinary computer, wired to the Internet."

"Nevertheless, it is government property and not for anyone's personal use. It's a violation of federal law for you to touch it, and I'm going to have to ask you to log off immediately."

"What if we say no?" said Dylan. "What if we refuse?"

"Then I'll have to take the computer away and secure it," the man answered, and then his arm jerked forward. He had a gun in his hand. "I have no interest in restraining you or causing an incident."

Dylan backed up a step. "What are you going to do, Agent Grady, shoot us in an airplane at forty thousand feet and risk a possible decompression, like a blown-out window that could suck us all out?"

The man laughed. "I've been in the CIA for twelve years, Mr. Hatfield, or whoever you are. That may not be much to you, but it's enough to pick up a few tricks. Like knowing how to shoot and kill someone so the bullet doesn't exit the body."

"Fine," Dylan said. "But all three of us? You're going to make a perfect shot at all of us in a split second's time?"

"No, but I'm sure two will be plenty. Connelly?"

He cocked his head sideways, and the second agent appeared, his eyes bleary from sleep. As he stood and took in the situation, his gaze became sharp and his movements deliberate. He moved to Grady's side.

The two groups faced each other, poised for the least provocation. Finally, Abby said, "Dylan, let's obey them. It's what God would want."

"What?" Dylan replied.

"Let's do this the right way." After Abby spoke the words, she inwardly whispered a prayer, then took a step toward the CIA men. The gun in Grady's hand rose in anticipation, but then stopped when she moved no farther. "Agent Grady," she said, a grimace of pain crossing her features, "I'm asking you to change your mind."

"I can't just—"

"Please, allow us to monitor the Internet through your communications terminal."

"It's not up to me."

"You know the crisis our country's facing right now. Well, unless a miracle happens soon, there may not be an eastern seaboard for us to land on when we return. There may not be a Dulles Airport, or Capitol building, or your CIA headquarters. Everyone you know and love within miles of the Atlantic could be dead. The country you serve could be decimated. And all we want to do is to try and find a solution. You know the president urgently wants to speak with me about preventing this disaster. Now, do you want to go down in history as the man who allowed America to be destroyed because he couldn't bend the rules regarding the proper use of one laptop computer?"

His silence, combined with his tense body and flushed cheeks, revealed that Agent Grady had been thrown into a state of utter bewilderment by Abby's words.

"Please," she repeated. "You can look over our shoulder and make sure we don't access anything sensitive or classified."

At last Grady lowered the weapon. "If I don't like something you're doing, you either stop right away or I place you in restraints for the rest of the trip. You hear?"

Abby and Dr. Skinner both nodded, while Dylan stood stock-still.

"One more thing," said Dylan, "as long as we're at it. We need you to speak with the captain, and tell him and the copilot we may be asking for their help. In fact, given what may lie ahead of us, you all may be asked to show a great deal of flexibility. But we promise to fully explain any deviation we ask you to make. Deal?"

Agent Grady stared at Dylan, thought for a minute. Finally he said, "All right. Let me go talk to the pilot and explain the situation back here and see what he says. I'll be right back. Meanwhile, everybody take a seat. Connelly, you keep an eye on things."

"Will do," said Connelly, walking over and sitting down near the computer as Grady headed toward the cockpit.

Less than ten minutes later Grady returned and faced Dylan and Abby. "Okay. Here's the deal. I had a conference with the pilot where we discussed the exceptional circumstances of this flight, our country's crisis, and you three people. He said you can count on his assisting you as long as you realize he's still in charge of this aircraft. And Connelly and I will make sure the pilot stays in charge the entire way, by force if necessary. Understand?"

Abby nodded, then got up to return to the laptop.

Dylan took a deep breath. "We understand, and thanks for your help." He reached out to shake Grady's hand.

Grady accepted Dylan's hand with a blank expression. "Roger that," he said.

CHAPTER
_57

During the two hours that followed, leading up to two o'clock in the morning, the U.S. intelligence community flew into a frenzy. First responders of every variety were deployed in every community east of the Appalachians. Spy satellites conducted complete photographic surveys of the Eastern Continental Divide and the most notable mountaintops along the coastline, including Mount Washington in New Hampshire, Mount Mitchell in North Carolina, and Mounts Marcy and Algonquin in the Adirondacks. In addition, their photographic functions were augmented by special radiation-detection sensors in overflying U2 spy planes.

All sources soon reported no abnormal activity or radiation detected.

The mosques and headquarters of six fundamentalist Muslim mullahs with suspected ties to terrorism were raided by the FBI, resulting in the detention of thirty-six suspects.

The ports of New York, Washington, Baltimore, and Boston were shut down for a period of one hour before and after two o'clock that morning. Thankfully, it was not a busy navigation period to begin with.

Meanwhile, Washington was essentially drained of key governmental leaders. The president and first family were flown by helicopter to Andrews Air Force Base, where as a precaution they boarded the E-4B, the National Airborne Operations Center—essentially a flying command post and disaster survival refuge housed in a retrofitted Boeing 747. On board, he was awaited by the Secretary of Defense and the Joint Chiefs of Staff. The jet took off immediately, performed an unusually steep tactical takeoff to rapidly reach its maximum altitude of 45,000 feet, cruising at 700 miles per hour in a wide holding pattern over the plains states.

All over the District of Columbia, several dozen Blackhawk helicopters landed simultaneously in parks, parking lots, and even one residential cul-de-sac, not bothering to slow their rotor blades before taking on families, who jumped aboard with a suitcase apiece and their heads held low. The choppers took off and flew the passengers—senior leaders of Congress, Supreme Court justices and their families—to the Mount Weather Emergency Operations Center in Bluemont, Virginia. Mount Weather was a secret 200,000-square-foot underground facility boasting the means to sustain the leadership of the federal government in safe conditions for a minimum of thirty days.

In one of the lesser known aspects of the Government Continuity Plan, other nongovernmental citizens deemed of high national priority were also flown to Mount Weather. They included several constitutional experts and leading law professors from Georgetown University, pioneering doctors in the fields of trauma, heart disease, and cancer research, leading naturalists and horticulturalists with the National Botanical Gardens, and even the pastors of the president's and vice president's respective churches.

However stressful, their plight was negligible compared to that of ordinary Americans, who also heeded the warning and tried to flee westward during those final hours. Major highway hubs in every one of the region's major cities crawled to a standstill, jammed with hundreds of thousands of escaping families. Gasoline supplies quickly depleted in these cities as motorists topped off their cars' tanks. Grocery stores reported the predictable run on the basic staples, items such as cereal, bread, milk, water, and batteries.

Then, as the final minutes ticked down toward the terrorist-designated deadline, all of them—whether in high-flying aircraft or underground bunkers or stuck in traffic sitting in their cars—huddled before their televisions, listened on their radios, stared at their BlackBerries and Treos and iPhones, checked their watches, called loved ones.

And prayed.

ABOARD THE E-4B, NATIONAL AIRBORNE OPERATIONS CENTER—MINUTES LATER

Ignoring the strong advice of his Secret Service detail as well as the 747's pitching motions resulting from a recent encounter with air turbulence, the president sank to his knees and lowered his head.

Above him, a computer screen counted down: *fifteen, fourteen, thirteen . . .*

Unbeknownst to the president, behind him three of the Joint Chiefs did likewise.

The space fell deathly quiet—all except for the buzzing, distant voice of someone counting down the last ten seconds over the speaker system.

". . . six, five, four, three . . ."

Without looking up, the president reached out and took the hand of his teenage son, who sat nearby, sobbing quietly.

". . . two, one, zero . . ."

Nothing was audible now except for the steady drone of the aircraft's engines. The president looked up, blew out a long breath, and rose to his feet. He said nothing, nor did any of those around him.

There was nothing to say. Nothing to do but watch the rows of monitors bearing feeds from assorted points of interest: the Capitol, the White House, Times Square, the top of the Empire State Building, Boston's Copley Square, and Miami's beachfront. Somewhere in the room, a speaker issued the tiniest hiss as an audio feed from NORAD in Colorado Springs watched from space for heat blooms.

The president kept his eyes fixed on the countdown monitor as it entered negative territory, counting off five, ten, fifteen seconds after the deadline's passage.

Still, the only thing he could hear was the beating of his own heart.

He looked around to the Joint Chiefs for a clue as to when folks would start drawing conclusions. The Chairman locked eyes with his, and the president shrugged questioningly, holding up outstretched hands for some kind of verdict. The man was starting to nod his head almost despite himself, like some kind of nervous tic.

"NORAD?" asked the Chairman.

"Yes, sir," came a woman's voice, barely scratched by static.

"This is Pete Cockburn, with the president on the E-4. Anything to report?"

"Please stand by."

Struck by the irony of essentially being put on hold at such a moment, the general shrugged. "Roger . . ." he said dryly.

The president laughed mirthlessly at the irony.

"General, NORAD has no major explosive events to report over the watch area."

The cabin filled with a loud sigh—six pairs of lungs emptying themselves all at once.

The president looked to his highest military advisers. "So are we in the clear?"

The Chairman cleared his throat. "Mr. President, so far it's good news. But I would caution everyone that although the time stated was quite specific, there could be minor variations, even calculation errors. Or some kind of multipronged attack could have only now begun. I wouldn't celebrate for an hour or two yet."

"Good point," said the president, even though the relief on his face was unmistakable. "I don't know whether to feel grateful and relieved or incredibly ticked off that the whole country's been taken for a huge ride."

"Sir, if something had gone off just now and we had done nothing, that would have been by far the most irresponsible course."

"True. True. Well, please keep watching and listening, would you? I'm going to my private cabin to tell the first lady there'll be an America to land on after all."

CHAPTER

_58

In all of her seventy-five years, Luci Holliman had never been more physically uncomfortable than during those moments on the beach, kneeling in the sand. And yet paradoxically, never before had she been more oblivious to the signals coming from her weathered body. Just then she was in the throes of a joy more powerful and complete than anything she'd ever experienced before.

The countdown had faded away, carried by the soft voices of others on all sides of her. Now that it was over, a vague sense of anticlimax seemed to wash over many of those kneeling there. A few of the prayer warriors stood, looking around them intensely. Quiet conversations were breaking out across the sand. Reporters were now taking the liberty of approaching the line, their cameras lifted to shoulder height with their lights piercing the darkness.

Two police officers with flashlights had begun to gently usher some of them from the beach. A certain mood of suspense had been broken.

But Luci Holliman remained in place. She frowned, trying to sense the reason why. Was it fatigue? Laziness? The difficulty of rousing an old woman's bones after so much time in one position?

The answer came to her then: *No. There's something else. The mission is not complete.*

A finger tapped her shoulder. She turned; it was a female police officer. "Ma'am, we're trying to clear the beach now, for everyone's safety. It appears the deadline has safely passed."

Luci smiled. "Thank you, but I need to stay right here. I don't believe we're safe yet. Not at all. I feel the Lord telling me so. I'm being commanded to stay and keep praying."

A woman nearby got up from her knees and walked over toward Luci. "You know what? I feel that very same caution. But then I saw folks leaving, and I thought it was just me." The woman sank back down next to Luci.

The police officer turned and wandered off, shaking her head.

ABOARD THE GULFSTREAM OVER THE EASTERN MEDITERRANEAN

With the laptop behind them broadcasting streaming live video from the U.S., Dylan, Abby, and Dr. Skinner had spent the last few minutes praying as they never had before. When the final few seconds of the deadline passed, they all opened their eyes and looked at each other, then at the laptop's screen. A news anchor was nervously pitching the lead to correspondents positioned along the

Atlantic coast. So far they were all standing before their cameras, eyes wide with fear yet very much alive, totally unaware of any catastrophic event.

"Thank you, God, for your mercy . . ." said Abby under her breath, though something within her seemed unsettled still.

"Amen to that," Dr. Skinner added.

Unable to verbalize anything, Dylan sighed like a man given a reprieve from execution.

They continued to watch for several moments longer as a tentative *all clear* seemed to quietly sweep over the nation.

"Is it possible there was a mistake with the time Nirubi quoted?" Abby asked.

"What did he say?" Dylan said. "I've forgotten, exactly."

"If I remember right, he said 'two o'clock local time.'"

Dylan frowned, glanced at Skinner, then back at Abby. "He didn't say 'a.m.' or 'p.m.'?"

"No, but most foreigners use the twenty-four clock, so I think it's assumed he would have said fourteen hundred hours if he'd meant two in the afternoon."

Dylan shook his head. "But what about this 'local time'? Why didn't he say 'eastern time'?"

"Maybe because eastern standard time is an American term," Abby replied.

"Yeah, but still. It makes you wonder . . ."

Abby turned back to the laptop. "Hey, check this out. Listen to what this person's saying."

On-screen, a correspondent stood on the darkened edge of a beach. "Strangely, Brian," she said, "despite the deadline being over, many of the people are still here. They remained rooted to their stations all night, and this morning refuse to leave. I asked one of them why she wasn't celebrating and on her way home, and here's what she had to say."

The video shifted to a taped segment, showing a matronly woman in rumpled clothes, squinting in the glare of a camera light. "Frankly, I just don't feel like I've gotten a release from the Holy Spirit to go home," the woman said. "And it seems everybody else out here feels the same as me."

"So how long are you going to stay?" the correspondent asked.

The lady shrugged. "Until I sense God giving me an *all clear*."

"Brian," the correspondent continued, broadcasting live again, "it seems it's been that way throughout the numerous sites where these people have stationed themselves. Even while the administration hesitates to declare a national 'all clear' just yet, these folks seem to mirror that mode of caution. I suppose only time will tell if what they're sensing is justified. Back to you . . ."

"Great!" Dylan exclaimed. "Just when I thought the suspense was over."

"Yes, but imagine their courage, their determination," Abby said, a glow of wonder spreading across her features. "I have never been more proud of people I don't actually know! I mean, in the face of probable death, they're staying. They're using their faith and waging war in the Spirit. What heroes!"

"You helped make this happen," Dylan said with a smile and a hand on her shoulder. "I'm so proud of *you*."

"Well, you played a huge part," she replied. "You and Dr. Skinner. By the way, where did he go? Restroom?"

"He went to lie down in one of the berths. After the deadline passed, he decided to get some shut-eye."

Abby nodded, then settled deeper into her seat, trying to relax her tense muscles. "So what do we do now?"

"I guess sit back, wait to arrive back home," Dylan said.

"I feel like I'm supposed to keep going. Do something . . ."

"How about checking some more email messages, see if there's anything important we should know?"

"Good idea," she said.

They both returned to the laptop, where Abby began scrolling through the file names on the screen. "Man, how am I gonna know which ones to read? There are so many messages here."

"The same way you chose which spot in all of western Europe to look for the summons: by trusting God to point out the right one."

"Right," she said, exasperated with herself. "Please, Lord, bear with me one more time . . . I'll just scroll through the most recent messages, scan the subject lines, and see what grabs my attention. Look, here's an interesting one: 'warning from a mountain pastor.'"

FROM: *Rev. Walter Landers*
TO: *Abby Sherman, MyCorner.com*
SUBJECT: *Warning From a Mountain Pastor*

Ms. Sherman, I live in a church parsonage along the crest of the Eastern Continental Divide, right near the highest point in Maryland. Since yesterday I have kept a close watch on a group of very suspicious-looking folks who seem to be hiding out in a secluded part of the forest near my home. I have photographed a banner in their possession which, if my rough translation is correct, says, The Great Satan Is Dead. By the way, I read this on the banner before Sheikh Nirubi used that expression on his Internet warning, not after. I also saw them preparing whole bundles of automatic weapons. So far, no law enforcement agency has seen fit to answer my reports. I suppose they're quite busy. And yet I feel this is important. It seems they had assembled a staging area, and the choice of location was far from accidental.

Well, Ms. Sherman, it is now several minutes after two o'clock, the designated time. I spent the final seconds in the trees, watching these people, who I am convinced are somehow associated. And the strange thing is, they didn't even stir, let alone seem to be watching the countdown, while the rest of the country was ticking off the seconds together. In fact, most of them were asleep.

I know I'm just one person, a small-church pastor out in the middle of nowhere. But if you can share my warning with anyone in a position of influence, please tell them with all certainty that the deadline was some kind of ruse. These folks nearby are still poised to do something terrible, I just know it. But apparently their signal hasn't yet been given.

We are being tricked, my dear sister. Please heed this warning . . .

"Wow," whispered Abby after finishing the message. "That's really disconcerting. Dylan, what do you make of it?"

Dylan finished reading the message, then replied, "I say strike number two against this whole thing being settled."

"I'm going to keep looking, just in case this trend picks up any more steam."

FORT MEADE, MARYLAND—MINUTES LATER

Deep within the NSA's cryptology center, a morning-shift junior analyst charged with sorting through the prominent search terms received by sources deemed to be "of interest" sat down at his desk and wrote down four lined entries.

Wave of death.

Ancient peak.

Atlantic coast.

Tsunami.

He'd spent four hours the day before, analyzing a different list of words and had produced nothing. His final step, now that the threat seemed to be waning, would be to *wash* the terms through the agency's exhaustive computer program known as the "Word Laundry." It consisted of one of the world's largest databases, designed to find patterns among groups of words by sifting them through millions of terms in one hundred different languages, like a grain of sand on a vast beach.

He entered the words, started the program with a simple click of the mouse, then went next door for coffee.

When he returned, he took one glance at the screen and frowned. He sat, thought for a moment, and looked again for good measure. He made a few calculations on a note pad.

Then his face went white, and his hand groped for a nearby telephone as though he'd been struck blind.

CHAPTER

_59

At first, Grady and Connelly were closely monitoring Abby and Dylan's use of the laptop, the "government communications terminal" with its classified status. But after a while, seeing the two could be trusted and were not up to anything sinister, the agents backed off, went and took seats outside the cockpit door.

Abby, meanwhile, continued sifting through her email.

"Here's an interesting one," she said to Dylan, who sat fighting off sleep on the couch nearby. "It's not from America; it's from the Canary Islands."

FROM: Isabella Ignacios, novice of the Convent of La Madre, Santa Cruz de la Palma, Canary Islands

TO: Sister Abigail Sherman
SUBJECT: please heed a desperate warning

Dear Sister Sherman,

I am only 15 years old and a humble novice in the service of Christ Jesus, yet I have seen and heard things which only I have witnessed, and I believe after seeing your VideoCorner clip that you are the only one He has ordained to hear my warning. The sisters of my convent do not believe me, even though they know me to be a person of honesty and devotion.

Sister Abigail, a strongman, a demon of death and destruction, has come to my island of La Palma. I cannot put it any more plainly than that. I have never been given to unfounded visions, but after a week of almost constant fellowship with the Father, I was given a vision which has been a great burden to me. I felt the arrival of darkness almost like an eclipse upon my soul, and it was revealed to me that a grievous evil would be wrought against many from the shores of La Palma.

Sister, if you receive this and are inclined to respond, I would be overjoyed to hear from you. Until then, please consider me your faithful sister in Christ . . .

Abby let out a low whistle and leaned back in her chair.

From his perch over her shoulder, Dylan raised his eyebrows. "'Like an eclipse upon my soul.' I can say, I know the feeling."

"Me too," said Abby.

Suddenly Dylan's hand, which had been resting on her wrist, a sign of the growing affection between them, became a tight grip.

"What's the matter?" she asked, and then seeing the expression on his face, she bolted upright in her seat. "Dylan?"

"Abby, where have you heard of La Palma before?"

"I don't know. I don't think I ever have."

"Well, I have. What was the term your mother told us to be looking for?"

"Ancient Peak."

He nodded. "Ancient Peak. And what language do they speak in the Canaries? Spanish, right? It's part of Spain. What does 'ancient peak' mean in Spanish?"

"I don't know. Something *vieja*, I suppose."

"Good guess. Cumbre Vieja, actually. Go online, find a search site, and type in the words *Cumbre Vieja*."

He waited while she quickly typed it in, hit Enter, then started reading.

"'Cumbre Vieja is an unstable volcano on the island of La Palma, in the Canary Islands, believed capable of releasing a vast quantity of earth into the Atlantic during its next eruption, a quantity catastrophic enough to send a three-hundred-foot wall of water crashing into the Atlantic coast of North America at speeds of over six hundred miles per hour.'"

She turned to Dylan, feeling as though she were about to faint.

"A *wave of death*. So it never was a turn of phrase. It was literal!"

"Is this a joke, Dylan? Please tell me this is some kind of joke. Some whacked-out urban myth."

"It's not a myth," he replied, shaking his head. "This is real. In fact, according to the Homeland Security people, it's listed as one of the scariest scenarios out there."

"Oh no . . . and my mom's message about it being a tsunami. But what about the thing she said, remember? Something about how tsunamis happen on their own time?"

He looked her straight in the eyes, his face grim. "That's where the bomb comes in."

Abby turned pale at the thought, turning back to the laptop. "The landslide from Cumbre Vieja is thought to be imminent," she said as she scanned the article, "because it's from a fault line that's already slipped before, and they think it's poised to slip again. Any eruption, or even excessive flooding, could trigger the landslide that would then set off the tidal wave."

"Even a low-yield nuclear weapon could be powerful enough to give that fault line the shove it needs to go sliding off," added Dylan. "And a bomb was never found in any ship crossing the Atlantic. What if that's because it was never meant to cross it in the first place? What if it left the Mediterranean but stayed on that side of the Atlantic?"

"As in the Canary Islands. Which are on the African coast . . ."

"Bingo."

"It's a brilliant trick. They didn't have to go to the trouble of smuggling a device onto American soil. All it took was getting through on a casually screened tourist island. Meanwhile, everyone has been running around on the American mainland looking for bogeymen. According to the article," continued Abby, "the tidal wave would cross the ocean in six hours and would wipe out every-thing on the Atlantic coast from the Caribbean to Nova Scotia, for twenty miles inland or even more."

"New York, Washington, Boston, Baltimore—they'd all be gone."

"This is insane," Abby muttered. "Tell me I'm in a nightmare brought on by bad food or not enough sleep. Tell me some sick hacker planted this story and we just got taken in by the lie."

"Sorry. I wish that were the case."

"But if so many people know about this possibility on La Palma, and an explosion had gone off on the island, wouldn't we have heard about it already?"

Dylan acknowledged her point with a solemn nod. Staring at the floor of the plane, he began processing the information bouncing back and forth in his head. "Remember that this whole plot has been one huge misdirection play, as they say in football."

"Go on," said Abby.

"So if Nirubi meant two o'clock La Palma time, and if he wasn't using European or military time but meant two in the afternoon—"

"That's what, five hours ahead of Eastern time?"

He nodded.

"So nine o'clock eastern . . ." Abby spun around in her chair. "Dylan! That's an hour from now!"

CHAPTER
_60

The Chairman of the Joint Chiefs stood before his Commander in Chief, swaying slightly, though it wasn't clear whether this was because of the tilting of the aircraft or the nature of his message.

The president sat at his desk, staring at the general, holding an emergency communiqué from Fort Meade, which detailed the cryptographer's findings, along with corroborating evidence in the form of a thermal satellite scan of Cumbre Vieja that showed recent digging activity along the volcano's spine.

"Can we reach it in time?" the president asked in a plaintive, almost childlike tone.

"No, sir. If the time differential is factored in, the weapon would detonate in one hour. We have no assets close enough at this moment to make any sort of ground incursion in the period required."

"How close are our bases in the Azores?"

"Two and a half hours away."

The president's face went taut. "How many people on La Palma?"

"I'd have to check, sir. Probably around a hundred thousand. The Canary Islands are a tourist destination belonging to Spain."

"I'm well aware of that, thank you. That Abby Sherman girl who stirred up all those prayer warriors—did she and her Special Forces friend ever get brought back from France?"

"Sir, the plane bringing them back to the States is somewhere over the Atlantic, just southwest of Gibraltar."

The president's eyebrows knitted together. "Wait a minute . . . Where are they?"

"Near Gibraltar, sir."

"General, I need to talk with the commander of Operation Mystic Sender. Get him on the line. Now!"

ABOARD THE GULFSTREAM OVER THE ATLANTIC OCEAN

After speaking to Agent Grady and getting permission to talk with the aircraft's captain, the cockpit door opened and Dylan was allowed to approach the one behind the controls. "Captain, how far are we across the Atlantic?" he asked.

"A little over five hundred miles west of Gibraltar. Why?"

"Doesn't that put us due north of the Canary Islands?"

"Right on the money. In fact, if it was bright enough, you might be able to see one of the outermost islands."

"Which island would that be?"

"Ah, I'm not quite sure." He bent over and checked his map. "La Palma."

For a moment, Dylan simply stood there and smiled. "God, you are a resourceful Creator, I'll give you that," he said under his breath. He moved closer to the pilot, crouched down, and began to speak in a clipped, fervent tone. "All right. Here's what I need you to do. If you were to radio in and talk to the president, he'd probably tell you that La Palma Island in the Canaries is about to become the most important spot on the planet in the next hour. The survival of the country may depend on it. That might sound crazy, but it's the truth! Please trust me on this."

Both the pilot and copilot turned and gave Dylan a scrutinizing look. Then the pilot slowly nodded and said, "Okay. Hang on while I call someone from the administration."

Just a few minutes later the Gulfstream had been given a new mission, had suddenly changed course and was now heading for La Palma, streaking across the sky at breakneck speed, the pilot and copilot in high-alert mode.

Dylan had rushed back to the cabin to fill in Abby and Dr. Skinner on his conversation with the pilot and then quickly returned to the cockpit.

"All right," he said to the pilot. "My commander's orders are for us to call the closest radar facility and demand they patch us through to the op center, wherever that may be. Tell them you're a government aircraft with presidential clearance and you have an urgent message for the National Command Authority."

"You got it," said the pilot.

Dylan turned to the copilot. "Can we open this plane's doors in midflight?"

"What altitude are you talking about?"

"Anything under ten thousand feet doesn't matter. I'm HALO qualified."

"Well, with a password override from the cockpit, we should be able to open the doors."

"Great. Where are your parachutes?"

"Passenger chutes are in the galley, overhead bin three."

"What type are they?"

"State of the art, of course. Nylon ram-air models."

"Perfect. Is there any way I could jump with some kind of radio link with you guys?"

"What do you mean?"

"I'm going to jump out in a few minutes, but I need to maintain radio contact. Is there any way we could rig that up?"

The two pilots exchanged glances. "We have walkie-talkies, range of about ten miles. Are you sure about this? You know, you may not make it."

"No other choice. We're running outta time. So could you stay within that ten-mile range for, say, twenty minutes?"

The pilot glanced at his fuel gauges. "Over La Palma? Yes, but no more than that."

NATIONAL COUNTERTERRORISM CENTER, VIRGINIA—
MINUTES LATER

Because McLean, Virginia, is over twenty-five miles from Chesapeake Bay and nearly a hundred miles from the Atlantic shore, the few remaining suits who had not been officially evacuated and who had once been hard to keep close by suddenly became quite anxious to remain close. In fact, several asked if their families could be found housing anywhere on the complex, an amazing presumption universally met with stares of disbelief.

David Ashman, who knew firsthand that the headquarters' residential amenities consisted mainly of employee showers, remained in attendance and had now, by default, assumed authority over the operation at Langley.

"David, we've received radio contact from a government aircraft with Abby Sherman and Dylan Hatfield on board. You're not gonna believe this, but they're approaching the Canary Islands, and somehow they've been fully briefed on the situation."

Ashman cocked his head forward in amazement. "What's that?"

"Dead serious, David."

Ashman's face turned a bright shade of red. "Where's Agent Clayton?" he shouted. "The one who ran Hatfield for the CIA? I want him up here ASAP!" The room seemed to jump to a new, more intense level of activity. "What's Hatfield planning to do? Is he going to get himself on the ground and attempt some kind of intervention?"

"I think he means to do just that, sir—to parachute out, get down there, and try to locate the device."

"All right," said Ashman. "I want maxed-out satellite coverage of that volcano. We already found the thermal reading on that digging, right? Now I want real-time video on the entire mountain. And someone contact La Palma through the Spanish Air Force and request helo support. Now!" He was pacing with excitement. "C'mon, people! Let's move it!"

CHAPTER

_61

"What are you doing?" asked Agent Grady at the strange sight of their kneeling down in the center of the aircraft's cabin.

"We're praying," Dylan responded without looking up. "Do you want to join us?"

Grady took an involuntary step back. "Oh, that's all right."

"I will," broke in Connelly. "I doubt whether I'll get fired for it." He stepped forward and joined the small circle just as Dylan began to pray.

"God, you know how quiet things have been between you and me lately," Dylan began. "It's been a dry spell, to say the least. But the strange part is, when I look back on the last few weeks, it's so clear how you've been guiding us right through the despair and the silence. Even through my stubborn insistence on doing things my way." He leaned back, took a deep breath. "But I'm here to tell you that I want to follow you more than ever. And to ask you—please show up today, please help us. If you don't intervene, then I don't even want to think of what might happen. We need you, Lord. We have no other place to go, nothing else to put our faith in. My strength isn't enough. My training isn't enough. Not even close."

Abby now lifted her face skyward and smiled. "God, I was so silly to doubt you. Forgive my unbelief, because now in hindsight it was so childish. You led us to the summons. Your Spirit guided us across half a continent to just the right place. How incredible you are! And now you've raised up the Warriors spoken of in the summons. They're at this moment asking you for the same thing we ask of you now. We beg you to spare the lives of our country-men. So please guide our path, and bless Dylan's mission . . ."

After they had finished praying, Abby began to feel, instead of a painful sensation, the onset of a deep euphoria. A sense of peace and comfort came over her and seemed to fill the whole interior of the plane. Dr. Skinner said he sensed it too.

"Do you two remember what I challenged you about?" Skinner asked as Dylan began pulling on his parachute. "I urged you to work on learning from each other's modes of warfare, your two respective specialties. Well, what you're about to do is the epitome of that. We have thousands praying for us across America right now, and we'll continue doing so after you've jumped, Dylan. But you need to stay in constant touch with the Father while doing this."

"Yeah, but I have to think about what I'm doing at a hundred miles an hour!" said Dylan.

"Sure, but you can still operate while in a constant state of prayer, like keeping an open channel on a radio. And you'll feel His presence with you every second of the way."

Dylan nodded, absorbing the suggestion. Then he looked up, his face set. The parachute was ready. "Gotta go."

He walked toward the cockpit. Once there, the pilot leaned forward and pointed down at the island so Dylan could get an idea of where they were. From their altitude, it looked like a giant comma with the volcano's cone clearly visible, dead center in its upper curve.

"Look straight down from the middle of the volcano's southern slope," the pilot instructed, "and you'll see the ridge that runs down to the tip."

"I see it," replied Dylan.

"Okay. You see that tan smudge about a third of the way down? That's a clearing in the forest. And according to the coordinates I just received, that's the spot you need to aim for. They recorded fresh signs of digging in that area. A chopper is already airborne and coming our way from Tenerife, the main island. Once you've located the bomb, the chopper will pick you up and carry you out so you can dispose of the device offshore. Got it?"

"Got it."

"Now let me enter the password to open the door for you. Godspeed, my friend."

They shook hands, and Dylan backed out of the cockpit.

From that moment on, everything began to take on a choppy kind of altered state, a feeling of slow motion that Dylan often experienced during moments of great stress combined with exhilaration. His brain seemed now to process life in five-second blocks, rather than streaming in real time as his body switched into autopilot.

The jet's speed was reduced, its engines becoming a distant hum. A rumbling noise signaled that the captain had lowered his flaps to gain more control and make it safe for Dylan to leap from the aircraft.

Tethered to the wall, the copilot wrestled with an unwieldy release hinge, yanked with all his strength until the door swung backward. Immediately a roar of freezing wind rushed into the cabin. Through the open doorway, blue sky raced past fragments of cloud.

Dylan strapped on a pair of goggles scrounged up by Agent Connelly, made sure he had the walkie-talkie as well as the gun and ammunition returned to him from Agent Grady, then suddenly did something he'd been thinking about for days.

He stepped over and took Abby into his arms, then kissed her tenderly on the lips.

For several head-swimming seconds, time slowed down even more, the threatening world of open sky and far-flung earth and danger momentarily forgotten. It was now replaced with a world of soft skin and warm breath, and an affection he'd longed to explore long before then.

She pulled away first, slowly, and caressed his cheek. "Dylan," she said in a halting whisper, "please, promise me you'll be careful. We'll be praying . . ."

"I promise," he said. "I love you, Abby." Then, turning to give Skinner a thumbs-up, he took three quick strides and, without a second's pause, threw himself from the plane.

CONVENT OF LA MADRE—THAT SAME MOMENT

Everyone at La Madre knew some victory had been achieved when Isabella's countenance brightened like their cloister walls at the dawn of a summer day. The cloud that had followed her for the previous week simply evaporated, replaced by the luminous charm and ready smile they had always loved.

So no one tried to stop her when a low hum passed overhead as they sat at Matins, and Isabella, who had looked up at the sound, gasped with joy and ran laughing out of the chapel. On the terrace outside, she kept running until colliding against the outermost stone railing, nearly doubling her in half.

A plane was circling overhead. She had felt its coming, and now that it had arrived, she was so overjoyed that she felt capable of jumping up to the sky and wrapping it in a big welcome hug.

Staring upward, she saw a dark oval along the plane's side. While she tried to understand its shape, it spat out a tiny dot. The minuscule form plummeted almost sideways, causing her to stare at it in wonderment until a blue square sprang to life above the dot. The knowledge flew into her stunned mind.

A parachute!

Laughing, she sprinted around the side of the chapel and the outer buildings for a better look. Jumping and shouting so loudly that the other nuns began streaming out of the chapel to see what was happening, Isabella watched the parachute disappear along the mountain ridge at the southern end of her horizon.

CHAPTER

_62

SKIES OVER LA PALMA

Dylan had jumped many times on missions, and his free-falls had always wound up among the highlights of his adventures. However, something about this jump felt far, far different. Had he been able to spare enough mental capacity to ponder the subject just then, even while committing his thoughts to aiming himself toward the appointed landing zone, he might have arrived at some reasons why.

It might have been the tingling sensation still lingering on his lips, the delicious taste of a kiss that had sent a shudder down his spine. Even better was his feeling closer to Abby than ever before.

It might have been the danger associated with Dylan's awareness that the survival of millions of American lives may well depend on his performance in the next few minutes. He had done his best to banish all thought of his work's ultimate consequences. But as often happened, the thought kept resurfacing anyway, bobbing just in and out of the boundaries of his conscious mind.

Or it might have been the sheer beauty of the jump itself. Never before had Dylan glided over a landscape as exotic and brilliantly colored as the one below him. Even as he tried to ignore his peripheral vision, it continued to flood his senses with the incredible experience of soaring so high above such unspeakable beauty. The Atlantic shone cobalt blue like a precious jewel. The island was bright green and intricately detailed with its perfectly placed volcano cone and bisecting mountain ridge.

The splendor all around him conquered his iron concentration and ignited a rush of gratitude to the Creator of it all. Even in such peril and stress, it humbled him that he was carrying out such a mission in these magnificent surroundings.

The jump's uniqueness was also due to the presence of the Holy Spirit, which he sensed now more than ever before. The impression was so intimate that he almost felt another person was strapped to the chute beside him.

All of these matters hovered somewhere far behind the ever-flowing, internal commentary of Dylan's tactical mind.

At the moment he was attempting to orient his approach to the central ridge. Balancing his trajectory with the wind's direction was always a tricky job along an island coast. Only through the deliberate adjusting of his toggle lines could he hope to weather the capricious shifting of the wind as he approached his target.

So far, so good, he told himself as his chute flapped above him and the giant teardrop of La Palma swiveled far below into a larger perspective. As he observed his target, it occurred to him that this would also be the most unforgiving jump of his career. If he was forced to approach the mountain from a right angle along its side, he would have but one shot at coming to rest precisely along its spine. One miscalculation or sudden gust, and he would go sailing into the ocean.

His best chance of success was to approach the ridge along its length, thereby giving himself an extended landing zone. Problem was, that would require him to make his final turn over the volcano's rim, and such a formation would mean highly unstable and powerful winds.

Something flew over the sun, causing a sudden dimming of light and briefly diverting his attention. He looked up and saw the Gulfstream, flying in a circling pattern above him.

He glanced at his watch. *Eleven minutes.* He was cutting it close . . .

It was time to come in toward the volcano, at an almost oblique angle to his desired landing. It might not have seemed like the most direct route, but experience told him the best way to weather the cone's strong winds would be to ride with them, breaking away only at the final second. That would require entering their stream essentially from behind.

He began to pick up speed, the volcano growing ever closer. His chute was flapping louder now as he neared the summit. He drew closer to the earth, knowing he was fast approaching the moment of truth and that it was imperative to maneuver perfectly. He pulled the left toggle line, but the wind caused him to dip too low. A quick correction brought him level again, yet still lower than he'd wanted. He turned away to gain back the altitude for another attempt, readying himself to try once more.

Tugging gently on the toggle lines to familiarize himself with their tension and resistance, he shot down into the winds' path.

This time Dylan swept into the currents just as he needed to and swiftly began circling the volcano. The speed and tug of the turn's g-force against his limbs brought a grimace to his face.

All at once the rim came speeding toward him, its wooded slopes and jagged rocks rushing up and flooding his senses. The caldera was huge, he reckoned with a glance, probably ten miles across. Under its overhung crown of bare stone, the volcanic valley was thick with an evergreen forest.

He looked away, southward to the ridge he needed to reach. The feeling of being suspended impossibly high above an ocean of space suddenly overwhelmed him. But he forced himself to concentrate on his next turn, to position himself directly over the target.

He pulled his lines forward and allowed himself to lose altitude, picking up additional speed. Then he pulled hard to the left, turning forty-five degrees to the south. He gritted his teeth, knowing that if he failed to leave the caldera's currents and missed his turn now, he would be done for.

Seaborne winds from the west suddenly buffeted him violently, the lift of the ridge's gigantic wall heaving him upward. Chastising himself for not foreseeing the problem, he fought to keep his glide path headed straight southward along the ridge's center. Manhandling his lines to stay on course also caused him to lose altitude prematurely.

Rounded shoulders of earth rose up to meet him, darkened in places with pine trees. This was his general drop zone, yet he had to travel farther along its clearing before landing. He pulled his lines again to steal more lift and managed to squeeze out one more upward surge.

It was now time to brace for landing. Desperate for a little more altitude, he slowed almost to a stall in his effort to steer the chute skyward again. It didn't work. Luckily, a broad meadow now lay open before him. *Fifty feet, then twenty.* It began pulling the lines . . .

He seemed to enter a surface-level river of air right at the last second, and the gust nearly collapsed his canopy. The impact buckled his ankles and his knees, hammering needles of pain throughout his body. He lost his balance and felt the chute drag him across rough terrain. He felt powerless, and the thought of all that was at stake invaded his mind again. He tensed every muscle of his body and dug his heels into the soil. The momentum pulled him another ten feet before his weight finally stopped the advance.

Suddenly the clock's ticking reentered his thoughts. He threw himself into action, ignoring the agony in his lower joints as he unshouldered the chute and whipped out the walkie-talkie.

ABOARD THE GULFSTREAM OVER CUMBRE VIEJA

"Abby! Abby! Can you hear me?"

The voice was faint and coarsened by a gravel bed's worth of static, but it was him, and by listening closely Abby could indeed make out his words. She pumped a fist into the air, matching Skinner's gesture next to her, and raised the receiver.

"I hear you, Dylan! Are you okay?"

"Yeah, I'm a little beat-up, but I'll make it!"

"Look, you're a little farther than we wanted, but that's okay! Just remember: we have five minutes!"

CHAPTER

_6 3

NATIONAL COUNTERTERRORISM CENTER

On the room's wall-mounted, oversized plasma screen, the central ridge of Cumbre Vieja glowed like a giant green-and-tan organism bristling with grassy capillaries. Dylan's billowing runaway canopy, thankfully a bright blue color, was easy to make out. Even Dylan himself was visible—as a tiny dark line against the ridge's sloping flank, his position tracked by needle-thin red crosshairs that moved with him across the landscape.

None of that technological mastery meant anything to the center's occupants, however. With the final six hundred seconds counting down, David Ashman and the analysts, as well as the liaisons and military attachés, were all on their feet, in the throes of their individual, habitual responses to crushing anxiety: clenching fists, pulling on hair, biting nails, pacing, guzzling coffee, tracing wild gestures in the air.

Ashman glanced at another marking on the screen—a bright red dot placed electronically on the site of their positive thermal reading for a recent excavation. It lay in a copse of trees, its distance from Dylan hard to estimate due to several dips and rises in between.

"Foxtrot Twelve, inform Miss Sherman that if he faces due south, the target's at one o'clock, half a klick as the crow flies." Ashman covered the mouthpiece and turned to an operator at his left. "Jerry, we need a more accurate distance. Can we get a laser range finding or anything?"

The operator shook his head. "Not from the bird, we can't. But, sir, you gave him a good estimate."

Ashman nodded and uncovered the mouthpiece. "Just tell him to run like crazy!"

CUMBRE VIEJA

Dylan didn't need that last instruction. The excruciating pain in his knees and ankles was gone now, banished from his awareness by sheer force of willpower. He was now soaring in a whole new sort of flight—sprinting across a treacherous landscape.

Before him lay a mixture of meadow and thin forest marked by obstructions such as half-rotted logs, sharp rocks, deep ruts, and holes. Running across the ridge, he pitched headlong into a dirt bank, his foot the victim of a grass-covered channel in the ground. The ankle came screaming back out of his denied sensations and doubled its agony. He grimaced and stood up as quickly as he could, gasping for breath.

He raised the walkie-talkie and shouted, "Abby, I lost my bearing on that fall! Where am I going? What direction?"

No reply came. He clicked the Speak button once, then twice, but still nothing. He'd lost them! With a frustrated growl, he threw the unit to the ground. He looked around, desperate to regain his bearings and figure out the right direction. The pounding of his heart and the urgency of the situation were conspiring to wipe out his faculties.

Please, Lord, you didn't bring me this far just to let me fail!

He began pleading with God, inwardly groping for another dose of that confidence he'd felt just moments ago. Instantly he was brought back to another mountaintop, back in Italy, when he and Abby had cried out to God in a moment of helplessness. What had been the solution then? He fought to remember. Then it came back to him, but in faint shreds . . .

Just keep moving. I will guide you . . .

Blind faith.

Okay, then. Blind faith it would be . . .

OCEAN CITY, MARYLAND

Luci Holliman closed her eyes against the beach's onshore wind, raised her hands in the air, and began to pray out loud. Beside her kneeled a long row of nearly two hundred others who had spent the night calling out to God. For the last four hours, they had been taunted and jeered at by cynics who were unconvinced of any danger. The believers had not responded, but instead continued to pray.

Now was the moment they'd been waiting for. As one, they started to pray for direction.

Direction—none knew exactly how the term applied, what made it matter. Was it simply instructions from God? Most of them knew it was something more. Something much more specific.

LA PALMA, CUMBRE VIEJA

Stirred by an odd yet powerful notion, Dylan did something crazy, but the only thing he knew to try at that moment. He began to run. Blindly.

He merely started moving, shutting down his mind to allow gut instinct and faith alone to guide him, and he found with each yard gained that he was becoming more and more confident of his direction.

A rhythmic *chop-chop-chop* grew louder, coming from straight ahead of him. The evacuation chopper. He sighed in relief and seemed to shift into some kind of overdrive. As he moved in the direction chosen for him, something within assured him that no hidden encumbrance would keep him from what he needed to do.

A few seconds later he stopped in his tracks, looked around for any sign of digging, disturbed earth, footprints, trampled vegetation . . .

A stick, leaning straight against a tree trunk, caught his eye. It appeared out of place, unnatural. He rushed over and with his foot cleared the ground of leaves and loose dirt.

Yes! There were footprints!

He threw himself onto the spot, digging farther down, frantically shoving aside the dirt, knowing the clock must be ticking down to its final seconds. The thought of being just moments from victory when the white-hot flash came shooting out from under him to not only vaporize him but soon after drown millions—the crushing despair of such an outcome roared back to torture him.

Pushing away the dreadful thought, he continued clawing at the earth. His ears filled with the thunder of the nearby chopper as he dug. Soon he was kneeling three, then four feet down from where he'd begun.

Then a downward thrust of his right arm struck something hard. A metal shape, shrouded in something softer like leather. He reached down, burrowing with his hands, grabbed hold of the thing and pulled it out.

A backpack. Containing something very smooth, very heavy.

He unzipped it quickly for a look. Stainless steel reflected blue sky back at him. The radioactivity symbol filled one panel.

This was it! "Yes!" he cried.

Zipping up the backpack, he thought he heard noises from inside—clicking, spinning . . . or was it only his imagination?

Without thinking, he was on his feet again, running, grasping the backpack with one hand and waving wildly at the chopper with the other.

The chopper hovered fifty yards away, forming a crater in the grass with its rotor wash, throwing off branches and clumps of earth. Dylan beckoned it closer. The tail swung around and rose behind it, giving the craft a nose-down bent as it flew over to him. Now only twenty yards away, the chopper leveled off and began to drop down . . .

There was no level ground! The slope's steep angle would not allow the helo's runners to descend any lower than six or seven feet in the air. Dylan glanced around. Up ahead, fifty yards downslope, the terrain flattened somewhat. He pointed, then broke into a run again.

He heard the chopper close behind, pursuing him, and ran, holding the backpack tightly to his chest. The chopper pitched right, then left, and the rotors' hurricane force engulfed him. As he drew near, he saw the shelf he'd sought was too small. There was no room for the descent, nor adequate space for the runners to come near enough to the ground. Worse still, a sheer edge was approaching him with every step, offering nothing beyond but a dizzying drop to the rocks below!

He had no choice. He looked over—the runners were now at head level, only five yards away. He quickly shrugged on the backpack as best he could, then threw himself across the void, his arms outstretched.

He felt the slippery metal strike his forearms, hard. Wincing in pain, he curled his hands around the runner, gripping it just in time. Pulling himself up with every ounce of strength he possessed, he reached for the vertical bar attaching the runner to the chopper's fuselage and wrapped his arms around it.

Gravity now yanked hard against his hold on the bar. As he looked down, the shelf gave way to a plunging cliff, distant hillside, and ocean.

Good! he thought. *That's where we need to go anyway. Open water . . .*

CHAPTER

_64

ABOARD THE GULFSTREAM

Obscured from the sight of Dylan's fate by the need to make another positioning turn, Abby, Dr. Skinner, and Agent Connelly now held hands in the sharply banking aircraft, openly, unabashedly shouting out their prayers.

They knew the final seconds had elapsed. Now they'd entered the equivalent of overtime. Detonation minus twelve seconds.

Abby's prayers were beyond the point of coherent phrasing and organized thought. The urgency of the moment had shredded her entreaties into raw pleading. "God, please, please, *please* . . ."

"Will we see anything when it goes off?" Skinner called up to the captain.

"I doubt it" came a strained voice. "I've taken us to the opposite side of the island, to get away from the explosion."

Their turn eased, and the plane leveled off. They were now able to see the Cumbre Vieja ridgeline.

"Then what in the world," shouted Skinner, "is *that*?"

He was pointing out a left-side window. There, shooting out over the volcano's massif, flew the yellow oval of a helicopter fuselage at top speed.

"Have they already dropped it?" Abby asked pleadingly. "Is Dylan still hanging on?"

"You see that dark spot just above the runner?" said the captain.

"Yeah . . ."

"That's Dylan!"

Abby screamed for joy, leaped up, and struck her head against the cabin ceiling. Rubbing her scalp with a pained scowl, she peered through the window. "Why are they dipping so low?" she asked.

"Because they haven't dropped it yet!" yelled the captain.

"Why not?"

Skinner turned to her, his face bright with realization. "He wants it as far from the volcano as possible. The shock waves could—"

"Fry my avionics!" the captain interrupted, finishing Skinner's sentence. "Hang on!" he shouted. "We have to get out of here!"

SKIES OVER CUMBRE VIEJA, SPANISH AIR FORCE HELICOPTER

Despite crying out in pain at the metal bar and the runner gnawing away at his joints and tendons, despite his elbow-lock on the bar cramping up as his strength drained out of him with the bomb-laden backpack now dangling midair from his free arm, Dylan knew he would hang on for as long as it took. His joints could recover. Every second now meant a measure of safe distance from La Palma. He knew that if they released it too close to the island, especially its western flank, the resulting explosion could still set off the catastrophic slide. He risked a quick loosening of his hold and frantically motioned out toward the ocean. A nod from the pilot and the craft swerved into the new heading.

Just seconds later and the chopper dipped sideways in an unmistakable signal. It was time!

With the backpack grasped tightly in a fist, his fingers almost refused to open. With great effort, he forced them apart.

The strap slipped loose, now consigned to the winds. Sweet relief shot up Dylan's arm and into his shoulder.

He allowed himself the briefest of glances—the pack was already a tiny brown speck against an eternity of blue, its straps flapping wildly in the wind.

ABOARD THE GULFSTREAM

The captain didn't wait for his passengers to find their seats, but pushed the levers of the twin Rolls-Royce turbofan engines to full throttle. The jet shot forward as though it had been standing still in the air.

Dr. Skinner managed to throw himself to the floor and grab a table post, hanging on with all his strength. Abby went tumbling over a chair and into the rear of the cabin.

They were tossed into a steep bank that glued them to the floor. Abby began crawling back toward the front, feeling three times her normal weight, when a flash like lightning lit up the cabin, accompanied by two awful sounds: a low, almost subsonic rumble, and the captain's cry of alarm. The plane shook violently. She looked up and saw Skinner clutching the table and staring out a window with an expression that made her blood run cold. Scrambling forward on her knees, she reached a window of her own and peered out.

What she saw was a portrait of apocalypse. A huge circle of the sea was vomiting into the sky a dome of white foamlike spray that spread wider and higher with every passing second.

"Hang on!" shouted the captain. A cacophony of warning bells and beeps rang out from the cockpit. The plane felt as if it was sinking, not descending or banking but sinking in midair. The sensation yanked a fierce tug on Abby's stomach.

In the next instant the plane pitched nearly upside down, and alarm shifted into raw terror . . .

NATIONAL COUNTERTERRORISM CENTER

A white dot shot out across the on-screen shape of Cumbre Vieja and bloomed into an umbrella-sized sphere. It almost seemed like a blowtorch had ignited on the screen's other side, its point of impact warping the pixels as it traveled outward.

The surrounding monitors flashed with a cavalcade of raw sensor data, out-of-control telemetry readings, and the stacking collages of satellite photos.

"We have detonation," a somber voice called out.

"How far?" asked Ashman. "On the island?"

"Too soon, wait . . . No, it looks like ten miles east."

"East? You mean on the safe side of the island?"

"That's correct."

Ashman was so overwhelmed with relief that his body gave way and he began to sway backward. Only the end of the conference table stopped his fall.

In the resulting din of raucous shouts, leaping colleagues, and wild high-fives, nobody even noticed.

DYLAN'S HELICOPTER

A brown hand reached down and took Dylan's wrist in a strong clasp, yanking him up into the cockpit. Normally Dylan would have hesitated to entrust his life into the grip of a complete stranger, but in this case his beleaguered joints demanded that he not be choosy.

As soon as the door slid shut, however, his gaze was drawn to an airborne shape flying erratically in the distance. In front of him, the chopper pilot pointed toward it as well, commenting in a grave Spanish tone.

Then Dylan recognized it. The Gulfstream! Without thinking, he reached forward and grasped the pilot's forearm. "We can't land!" he cried. "Do you understand me? We have to go and help!"

ABOARD THE GULFSTREAM

Inside the floundering plane, Abby's whole world slowed to a benumbed carousel of chaos. With its controls and electronics knocked out by the blast, the aircraft followed a path that no longer made aeronautical sense. Its once nimble shape was near to stalling speed, its wings rocking wildly to either side. The Atlantic waters, now far from the explosion site and nearly a minute past its climax, churned alarmingly close beneath their windows.

And yet somehow all Abby seemed capable of focusing on just then was the majestic presence of God. For some reason, the extreme danger surrounding her, this brush with death, now loomed as the natural culmination of the past days' spiritual roller coaster. This blissful countdown to eternity, this betrayal of earthly hope, had been the child to which she'd been giving birth all this time.

Sitting next to Dr. Skinner and watching the copilot wrestle open the cabin door, she stopped him in the middle of passing out parachutes, snatched up his hand, and flashed him a smile. "Don't worry!" she said. "We're almost at wave-top level and we're approaching stall speed! We won't need them."

Then the plane pitched sideways, and the copilot was thrown out the open door, propelled by gravity at the plane's sudden turn.

"He'll be fine!" she shouted to Skinner. "Come! Let's follow him."

Dr. Skinner looked at her as if she were caught up in some suicidal euphoria. Without hesitating, she crawled over to the door, waited for the plane to right itself again—which it did three seconds later—and then launched herself out of the aircraft . . .

Those first few seconds of free-fall were strangely liberating for Abby. Despite having no parachute, no warm clothing or jumping gear or goggles, she held out her arms and simply allowed the wind to take her.

She felt a bright sun wrap her in its arms, the wind tug at every inch of her, and she saw the coastal sky embrace her plummeting form. Above her, the plane thundered past, disgorged Skinner, then entered a dive and executed a graceful spiral into the sea.

She breathed a prayer for the remaining captain.

Thankfully the water was only feet below. She was briefly aware of a great blueness rushing up to meet her, faster than she'd ever dreamed possible.

She struck hard, with enough force that she would have been seriously hurt had her fall been even slightly crooked. She felt her feet explode with pain, then coldness on all sides.

Then blackness. And peace.

CHAPTER
_65

Abby awoke to dim lights, curved neutral-colored walls, warm blankets about her, and a telltale humming noise from somewhere not too far away. And the face of a smiling girl she didn't recognize. She opened her eyes wider, turned and looked straight into the gaze of Dylan, who was kneeling beside her bed.

She smiled and tried to ruffle his still-tousled hair, but he caught her hand and held it.

"Hey. We did it," he said in a breathy voice. "This is a friend who helped. Abby, meet Isabella. Without her, we never would have known. We never would have figured this whole puzzle out—in time, anyway."

"Isabella, it's so nice to meet you," said Abby. "You did a great thing today."

"Lord Jesus did a great thing," the girl corrected, beaming.

Abby shifted her eyes to Dylan. "Where am I? It looks exactly like the plane we were on before."

Dylan chuckled and held up a small cushion at the bed's foot. It bore a circular motif, a bald eagle, and letters she could not make out at first . . .

United States Air Force.

"What?"

"It's a C-37, the same model, except configured for medical transport."

"They sent it for us?"

He nodded, amused at her astonishment. "You forget, the eyes of the world were watching," Dylan said. "The bomb went off safely. The wave of death was stopped. And some people seem to think you played a part in stopping it."

"Like Isabella said—it was God."

"Well, you did a decent job of letting Him use you, and so did a whole lot of other people."

Abby closed her eyes, and a peaceful smile washed over her face. "My body feels like it got hit by a truck," she whispered.

"I know. I jumped in after you."

"You did?"

He grinned and said, "You think I'm going to let you go through all this only to drown right in front of me?"

She squeezed his hand. "This jumping out of airplanes is getting to be a nasty habit with you," she said wryly.

He nodded, rolling his eyes good-naturedly. "I suppose I'll have to work on that. If you'll stop putting us in mortal danger."

EPILOGUE

Hi everyone!

Abby Sherman here. Sorry it's been so long since I've posted.

I suppose there's no need to hash over what everybody has seen on the news. It's all so wonderful and thrilling!

I do want to let you know that my mom is fine. She and I were reunited in Washington the very next day in, of all places, the Oval Office! Dylan and Dr. Skinner were with us too. The president was a character, treating me like a snobby guest who had kept turning up my nose at his invitation. So that's why all those government guys were chasing us!

We had lunch in the Rose Garden. What a trip! The first lady gave me a hug, then her husband did too, not to be left out. He wanted to say more, but his National Security Adviser was there and it seemed he couldn't really speak his mind.

But the president did ask me to pass on his gratitude to all of you who heeded the summons and took a stand on that fateful night. He said the nation is grateful for your courage and leadership. I am grateful too. You rose to the occasion in every sense of that clichéd phrase. I'm so proud of you all! More importantly, so is God. He awakened a mighty army of Warriors that night, and you know that things will never be the same now.

To tell you the truth, I'm not sure the president, and especially his advisers, knew what to make of everything. At one point he called me and Dylan aside. "You have to understand," he said, "every hour of the day I have generals and all kinds of experts stumbling over each other as they try to paint for me the big picture of global warfare, hoping to nail down what makes our enemies tick and discover the root causes of world conflicts. I can't tell you how many briefings I've been handed that try to explain why different nations and cultures attack each other in the first place, and what's the source of it all." Then his voice lowered, and he leaned closer to me. "But this notion of a spiritual war behind the scenes of human history, the ancient rebellion that provokes all the others? I mean, I've heard it described in other contexts, but never in these terms, never as a strategic, geopolitical reality. I guarantee you, a lot of the brass will be chewing on the implications of all this, and for a long, long time."

So remember, everyone—there'll be other attacks, other battles. Like the brave brothers and sisters who came before you centuries ago, you obeyed Him and came together to do a mighty thing. And like me, I know you'll never go back. Not after this.

What you did was life-changing and history-making. And we're just getting started . . .

—Abby